Borneo
Fire

SCEPTRE

Also by William Rivière

Watercolour Sky
A Venetian Theory of Heaven
Eros and Psyche

Borneo
Fire

WILLIAM RIVIÈRE

SCEPTRE

Extract from 'The Waste Land'
© T.S. Eliot
from *Collected Poems 1909 – 1962*, published by Faber and Faber Ltd.

Copyright © William Rivière 1995

First published in Great Britain in 1995 by Hodder and Stoughton
A division of Hodder Headline PLC

A Sceptre hardback

10 9 8 7 6 5 4 3 2 1

A CIP catalogue record for this book is
available from the British Library

ISBN 0 340 618523

Typeset by Hewer Text Composition Services, Edinburgh
Printed and bound in Great Britain by
Mackays of Chatham plc, Chatham, Kent

Hodder and Stoughton
A division of Hodder Headline PLC
338 Euston Road
London NW1 3BH

Be not afeard: the isle is full of noises,
Sounds and sweet airs, that give delight, and hurt not.
Sometimes a thousand twangling instruments
Will hum about mine ears . . .

The Tempest

Burning burning burning burning
O Lord Thou pluckest me out
O Lord Thou pluckest

burning

The Waste Land

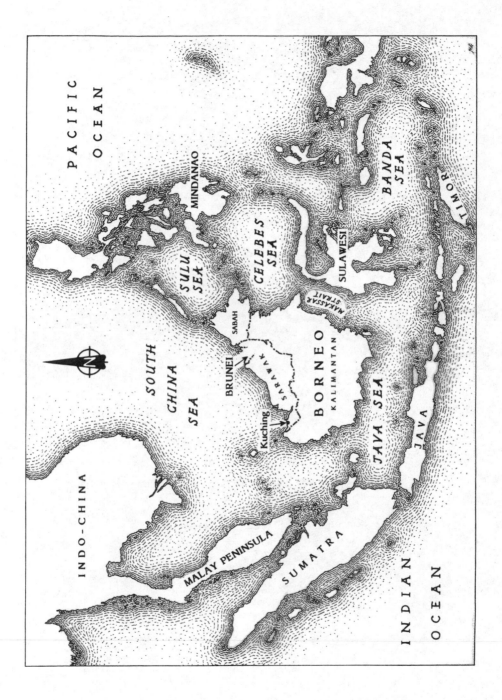

ONE

In the interior the fire had started to burn, but outside the forests no one seemed to be aware of it.

Philip Blakeney knew there was a fire because the pilot Yusof Badawi had been flying from Balikpapan to Sandakan and had seen smoke.

'A lot of smoke,' he insisted to Blakeney a couple of days later when he was back in Kuching and ensconced on the Englishman's weatherbeaten, rickety verandah. 'Not the plume of smoke the farmers make when they're clearing a hectare or two. Where? Difficult to say. The Mahakam region. But to be more precise . . .'

Yes, Blakeney made himself recognise, people living along the coasts of Borneo or at down-river settlements would be reluctant to know about the fire. The clingers to the island's periphery, to its outside, would not want to acknowledge the conflagration, not wish to confess to it. And he was right, he discovered, when the day after his conversation with Badawi he rang up the Forestry Departments of Sarawak, of Sabah, of Kalimantan.

Three times he was given the same response. 'What fire?' the voices asked. 'There is no fire.'

Philip Blakeney lived on a quiet lane a short way up-river of the Astana, where the white Rajahs had held court and now the Chief Minister reigned. His house stood on stilts like all old Malay houses. The stilts held the floor up clear of wet season floods, and when it was dry you could sit below on the rotting cane chairs in the latticed shade, for the building had once been a grand one for Kuching and had the remains of fine lattice-work. Down there in the dusty mud the neighbours' pullets and bantams scratched. Cats came too – the ugly Bornean cats which have short tails with a twisted lump at the end.

The house had long ago been painted green and white. It had a shingle roof, it had carved eaves, it had gables with pinnacles. The staircase came up through the verandah floor, and there it was always shady because the first Blakeney to live in Sarawak, Philip's father Michael, who had been a District Officer under the second Rajah and a Resident under the third, had planted trees – an areca palm, a nutmeg tree with dark green shiny leaves like a bay, a jacaranda, a frangipani, a mangosteen. From the verandah, through the garden foliage you could see the ironwood walkway that led over the swampy ground to the paintless hut with the palm thatch they call *atap*. There along the riverside the nipah palms grew luxuriantly, tented the unclean rivulet where the *sampan* was moored. Beyond, the brown Sarawak river brought down its balks of timber and treetops and clumps of sedge, when the tide set up-river brought them back inland a little, with the ebb floated them again toward the sea. Also you could watch the *tambangs* being rowed back and forth with passengers, and sometimes there was a yacht anchored in the reach. The other side of the river stood the dilapidated Brooke Dockyard, the big glossy new mosque, the bazaar with its portico, the market where the fishing boats moored.

Tall, gaunt, bald, Philip Blakeney sat in his saloon and looked out at the woodsmoke wafting up from a nearby garden, saw how in the damp evening air the smoke hung seemingly motionless in the fronds of the trees, clouded warm and grey in the sultry greyness. He worried about the smoke Yusof had seen, about the answers the Forestry Departments' officials had given him.

His father had called their principal room the saloon because with its woodwork and its five-sided bay window and its brass lamps it reminded him of turn-of-the-century yachts' cabins, of dinners after regattas at Cowes. But now the trouble was that with his few political friends either long out of office or dead, what could Philip do? And no Edwardian skipper would have accepted paintwork so tatty, brass so long unpolished, cobwebs at the cornices. He frowned, reached across his desk, pulled pen and paper toward him. He would write to his son in Timor. He wrote *Dear Hugh* and the date. But then he mused. Above his head, the brass propeller of the fan slowly turned.

What were these facts, or why was it that facts in Borneo could seem subtly different from facts elsewhere? For surely a forest fire, if merely by virtue of its brute size and high temperature and unvanquishable destructiveness, should be a phenomenon difficult to be oblivious of . . . And yet already he thought he could see how invisible it would appear.

The ruffle of hair at the back of his head had been grey for twenty years and when he walked it was with a stick; but he had seen fires. In the interior there was a hill where seams of coal had been smouldering for as long as anybody could recollect – once he had reached a scarp from which it could be seen. Of course the logging companies would put the blame for the fire on the slash-and-burn farmers. Who had actually started the blaze – there was a supposedly simple supposed fact never likely to be ascertained. And of course the state governments would back up the companies – ministers granted timber licences to their allies, to their relations, some even held concessions in their own names. The authorities would perhaps declare that the fire was natural, or was insignificantly small, or was an act of terrorism, or, yes, didn't exist. Undoubtedly they wouldn't explain why hills and valleys which had been logged were more vulnerable to fire than primary forest, or why they were taking no measures now to control this one. And yet – what was it? There *was* something nebulous, sometimes, about events.

He thought about Hugh whose indignation had been inflamed by the atrocities committed by the invading Indonesian army in East Timor, fiery Hugh who for weeks had been compiling a dossier on the outrages of that occupation. He thought of Hugh's mother Danielle who – he couldn't dispel the uneasy gloom with which he recalled this – with her second husband was expected to sail up the Sarawak river any day now, drop anchor right before his jaundiced eyes, damn her. He thought again about the nebulous. Facts could seem to exist astonishingly faintly in Borneo. He'd spent the best part of his life here, ought to have enough experience to go on. Unreal . . .

Borneo had impinged itself upon the world extraordinarily little, when you considered how vast it was, bigger than the British Isles, with a coastline of – what? – well over five thousand kilometres it must be. Was this passivity anything to do with his presentiment? It was an island which from the beginning of recorded history had uncommonly little recorded history. An island whose peoples had never inflicted on other lands either governments or creeds. Yes – a quietude . . . Borneo had rarely sent its peoples abroad, though it had received Chinese, Bugis, Javanese, Malays, Hindis, Portuguese, Tamils, English, Dutch, Japanese, and almost all of it was now under the sway of capitals far away across the seas. Patient, yes, and quiet. Even, for all its size, slightly invisible. Look at the way the European mariners of the Renaissance almost ignored the place in favour of the Moluccas. And in 1945 the Allied advance swept from New Guinea to the Philippines; till the end Borneo was given scant attention.

Philip knew all about that. He'd been one of the first British soldiers dropped into the Tamabo Range to prepare resistance to the Japanese. Had been something of an island hero as a young man, M.C. and all – though he was forgotten now, a relic left over from a Sarawak that had ceased to be. However, dinner parties were still on occasion amused by his tales of how it had not invariably been possible to restrain the tribesmen from attacking their oppressors until the time ordained by High Command, nor always to regulate the uses to which the trophies of these fights were put. Yes, the Japanese had treated the Dayaks with such contemptuous savagery that – oh, it was of course to be most fulsomely deplored – the ancient habit of head-hunting, recently and with difficulty suppressed, had broken out again. Quite a recrudescence, he was ashamed to say. So several longhouses proudly displayed the crania of Emperor Hirohito's men.

Was it that so few of the island's events, from the fall of a single leaf to the mating of two leopards, had been observed by human eye? That so few of the observers had left accounts of their experiences? And few of these writers had been indigenous, so the whole gave the impression of having been regarded predominantly from the outside. He would write to Hugh – as he increasingly did in despondent, powerless old age when the things a man did not know, was never going to have understood, piled up like Mount Kinabalu. And anyhow with luck his letter would stimulate that ardent spirit and pugnacious political campaigner into writing back – if he hadn't been chucked out of the country or into prison; the Jakarta government was among the least scrupulous in Asia.

But . . . The way unrecorded occurrences outnumbered recorded by such a ludicrous margin – though doubtless there were African and Siberian forests where mankind had left as scarce traces of ever having thought or felt. Oh, he knew there were longhouses where they'd recite you their ancestry for twenty generations back, for twenty-five – but oral traditions were fragile, and since the war that village culture had been subjected to such violence that it would probably be more accurate to say that he *had* known such places and people, these recitals *had* been made. Still . . . Yes, the way so much time had been unseen, unheard, the forests always having been sparsely populated. Or anyhow, time had neglected to exist as the time of chronometers or of revolutions, as the time of the timeless moment of a transcendental leap or of divine patience and love.

The way things had of happening observed only by a dragonfly – off and on over the years in the forests – this had fascinated Philip, and it came back to him now. And if you chanced to be there when whatever it was occurred . . . If you saw a bore thunder up a river, or you watched an injured festering macaque die . . . Abstract . . . And would it be like that with this damned fire of Yusof's?

He would write to Hugh. But first there was something practical he could usefully do, he realised, and telephoned an acquaintance of his in Hongkong who worked for *The Far Eastern Economic Review*. And indeed a couple of weeks later, after Blakeney's suggestion had been acted upon and the few apparent facts checked, two column inches were printed under the headline BORNEO FIRE.

After his telephone call, Blakeney went on sitting alone in his dusty, twilit room. He bowed his brown skull over his mahogany desk, wrote to his son about his intimations.

The best part of a year later, when it was all over and Nasreddin and Bernstein were sorting through the Blakeney papers, they found almost a century of family letters, including the one about the fire which Philip dispatched to Timor and which Hugh kept and brought back to Kuching and left among others in a chest of drawers in his bedroom.

The Malay lawyer and the Jewish Norwegian anthropologist stood in the saloon, listened to the cataracts of rain drubbing on the roof, cascading down the jalousies. In the gale of wind, the trees thrashed their branches. The swamp was awash, brown water swirled along the lane.

'If you consider that Philip never went to the fire . . . Right from the start, how intensely he must have felt it!' exclaimed Akbar Nasreddin with soft sadness. 'He never set eyes on it. And yet . . . I suppose he was an eye witness of a different kind. What do you think? Or a – a heart witness. That word he used – abstract. You could say he saw the abstract fire.'

'He didn't need to go to the fire, did he? It came to him,' Thor Bernstein replied gently, grimly, laying a bundle of letters back in the writing-box where the revolver too had lain, had waited for so long. He straightened his back, looked around at the spears and shields and musical instruments and carved images, at the bookcases, at the monsoon wall of darkening rain. 'The abstract fire came here.'

'Of course!' impulsively Nasreddin mourned. 'To Kuching. Yes, you are right. To this room. That is what we saw, you and I.'

'The fire burned here. He burned in it here.'

2

In the beginning was a green island . . . But no, you couldn't even say something as straightforward as that, Philip Blakeney grieved with cheerful exasperation to his listeners, flaunting his helplessness with a hand in which fluttered the newly issued *Review* with the curt notification he was pleased to have inspired. For had Borneo before the last Ice Age not been part of the Asian mainland?

They saw him of a sudden frown, glance bleakly toward the river. Raoul and Danielle Kahn had been delayed, day after day had not sailed up the reach, not invaded. So this evening . . . It was very likely. What had he been . . . ? Ah yes, the seas around Borneo's shores were shallow, the island lay to the west of the Wallace Line. For that matter you'd have also to discount the fact that the overwhelming majority of its inhabitants had never known the island was an island, never conceived of it as a geographical unit at all.

Blakeney was holding court, in his humble way. Akbar Nasreddin was there, quiescent in a rattan chair, as he generally was. Yes, quiescent like a quiescent volcano, but one that had never erupted, never would erupt. Faintly, benignly, he wisped cigar smoke, day-long, night-long. He had a soft round body. He had a soft round face like a baby or a Buddha, a face that looked unlived-in – or perhaps it had been contemplatively occupied from before all time, you couldn't tell. Either he'd never thought or felt anything, or he'd thought it all before. Thor Bernstein was there, on one of his rare descents upon Kuching – had gone along to sit on his ailing mentor's verandah, as always vaguely conscious that one of these days it'd be for the last time.

Why Blakeney still had courtiers, the gossips of Kuching were at a loss to explain. He was a ghost left to haunt uselessly a Borneo the destruction of which, as the twentieth century neared its end, was almost complete: its forests felled; its *kampongs* and longhouse communities unsettled and dispersed; its myths and its crafts being forgotten; its tribes' animistic religions savaged by Muslim and Christian missionaries, the indigenous genii hounded from their shrines of rock and tree and waterfall, harried to oblivion.

The old fellow's adopted daughter, people said. Her nubile beauty. That explained the attendance of the younger men.

Our old heron, the habitués of Blakeney's verandah called him. So tall, so spare, so grey and brown, so solitary, so watchful. It had started with a consul's wife. For the duration of that lady's jewelled and drawling, her hatted and tippling residence, he had been *my darling old heron* to her – for even his last years had not been without their formal gallantries – and the appellation had stuck.

As for why people turned up . . . He didn't make speeches, praise heaven, but he knew an unfathomable sea of things. You could ask him the most recondite question you could come up with about *adat*, the customary law of the tribes, and nine times out of ten he could tell you the answer. You could ask him about the export of diamonds through Pontianak in any given decade. You could ask him about the different omen birds. Or about the war of 1859 between the Kayan and the Iban, and whether the Rajah was right or wrong to be on the side of the latter. Or about the murder of Sir Duncan Stewart, the second British governor of Sarawak, in 1949. About the plumage of the Malay lorikeet. About the organisation of a Chinese *kongsi*. Or hamadryads. Or waterspouts. Bernstein used to pick his brains about the *tiwah*, the death feasts, always said Blakeney was better informed than half of his anthropologist colleagues.

His not giving lectures – that was so wonderfully acceptable. And yet if you were intrigued by the *antohs*, the spirits, and their carryings on, which *were* fairly remarkable, he was your man. And he knew all about Schwaner's explorations of the Katingan river. Knew who Schwaner was, which no one else did. Knew how he came to be the first white man up the Katingan, knew

where that river ran, knew all this happened in the forties of
the last century. And he'd break off from talking to rout in his
chests and come out with the most extraordinary odds and ends
– a necklace made of bats' canine teeth, or a tiny fishing fetish
carved in bone, or a bezoar stone. He used to pride himself on
being able to tell a real bezoar stone from a fake. The genuine
article, the true elixir, had to have been hoiked out of a monkey's
gall-bladder, or the gut of a porcupine or somewhere, and he
could tell.

Blakeney had seen more than anyone, too. As a lad he had
watched a sergeant-at-arms tread behind the last Rajah and
hold over him the yellow umbrella of state. Then there were
his father's stories he'd tell, stories going back to piracy days,
to fights for stockades. Tales, too, of a Blakeney friend; an
exceedingly shabby east-coast sultan who had the old Malay
passion for the cock pit, had his lackeys carry his champion
fighting cocks down to the river each sunrise to be washed.
As for the horrifying things those old blue eyes had seen . . .
He'd been there that September of '45 when they liberated
Kuching prison camp. He didn't discuss such revelations much
– or only with Akbar and Hugh. Neither would he have dreamed
of rehearsing his bravado at the capture of Kapit earlier that
campaign, or at Sibu where by repute his courage went well
beyond the disdainful, impressed some observers as slightly mad
– certainly got him decorated. Anyway, gruff good humour was
the tenor of his old age, and it was maintained with very nearly
immaculate consistency very nearly to the brink, to the end. The
visions of horror, the knowledge and the self-knowledge, stayed
interred in his furrowed brown walnut of a head.

He was old, Blakeney said, letting the *Review* drop onto the
boards, and the year before he'd had a stroke, perhaps it wasn't
time that could be disconcertingly unreal, probably it was him.

Or possibly not . . . As far as this interglacial went, time out
of mind the green island wearing the equator like a belt round
its middle had lain on the blue sea, had not needed written
history while its fabulous generations were recorded in chants.
The night singing of the longhouse women weaving mats by
lamplight sufficed – Akbar, Thor, he appealed, he wasn't wrong
was he? And if, as you lay unsleeping on the planks, you desired

more eloquence – there clamoured the sudden baying of dogs, there belled the wind echoing off a limestone cliff, there fell the crash of a branch, in a lull forever the forest's patterings, rustlings, shrieks, mews.

Of course, here you didn't get the ancient Buddhist temples which decayed in the green lands of Java, Sri Lanka, Cambodia. A few Hindu bits and pieces dug up by archaeologists in the south-east of the island. A statue of Ganesh of the sixth or seventh century found at Limbang. A statue of the Buddha in the late Gupta style found at Santubong. Not much . . . Nothing! And it wasn't a climate in which anything that wasn't stone or metal or china lasted long. Things were flooded, things were overgrown. They were devoured by ants, they rotted. All of which was his roundabout way of suggesting to them that in Borneo knowledge, even existence itself, could seem more precarious than elsewhere. Somehow here transience triumphed with more than its customary effortlessness – did they follow him? In the forests the shadow of oblivion could fall on your mind with a suddenness, a dark . . . ! A warm, damp, everlasting death. He defied them to claim they'd never intuited it. Oblivion was here most swift, utter, universal. A dim, crepitating endlessness, with here and there a shaft of brilliant sunlight lancing through the leaf canopy, with birds one ceaselessly heard but rarely saw. An oblivion – you could sense it in your head, yes, right inside – with the texture of mulch, the odour of mulch too.

Take the fire. Take the fire, if they wanted to feel how – he hesitated for the word – how faint knowledge could be. Take people's indicative reluctance to talk about it.

Naturally the local newspapers were all in the contaminating grip of the political parties, you couldn't expect them to be up to much. But . . . With his heel he jabbed at one of the offending sheets strewn around his chair. On this occasion they were outplaying even their own standards of feebleness. This one – his foot thumped his contempt – had mentioned a report of smoke. But the following day it had stated that the situation was being officially monitored – good, eh? – and there was no cause for alarm. Sitting here on his verandah they all had some grasp of what seemed to be happening, and each knew more or less what the others thought. Doubtless dotted all over Borneo knots of friends were worrying about the disaster. But as for a general picture, a general agreement – nothing! Extraordinary, when you mulled it over, people's ability not to know what was going on. Because even the earliest intelligence of the fire gave rumour of an occurrence considerable enough, you might have reckoned, to be awkward to ignore.

Of course information emerged in a way that was haphazard to a degree, Bornean to the uttermost. Yusof Badawi had chanced to be their own first informant – uncommonly quick, uncommonly reliable. But from the fire, from that blazing centre, awareness must be spreading outward in all directions. Haphazardly . . . A pilot would speak with a forester, or a longhouse chief with the skipper of a river boat, or a trader with a hunter, and eventually somebody would go down-river as far as a bazaar where there was a telephone. No? So one way and another . . . His own latest news came from the son of an old friend. A Kayan who worked for the Sarawak Indigenous Peoples' Alliance – yes, that was right, the organization the State Government had declared illegal – on the upper Baram river. It appeared to be a fact, appeared to be a figure, might be roughly accurate. About five hundred square kilometres had already been burned. Difficult to imagine, even in an island where you got used to long distances and wide areas. And this was only the start. Those senseless advancing regions of flame . . . !

Of the three men on the verandah, Thor Bernstein was the one not to have been born on the island, and suddenly he felt it, felt cut off from them, even detached from this unseen conflagration of theirs. Born several years after the freeing of the prisoners of war at Kuching, after Blakeney's eyes had seen what hands had done, he was cut off by generation too. Restlessly he stood up, sauntered to the rail, idly contemplated the trees, the river. Perhaps the tittle-tattle had shrewdness, Cassandra's presence in the ramshackle house accounted for some of his loyalty, that of Yusof Badawi, that of the Chinese Christian priest Stephen Chai. Certainly Bernstein found himself musing that on Mission Hill evensong must surely be finished, she'd be coming back over the water soon, might be aboard that *tambang* crossing now.

Restless by nature, sometimes he felt rootless too. A family of religionless Viennese Jews who in 1938 had welcomed the providential offer of sanctuary tendered by their cousins in Norway, and had then had to decamp to Sweden for a few years. His first degree from Harvard. Post-graduate research at Paris. Even by mongrel standards he was cosmopolitan. And his strayings it seemed would never end. Fieldwork in Burma, made complicated by the government's inhospitality. Years in Japan made comfortable by the salary a Kyoto university paid; made melancholy by his unease in that society; made distant and sad now by his estrangement – he was learning how to confess to the word, to the apparently solidifying fact – from his wife Keiko-san. The determination to do some work on Bornean death rituals – oh, nothing to rival Metcalf's study of the Berawans, but workmanlike he had hoped. Only now . . . Somehow he seemed to have run out of steam. And that people everywhere were banally awestruck by the number of languages he spoke was no recompense for not really having a tongue he could call his mother's – she was perishing, senile, in an Oslo nursing home – or his own. Inexistent, it made him feel.

Not at home in Japan, Bernstein had started spending his vacations wandering in the Malay Archipelago. Then he had taken six months' sabbatical, had travelled alone in the interior of Borneo and had been happy among the Ibans and Kenyahs and Muruts, had not expected or wished to feel at home, but had rejoiced in the forests and rivers and hills. He had begun to make notes about death rituals.

A year later he had been back, on extended unpaid leave of absence. And now two further years had passed. No, more. And he was beginning to have money problems. And it was no longer a society he did not feel at home in, it was his research he suspected dejectedly. Or it was his discipline. Or, it could seem, it was his thinking, his mind. It had been, no doubt, admirable to start by living among several different tribes. But a decision as to which death rituals he should make an analysis of was embarrassingly overdue. And there was absolutely no excuse for idling away so much time on his island.

For Thor Bernstein had an island. He did not own it. Such a branch of driftwood of a man was not likely to be territorially acquisitive, had perhaps lost the ability very convincingly to possess. But he had in a manner of speaking adopted it.

This island lay about a mile off the north-east coast of Borneo, and there were farther islands in the offing, cloudy on the Sulu Sea. When he was feeling hard-up, or loveless, or intellectually at a loose end, or when he felt particularly inexistent, he would retreat to the hermitage he had built there, a little hut among the sea-almond trees along a cove. A senior colleague of his at the university in Kyoto, who sympathised with him in the decay of his marriage and who believed he had a distinguished academic future before him if he would only concentrate his dispersive curiosities, readily supplied him with grandiloquent documents relating the important, the almost official nature of the talented Dr Bernstein's research. These documents the Sabah Immigration Authority courteously translated into renewed residence permits, so there was little apparent cause for his idyllic withdrawal ever to end. Under the tropical sun his brown hair had bleached till it contrasted arrestingly with his brown eyes, made him look more Austrian than he was, confused his identity further still, made him seem perhaps the Norwegian he had never very profoundly been.

Idyllic . . . But it was an odd choice of island for an anthropologist, being uninhabited until the scholar took a boat from the *kampong* on the mainland – which was a charming village of wooden houses over the shallows beside a river mouth – and chugged across the azure strait and nudged his vessel's bow onto the sand. Perhaps too his benevolent colleague might have fretted if his protégé's letters had not all been stalwartly cheerful and much concerned with burials, if he had known into what melancholy the hermit could descend after a few islanded weeks. But idyllic, certainly . . .

Behind Bernstein, Blakeney was talking about how when the Malays first came to Borneo they were Buddhists, but by the fifteenth century the coastal sultanates were Muslim.

'Sometimes I'm afraid that whoever I was in those days forgot to change religion,' Nasreddin remarked. 'That in the mass apostasy he was . . . I don't know – but . . . slow . . . absentminded. Oh, I dare say my spiritual forefather went along with the general conversion. Unsafe not to. But only superficially, perhaps. His heart was not changed.'

It's too late, Bernstein reflected; Philip's *A History of Borneo* won't get written now. With those gold-rimmed spectacles of his on his nose he'll go on leafing through his notebooks, go on rereading his books by Lumholtz and by Bock, by Low and by Runciman, by Harrisson who was his friend. Akbar and he will sit here nightfall after nightfall. They'll go on lending each other books of poetry, go on reading aloud paragraphs from the newspapers which are particularly ludicrous or inane. Well, he mused, grant me such a peaceful old age. But perhaps Philip was not very peaceful. In his exasperations there lay a hardness, in his too conscious unknowing a despair . . .

A ketch under power with the French tricolour at her stern came into the dusky reach. The muezzin was calling.

Blakeney heaved himself to his feet, stood leaning his shoulder against one of the verandah uprights. 'Here they come,' he said. And he thought: Extraordinary! To have a head with the medley in it that mine has! Because even now, with the past returning to him with a blatancy that made it banal before it had finished arriving, a dispiriting cliché before the yacht had so much as dropped anchor, he couldn't help remembering not his marriage to the woman now standing on her second husband's foredeck but the Chinese rebellion of 1857, how the ketch was now passing where that night the Rajah swam beneath the rebels' boats. A ragbag, his mind. There at the Court House the president of the Chinese *kongsi* sat in the Rajah's chair, Nicholetts's head displayed on a pole, to hear the oaths of sudden loyalty of, among others, the timorous bishop. Up the reach the ketch crept, past where on the night of the rebellion one of the Middleton children was beheaded, the other hurled into his parents' burning house. They found Mrs Middleton the next day, wandering in the fringe of the jungle, half crazed. Ah, ravellings . . . 'Looks like Raoul has decided to anchor this side.'

Bernstein nodded, but he too had his distractions, had his absence, only appeared to be watching the ketch slow down, edge in toward the nipah shore. What he saw was the slope of mighty trees towering over his hut, what he heard were Sulu Sea ripples lapping, the fluttering of leaves, insects' hum. Against his blue heaven, the forest shimmered its jades and emeralds. On his sand, the sea-almond let fall its russet leaves. Out from his island's crest, a white sea-eagle soared.

3 ∫

Time out of mind the green island lay on the blue sea. The Chinese junks came to Brunei and Santubong, they sold their metalwork and their silks to the coastal Malays, to the inland peoples they sold jars and beads, from them purchased birds' nests and rattan and beeswax and the beaks of hornbills.

The Mongol emperors of China contemplated, it seems, the annexation of Borneo – but didn't do anything about it. Kublai Khan dispatched a fleet – but the chief object of his admiral's ambition was Java. The insensate spoliation lay centuries in the future. By the time the Majapahit kingdom of Java declined, the Bornean down-river sultanates were of some magnificence, but hadn't yet come to regard the hills and forests and rivers behind their backs simply as potential wealth, though the conviction that the native tribes were inferior to themselves had taken hold.

For centuries Islam clung to the skirts of the island, the body within was scarcely touched. The tribal religions were not affected, rocks and trees were still shrines, birds were still infallible omens, the longhouse wise men who dressed as women practised their hierophancy. The spirits of the forest flitted and vanished undisturbed, they endured. The tribal graves were not defiled. Dead chiefs lay in their ironwood tombs carved and painted like boats, rotted with their paddles at their sides so they could scull to the next life. Christianity had not been heard of.

By the time Malacca fell to the Portuguese, the European hunger for Eastern spices was becoming peremptory. For more lasting riches also. When the two remaining ships of Magellan's fleet anchored in Brunei Bay, Antonio Pigafetta wrote of a city built on piles over the water, of the women going to market by *sampan* at high tide, and he was vivid too about the Sultan's gold and china, his silver candelabra, his hangings of silk brocade, his courtiers' jewelled rings and gold daggers, two pearls as big as pigeons' eggs which the delegation was not permitted to see. Ceremonial journeys to and from the palace were made by elephant – the descendants of animals presented by a sultan of the Malay peninsula, shipped across.

Sultan Hasan, the ninth of the Brunei dynasty, early in the seventeenth century ruled all Borneo – what it amounted to was, he bullied the peripheral fiefdoms – but he was the only man who ever did. After that it was all faction and corruption, judicious murder and counter-murder. The Malay sultans secured their thrones by the elimination of rivals, financed their lawless governments by extortion from the Dayaks. Nowhere was justice to be obtained. Never was there peace. The lineage of the Prophet, the noble *sherips*, postured, plotted, embezzled, squabbled. When Sarawak was ceded to James Brooke in 1841 and the adventurer was proclaimed Rajah, the Sultan of Brunei was simple in the head and had two thumbs on his right hand. It was his Uncle Hassim who enlisted Brooke's efficient help in suppressing a revolt, and who obtained for him his reward, his tenuous sovereignty.

Not that it was a bit surprising that people had taken it into their heads to rebel, Blakeney would remark to his verandah of listeners. Nothing astonishing about it – though for grandees the usual form of death was strangling, and for lesser malefactors there were some pretty frightful ends, including being strung up by your ankles with your legs splayed so the executioner could chop at your crotch and you died being split in half. Had they seen, in the museum at Singapore, one of the swords used for this edifying purpose? It was in a cabinet, labelled. Beautifully made.

'Those were the days . . . ' Akbar would puff his cigar till his imperturbability was almost invisible, his laconic voice grew oracular. 'Those were the days, were they not, when in England if you annoyed the monarch you were hung, drawn and quartered?'

Depressed by the rapacity of present potentates, that of their predecessors had come to haunt Blakeney. It seemed all was foreshadowed, all! The Malay system of enforced trade, called *serah*, had been carried to extremes of brutal greed sufficient to make some communities retreat up the rivers into the hills – the unknowable interior serving, not for the last time, as at least a temporary sanctuary – and to make the less timid stand and fight. All a village's produce, rice, rattan, what-have-you, had to be offered for sale to the local Malay princeling at whatever price he considered fit. If there wasn't enough rice, you had to make up the deficit by selling children into slavery. The pretty Melanau girls were particularly valued for Malay harems. Naturally, the tougher tribes were handled with more circumspection. The Brunei government would sell weapons to the Ibans and the Kayans, urge them to attack their neighbours, get paid with half the loot when defenceless settlements had been sacked. Not much of a place by then, Brunei. Poverty-stricken populace in hovels. A ruinous filthy palace, half-savage aristocracy. Altered again now of course. Oil. Splendid. But if you thought of the present elites of Banjarmasin and Kota Kinabalu and Kuching . . . If you observed the barbarity – no other word for it – with which they dished out timber concessions for what had been the ancestral forests of the tribes, felled and sold, felled and sold . . . Not to speak of their avaricious ways with dams and mines. And the standard of living in the interior as low as ever, lower in some respects. Foreshadowings . . . Money always ended up on the coast, seemed to be centrifugal.

That rapacity more soulless than that of eighteenth- and nineteenth-century sultans might yet batten on the great vulnerable island, that for the oppressed its forests would not forever be an inviolable refuge, would have seemed inconceivable to Michael Blakeney when from the deck of a steamer one China Sea daybreak he first saw Santubong, his son would muse. The mountain rising three thousand feet from the sea. Then the Sarawak river pushing a fan of brackish brown out into the salt blue. The little ship crossing the bar, coming up the river on the last of the flood tide. Twenty miles of nipah mire on either bank. Then to port the Chinese shop-houses, to starboard stocky little Fort Margherita on its knoll with canons and flag, then again to port the wooden church on Mission Hill, the Court House down by the water.

Utterly charming it looked, he had told his son. But ... That predators would come who'd make an Illanun raiding warrior with sword and spear look tame – how could young Michael Blakeney, newly appointed by the Sarawak State Office in London and going out to begin a humble up-country job, have foreknown? Unruly tribes were all he'd been told to fear – he who lived long enough to witness a war-time ravaging, but not that of the subsequent peace. Oh, and he'd been most fervently instructed always to sleep beneath a mosquito net. And that the sea snakes were dangerous but very few of the land ones – they'd enlightened him on that point. The year was 1897. He'd just come down from Oxford. He was twenty-two.

A father who, during the reign of the second white Rajah, had fought with the expeditionary force sent up the Batang Lupar against Banting and his rebels who had been raiding peaceful villages – well, anyhow, villages loyal to the Rajah. This was one of the glories of Philip's childhood. Or rather, on that occasion his father had not fought. As the expedition lay at Nanga Delok, cholera broke out in the camp. About a thousand men died. The Dayak fighters dispersed to their villages. Give him a good old-fashioned baptism of fire any day, the elder Blakeney would expostulate to his rapt child – for the man who later planned *A History of Borneo* had been a boyish connoisseur of sea fights, river and stockade fights, mutinies, brigandage, shipwrecks, explorations. But to hear about Banting he'd lay aside whatever book it was – the story of the battle at Merudu Bay, that was a favourite of his: how the English cut the boom across the river, how Serip Usman's fort was set ablaze, how his wife, who came of the royal house of Sulu and was famous for her power to walk upon the sea, died of a broken heart and was buried where her husband had made his last stand.

Yes, it had been a failure of an especially hideous kind, that expedition, Michael Blakeney would recall. That struggle against men's horror and men's putrefaction ... Still, it had been while falling back with the survivors of the Sarawak Rangers and of the Malay contingent that he'd got to know the Rajah Muda, the heir. Trying to organize a more or less orderly withdrawal, they'd spoken several times.

A father who a year after the epidemic at Nanga Delok had joined the detachment which left Simanggang under Baring-Gould and pushed up into the Pan Range and defeated the rebels there. An uncle who away across the South China Sea was a rubber planter in Perak, who had once perched his small nephew with him on an elephant's howdah to ford a river. Who had another day taken the enchanted child on a rafting party. They had poled their indolent down-stream way through an enfilade of forest trees, had drifted out onto a lake spread with waterlilies in pale flower where off a sandbank a flock of white egret rose. These, before his summary expulsion from the garden of innocent earthly delights to an English school, had been Philip's joys.

As a junior government officer, Michael Blakeney had kept a *nyai*, a local girl who was his mistress, his housekeeper and his language teacher – a line of conduct the old Rajah approved of for the young men in his service, European wives tending to become more mem-sahib than was in his multiracial state's interest. That concubine and her children had been dismissed, had been provided for, were perhaps regretted, when the second Rajah died and the third succeeded. The District Officer was in Kuching that July day of 1918 when his old comrade-in-arms of the Batang Lupar débâcle was rowed from the Astana steps in the state barge which had been a present from the King of Siam, walked beneath the yellow umbrella to the Court House to take his oath of accession.

Michael Blakeney was married by then. Kitty sat beside him on the platform in the Court House. She sat among the members of the Council Negri and among her husband's brother officers and their wives to watch the third Rajah lay his hand on the sword of state. She heard him take his oath. She heard the Datu Bandar pronounce fealty. When everyone in the Court House repeated it, she murmured too. She raised her voice in the European cheer, felt her heart's rataplan when the Dayak chiefs shook their spears and roared their war cry and outside it was taken up, it echoed from the bazaar, from the grassy *padang*, from the boats.

Philip had just been born. His brother Andrew was three. Then in the twenties Kuching was gay, there were regattas, there were race meetings. The new Rajah and the Ranee Sylvia gave roulette parties, they gave dances, every Sunday they gave a swimming party with curry and gin slings. The Ranee kept two baby orang utans, one called Gin and the other called Bitters, and whether her liking for his father was ever carried indecorously far Philip could never establish. Some of his parents' friends who were still alive after the war would smile, say Ah, well, maybe. Certainly they were terrific friends. Who knows? One hot starry night when the dancing went on late. Others would raise their eyebrows. Would protest, Good Lord, whatever makes you suspect . . . ? The Rajah kept a boa constrictor and a porcupine, and that Kitty Blakeney was one of his mistresses appeared to have been a fairly open secret among habitués of the Astana in those years. Whether this had anything to do with his father's promotion to Resident on the Rejang river – here was another matter concerning which the dilettante historian had to resign himself to knowing he'd never know. Nor would he ever be able to ascertain whether it had anything to do with Nerissa's birth.

The man in whose mind a country's tragedies were shadowed, to whose vision his dead stole back with too insatiable loyalty, heard Raoul Kahn's anchor chain go rattling out.

The trick with the past was to limit your contemplation to its acceptable aspects. Think about the living. The living were nothing, were child's play. Danielle on the foredeck of that ketch was nothing.

Or the long-dead past, that was all right. The dead, dead, dead past. Sung dynasty coins dug up. A T'ang dynasty jar he himself had seen in a longhouse. That sort of thing.

Blakeney frowned at the effulgent sunset beyond Mount Serapi. The river was burnished silver now and streaked with glinting flames, lay under mist which wreathed among the shore trees too where the first bats of the evening flew.

Difficult, though, to shake things off. Once in the Tamabo Range he'd got lost, had seemed then to see through a rent in the veil, see absolute moral solitude. Was he afraid he might be condemned to some such vision again, was this what reports of a distant conflagration were doing to unsettle him? Miles of flame. Emptiness, the inane . . . Or the lost soul lying on the forest floor, ants getting to work while you were still alive. There were scenes it would have been agreeable not to see, would be agreeable to forget. In 1945 in one inland village the Dayaks got hold of a couple of stray Japanese, broke their wrists and ankles, left them to drag themselves about on the ground till they died, left them to the pigs, the dogs, the ants, the blow-flies.

'What kind of a man is Raoul Kahn?' asked Thor Bernstein.

'Oh . . . ' Wearily Blakeney marshalled his good sense. 'Raoul's fine. He's an excellent seaman, I'll say that for him. First rate. Sails in the Andaman Sea, sails in the Java Sea. None of your usual shilly-shallying between Antibes and St Kitts. Sails in the Banda Sea. Rich, very. Paris stock exchange. Cassandra doesn't like him, but really he's, oh, he's all right.'

She was crossing the river now or she'd already crossed it, had seen the French ketch moored, had decided that during the Kahns' sojourn she'd pass a lot of her time on Mission Hill. Yes, very likely she'd discover she had to do church this and church that.

'If you wait a few minutes you'll meet him,' he concluded to Bernstein. 'Far better suited to be Danielle's husband than I ever was. A couple of years younger than I am, but he looks only about fifty-five.'

Raoul who with Danielle was making his yacht shipshape, would leave a riding light to gleam on the river, row his dinghy ashore to the muddy creek, walk up the garden in the sultry dusk. Raoul who would lounge here in one of the infirm rattan chairs with a glass of whisky in his mariner's calloused paw. Raoul thick-set, Raoul ruddy-countenanced, of a practicality one was constrained to admire, of pitiless good cheer. Raoul whose brutally conservative politics made Cassandra downright messianic. Whose voice was far too bluff – bellowing like a bull at the Bourse had tuned him, or bellowing in Sunda Strait gales. Who always seemed to be letting his fellow men know they were to keep the change.

'Philip!' They heard Cassandra's soft call, heard her steps on the stair, heard her kick off her shoes. 'I bought a bag of rambutans in the market, aren't I brilliant?'

In the sixties, when she had been orphaned, Akbar Nasreddin had been instrumental in bringing the little girl – she had not yet been two – under the protection of her father's friend. To have both parents killed within a year! It still made him shake his head at the world's cruelty. Well, poor Philip had been the right surrogate father, he who knew more than it was pleasant to contemplate about the slaughter of those held most tenderly to the heart. Since then, Akbar had been a kind of *de facto* godfather to her.

Smiling, he turned to the door. She might have inherited her height from her English father, but she had her Iban mother's fine bones, sheer black hair, eyes set wide, brows arched high. Her sarong rustled. She was wearing a necklace of leopard's claws set in silver, it gave a pre-Christian air to a young woman who was an assiduous frequenter of the ugly modern church which stood on Mission Hill in the old wooden one's stead.

That Philip's eyes should light up when he beheld her once more embowered in his verandah's bougainvillaea and roses was a matter of course. But the brilliance of Thor Bernstein's look – how often could he have met her? a dozen times? scarcely – Akbar had not expected, avuncularly noted. And Hugh, what would Hugh think? Apparently, presumably banished Hugh?

'My darling, they've come,' Blakeney lamented happily, for his old friend was correct, her presence would usually waft him from his doldrums. 'Raoul and Danielle. Shall we hide? Or we could run away.'

'Absolutely not.' She was blithe, she tapped her foot. 'This is our ground. We'll defend it. Don't be afraid, I'm not going to abandon you to their mercies. I'll stick by you, close, close.'

4 ∫

If Akbar Nasreddin had ever had a talent, it had not been for living.

Not that he had lived what is called badly. 'But I've often displayed quite a flair for *not* living,' he would claim with his wry placidity. 'Yes, for not being there when whatever it was that was vital occurred. Or, if I happened to be present, I was absent too, if you see what I mean. I've always been looking the wrong way. Not listening. Thinking about something else, something not important at all.'

On one occasion in his life Akbar had not been absent. The formal photograph of his wedding showed bride and groom sitting in state in the Malay fashion, she wearing the embroidered *songket* which was her pride, he with a *topi tarbus* with a tassel on his head. She had been all shimmers of red and gold, and his solemn headgear had been red and green, but the picture was black and white, you had to imagine the lustres, the sumptuousness. He'd omitted the intricate silver belt his father and grandfather had sported at their weddings, but apart from that ... This least obtrusive of men had got married with all the conventionality he could lay hands on. As if – but for him it will have been the most suppressed of hopes – to perform scrupulously each and every formality made the soul, wretchedly overt in its dozens of kilos of flesh, a little invisible, gave a ghostly liberty.

A low dais, a middle-aged bespectacled groom, a youthful bride already modestly plump ... At his most captured, you could see the reluctance with which his eyes had looked through their lenses at the black box on a tripod and its lens. Transfixed supposedly in the act of living, there was something terrible in how unnatural to him it was.

Of such a man you could believe that if the past were to chug up an equatorial river in a French ketch and anchor before him, it would not be his past. What even he, prosperous, peaceful, puffing his cigar, sipping his whisky like a Christian, was only on the threshold of being haunted by, was that if the dead came to him on a verandah at nightfall they would not be his dead.

Philip Blakeney might, as a child, have been able to chart with his finger the courses of Albuquerque and Drake. Might have informed you that the latter bought six tons of cloves at Ternate. Might have described how the lust for gold and for spices possessed men till they scorned cyclones and reefs, sea monsters and tidal waves, how typhus and diphtheria were, until they broke out on board your ship, mere haze in the adventurous mind's eye. He might – for his inability to distance himself from feelings marked him young – vividly have put you in a boat off the island of Krakatau when it blew up. Or aboard the sailing ship *Sultana* off Palawan when she was struck by lightning which fired the cargo of cotton in her hold, so that by the time her cutter and longboat were hoisted out the ship was blazing from stem to stern. Or in a hundred other dramatic circumstances. As later the man, the boy could be deflected from one story to another; but he was always present somewhere. Akbar Nasreddin was not. He was absent everywhere.

As a boy Akbar had not lost himself for hours following the serpentine ways of the desire for cinnamon and pepper and cloves, for gambier, for dammar, for gutta percha, for camphor and cassia and indigo – or, if he had, it was to marvel at some men's singlemindedness, the European's readiness to leave his bones on Asiatic shores, the relative scarcity of Malay bones paving the North Atlantic. Possibly he revelled in more intrinsic ways of losing himself. Anyhow, his own mind was incorrigibly plural. Most of his thoughts were generally elsewhere. Not often, it was to be confessed, hovering around his obese wife. But creditably frequently haloing his daughters Zahrah and Sukinam who were married but to his relief – yet even this was a mild sentiment – still lived in Kuching.

Plural his mind, multifarious his distractions, gentle his feelings. You'd see him immobile, the smoke of his cheroot pluming
up unwaveringly. Blakeney would be talking about one of the
side-shows of Bornean history. The Field of Stones called Jallan
Batoe off the Benangan river – no one else would have a clue
where these pinnacles towered, but of course he'd have been
there – where the Dayak chief Soro Patti held out against the
white men and their guns. Or it would be the dugong. He was
great on the dugong. It was just about extinct, the poor harmless
old brute, did they all know? Still on the *Protected Species List*, as
was only politic; but the last ones in Bornean seas were dying. Bit
of a war memorial, that august *List*. Pages of it commemorative
only. The clouded-leopard was on the way out too, almost no
habitat left. The rhinoceros also – hunted for its horn, which
the Chinese, seduced by its priapic shape, were convinced was
aphrodisiac. They ground it up, made a paste he'd heard. So
Blakeney might suggest that everybody raised their glasses in
memory of the persecuted dugong. Might as well dedicate a
moment's memory to leopard and rhinoceros too while they
were about it, the rate they were being shot. You'd lift your
glass to your lips. And if you happened to glance at Akbar
Nasreddin as he did likewise . . . It wasn't that he gave the
impression that he was more present somewhere else. He wasn't
oblivious, either. Extraordinary, his tranquillity. If there was an
instrument which could measure intensity of living, if you could
plot degrees of this intensity from faint up to middling and then
up to vibrant or passionate or whatever, he'd have been right
down at the bottom, at very faint. Naturally you assumed he
lived an abstract life of inversely proportionate intensity. But
you couldn't tell.

Reflecting on this impression he feared he gave others, knew
he lamentably gave himself, Akbar remembered that Christmas
Day of '41 when the Japanese occupied Kuching. He hadn't lived
through that doubtless momentous event with much fervour.
Not with the curiosity other schoolboys had shown. Not even
with much taking of sides. Feeble, his concern only with inciden-
tals. His parents talking about nothing but provisions, he recalled
that. His father's concern not to be apprehended at his job, his
resolve to have held no post in the Rajah's civil service.

One day later in the war Akbar Nasreddin saw an Englishman hauling a bullock cart. The man had been a government officer, now he was a prisoner. The boy stood under a rain-tree by the roadside; the skeleton dressed in tatters with unkempt grey hair and oozing sores dragged at the cart. Generally, when the people of the town saw one of its former administrators labouring in its public places as a slave, politely or in shame they turned their eyes aside, some even ran away. But this time a little Chinese girl scurried out of the jostle, shoved a bunch of bananas into the skeleton's hand, scampered away again. Jolted, for a moment Akbar stared, confronted face-on the slave cramming a banana into his mouth, heard Japanese yells. Then quickly he looked away.

Too easy, was it, he brooded, to conclude he'd been looking away ever since? But if it was the case?

He'd measured out his life with the births of daughters, the births lately of grandchildren. He'd measured out his life with the short journeys between his house and his office and the Court House, first in a rickshaw, then steering his old rattletrap, recently in a Ministry of Justice limousine driven by a fellow with a cap, with white gloves clean every day to lay on the wheel. He'd measured out his life, for pity's sake, with cups of tea.

Next year he would retire. After that, nothing would ever change. Diffidently he'd visit his daughters, with woeful ignorance and courteous falsity praise their husbands' new Japanese cars. Steadfastly he would visit Blakeney. When the newspapers reported things uncommonly bad, Philip would mutter, *They went to sea in a Sieve, they did, In a Sieve they went to sea*, and they would sip their lime juice or their Laphroaig, and Cassandra would come back from evensong.

On the March occasion of her returning with her bag of rambutans and her wonderful loyal love for Philip, her admirable confident gaiety, Akbar peered through the misty gloaming at the much older female figure who, beyond a few fruit trees, stood by the inlet holding a torch while her husband moored their dinghy.

He had been home from Gray's Inn – English professional training had been customary for Malays of his class in those days – when in 1949 the then Danielle Vernet from Saigon had first made her entrance on the Kuching stage. With her in his eyes, Akbar had learned what a cloche hat was, how fetchingly a dark green one might perch on a glossy raven bob. Bewitched by her, and being already an avid reader of novels, he had precipitately understood what the word vamp meant, and had started to form opinions on matters he had not previously considered, such as make-up and chokers and cigarette holders. In the vicinity of the dashing Philip Blakeney, whose tragedy and whose audacity all Sarawak had discussed, and of his fiancée, he had felt . . . Not sexual jealousy, not precisely that. Erotic admiration was more like it. The determined hope that he too – one day – with passion – exalted – he too lightheartedly . . .

At Kuching a year after the fighting was over, Blakeney had stood near Lord Mountbatten when he signed a proclamation restoring civil government. He was already a District Officer by then – appointed by the Rajah who had been his father's friend and, though he hadn't yet discovered this, his mother's lover. He spoke Iban, he spoke Malay, and that he should make a career in the Sarawak Service had always been the plan. That the man who in the crucible of Bornean history had been burned so cruelly should wish to give his life to the reconstruction of that devastated society was widely remarked upon as a moving testimony. The cession of Sarawak to Great Britain was a miserable business – all overt partiality and hurried bungling, couldn't have been worse. But it didn't bother Blakeney much. He was happily at work up the Baram river when he became a servant of the Crown.

That, along with being a good soldier and a good administrator, he was also a hopeless romantic was less widely discussed. In Sarawak for years not a soul knew he wrote verse, and then that soul was only Akbar Nasreddin. Their progression from being acquaintances to being friends occurred around the time of the Englishman's divorce and the Malay's marriage. So did the latter's realisation that he never had lived, never would live passionately.

Had the hard-bitten late-middle-aged millionairess now so disconcertingly before Akbar's eyes been a reader of her first husband's poetry? When she was not this bronze-faced, steel-haired, commanding consort of a commanding man . . . When she was the slender and reputedly penniless bride from French Indo-China who had enchanted Kuching; in one stroll had almost caused Sibu bazaar to burst into flames again as it had twenty years before; had one sunset at Kapit made Fort Sylvia, which customarily resembled a shabby cricket pavilion, seem an outpost of sophistication, a citadel of gaiety, made its hurricane lanterns scintillate . . . A reader of those war poems which on the other side of the world were sporadically being printed in *The Cornhill, The London Mercury, Poetry Quarterly*, one of which appeared in *Penguin New Writing*, another in *Horizon*?

Akbar Nasreddin had, since, been allowed to borrow the poet's tatty copies of these publications. He had at the time on the Baram seen Danielle, paddled by her husband's boatmen and wearing a straw hat, so ravish the senses – well, his bookish callow senses – that her *prahu* seemed a barge glowing on the water. Now he tried to imagine whether she would have had a book in her languid hand. Anyway it must have been about then that Philip gave up writing – or at least stopped being published. It had been a bitter disappointment to him, Akbar knew, the way in the fifties his literary career, which it had appeared might be beginning, had petered out. Maybe the editors who had thought he was worth a chance lost their jobs. Maybe fashions altered. Maybe the Baram was too far from the Thames. Maybe he lost heart. Anyhow, here Danielle Kahn sat in the lamplight. On a rattan chair. Exclaiming, 'Philip I *knew* we could depend on you. As we rowed ashore, I was reminding Raoul. Always the *finest* whisky.' Among the climbing roses, the Chinese jars. Always a jumble of Bornean bits and pieces that verandah, despite war-time depredations. Among the embossed gongs, the intricate mats, the carved masks, the clusters of woven baskets slung from rafters, the swags of hammocks.

A shame Kahn's joviality was so reverberative, it reminded one how meagre was the pension on which Philip subsisted.

Akbar's pursed, podgy lips emitted a billow of tobacco smoke. Thus shielded, he blinked protectively at the man of passions through whom he had made his own tentative essays at living. He didn't look much like a man of passions any more. Withered shanks. Scrawny throat. His walking stick was propped against the doorway. He was talking about which tribes in which decades, when building a longhouse or a chief's tomb, began to substitute a water-buffalo for the sacrificial slave buried alive under the king-post.

In the warm night, Akbar shivered. Danielle might appear to be here, every stitch she wore what Paris recommended for the tropics and for yachting, but she wasn't really, hadn't come back very really. Only the dead.

Most intensely the dead. Andrew Blakeney in uniform. Nerissa Blakeney. Had Philip by a casual mention of their names or in silence invoked them? Called to them with that inaudible cry of his that never changed? It was a racked cry, a cracking cry, unforgiving, unrenouncing, a cry of undying love and of immitigable pain.

Perhaps Akbar's perennial absentness was to be of some use to him at last. Perhaps he, more than undeniable solid souls . . . Possibly in the end he, nebulous, was more in tune with the absent, the nebulous, sensed when ghostlily they came. Was the life he'd been waiting for, no, years back had given up waiting for, about to begin? A spectral life, naturally, being his. A communion with shadows. But something. Some dream.

They were the dead for whom Philip had fought the Japanese. He had fought for the Borneo of his youth which the war had annihilated. He had fought not knowing if they were alive, had won through too late to save them, save the lost island in his mind.

Akbar had only seen Nerissa once. In 1938, probably, he had worked out. If so, he had been twelve. She must have been about sixteen. It was at Kuching race-course. Very simple in those days – thatched huts and awnings, posts and rails. Andrew had just ridden a winner. In the unsaddling enclosure the Blakeneys and a few friends had clustered around his steaming horse. She was there, merry, in a blue dress.

Long years after, Philip had told him how, it must have been that same year, he had spent some time with his sister at a bungalow his father had built on a hill toward the headwaters of the Rejang. It wasn't an easy place to get to, but in the absence of anything in Sarawak you could call a hill station its breezes had a pleasant freshness. She'd been on holiday from her English school. He'd been about to go up to Oxford.

One morning they went to bathe in a favourite pool of theirs. After swimming, Philip sat in the shade, looked at the butterflies. But Nerissa was suddenly overcome by gaiety or happiness or something. Dressed again, she went galloping along the water's edge past the circling trees, she leapt the little stream where it flowed in. With her brown hair blowing, she ran on round the pool. Wildly she rushed past her brother, jumped the stream where it flowed out the other side, ran exultantly on round. He watched her. He thought: She'll fall in love. Already, she's gone.

Long after again, on the verandah of the house where she was born, old fat Akbar Nasreddin seemed to see her shade very clearly. A girl in a blue dress, a white girl with brown hair – simple enough. Of all spirits apparent or dispelled, hers was the most present to him, the most vivid.

The minute passed. In his unquiet mind, the communion with shadows which had seemed so inspiriting, which had seemed a calling, a new life, came to him now as the most deathly of initiations, the saddest beginning ever dreamed.

5

At the outbreak of war between Britain and Germany, Philip Blakeney was at Magdalen. He had joined the army a couple of days earlier.

He was the dreamy kind of undergraduate. Of Oxford on the eve of war, later he'd recall the autumn mist at dusk coming up from the river, the deer walking over the yellow elm leaves on the grass in the Grove, his saunterings along Addison's Walk. But he was capable of swift, elegant action too. In the early spring of '39 he rode in the four Grinds, the University race meetings on tented fields at Somerton and Tew, twenty or thirty horses in a race, watched it seemed by half the beautiful girls in England. *The Cherwell Magazine* and *The Oxford Magazine* published his verse. He trained with the Cavalry Squadron. Armed with swords and rifles, mounted on horses from a livery stable, they practised on Port Meadow the lessons of the South African War.

Two years later, at the time of the Japanese advance against the French and British and Dutch possessions in the Far East, he was a lieutenant who'd been mentioned in dispatches a couple of times and was now in the vice of a longing to go to Sarawak and fight to defend the place or, failing that, at least get his sister to safety.

There was no defence of Sarawak to speak of. The Rajah was out of the country. The 2/15 Punjabis were all there were. They put up a brief resistance, blew up the aerodrome, retreated inland. The idea was to cross the island to ports from which they might be taken off, but they never made it. After a cruel march, three months later they were caught by the Japanese. In the years in prison camp, half of them died.

What befell the Europeans on the Rejang, including Michael and Kitty Blakeney, their son Philip did not discover for several years. Nor what happened to Andrew, who was with the tiny garrison of the Miri oilfield when the Japanese invasion force of ten thousand men appeared offshore. The last news to emerge was that, with the oil company officials, they destroyed the installations, in three ships sailed for Kuching. They were attacked from the air during the voyage, but they got there, a few days ahead of the invaders.

After that, no more intelligence reached the outside world. Sarawak was immured in war, was an oubliette. What part Andrew had played in that Christmas Day loss of Kuching, whether he was alive or dead, Philip could not discover. Nor whether Nerissa was alive. She had not left when most of the European women were sent away at the beginning of the emergency. She was nursing at the hospital.

Early in '45 Philip Blakeney parachuted into the highlands of the Kelabits as an agent of what was known as Z Special. His first evening in the longhouse at Bario he met David Matlaske who, killed in action twenty years later against the Indonesians, bequeathed him his daughter Cassandra.

Blakeney had never been in the Tamabo Range before, three thousand feet above the sea where the streams were too slight to be navigable, just rivulets that only bore small fish, though the eels and crabs were good, where the grass harboured cuckoos and quails and warblers. In the high moss-forest it was too sodden for the trees to grow handsomely, they were gnarled and fronded. If you followed the Kelabits' winding ways in the wet season it was like pushing through water, everything was overgrown with puffy sponges, you fell into pits of slime. But then at a ridge, if the clouds cleared, you could stand and shiver and gaze out over the far inviolate summits and watch a serpent-eagle wheel.

To be back in Borneo was something, though it did not alleviate the dread that his family had not survived, nor make it any easier to stop thinking of the evil reputation of the Japanese in the matter of the treatment of prisoners.

Lying at night on a mat by a smouldering longhouse fire, he thought about Nerissa. He listened to the dogs, the wind, the owls. Lying beneath the shadowy slung fruit baskets and fish traps, hides of clouded-leopard and honey-bear, spears, a hen and her chicks slung in a basket to be safe from civet and mongoose, hearing the sudden battering of dark rain on the *atap* thatch, he was a long way from knowing what he longed to know, a long way from whom he longed for.

Outside, the creatures of the night were afoot – tiger-cat and badger, lemur and tarsier and loris. Bats and cockchafers and moths flitted darkly.

For his father and mother Blakeney disciplined himself hardly to hope. When Z Special agents were first dropped into the mountains, one of their orders was to locate and succour any Dutch, English or Australian civilians or escaped prisoners of war surviving in the forests – but it appeared there weren't any. The *penghulu* of Bario said none of the pre-war whites were left in the interior. There were, on the other hand, a few recent arrivals, airmen who'd crashed behind Brunei Bay and escaped inland. Some were alive.

That Andrew and Nerissa might be alive in prison camps in Kuching he could not help hoping. He would pray until the cocks in the rafters began to crow and in the foredawn translucency the gibbons in the trees began their call of *wah wah wah*. At least that their deaths had been merciful, he would pray. He would beseech the night, beg the God he did not believe in, his mind loathsomely aswill with images of sadism and of suffering, aswill with hatred for his enemies. He would clench his brain on its horror, or the horror would clench his brain. Weeping, he would try to will the world his way. Incensed with hatred of the human mind, he would deride his powerlessness, his futility.

Yes, by the end of the war he was well schooled in patience. Severely schooled in knowing and not knowing too. Schooled in the vanity of wishes. He'd been beguiled by the baited hook which is belief in action and, impaled, he twisted a long time before the Fisher reeled him in.

Why did the peoples of the interior so promptly support the first half-dozen defenceless Allied soldiers who came winging down into their highlands? Recollections of the justice of the Rajahs of Sarawak maybe. And the Japanese had treated the tribes with even more contempt than had the Malays. More persuasive probably was the fact that Harrisson, Blakeney, Matlaske and the rest started handing out arms. Parachute cloth for the women. For the men, rifles, carbines, Sten guns, Bren guns, hand grenades. They had nothing like enough to go round the warriors who'd come walking up hill and down dale to profess their loyalty. They promised more weapons would be dropped. When punctually this occurred, their prestige was unassailable, far-flung villages rallied to their cause.

In a leafy hut, their aerial suspended between two trees, Blakeney and Matlaske struggled with their simple radio – for soon information well worth transmitting back to Darwin began to be relayed to them, details of Japanese positions around Brunei Bay vital to the planning of Australian air attacks and eventual landings at Labuan and Tarakan. They cranked their portable generator, tried to instil in Kelabits the knack of such mechanical labour. Hampered by storm disturbance from the mountains, wearied by two heavy volumes of code, they cranked, they sweated, they ciphered and deciphered, attended by mosquitoes, by leeches, by sand-flies, by ants.

The young man whose name was still on his door at Magdalen – casualties were heavy among the volunteers who'd entered the war at the start, but so long as you were alive the college kept your rooms for you – soon wearied of the noisy longhouse. The endless need to be jovial, the endless volubility and mirth – how he longed for peace! His austere spirit winced from the crowding, the clamour, the horseplay, the tireless recitations of monotonous music. He didn't like the gruelly *borak* they were obliged to swig all evening, disliked feeling drunk. On the Rejang, when travelling with his father, he'd been fêted in longhouse after longhouse and had been fascinated – but on those expeditions after a night they had set forth again. Harrisson and Matlaske, extroverts, took to the Bario longhouse happily, with passing irritations only. But they hadn't got their families in enemy hands or graves.

A chicken-coop society. And it was from his own forced amiability that he longed to flee. Five years later, sojourning idyllically in Baram longhouses with Danielle, Blakeney remembered his anguish in the Tamabo Mountains with a shudder. It was to return to a mind diseased by dread and hatred, it was to walk back in under a shadow, to be overcast. He had been imprisoned in his head. His head had been imprisoned in those cloudy mountains. The circle of skulls hung in rattan from the beams in the place of honour over *penghulu* Lawai's verandah at Bario were not more appropriated, were not more uselessly propitiated, were not less free.

To be away into the forest! This was some relief. It was a release, gave some feeling of taking action. It promised that he might escape from the interior where he knew nothing – knew a horde of details about troop deployments, knew a defective radio with disgusting intimacy, knew the pettifogging intricacies of ciphers, knew the differences between buffalo-leech and tiger-ant, deer-fly and tiger-hornet; but knew nothing that might ransom a soul in the toils of demonic imaginings. To escape from not knowing to knowing, from thinking to doing . . . !

The forest promised a passage out. It was the coast he longed for, it was Kuching, the outside. There truth lay. The very opposite of what Hugh had begun to ache for, as soon as in Timor he had received the letter about the fire, Blakeney observed a generation afterward, bringing to mind his son who was five years older now than he himself had been then.

Yes, his letter had accomplished the effect he had hoped for. At his father's report of this new environmental catastrophe Hugh had been inspired, he had written back. Timor would have to wait a few months. Of course, he would go back. Anyhow, already he had a pretty dramatic report to publish. He would be in Sarawak soon, soon. This fire was to be witnessed, whatever the difficulties, his father was to wait and see. Witnessed, described, accounted for. Mapped and photographed if possible. Hugh had been all ideas, all resolution. The interior! That inner burning! And at Bario in the old days, the sombre reader of this enthusiasm recalled, the people had been terrified of fire. Their hearths were of baked clay, but on occasion embers would roll out. Longhouses were burned – it was not unknown; the loss of jars and gongs was a great grief.

And in those times people believed a fire could be caused by somebody mocking an animal, deriding a toad for its ugliness, say. Or, if it were not burned, a guilty longhouse would be petrified. Blakeney had seen the sad charred logs left after fires. He'd seen abandoned ruins rotting, overgrown. He'd dreamed of coming out of the jungle and finding a longhouse turned to stone. The water-buffalo rasping its mud-caked hide against an upright would make the ramshackle tenement shake no longer. Stone, the buffalo. Stone, the posts. The women husking rice, their bark bins – stone, stone.

Outside the longhouse, Blakeney liked the shady grove of fruit trees: mango and mangosteen, jackfruit and paw paw, pomelo and lime. Then the canes set in a weir to direct the slivers of up-river tiddlers and eels toward the cone-shaped rattan traps . . . Out fishing or hunting he felt the beginnings of release. A rice field left to its natural grasshoppers, frogs, butterflies, bees, dragonflies . . . A clearing which after a few months was a paradisal tangle of scrub, sedge, pink-flowering tea bushes . . .

In the high moss-forest, red rhododendrons flowered. Travelling with his Kelabit guides to gather information and drum up passion for the coming fight, he stumbled into mud pools with moss floating on them, which luckily were often only a couple of feet deep. Foliage hung in dense mats, in festoons: with his *parang* he hacked his way through. He clambered over hummocks of moss, of orchids, of insectivorous pitcher plants named after Nepenthe the goddess of sleep, oblivion plants shaped like Georgian claret jugs. To get out, to cut through! To descend, emerge, act! His companions and he cut at the binding mosses. He was a mummy trussed in ignorance, in horror. He was webbed in a cocoon, the interior wouldn't let him out. He yearned to be reborn, to fly free. That he never was, never did – this couldn't assuage his desire then, mollify his despair later. To take action, however sanguinary, however long too late, inanely consolatory . . . !

Z Special had been two months based at Bario when a party of Kenyahs reached them after making the journey from Long Nawang. In this way, Blakeney learned of his father and mother.

For the Europeans on the upper Rejang when the Japanese occupied the coast and the lower rivers, the only hope was to escape south over the high watershed. Men, women and children, they made their way up from Kapit to Pelagus, then up the rapids, on higher to Belaga. There they left the river. After climbing the mountains and crossing the frontier into Kalimantan, they found sanctuary at the lonely settlement of Long Nawang. The Kenyahs received them hospitably. There was adequate food. There was shelter.

Five of the younger and fitter men set off to walk through the jungle to Samarinda. After eighteen days' trudging they made it, later were flown out to Java.

The rest, sixty-odd of them, remained at Long Nawang, including Michael and Kitty Blakeney, not young, not fit. They were a heterogeneous bunch. English and Dutch civilians, an American missionary or two, boys and girls. In time the Japanese reached them, murdered them all, buried them in one grave.

When in June the Australian Ninth Division landed in Brunei Bay, chiefly on the old coaling island of Labuan, Z Special and their tribesmen fell with scattered ferocity upon the inland Japanese and their collaborators.

It was a motley force. Allied lieutenants and corporals, with their wild bands of Iban and Kenyah, Kayan and Kelabit warriors, fought their remote campaigns, lorded it over strategic hills and rivers. Z had a good thousand men armed with weapons dropped from the air, another thousand or so wielding shotguns liberated from stores of sporting weapons the Japanese had confiscated earlier in the war. Then there were the irregular units of nomadic Penans armed with the *sumpitan*, the blowpipe, who could bring a monkey down from a treetop and now hunted the *Orang Gippun*. They smeared two types of poison on their darts, both obtained from saps. The glycoside venom attacked the heart, the strychnine the nervous system. The flight of their shafts was so silent that, if they missed, their prey remained unaware, ghostlily they shot again. It was best to shoot at the back, so the stricken man could not quickly cut the barb out.

Matlaske was with the force deployed on the east slopes of the Crocker Range, harrying the enemy along the Tengoa valley as they tried to obey their standing orders and fall back on the Sapong rubber estate in British North Borneo. It was here that he first saw suicides. Later the sight came to be common in the valleys toward Sapong. Too tired or ill or starving to keep up with their columns, the Japanese were killing themselves. Hanging themselves with their belts from the branches of trees, usually. It made Matlaske's pursuit ghoulish. He'd lost touch with Blakeney by then. But when at the end they came to Sandakan and freed the survivors in the prison camp there, when he saw those wraiths, when he heard their stories, heard of the death march from Sandakan to Ranau in the foothills of Mount Kinabalu, he couldn't stop thinking of Philip.

Harrisson had sent Blakeney over to the headwaters of the Rejang to liaise with Sochon who was in command there. He spoke Iban, didn't he? He'd be useful. And Harrisson knew he'd get to Kuching sooner that way.

Blakeney flew from Labuan in a sea-plane, skidded down onto the Rejang in a rainbow of spray in front of the longhouse which was Sochon's headquarters. After that they fought their way down the river with a small army of Ibans it was not easy to restrain. They took Kapit, they took Song, they took Kanowit, at last they took Sibu. The torturing thing was, it was Allied strategy to leave Kuching to liberate right at the end, for the sake of the civilians and soldiers imprisoned there who might in last-ditch brutality be killed. That was Japanese policy in many of the territories the Emperor of the Sun was being forced to relinquish.

6

'Yes, Hugh is dead set on seeing the fire. He wants to *know*,' his father remarked when, a couple of March evenings after the Kahns' anchoring off his shore, the newcomers' engagement to dine with Malay and French diplomatic company at one of the swish new hotels left Cassandra and him in their habitual peace. Akbar Nasreddin was there, a volcano wisping. Restless Thor Bernstein had departed – for his island, or somewhere. 'Oh, I can understand it very well. I remember from '45 . . . The wish to *know*. The wish, if possible, to have an effect. Or to appear to – in your own eyes.'

'Unless I'm much mistaken . . . ' Akbar puffed. 'Wasn't your ploy to get Hugh back skirmishing here? Here where the powers of the land, when he irritates them yet again, are likely to treat him a good deal more humanely than those in Timor.'

'Ah . . . Was that my . . . ? You don't think that when I wrote to him about the reports of the fire I was just sharing my perplexities with him? The way any man might do with his grown-up son? Oh, by the way, it seems it's a lot bigger than we thought, this fire. Well over a thousand square kilometres gone up in smoke, the last I heard. Not easy to conceive of. Or . . . You wouldn't allow that I was simply picking the best man for the job, the best man to go and have a look at this hell they've made, see if anything can be done about it? Given Hugh's – what shall I call it? – his determination, always? This rage to find out, to take action – I have a feeling for it. Perhaps I wanted to give him his chance. He is my son, after all. Some fools never learn – I can hear you thinking that, Akbar. Well . . . To an extent I live imaginatively through him, these days.'

I've always done my surrogate living through Philip and now he says he lives through Hugh, Akbar Nasreddin reflected ruefully. He wants to give the young man this splendid chance. Wants proudly to watch him in action. See if he can – well, in this case, see if he can snatch something interesting out of the fire. While I . . . Oh, I'm at more removes from the real thing than ever.

Glowingly Cassandra Matlaske – it had been Philip who insisted she bear her real father's name – meditated on Hugh Blakeney's achievements. Her distress on his account she managed this evening almost not to feel.

Flecked with moments of glory, his twenties had been. In the newspapers of several nations she had seen reports and pictures of his dare-devilry. Reuters' men had photographed him as his inflatable dinghy with powerful outboard engines dashed alongside Scandinavian and Japanese whaling ships, alongside ships dumping nuclear waste. Once the front page of *The Herald Tribune* had shown him as, from his tiny speedboat cockling in a ship's wash, miraculously he scaled the hull, planted the Greenpeace flag to flutter defiantly there.

In the last century he would have been a famous explorer, and in the last war a commando, Cassandra had never doubted it. Tall Hugh with his father's blue eyes, with his tussocks of brown hair which had flamey glints, it was tawny, that was the word. Hugh who together with his moments of glory had also decorated his time with honourable disgraces, reversals which would not long set back any of his numerous causes.

Flung out of Burma on account of his concern for political prisoners there, the authorities all too justifiably concluding that his was the hand writing Amnesty's bulletins, he had come inadvertently close to curtailing Thor Bernstein's research in that country, they having been observed in vivacious confabulations in the shabby grandeur of the bar at the Strand Hotel in Rangoon. His name was on the list of those no longer to be admitted into China too – on those grubby airport files wherein are the world's few eloquent and uncowed. Unfortunately, the Sarawak authorities also took a baleful attitude toward Hugh, cramped him with prohibitions to travel in the interior which he by and large contrived to transcend, because of his dogged agitation for the rights of the indigenous peoples. Soon perhaps they wouldn't let him into the state at all. What they needed was some slight further trouble from him, an excuse, and then that he had been born here would no longer avail him. His campaigning in defence of the sold and speechless rain-forest had made him enemies in high places too.

On the lamplit verandah Cassandra said to her two ancient listeners, 'If Hugh comes – and he will. If he decides he wants to go to the fire . . . ' Her voice was soft, but with pride it could lilt, could quiver. 'They won't stop him.'

'Is it a good idea, I wonder . . . ?' Akbar's instincts were cautious, protective. 'I mean, to pitch him into a situation where his nature will be to . . . to charge right ahead . . . to take risks . . . '

'Can't stop him.' Emotion usually made Blakeney gruff, dismissive. 'Disloyal to try to distract him. One's got to be let . . . I mean, if you want to see what's to be seen. Even if it's just a matter of waking up from an evil dream, like it was for some of us. Waking up to the knowledge that the evil dream is true, is all there is. All there will be, can ever be. I think, if you want to feel what's to be felt . . . Taste, taste . . . '

The sharpness of his 1945 lessons in revelation was present to his old friend, still mildly and for the most part vicariously living. It was also present to the daughter he had inherited from his other friend who had lived vitally enough all right, had pursued his way through his forest with hanged men here and there to his left and now and then to his right, himself now dead twenty years. Between the three on the gloomy verandah these discoveries trembled in the warm air, came wafting in the smells of woodsmoke and mud and lush greenery, visited with the whine of mosquitoes and the fluttering of moths, shivered unseen, seen.

It hadn't only been his wild Iban warriors who'd been difficult to restrain when they came storming down the Rejang, Sochon had said afterward when he'd got his D.S.O. and Blakeney had got his M.C. and the pick of the triumphant Ibans had, in addition to some enemy heads, got medals too. The desire to reach the sea and to get along the coast to Kuching and to know had been on Philip like a madness, his commanding officer had recalled. Yes, madness the way he went for Kapit, went for Sibu, reach after reach of the wide tumid river with the forest grand along its shores, and the Brahminy kites which the Ibans believed were the kings of the omen birds overhead. And then, yes . . . to know had been more cruel than to have been shot in one of those fights would have been.

Some were lucky. Some found those whom they loved alive.

Some found them alive, but scarcely sane.

Some found them alive, but dying. Dying of typhus, dying of beri-beri, dying of malaria or cholera.

Some were luckier than they might have been, had to count themselves lucky. When David Matlaske fought through to Sapong, one man with him had been a rubber planter there. Most of the estate workers were dead. Those who were alive were foul with ulcers, scabies, yaws. The pigs had dug up the graves, human bones lay everywhere. But this man's wife had survived. His youngest daughter had died right at the end, of malaria. But hidden in the jungle, planting *padi* and catching fish, his wife and the other children had survived.

One friend of the Blakeneys' had slaved in Singapore Docks, and he survived – one of the eighteen who did, out of the two hundred in that labour gang when they began. Another man was one of a detachment three thousand strong sent to build a railway across Sumatra – but he was one of the two thousand two hundred who died. Philip's uncle Claud Blakeney was in the column marched north to build the Burma–Siam railway. At Three Pagodas Pass he died of cerebral malaria.

In the prisoner-of-war camp in Kuching, toward the end they were burying ten a day.

Andrew Blakeney's imprisonment had not lasted long. Perhaps because right from the start he maintained a dignity his captors found offensive, or he tried to . . . Perhaps because he was uncommonly good-looking . . . Perhaps because they thought he knew things about the Miri oilfield, or for some other reason, he was one of those the Japanese tortured. Day after day he was taken aside, one of the ghosts still alive told his brother. They did such unspeakable things to him that one night he got hold of a bottle, broke it, made enough of a mess of his throat to bleed to death before morning came.

Philip Blakeney wrenched his mind away. His son's lessons in knowing, however adventurously sought, were not likely to resemble in horror his of that September.

'Caz my darling,' he asked, because this too had been haunting him, 'if Hugh turns up . . . ' He was hesitant. 'When we next see Hugh . . . '

'I shall be delighted to see him.' Her voice rang impeccably calm. 'I look forward to it,' she elaborated steadily. And, when Akbar lumbered up from his creaking chair, when he declared it was time he left them in peace, 'May I walk with you as far as the jetty?'

Philip Blakeney had been possessed by diabolical knowledge for forty years; more than half his life, more than half of him, was in the hands of that tyranny. Now again he was left alone in its grip. His parents' carcasses among dozens dumped in a pit. Bonfires of the victims at Three Pagodas Pass – they tried to contain the diseases as they could. Andrew. Andrew.

After the known, the unknown. He'd been possessed by the unknown for forty years too, by that omnipotent evil, that master of imaginative ceremonies. Hearing Akbar's and Cassandra's voices fade down the lane, he stared at his lamp, at the circling moths. Of Nerissa he had found no trace.

Nothing.

She had not been interned. There was no record of her living or dying. None of the survivors had seen her.

Maybe she had managed to get herself shot when the Japanese occupied Kuching Hospital. Possibly she had killed herself. Philip could imagine her doing that. But probably at the beginning she had not conceived how vile life in enemy hands would be.

It was most likely she was taken as an army prostitute. 'Comfort women,' that was the euphemism. Polite, the Japanese. Chinese and Korean girls, Philippine and Malay girls, Burmese and Javanese girls, and a few European girls too, all over that famous Co-Prosperity Sphere. After the war, facts began to emerge. They emerged slowly and patchily, because in a lot of military brothels at the end of the war the surviving whores were killed lest they should talk. But word came . . . Word of dozens of men a day. Of tortures. Of how when the girls became diseased or pregnant they were shot in the vagina.

The beginning of Blakeney's madness in the possession of the unknown had been when peace came to this territory and that of South-East Asia, it had been his desperate searching, his hope Nerissa might still be alive somewhere, might have been kept as a general's toy, anything, anything, might somehow be alive. Since then, the known and the unknown had battened on him with equal wolfishness. In time he'd more or less convinced himself that she'd found the means to commit suicide – early, he prayed, early.

It was as he had said a few moments before. That September he had woken from an evil dream to find it true. Unknowable, but true – that was the twist. Left alone on his verandah, he supposed that with his death it would end. He watched the moths battering softly at his lamp. The horror and he haunting one another – this must end, it must. Ends came, didn't they, death was good, a grace, oblivion came, didn't it? The goddess Nepenthe would come, would hold out to him her flask of forgetfulness. Then after further years he would be forgotten. It would be as if Andrew and Nerissa and he had never lived, and that would be good. That was the best that could be hoped for. Evil beyond knowing – that was their particular twist of fate. Evil victorious, evil unknowable but true. Their twist.

There was not much traffic on the Sarawak river at night. Akbar and Cassandra were the only dim figures waiting on the jetty. When a *tambang* approached, its lantern glimmering, he said goodnight.

'One thing . . . ' She hesitated. 'They won't want Hugh setting off into the interior. They'll try to stop him. I wondered . . . Oh, I hate asking favours of people, but . . . You're a sort of godfather of his, a sort of godfather of mine. You're a judge, you've got friends in politics.'

'My dear girl, you overestimate me,' Akbar said hurriedly, secretly flattered, as on occasion before, that she who was so serious about her Christianity should honour a nominal Muslim like him with this accolade.

'I wanted to ask you . . . Is it possible to have Hugh left alone?' Slim, dark, she stood on the jetty in the moonlight. She twined her fingers. 'He won't do any harm. He's never done anything wrong in his life.'

'Cassandra, I absolutely agree with you.' Flustered by doubts, thus far he could be forthright. 'But unfortunately that's not what the Forestry Department thinks. At the Ministry of Development they don't like him either. That article in *The Economist* about dams that don't work – remember? Ah, here's my little ferry.'

The boatman stepped onto the slipway. Patient, silent, he waited for his passenger to embark. The lantern shimmered on the sliding water, on eddies, on sticks.

'And I wonder . . . ' As timid as he was fond, Akbar peered worriedly at his companion. 'Do you, do we, really *want* him in trouble here again? Has it occurred to you that it might not be that bad a thing if he were prevented from . . . from involving himself too deeply?'

'Yes. It has occurred to me.' With a breath of laughter, she tossed back her head with its black tresses. 'I wrote to beg him to keep out of this, to keep away. When he next wrote, he said I should have known him better. I wrote back, I apologised for having asked anything so cowardly.'

'You write!' Akbar could not help exclaiming, but just managed to bite off his, You write to each other still!

'We write,' she assented, with wryness in her gravity.

The old lawyer embarked on his *tambang*. Despairing of another passenger so late at night, the boatman pushed off.

But just as he was about to duck into the low cabin, Akbar checked. Sauntering along the lane, they had spoken Malay. But now in English, for discretion's sake, he called, 'Please! Think about it, Cassandra!' The *tambang* was turning. Stoutly, wobblingly he turned; he called over the cabin roof. 'If Hugh had to stay in Kuching . . . Better . . . !'

'No!' Her call was in English too. 'Never! You must do what I ask. Leave him be!' Faintly it reached him. 'Let him go!'

TWO

5

Singapore
3rd December

My darling Cassandra

You didn't say I mustn't write. And when I told you I was going to ask you again you didn't say I couldn't.

Why, why did you say no? But no, you didn't exactly say no. You said you didn't see how it could be possible. I keep reminding myself that you just said wait, let me think, not now. Well, you did say no.

One of us is mad – I wonder which one? I only asked you because I already felt married to you, I knew my soul was married to yours. I still know it. It had come to me with a clarity I'd never seen before, it was a resolution of all doubts, a going beyond all half measures. I know faith is a ridiculously low form of cognition, but in this instance it's all we've got to go on. You make sense of me.

I keep trying not to think: If she hesitates she's superficial, chuck her. I keep trying not to think of all the rest of my life without you. I try to know you need time, then you'll understand that to love one another is our only hope. Then if I feel more sanguine I think: Well, any illusion so long as it's effective.

I'll wait, I'll do anything you ask.

Hugh

Kuching
20th December

Dear Hugh

It is true that I did not forbid you to write. It is even true that in time I should have begun to long for word of you – for word from you, yes, I confess it. But the swiftness with which your letter came appalled me. My spirit had not begun to find the peace it yearned for. I am still struggling to desire peace wholeheartedly.

This is why your letter has remained unanswered for so many days. Hugh, one thing I beg of you. Do not telephone. You must not.

You know the little hut by the water where the *sampan* is moored. When I was a child it was my hide-out. I have taken to retreating there to pray. The house is alive with your presence. But the hut – have you ever done more than glance inside it, I wonder? I walk down the garden, I climb the rickety ladder. When it rains, the *atap* leaks a bit, but there is no furniture in the room to be spoiled. There I feel a little distanced from you, a little safe.

You ask why. *Why?* My brother, are you mad? You are my brother. Am I mad to know this? Of course I know too that we have no drop of blood in common, but I cannot remember my real father and mother. I have always loved your father as my father. One of my great joys for which I have given thanks to Our Lord is that you have never begrudged me your father. Do not undo your generous love now. Before the law we are brother and sister. Before the Church . . . I have not yet summoned the courage to speak to my spiritual adviser on the subject. I pray that God will give me the strength not to wish to enquire. In the eyes of God, Who gave me to you as your sister, how can I believe that I could ever be anything other than that, could be your wife?

That my parents were dead and that Philip was my father now – I have always known this, it is the first knowledge in my heart. That my name should be Matlaske was his idea, his charming insistence, but Hugh, Hugh, this does not mean I am not his daughter. Akbar saw to the legal business of my adoption, and I am sure it was all correctly done. And that in France a boy was growing up who was my older brother, whom one day I should learn to love as my brother – I cannot remember a time when I did not know this. When I was adopted, did Danielle not tell you that you had a little sister, away in Paris did you not think of me sometimes? You have told me you did. It has warmed my silly heart to think of this.

Now I remember the first time I conceived of you – or it must have been one of the first times, I was very young I think. Philip took me up to the Fourth Division with him to visit the caves at Niah which had only been discovered a few years before. I held his hand, I stumbled beside him over those crags of guano in the dimness, he had a torch, he shone it before our feet. I am probably muddling it up with later visits, but I think I recall him showing me a cavern bigger and more dusky than a cathedral, the Dayaks with baskets and torches shinning up their spindly poles to collect the swiftlets' nests. He explained to me how they sold them to the Chinese who made them into soup. Then at nightfall we stood at the cave mouth, we looked out over the rolling miles of forest and the twilight was darkened by the multitude of bats which flew out and then it was darkened again by the returning swiftlets. He told me to stand still because they never hit you. Wave after wave of birds flew toward us over the trees, and suddenly I heard him talking of you, telling me about his little boy, how he had brought you there when you were still really his. I stood holding his hand and I imagined you standing there and holding his hand a few years before, I wished you were holding his other hand now. I looked up at Philip, for the first time in my life I saw tears in his eyes, I was awestruck, cloudily I was aware he was grieving for you, for David perhaps and for you. The air was clamorous with rushing wings, then the last wave broke behind us in the gloom and it was true what he had said, true that none of the birds had brushed us, and the sky was hushed and night fell.

It is wrong to have written so much, I feel that now. I have let myself be carried away. The joy of seeming for a moment to talk with you! And I did not like to think of you alone at Christmas in a hotel with no word from your sister.

If I did not reply when you said that one day you would ask me the intolerable question again, it was because I was dumb with fear or I did not trust myself to speak, not because my answer might ever be a different one. This is true. Please, please believe me.

And that terrible hour on the river in the *sampan* – how can you claim I did not say no? It seems to me that I screamed in a whisper *No No No!* I implored you not to insist, I implored you to go away, to forget your mad cruel idea, to forgive me.

You are probably right that I am superficial. Our only happiness, almost our only hope of sanity, will lie in our agreeing that I am.

I pray God to protect and comfort you.

Your sister

Cassandra

Singapore
25th December

My darling Cassandra

If by your spiritual adviser you mean that fat little priest of yours, that Stephen fellow, have the decency to leave him out of this. I don't like him, don't trust him, don't want him nosing around us.

I've got no idea what Church or State might think of you and me – though I scarcely see how they could object, since we're brother and sister only on paper. I haven't got enough respect for Church or State to care much. And if they make a fuss, to hell with them. For that matter, supposing Philip and not David had been your real father – I wouldn't love you differently or love you less, and I defy you to pretend that your feeling for me would be merely sisterly. I'd commit incest with you happy in the knowledge that we were more profoundly married than in any union Church or State could fix us up with.

You talk about the eyes of God. Cassandra, I've had passions that came and went, but now I know I'm in love with you. If God exists, my soul is married to yours. If God doesn't exist, my soul is married to yours. You notice, incidentally, how high above theology we fly.

I've been trying to make some headway with the Timor plan, but the bureaucracy is a hopeless tangle. The Indonesian Embassy here make all manner of trouble for journalists who want to go to Dili. As for the trips I want to make into the hinterland, you can't imagine the excuses they come up with to deflect one where they can control what one hears and sees. It's going to take weeks to organize, so today I decided to go and meander about in Java for a bit. I haven't been back for years, and Singapore is depressing. I dare say it used to be as romantic as Philip and people say, but they've bulldozed most of the old white bungalows, the old Chinese shop-houses, the old bazaars. Write to me *Poste Restante* in Jakarta. Write to me.

I went to Raffles a few nights ago with a man who writes for *Le Monde*. Drank bourbon, too much bourbon. Hot night, we sat in the courtyard. I told him about you. Wished I hadn't.

A godawful Christmas Day today. Usually I only go to Saint Andrew's to read the memorials – there's a lot of history to be learned from church walls in the East, Philip taught me that years ago. But today . . . The bells were ringing, there were going to be carols, I suppose it brought my childhood back or I wanted it to. So even a creedless wretch like me . . .

I went in. The service began. I found I was praying. Let her not condemn us for the sake of a superstitious taboo or a legal quibble, I prayed. Let her love me as her heart inclines, as I can't believe I haven't seen, haven't felt. Then I remembered that you were very likely praying for me – praying with all your sweet sincerity to a God believed in, not just mouthing your desperation as I was. I thought how you might be praying for our love to fade away, to be what you'd miscall transcended, and I hated your prayer, I hated your religion and your sincerity, I came close to hating you. The idea that you might go to a priest for advice made me sick with anger. My mind was snarling abuse of Christian notions of virtue. Blundering out of my pew, I trod on someone's foot.

I'm more calm now. It's evening. I'm in a restaurant. Cassandra, won't you pray less and love more? Or if you pray, my darling, pray that our love burgeons and flourishes. If love isn't perfect, shouldn't it be encouraged, trained to grow toward perfection? I'm not going to love another woman as I love you. I dare to believe you'll never love another man with this love. Be gentle, think again, don't blight us.

Cassandra, with all my heart and with all my mind,

Hugh

Kuching

21st February

Dear Brother

I made myself promise I would not write back to you for a month, and it was a correct decision, because look, the habit of abstinence is a healing one, I have successfully let much of February too elapse tranquilly.

I write now because Philip tells me he has written to you about a great fire which they say has broken out in the interior, in East Kalimantan it seems. Hugh, please, I ask you not to take this opportunity to come back to Borneo yet. I am not ready to see you. I do not trust my whirligig of a heart. As for my mind, it never ceases to sing your praises, but it had best be left to do this out of your earshot.

I have reread your letters – unnecessarily, since I have them by heart. The things you say! So faith is a low form of cognition, is it? I know you are far cleverer than I am, I know I never went to university – but it appears to me that you and I base all our thinking on faith. And all this wild talk of incest! And your idolatry! But at least you do not write what you think will please me, and this is typical of your superb disdainful honesty – and, yes, it pleases me.

Do not insult Stephen Chai, he is a wise and good man, his sisters and he are my friends. I have disobeyed you and broken my first resolution, I have gone to him for advice. In his view, as in mine, that God first gave me to you to be your loving sister is a grave impediment to any other love, and he counselled me to pray earnestly to Our Saviour that my wayward longings should return to their proper channel. It is not his initial opinion that the Church would have an irrevocable opposition to our marriage, there being no consanguinity, and if in time it is the Lord's wish he will consult an ecclesiastical lawyer to ascertain this. Our case is so unusual, he says he cannot think of a precedent. He prays every day that God will show us what is right.

It is fair that you should know this. But even to write of these matters pitches me back into a reprehensible agitation.

I am in the *atap* hut by the water. Still every morning and evening I come here to pray. The room is utterly bare, which

I like. I had to bring pen and paper with me. I am kneeling, I am writing on the floor, there being no table or chair. A cock is crowing. Also I can hear a fishing-smack chugging up the river. Sunlight glints through the ragged thatch, between the slats of the walls.

Ever since your leaving us, Philip has been all discretion, all kindness. That he misses you I know – but then he is sadly accustomed to your flitting between half the countries of the world, for so many years to miss you has been his only way of loving you. That he saw our love was tempted to change, he saw us wavering, saw the abyss beneath our feet – can I doubt it? That in your sudden departure he saw our crisis, our stepping back from the brink – something of this he has intuited. And though Heaven knows I have never been much of a Bohemian, my ever more cloistered existence these last eleven weeks, my silences and tears, my retreats to this hut . . . Eloquent enough.

One evening he said a terrible thing about the war. He said that either God created in Doctor Faustus the overriding need to sell his soul to Lucifer – a point of view which my whole mind spurns – or Faustus freely chose to make his hideous bargain. Whereas when in 1945 he discovered what had been done to Andrew, and when he was forced to consider the probable fate of Nerissa, his soul was bequeathed to the Devil without his consent, against his every prayer, in return for a diabolical knowledge he was constrained ever more deeply to understand. Yes, an involuntary Faustus he said he was.

You are irreverent from high spirits and I have trained myself not to let your levity make me wince, but sometimes Philip's despair terrifies me. Since I can remember I have prayed that in the end he may find peace. Since he said this awful thing I have besought grace for him with a fervour which can only come from God.

My prayers go with you too. When you were what you called meandering about in Java for a bit I prayed that the beauty of the island might be some consolation to you. Now that you are in Timor I pray that by the efforts of you and others like you some belated justice may be granted to the suffering people there. Akbar and Philip say that over the last few years the Indonesian army has killed more than two hundred thousand East Timorese. Can this appalling figure be true?

You are not easy to pray for. If you recall what you wrote to me on Christmas Day, if you recall the hard things that often you have said to me, you will understand why.

Hate me for praying for you! Hugh, Hugh, this is unjust. At first in my misery I made myself pray for you to dislike me, but it was a false, wrong prayer for which I have begged forgiveness. Since then I have prayed that you should love me as your sister. But I know you too well, I can sense your spirit trampling contemptuously on my prayer, calling it pusillanimous. My heart recoils, I cringe. Have mercy on me.

I pray too that I may love you as my brother. I keep praying this. What more can I do?

Cassandra

Dili
9th March

My darling Cassandra

Don't be absurd, of course I'm coming back to Borneo. Don't you know me better than that? Coming back to get inland to this fire, coming back to marry you.

Yes, unfortunately the evil news which seeps out of this island is true. My friend from *Le Monde* and I drink our bourbon in a dump called the Hotel Tourismo here. Off to Viqueque in a day or two I hope – though our every move is obstructed. A massacre has been going on there. A village festival was attacked by some Indonesian soldiers, who abducted and raped several Timorese girls. The villagers then killed the soldiers. You can imagine the reprisal. In a few weeks it seems they slaughtered five or six hundred people – burning them in their houses, parading them on the river bank to be gunned down.

You believe Stephen Chai prays for God to guide us? All he begs his maker is that you should fall out of love with me. Still, it's good he's had the decency to confess that the Church will smile on us.

Just to show you I can be polite about Christians: the bishop here, Carlos Belo, is a dignified man. Catholic not Protestant – but approximately your religion. He asked the Pope not to come here and sanction the invasion. Naturally the Pope came and naturally the Indonesians were delighted – but it was a stalwart request.

My darling, if that day in the *sampan* I frightened you, forgive me. I wanted you forever, and I knew you wouldn't let yourself have a love affair.

I've had affairs. I don't want another. I want to marry you.

I should get to Sarawak about the end of the month.

Hugh

Kuching
17th March

Dear Hugh

Come then, my brother, and let us see what Providence decrees. At least you will always be my brother. From this I take heart.

One thing, Hugh, please. The intolerable question – do not put it to me again. Believe me, there is no need. It is always here, with me, I have almost become it. Some nights when I cannot sleep I twist myself in mad arguments, I think that as God did not need to make me your sister in order for me to be your sister, so He will not need to make me your bride, my soul being already wedded to yours. Then even if it is not yet dawn I go down to the hut to pray. Slowly some peace comes.

Hugh, I have told your father everything, told our father everything. I hope I have done right. I hope you do not mind. Everything, I confessed. It came so naturally. We had taken up again our old ritual of rowing the *sampan* on the river at evening. He said how pleasant it had always been to scull the old boat with you and with me, and I said the last time I had rowed had been with you and suddenly I found I was crying and telling him everything.

He listened in silence. At first he looked stricken. Of course he had suspected – but to hear the full truth, sense its force . . . I was afraid, he looked as if he were being made to contemplate something that appalled him, made to see something hidden from me. But quite soon he recovered his equanimity. 'If an old sceptic's blessing is any good to you . . . ' he said.

Your mother and Raoul have arrived. I find him rather lacking in gentleness, as you know, but no doubt this is a mistaken sort of sensitivity in me. To see Danielle again is lovely. Sometimes she can appear to me a little formidable too – probably this is the effect of my always seeing her beside him, and the effect of my provinciality and inexperience. But one evening when we were all on the verandah suddenly I wanted to kneel before her chair and lay my head in her lap and tell her about you.

Last night Philip and Akbar were talking about you. I was

relieved to find how calmly I listened and talked – almost with my old unabashed happy pride in you, the simple adoration your sister lavished on you. I even summoned the courage to ask Akbar if there was anything he could do to make it easier for you to travel in the interior. Wasn't I good?

When you come back, be gentle with me. If you are contemptuous of my prayers, you despise me. Touch my mind gently, it feels as if it were made of glass.

Cassandra

2 ∫

What came to be called Confrontation began when on an April day in '63 a platoon of Indonesian soldiers attacked the police station at Tebedu in the First Division of Sarawak.

It suited David Matlaske down to the ground that the President in Kuala Lumpur, Tunku Abdul Rahman, wanted the British to stay and help defend the nascent Malaysia. Some Argyll and Sutherland Highlanders were there, some Royal Green Jackets, some Gurkhas, some SAS. He was a major in the Queen's Royal Irish Hussars by then, a major the regiment expected to see promoted again before long. He was thirty-nine. It was splendid to be back in Borneo. It was splendid to see Philip Blakeney again.

Headquarters was the Haunted House in Brunei. Photographs of Blakeney visiting Matlaske there survived, and of both of them at the former's bungalow up the Baram – Philip already going bald, as if the Devil had patted that involuntary Faustus on the head or as if his hair without had fled from his thoughts within. He already looked gaunt, halfway on his passage from dashing young officer to old heron. He had just got divorced, he had given up writing poetry, and these things or other griefs showed.

The British with their Iban Border Scouts had a fairly wild time of it in the jungle fighting. There were operations called Hell Fire, called Kingdom Come, wonderfully resounding operations. One small slaughter was called Blood Alley, and there was a Gurkha ambush of a longboat with eight Indonesians on board lightly named Guitar Boogie.

Matlaske had a wild time when he wasn't in the forests

ambushing and scouting. His Iban mistress was a renowned
beauty. Island gossip whispered that she had her wildness also.
Island gossip had even been heard to elaborate that she was one
of Blakeney's mistresses too or she had been, but afterward the
rumour died away almost to nothing. Her baby daughter was
christened in the Church of Our Saviour at Labuan, with Tom
Harrisson, who by then was Curator of Kuching Museum, and
the District Officer on the Baram river, Philip Blakeney, for
godfathers. A prophetic name they gave her, as it turned out.
Yes, tragically prophetic enough to satisfy the most ruthless
advocates of predestination, but this wasn't because David
Matlaske or his lover were readers of Homer, students of the
siege and burning of Troy. No, it seemed Blakeney was reading
an edition of the letters of Jane Austen and her sister Cassandra;
his guests picked the book up, liked the name. An illegitimate
new soul – but the parson was a friend, was broadminded, and
as it chanced in this little half-breed he acquired for his flock a
girl of the purest, sweetest Christianity. Then her mother with
her famous loveliness and her wild ways took the baby home
to her village, on what ought to have been a brief visit to her
family, but while she was there the Indonesians attacked, she
was killed. The survivors found the infant Cassandra lying on
the dust in the sun beside her mother, shot at twenty-two. Ants
were crawling over the baby. She had flies on her face.

Operation Claret was the name given to strikes across the
Kalimantan border. Matlaske's last success was an ambush on
the Sentimo river. It had rained torrentially for five days; where
they stood among the trees, the water was up to British waists
and Gurkha chests. On the second day a sizeable python swam
between the waiting men, on the third day the boat they were
waiting for came. Well, the next ambush was a success too in
its fashion. They were up the Ayer Hitam this time and it was
dry. Two boats came and Matlaske and his men in the trees
fired for over a minute. The leading boat sank, and the other
with its loathsome freight of dead soldiers drifted slowly away.
But the Indonesians counter-attacked and cut them off on their
retreat to the Sarawak border; after the fight in the forest, David
Matlaske was one of those never seen again.

Of course the survivors who picked up Cassandra where she

lay crying among burning houses, among men and women and children dead and wounded, were the scared villagers who after the Indonesians withdrew crept circumspectly out of the forest which had been their salvation. But it was really Philip Blakeney who took her life into his hands. He was the survivor, the man who seemed always condemned to survive, who saw himself forever in the act of bending to pick up that child lying fly-haloed on the dust, of lifting her, holding her to his heart. That possessed man had for twenty years been trying to contain the unbounded evil in his head, reduce it to the comprehensible, to order, to sanity. Now solitary and bitter in his forties, his legacy after Cassandra's parents' deaths was the suspicion that he truly *was* damned, evil would go on having its way with the world and him, all you could ever know after a tragedy was that another would fall.

He didn't hesitate so much as a day before setting in motion his adoption of the orphan. He picked her up, held her close. She, at least, must be saved. To that he would dedicate his remaining years and strength. Had Danielle not recently departed for France, deprived him of his eight-year-old Hugh? And in some ways, people said, Cassandra saved Philip just as undoubtedly as he saved her, because without his wife and son his temptation to follow Andrew and Nerissa might have been overmastering. For years he'd fought his horror and despair with his wife at his side, had wrestled with his familiar devil for her sake and for their child's – but without them . . . Yes, it was lucky he had Cassandra now.

The only person who knew anything worth knowing about Philip Blakeney's wrestling with his devil in those years after the war was Danielle, and she never talked about it much, except once briefly to Akbar Nasreddin. A little curtly, also, the occasion being a discussion of her divorce, and she not being unaware that his sympathies were with her husband. Curtly . . . With flarings almost of hysteria.

'Dear God, man,' the just still Mrs Blakeney imperiously growled, 'have you thought what it might be like to be married to a husband who can't make love without thinking of his sister being raped to death?'

Dutiful, frightened, Akbar sat immobile, his plump paw with

its plumply opulent lawyer's fountain pen suspended impotently over the minutiae of Hugh's custody. He might at Gray's Inn have trained as a barrister, but back in Borneo he had turned his hand to all manner of legal work.

'A man who abhors sex just as much as he enjoys it, sometimes for weeks won't touch me. A man who lies awake dreaming of horror and hatred. Who when he sleeps has nightmares, wakes me with his cries.' Danielle Blakeney lit her fourth cigarette of the interview. 'Of course I know I'm betraying him, don't you dare suspect I don't. I'm leaving him alone to face . . . ' She almost screamed, 'To face I don't know what! But if I don't get out he'll drag Hugh and me down with him into . . . ' She gestured her helplessness to express the void which terrified her. 'Your wife doesn't wake you with her screams all that often, I presume?'

So accurate was this understanding of his spouse's slumbers, her tranquillity lulled by her family, her religion, her plants and his salary, that Akbar did not even shake his head.

When Danielle divorced Philip she knew she might be abandoning him in a vortex in which he would circle downward and inward to death. But she wasn't new to the idea of suicide.

Rumour was cloudy by the time it reached Kuching after twenty years and a world war. Maybe mercifully cloudy. But it appeared that Vernet had left his wife and small Danielle in Saigon – perhaps his tour of duty up-country was going to be an arduous one, or already the marriage was ropy. And then . . . Not enough, it seemed, the pleasant bungalow by a river, not comfort enough in the isolation for months, the hard work, the heat, the marshes. Not enough the local girl, the maid who knew how to keep her pretty mouth shut. Not enough that handmaiden with the slender body of a child and hair softly heavy and blackly lustrous to her waist, she the wench who when he came back from work tired and sweaty washed him with water kept in a Shanghai jar, in the latticed shade slowly ladled the soft cool water, washed him slowly, silkily. Not enough, it seemed. No, Vernet had to go and convince himself he was in love with the daughter of one of the grandees of Indo-China. Yes, a daughter who lived in one of the great white pillared mansions which were the pride and earthly reward of the nabobs of

French colonialism, a daughter for whom an aristocratic fiancé had already been chosen – they could be watched waltzing together at the balls her High Commissioner papa gave, balls to which Vernet was courteously invited along with other junior officials till his disgraceful passion and the spoilt young lady's unaccountable vacillations came to be known. After that it appears to have been chiefly a matter of his drinking too much hard liquor alone at night in his gloomy bungalow where the mosquitoes were relentless. Not an uncommon problem among solitary Frenchmen too many miles up the Mekong, solitary Englishmen too many miles up the Irrawaddy – unfortunately not uncommon at all. Sad. Messy. Then one night the writing to the lady of rather a sentimental last letter. The drinking of a copious last glass of cognac. The pistol held to his brown and dryly swallowing throat.

Danielle was four. She scarcely remembered Vernet; only the story. His succumbing to the romantic or the vaporous, to the mortally passionate or the self-regarding, left his widow bankrupt. She took a job in a Saigon school teaching French. All Danielle's girlhood they were hard-up. Luckily before the Japanese army arrived she had been sent to France, cousins had found her a job as a secretary, so she was invaded by the Germans instead, which was bad but not as bad as the Japanese would have been. She wasn't a Jew.

From the age of seventeen to twenty-two Danielle Vernet typed business letters in Poitiers. She forgot how poor her mother and she had been. The East waited for her, like a mirage. Typing, she remembered the ferries on the Mekong, she remembered green river islands with pagodas and herons and egrets, villages on stilts over the shallows where you paddled from house to house by *sampan*, sun-beaten backwaters where the fishermen drifted patiently under their conical hats, the vast region of brown flood proceeding to the coast bearing rafts of water hyacinths. She did not wish to die typing letters in Poitiers, after the war she went back to the East. Her mother was still in Saigon, still teaching French. More hard-up than ever. And her character was beginning to ravel. She repeated herself, didn't finish her sentences. She was unnecessarily dogmatic in her views, would hold forth about the threat of communism until you stopped her. Through the stupefying afternoons she slept in her chair with her mouth open, flies buzzing, sweat on her moustache.

In Penang a few months later Danielle met Philip Blakeney – met him at the Eastern and Oriental Hotel, in the ballroom, beneath the cupola and its chandelier. She was perhaps a woman of hotels, of destinies turning in foyers, in ballrooms, on canopied terraces. Later, as an elegant but impecunious divorcée with Hugh at a Paris *école secondaire*, she was taken by a bore to a reception at the Ritz where she met Raoul Kahn, and he was a laying to rest of uncertainties too. He also was a release, was freedom. Naturally this freedom was circumscribed; but she didn't need very much. Just enough in which to be a tolerable version of herself and to love Hugh, enough in which to identify a tolerable self to be.

Standing on the foredeck of the ketch *Aigrette* as they came up Kuching river in the warm dusk, standing with grey in her hair and one brown hand on the grey wire of the forestay, Danielle Kahn was surprised by her fear. A return, yes. A rediscovery too. But not the first. Every few years the Kahns saw Blakeney, relations were what are called friendly, called civilised. A new discovery, perhaps? Or a last one . . . hence the fear. A last meeting with her long-ago husband, with her old flame, her man of night sweats and night cries – very likely, he was old, ill. A definitive discovery, a definitive losing . . .

In the days of waiting for Hugh to arrive from Timor there was a fair amount of cheerful coming and going between the verandah of Blakeney's shabby house and the cockpit of Kahn's trim yacht; Danielle had leisure to make her observations, had scope for her antennae. Akbar Nasreddin never changed, he was as flaccid as ever, just fatter. The girl, the adopted daughter of whom she'd heard so much in Philip's years of letters to Hugh, the saved waif . . . The girl who on Raoul's and her last visit had been alternately schoolgirlishly mute and then gauchely passionate on political subjects she only sketchily understood . . . She was more self-possessed now. Still tremendously innocent, of course, but a little better poised. She had progressed, it seemed, from studying at the Mission School to teaching the smallest pupils there. What adventurousness! She was nervous.

There quivered an anxious tension, didn't there, in her quiet gazing at one across the evening verandah? Danielle Kahn wondered why. The girl was accustomed to being the mistress of Philip's house, possibly felt threatened by his long-gone wife's return, was that it? She made a resolution not to tread on this wide-eyed and excessively Christian damsel's toes.

And her darling old Philip . . . ?

He had survived. No doubt in his walnut head the vortex of horror still turned, but he hadn't been sucked under. He was tough. Year after year he stood tall and motionless, he waited gaunt and grey, he watched the river flow. If we're not careful he'll become a veritable grand old man, Danielle thought with a sudden resumption of old liking, with a spontaneous, warm smile. There were things she would like to talk about alone with him, she realised; and smiled again, this time an inward, abstract smile. Well, when Raoul was busy one day . . . About Hugh and the fire, for instance. This decision of Philip's to send his only begotten son to see what outrages men were committing on his green land, see if anything could be done about it, anything saved. He's my only son too, Danielle thought. Not that Raoul, who for all his bluffness knew how to treat a lady, had not years before offered the idea of a child. He would have known how to pay nannies and nursery maids too, take a lot of the tedium out of family life. But Danielle had refused; had surprised herself by the prompt fluency of her refusal. 'A child, darling?' she had drawled. 'It's exhausting enough being married twice, do we have to jump *all* the fences in the gymkhana? Anyhow, I probably couldn't, now. Feel a bit infertile, you know, sometimes.'

But when Raoul went to lunch with a man who was trying to raise the capital to establish a palm plantation, when Danielle invited Philip but not Cassandra to sample her prawn curry and a bottle of white Burgundy under *Aigrette*'s awning, it was not their son's going to the fire they spoke of.

'He wants to marry Cassandra,' Philip said, and recounted the girl's confession of the evening before aboard the *sampan*.

'Good Lord!' Danielle had not seen her son for the best part of a year, her astonishment was genuine. So, hard on its heels, were her merriment and her smiling, 'Well, why not?'

Philip did not answer. He did not meet her eyes, seemed to be looking at something away in the blazing blue air toward Mount Serapi – an eagle, perhaps.

'After all you've said about what a glorious girl she is . . . ' Madame Kahn was conventional enough to be impulsively enchanted by the prospect of a beautiful bride for her handsome son. And truly it was high time his career as Don Juan came to an end, or his excesses were at least moderated. 'Is something wrong, Philip? I'd have thought you'd be delighted.' She leaned across the teak cockpit, gave his white cotton knee an encouraging pat. 'Of course it's all quite extraordinary and I expect hopelessly immoral, but I think it's a wonderful idea. She's madly in love with him, she can't not be.' The money side of things would be taken care of by dear Raoul, she would speak to him about it. 'There isn't any reason why they shouldn't get married, is there?'

Philip turned back to the curry, to the wine, turned back to her. Slowly he said, 'No, there's no reason at all.'

3

In her thirties Danielle was still charming to look at. She'll marry again, Philip Blakeney thought grimly as he accompanied her to Kuching airport for her irrevocable departure for Paris. Just a dull question of waiting two or three years before I know who my little boy's stepfather is to be, who will be making dutiful efforts to love and be loved.

The woman, a part of whose temperate contempt for Akbar Nasreddin was her suspicion that she was his idea of carnal grace, stood with resolution among the dust-blown airport oleanders, the Malay apple trees, the musk limes. Afterward the only deadpan comment of hers that day which Philip could recollect was, 'Broken marriages run in families.'

Pivoting on her well-formed ankles, a faint frown puckering her brow beneath her straw hat, she began to leave him. Docilely uncomprehending, Hugh held his mother's hand. Then suddenly he understood sharply enough what they were doing to him, with all his childish might he tore himself free, he grappled his arms round his father's waist. 'For God's sake take him,' Blakeney muttered, detaching his limpet son with horrible strength, twisting his head awry so the boy shouldn't see his tears.

It was about this time that his idea of writing *A History of Borneo* took more embracing hold of his fissile musings, as if his mind were a tree struck by lightning, a local landmark, a famous tree which now required an iron band blacksmithed around the trunk to stop it falling apart. If the cession of Sarawak to Great Britain had reflected credit on no one, the territory's subsequent cession to Malaysia was even shabbier; he would have liked to write a page or two that might set these manipulated records a little straight. It was in these years too that he began to be aware of facts as talismans. In his mind's nebulous and refractory elements, any phenomenon that had the decency or the sophistication or the guile to appear as a fact became an amulet worn to avert evil. Of course the scientists had a saner time of it, he would remark. Botanists and ethnologists and what-have-you, they went charging off into the rain-forest and hunted for facts and found hundreds and came back merry. But he, whose passions as a young man had been for philosophy and for poetry . . . !

He began collecting more methodically too, amassing things as well as facts. Tribal costumes, graven images, weapons, musical instruments, fish traps, jars, mats, baskets, gongs, fetishes . . . Débris of the dying cultures of the interior. In the name of National Unity the coastal Malays and Melanaus – these last having tepidly embraced Islam – while rehearsing platitudes about ethnic diversity were with their every policy undoing those frail societies, appropriating their forests, polluting their rivers, corrupting them with cash and missionaries. In the sacred names of Progress and Development the forest peoples were to be herded into Model Villages, Blakeney read in the government's plans, where as soon as the trees had been cleared they would provide the labour force for enormous plantations. Model Villages! Extraordinary, the Stalinist jargon the new capitalist ministers of South-East Asia employed. And as if a longhouse were not a model of cooperation and peace! In his *History* there would be a page about this too. And about how nineteenth-century belief in Progress was still alive, it had just changed continent.

But method, method. He would start at the beginning. First, the Po-ni mentioned in the histories of the Sung dynasty could be identified as Brunei. And how old were the Hindu deities which Spaan had found in the caves at Kong Beng, Mountain of Images, east of the river Telen? Erskine was the next literate man there. He wrote of how when his intrusion startled the bats the noise of their wings was like surf, of how he waded knee-deep in bat guano choking on the stench of ammonia. Then far back in one of the caverns he came to the Hindu pantheon carved in bas-relief arranged in a semi-circle, and high above was an opening to the sky so a shaft of sunlight slanted down to glimmer on the gods and goddesses.

Anything to silence the drumming of the Devil in Blakeney's ears, that barbaric blood-beat, that hellish music of horror and hate. His marriage had been an interlude, no more, dejectedly he realised. Danielle had helped for a while, she had been a distraction, an aesthetic and sensual delight. Now he was alone again in the grip of his brother's and his sister's deaths. The only difference was that now he had, in addition to the light humiliation of having been chucked by a fetching wife, the ache of missing his little son.

Action! He tried to keep busy. The Irish Hussars turned up; when David Matlaske first had a few days' leave he and Blakeney went back to the Tamabo Range. But Bario had changed. No one bought things with salt any more, they were all dependent on cash. At night no one drank *borak* – the Australian missionaries had put a stop to that. No one recited the Kelabit myths any more or played the old instruments or sang the old songs. Only Christian hymns were heard in the longhouse. Soon nobody would be left who could drill and carve a *sumpitan* or remember his own ancestors' names or interpret the symbols in the patterns of woven mats. Blakeney found the new conformity disgusting, he found his own nostalgia silly, there was nothing he could think with any conviction.

Days were not too bad. But Blakeney's nights in his bungalow beside the Baram river could seem very long. Sometimes sex was a good drug, but then other nights it was repellent or merely inefficacious. Luckily some of the local Kayan girls were pretty and willing. He did not follow his father's example and take one constant mistress. What he did do, chiefly in order to occupy a month's unwanted holiday, was by amateur sleuthing on a tributary off the Rejang to identify his own elder half-brother without himself being identified as a relation. The man's mother was dead; he was married, had grown-up children. With an envy he had not expected, Blakeney watched his brother in the morning mist leave the longhouse, untie his skiff, with his middle-aged wife paddle off toward their clearing, their *ladang*, to tend their rice crop.

When Blakeney was alone at night, when he could not sleep or did not wish to sleep because of the risk of dreaming, he sat on his verandah, sipped his whisky, smoked cheroots to keep the mosquitoes at bay. He did not light a lamp. Moonlight and starlight were enough. Across the wide Baram stood several of the lofty tappan trees which for some reason bees particularly favour, and occasionally Dayaks would come, and in the comparative safety offered by darkness would climb the trees with ladders of pegs and rope to collect the honey and wax. The tall columns and wide crowns of the tappans looked handsome in the light of the moon, graceful reflected in the silvery sliding river.

Around the bungalow he had planted trees – an Indian cinnamon tree, a rambutan tree because he liked the way the fruit matured from greeny yellow to dark red and he liked to eat them. Pandanus grew all over the place, and bamboo. Someone had once planted areca palms. There was a superb flame tree. When on his verandah it was impossible not to think, on occasion he would walk in his grove, to and fro, to and fro. One night he returned to the house, went to the writing-box which had been among the European bits and pieces his father left. It was a Regency oak writing-box with brass corners, and you could tell that it had been made for travellers because, in sockets, it had slender brass screws which if they were lowered would secure the box to a ship's cabin table, so you could write even in foul weather. Inside were compartments for letters and pens, a small sloping leather-covered surface for writing on. Beneath, there was a drawer in which lay a pistol and a few rounds which at the end of the war Blakeney had decided to hang onto. But the night he took it out, handled it, he put it back, shut the drawer.

In order not to think and not to sleep, lying under his mosquito net Philip Blakeney would name the things he knew. He might start with the rivers of Borneo or the hills, telling them name by name in an incantation which became an inventory of his world, a final reckoning, a summing up as if for the last trump. Then all the species of trees that he could identify, then the breeds of fish in the waters, their Malay names, their Iban and Kayan names when he knew them. His nights became nights of naming, of recitations as of the prayers of a rosary. Or he might name the birds. Water birds to start with. The frigate bird that wheeled over the sea all day. The curlew and whimbrel that started up from greasy mangrove swamps. The different heron and bittern and egret and tern. The snipe that wintered on the wet rice mire. Then he'd name the eagles; or the great number of pigeons, beginning with the pied imperial; or the numerous sun-birds or flower-peckers. Then if still dawn had not broken he'd go on to the snakes. Gliding tree snake, Malayan racer, keel-back, he'd name. The pit viper, the mangrove cat snake, the green whip snake . . .

On other nights Blakeney left his bungalow where Danielle and he had entertained their friends to dinner, where on sweltering afternoons beneath the mosquito net and the turning fan they had made love. He went down to the river, unmoored a *sampan*, paddled up-river keeping near the bank where the current was gentle. Majestic with stars, the Bornean night. Majestic the Baram rolling its flood to the sea, lonely the narrow stream into which he turned between forested banks. The *sampan* leaked slightly, he took a tin scoop, every half hour he drifted for a minute and bailed. A fish jumped, from the trees he heard a rustling, a scampering, then wings, a cry. An owl or a nightjar flew across from shore to shore. If he paddled near where fronds and creepers fell to the water he could see phosphorescent lichens gleam. On and on in the hot vibrant night, reach after reach of the stream, going nowhere. Nearly silent the splash and drip of his paddle, the ripples the hull made. Toward daybreak he came drifting back, guiding his skiff easily down-stream. Haggard, but alive. And in control of his mind. No nervous breakdown.

When Cassandra Matlaske lost first her mother and shortly afterward her father, Philip Blakeney resigned his post. Anyhow there was no future for a British civil servant in the new country Malaysia. He'd worked for twenty years, earned a subsistence pension, and the Blakeney house in Devon was let and made a pittance. He returned to the house in Kuching where Andrew and Nerissa and he had been born. The Regency writing-box came with him, and the collection of island artefacts he had been buying more systematically of late. He engaged an

Iban woman to keep house and to be a nanny for his newly inherited daughter.

So began the long last season of Blakeney's life, that of loving the absent Hugh and the present Cassandra. Prematurely old, to all intents and purposes useless except as a father, he survived among generations who did not remember, and did not trouble to find out about, the freeing of the country in '45, a relic known to hundreds of people about Kuching but not famous any more.

For five years he ran a small business exporting spices, mainly cloves. It never made a loss. He gave it up because buying and selling bored him. The cobra of despair lay coiled in his brain, it was always there but it didn't raise its winged head – or not till after many years, not till right at the end. Blakeney was very much the Englishman of the despised old school, pretty well what you'd expect of his race and class and time, and no doubt that helped. Certainly he kept his reserve to the end, beyond the end. He maintained his equilibrium right up to the last too.

Not that Danielle Kahn tried to limit Blakeney's seeing his son. Her dominant instinct was self-protection – yes; still, she wasn't trying to punish him for his suffering. But the distance between Sarawak and France . . . The expense of travel, too. All the same, every summer he'd leave Cassandra with the Iban housekeeper, fly to Paris, take his son to Devon for a few weeks. He couldn't afford not to let the family farmhouse, so they stayed in lodgings in a variety of coastal villages.

Blakeney was liked by his Chinese and Malay and Iban and Indian neighbours on the sleepy north bank of Kuching river where the wooden houses were enfolded in greenery, in that tranquil enclave where dedicated flyers coaxed aloft their kites which seemed mere scraps. They coaxed them up the sky on the day's last breath of a breeze and then kept them flaunting up there, by remote dexterity floated them on high flutterings when down among the breadfruit trees the faintest airs had died. He was liked by the boatmen on the *tambangs* crossing the detritus-burdened river. A distinctive apparition, with his old clean white shirts and checked shirts, with his invariable courtesy, with the dark pretty little girl who never voluntarily left his side.

He was well known on the south side of the river too, by the Court House with its Doric capitals, by the Post Office with its Corinthian capitals and the motto DUM SPIRO SPERO. Well known walking along Jalan Barrack, along Jalan Carpenter, along Jalan India and Gambier Road, always holding Cassandra by her hand, stooping to talk to her. Naturally when she grew older she went to school unescorted, but in her early years he accompanied her, though the housekeeper would happily have done so. Past the Cantik Pawn Shop; past the Min Heng Café with its round marble tables and grimy walls and white-vested smoking Chinese; past Joseph Tie and Co, Advocates; past The Sarawak Turf Club; past Klinik Doktor Sim. The Cantonese Mutual Aid Society would not distract them, nor would Chai Chin Phin, Licensed Pepper Purchaser, nor would the Horng Yann Beauty Parlour. At Teck Heng, Rattan Furniture Maker, Blakeney might stop so Cassandra could watch the men weaving, so she could clamber to sit on one of the chairs. At the spice stores they might sniff. At one of the Chinese goldsmiths they might say good morning to the guard, a venerable Tamil, long since a British private, dozing affably over his battered beloved Lee Enfield. At the Tai Tung Book Store they might buy a new exercise book and pencil for her satchel. And so they would arrive at the Christian School For Girls on the east side of Mission Hill.

After delivering Cassandra to her rompings and her gigglings and her solemn studies, often Blakeney turned aside into the graveyard. Of course he'd travelled to Long Nawang, been shown where after the massacre the sixty corpses had been heaped; but he couldn't keep on going back. And no one knew where Nerissa's lovely body had been thrown. But here Andrew lay, among Kuching's Christian dead. Here beneath the buttressed and creepered and ferned trees, here within the flowering hibiscus hedge. Somewhere underfoot Andrew's bones lay. His flesh and his tortured nerves would have rotted away.

Philip Blakeney knew the Christian dead of Kuching better than anyone. *To The Glory Of God And In Memory Of The Allied Prisoners Of War Buried Here. Dedicated Easter Day 1943.* And a few who were named, who had headstones or crosses. *Francis*

Terry Davidson, 27 April 1945, 'With Christ Which Is Far Better'. On Blakeney would move, from grave to grave. He was a familiar sight, stepping over the nameless mounds, stooping to read, stooping to scratch away lichen or moss. War dead, pre-war dead, post-war dead. Unknown dead – in the tropics a wooden cross doesn't last long. *In Loving Memory Of Emily Lydia, Beloved Wife Of H. Bateman, Died 16 August 1917, Aged 37 Years*. His head became an encyclopaedia of strangers' deaths – and of course a lot of them he had known or his parents had told him about. There were inscriptions repeated in English and Chinese, others in only English, in only Chinese. *Adelaide Julia Linang, Requiescat In Pace. Harry Arthur Byron, Of Tuaran, British North Borneo, Who Died During Internment At Kuching, 12 May 1945*. Philip Blakeney knew them all. Lilian Tan, who in marriage had been Mrs Reggie de Rozario – old Sarawak family. Esther Sawi; Fabian Chung Ah Luke, dead as an infant; Florence Chan; Yap Chong Lim who died in 1926 when he was twenty; Edith Klabu. And Rose Lance who was born in 1884 and died in 1902.

With time, it was the general wisdom that Philip Blakeney's good humour was becoming more natural. Not that he talked in a very unbuttoned fashion with anybody. But the acupuncturist Chuan Heng, to whom he resorted when his headaches were particularly troublesome, noticed that by the seventies he was feeling his way up his dim decrepit stairs less frequently. And when he was lying stretched out and Chuan Heng was planting fine steel needles in his hands, in his chest, in his bald head, his gruff confidences sounded with a fortitude it was hard to believe was assumed. Akbar Nasreddin likewise, who while at Gray's Inn had developed a taste for Keats and for Tennyson, and now by Blakeney was being lent volumes of Auden, began to hope that his friend at length might be sailing through an isthmus of sorts, might emerge to a more pacific sea. The blessing of Cassandra, of course, that was what it was. And as for the man himself . . . That she was his Angel come at the very last to save him – how could he doubt it? The innocent dragooned Faustus might escape damnation yet.

There were procedures. The trick was to follow them in the most disciplined of ways, without imagination.

Forget Dorothy Ak Augustine who had died when she was

seventeen, forget Rose Lance who had been eighteen, remember Cassandra Matlaske. Forget Nerissa Blakeney who had perhaps been nineteen or twenty. Forget David Matlaske's machine-gunned body oozing cruor onto the forest floor. Remember his daughter Cassandra who aged four months had heard gunfire break out all around her, had seen houses burned, had heard the dying scream, had been picked up from the dust.

Sometimes the thing could be done. For Cassandra there could be hope. Why not? DUM SPIRO SPERO, the Post Office admonished him when he went to buy stamps. But maybe post offices were not particularly intelligent, his jaundiced mind would remark. And Latin had never been much of a language for tragedy.

Blakeney's care for Cassandra's happiness and her education was tireless, excited favourable comment even from the sniffiest matrons of the Kuching bourgeoisie. He who had been so denuded of all defences wanted only to protect her, to live long enough to see her tucked up in the bed of affluent Sarawak society: That was why he encouraged her church-going: it was a bulwark against truths he wanted her to die without suspecting. He who had little liking for the new profiteering elite with their plantations and factories and concessions, with their Japanese and German cars, he who had been unhappy in marriage, longed to see her married into those ranks.

Things might very easily have gone that way. Cassandra Matlaske probably would have taken her place in the upper class of what was coming to be called a Developing Nation, had not destiny marked her for a more atrocious elevation.

4 ∫

Hugh Blakeney did not return to Sarawak until he had followed his grandfather and his father to Magdalen, but after his first Eights Week he came. Reserved, adolescent Cassandra began to worship him straight away, just as she worshipped the Chinese theology student Stephen Chai.

Already her life was all church. In a simple white frock she had been confirmed, her mind a shrine glimmering with candles of such irresistible sincerity that her sceptic of a protector, the man who tried to content himself with doubt because the alternative was to believe in an omnipotent malignity, could almost convince himself that her faith would cocoon her forever. Her days portioned out between school and Sunday school and choir practice – how safe!

Philip Blakeney gave her his family Bible with its soft calf covers and its purple end-papers and gilt pages, with its names and places and dates going back a couple of hundred years. He smiled to watch her writing her name on one of the fly-leaves already inky with births, with marriages, with deaths. *Cassandra Matlaske*, she wrote, *adopted daughter of Philip Blakeney, confirmed 27 June 1977, Church of Saint Thomas, Kuching*. Unreasonable to expect an angel not to be religious, he reflected with grim but adoring amusement. Her girlhood friends were all children she met at the Mission School, Chai's younger sisters Grace and Lily pre-eminent among them. When they visited her, Blakeney found their chit-chat pleasing, their simplicity soothed his fears.

Exiled to Paris, to Devon and to Oxford, as his mother before him to Poitiers, for Hugh Blakeney too the East had waited, as unforgettable and for the time being as unattainable as a mirage.

From rainy Augusts spent learning to ride Exmoor ponies, from days watching the rain beat on coombs, beat on the Western Approaches and shroud the Eddistone Light, Hugh remembered his father's stories of the Armada being sighted, Drake's ships being roped out of Plymouth at night against a head wind. But he remembered stories of the *Dido* more impellingly, because it seemed that it had been in his own half-lost and half-refound past that the first square-rigged ship ever to sail up the Sarawak river had anchored before the palmy village which in 1843 was Kuching. Back at his Paris school, Hugh partook of a myth too far away and too exotic for other boys. For him Keppel and Brooke went ashore. Wearing cocked hats and swords they marched to the royal palace which was a long low shed built on piles. Followed by their marines they climbed the ladder to their audience with the Rajah Muda Hassim, who sat chewing his *sirih* leaf and betel nut, one leg crossed under him, playing with his toes. In Hugh's excited reverie, as in his father's before him, on the Saribas river at the storming of Padeh the *Dido*'s pinnace, gig and two cutters fought their way through the boom, the forts were charged, were fired. But before he left his *lycée* to go to Oxford his interest in Brooke had changed. Now the question was whether, although the first white Rajah was a stalwart defender of the tribes' customary rights, his assertion of his dominion over the whole country was the beginning of the expropriation of the *Orang Ulu*, the people of the interior, from their immemorial home? Didn't this dominion, hardening from administration to administration, make possible the deleterious Land Code with its categories for ministers to juggle, the State's absolute control over Interior Area Land and Reserved Land for which logging licences could be freely written, its ability by fiat to shrink Native Customary Land?

His three Magdalen summers, Hugh Blakeney came to Sarawak. Tall, bony, dressed in white trousers and shirts, he sat on his father's verandah. Looking as if he'd just come off his college cricket pitch, handsome with his tawny hair, he talked.

Of course those who occasionally gathered on that shady and leafy stage where the elder Blakeney and then increasingly the younger held court were a reasonably educated bunch. Everybody was aware that the timber businesses of Kalimantan and Sabah and Sarawak were going to run down at the end of the century for the simple reason that no forest to fell would remain. Everybody knew that once the trees were gone the next wet season took the soil too, the hills became brown cascades, the rivers flooded their banks. It was not a mystery that when the next dry season came a logged region was a wilderness of mud slides and broken trees and dust, a desert where the forest would not grow again, where the creatures and plants were gone forever, where the longhouses and their cultures were gone and no man would come back to plant rice and hunt deer, where only flies and lizards bred, oh yes and the malaria mosquito – that disease was on the increase again, dengue fever too.

Perhaps people had grown apathetic, had started to give up, let themselves acknowledge the cause was lost. Certainly apathy about the timber business was one reason both Blakeneys later adduced for the general indifference toward the great fire – as if Borneo were already damned, so why make a fuss? Apathy about political chicanery had got to be a bad Sarawak habit too. That fracas in the sixties when there was an attempt to refuse to have Malay as the official language – why, when only twenty per cent of the population were Malay, thirty were Chinese, another thirty were Iban? They voted an Iban into power as Chief Minister and he was an honest man, but the Federal Government soon had him out of power and into prison on a trumped-up charge. Later when the job of Chief Minister had been given back to the coastal Muslims there was another pretty display, the country seemed to be back in the eighteenth century. A Chief Minister gave logging concessions to State Assembly men to make them millionaires overnight and keep them loyal when it came to voting, gave concessions to each of his eight daughters. The next Chief Minister, who naturally was his predecessor's nephew, did the same, dished out concessions to his sister, to his friends. The funny thing was, the man with the most extensive interests in timber was the Minister for the Environment. Or no, maybe funnier still was that neither of the Chief Ministers denied these accusations. They knew their fellow men. Neither of them had to leave politics, let alone go to gaol. Apathy . . .

Talk! Hugh Blakeney was eloquent all right. Well, if you think statistics are eloquence. Some listeners on the verandah thought the plethora of ·digits and computations gave the national disaster nothing but unreality . . . A disaster the official name of which was Development, needless to say, and which had the effect of making the rich get richer and the poor get poorer. The rich like that minister who made a speech Hugh loved to recite about cutting down the dark forest to let in the light of progress.

Anyhow, Hugh was all facts, all figures. In the seventies the lowland forests of Sarawak had been logged. Now they were felling the dipterocarp forests of the inner hills at the rate of a hundred and fifty thousand hectares a year, only that figure soon had to be corrected, yes even officially readjusted, to two hundred and fifty thousand. Did everyone know that in the last twenty years the area of Communal Forest Reserve had mysteriously declined from – but none of his listeners could remember the numbers. And were they aware of what so-called selective felling amounted to, that for every two trees cut down three more were irremediably damaged? He had heaps of reports he got this kind of stuff from. And that was the vehement, incisive way he talked. It made your head fuzzy to listen for long. Last year the industry had produced twelve million cubic metres of logs . . .

That even the one in ten of the replanting programmes which existed elsewhere than in governmental computers were derisory . . . Hugh Blakeney had sheaves of maps, photographs, apparent facts. The siltation of rivers, the fatal impoverishment of soils – well, at Oxford he was a scientist. As for invective! He was a fire-brand. Invective about forestry officials suborned with lumber company shares. About longhouse water supplies polluted. About wardens who exaggerated the numbers of the endangered species in their Reserves, firms that bulldozed their roads in there too until the whine of chain-saws was heard all over the land.

Not that Hugh Blakeney was all talk. He was all action too. He'd disappear for weeks up this river or that, up his father's old haunted paradise the Baram, where lumber camps now alternated with longhouses along the stately river which was changing colour in an ominous manner. He'd come back with notebooks scribbled from cover to cover, notebooks which had fallen into the bilges of longboats and *sampans*, been dried in the sun, notebooks bleached, torn, overflowing with impressions, facts. And indeed for those of his listeners who rarely or never ventured inland, such as Akbar Nasreddin, the photographs Hugh would hand round were depressing. Rather like photographs taken after an efficient modern battle when the dead had been carted away and the desolate land abandoned. A few trees left standing here and there, others cut off at ten foot or twenty foot. Brown hills with dust blowing off them in clouds, dust bowls sweltering, rivers clogged with mud and logs, a broken-down tractor, a deserted shack. Over the dead earth sometimes still a Brahminy kite hanging on extended wings, the kite the Ibans used to believe was the incarnation of their God of War. A waste land, irredeemable, where once the birds sang.

You'd look at Hugh's photographs and feel dispirited. You'd hear him declaring that sixty per cent of Sarawak's rivers, was it, were polluted, and there were not the fish there had been in happier times and there was hunger in some villages where there had not been before. You'd listen. 'This damned state has had a trade surplus for years,' he might say, 'so why are half the people of the interior living below the poverty line?' Of course he would know what the official poverty line was that year, three hundred ringgit or four hundred a month for a family, which no one else on the spur of the moment would be able to recall. No one would be able to understand how you could get the calories for mere survival into your children with less than a thousand ringgit, for that matter. And if as you listened you looked across at his silent sister who hardly knew him, if you watched her as she leaned against the rose-entwined rail ... He was a hero to her, right enough. He was Robin Hood, he was the Scarlet Pimpernel, he was worthy to be his father's son. For her he would have been the Cid and the Chevalier de Bayard too if she had known who they were – but the Mission School was unambitious. Well, she had been used to the Chai girls' chatter about tennis and boyfriends and choir practice.

And if then you glanced at Philip . . . It was heart-warming enough. Had his son not come back to him? In Paris, Hugh had grown to be a man. At Oxford, he had won a scholarship. Now in Kuching here he was, good-looking, well-informed, justly passionate and, best of all, replete with love. For although Hugh was invariably affectionate toward his mother and his stepfather, it was Philip who commanded his cardinal love, and rather moving to witness it was. They were in cahoots about a hundred matters, and they rejoiced in complicated issues to disagree about. You would hear them tussle away about Development for hours – how the tribes ought to have complete control over their land and resources, be allowed to develop in their own ways and their own time. They had jokes nobody else could understand. They were forever quoting things to each other.

It was difficult to believe that Philip Blakeney had truly overcome his own brutal lessons in knowing and in taking action. That in his son's rejuvenating company he could briefly forget them, you might surmise. That sometimes he would let himself hope that his experience had not been definitive, for Hugh things might fall out otherwise, his might be a different world . . . Once he started quoting from some book or other. *Action is consolatory. It is the enemy of thought and the friend of flattering illusions.* Usual kind of Philip philosophy; but heartened perhaps by Cassandra's charm and by Hugh who had appeared to him in his old age he said it quite cheerfully, with a much less ironic smile than anyone could have expected. And then Hugh chimed in with the rest of the quotation and that delighted the old fellow no end, fairly made him twinkle. *Only in the conduct of our action can we find the sense of mastery over the Fates.* But then there was another nugget he'd cite which said pretty much the opposite. Something about how all that was necessary for evil to triumph was that good men should do nothing. So how could you tell what he thought?

After Oxford, Hugh wrote articles for scientific magazines and for political reviews; in a year or two he was earning his living by researching environmental problems and writing about them. He still came to Sarawak whenever he was free, but he was in Africa so often and in the Americas so often that his freedom was not what it had been in undergraduate days. Cassandra Matlaske was a woman now, she was twenty, she was twenty-one.

The year before the fire, when Hugh Blakeney flew to Kuching and took a taxi to the bazaar and then crossed the river in a *tambang* and walked to his father's house, Cassandra wasn't there. She was at evensong.

Hugh dumped his suitcase, he washed, he talked to his father for a minute or two. But then he told him he'd be back in an hour, he was going to hear if their angelic chorister trilled her piety with conviction.

If he had not arrived late for the service, very likely Cassandra would not have noticed his unaccustomed presence in the congregation, but slipping into a back pew during a prayer he was conspicuous. She had known he was expected, naturally. But that the first thing he should do was to attend evensong was enough to suffuse her mind with a shimmering goldenness which the presumable fact that he had done so in order to see her did little, did irreligiously little, to eclipse.

The sisterly love in Cassandra's soul was all tranquil happiness till the service was over. The choir came down the aisle, she in their cassocked ranks. Hugh was at the near end of a pew. Was he possessed by devilry? Certainly his blue eyes were glittering with amusement as they met her dark questing look, her ghost of a smile, as his lips parted, as voicelessly but alas unmistakably he mouthed, 'I love you.'

5

Hugh Blakeney didn't have any trouble about knowing things. He didn't feel condemned to knowledge, like his wretched father.

No, for him to know was a straightforward enough process. He'd go to earth in a library in Paris or London for a day; he'd read report after report, souse his brain in graphs. To Hugh, knowledge was moral, that was the clue to his sanity. He left you in no doubt that the world was to be saved and that knowledge was to be the means of saving it, the only innocent means.

Of course, his native Sarawak was only a pocket handkerchief in all the blue and green and brown imperilled globe, but it was a scrap he loved with fierce tenderness. Once you had acquired the knack of weathering his blizzards of legal and scientific talk and his squalls of statistics it wasn't too bad. It was his father's relish for out-of-the-way facts but in a new guise. Philip might command a multitude of recherché details about *adat*, but Hugh could equal him when it came to those customary laws' abrogation by successive government decrees. A man who could get worked up about the 1875 Land Order! Either that or the 1933 Land Settlement Order, was it? Anyhow, his particular *bête noire* was a fiend called the 1974 Land Code (Amendment) Ordinance, which to hear him dissect and inveigh against was quite something. His most coldly clear flights of rhetoric were reserved for its Section Five – for his voice when he was moved was calm, cold, he just kept on bringing up facts and yet more facts, deploying them, arguing logically, always with impeccable logic. Apparently this Section Five laid down that the Minister could extinguish any native customary rights which might exist on State land. All the overworked politician had to do was to publish his order in the *Gazette*. Not much the natives living in the *Ulu*, the inner hills, could do to refer the matter to arbitration, especially natives who didn't read the *Gazette*, couldn't read any written page. *Upon expiry of six weeks from the aforesaid publication, native customary rights shall cease and be extinguished* . . . Hugh had it by heart. Quite soon you realised that his was a language of love. Of hatred for what some men were doing to the earth. Of love for the victim, of pity, of grief.

Not that Hugh hankered for the past. He knew you couldn't kill the gods Progress and Development. His worry was that they were mere slogans, they were just the latest official dressing up of a perennial exploitation; his concern was to make them do more good than harm. And as for idealising the past . . . He was unflinching when it came to the tribes' old habit of sacrificing a slave now and then. He knew that some of the pirate bands may have been fighting an honourable resistance against newcomers' determination to dominate trade in the archipelago; but just as often they were marauders who lived by pillaging those weaker than themselves, who when they captured a *kampong* or a *prahu* never spared a man's life, never allotted a woman any fate except rape and slavery.

On the taking of heads Hugh Blakeney was lucid too. One night in a Kuching café an innocent Californian traveller happened to remark to Hugh, who had befriended him in his bewilderment about which of the Indian money-changers to patronise, that maybe there had been something noble in a fight to the death between two Dayak warriors, the severed head borne home by the victor was a trophy not to be summarily despised. That Dayaks fought one another with ferocity he would be the first to acknowledge, the man dressed as if for cricket drawled – he had inherited his mother's drawl. But what had noble combat to do with head-hunting? Hugh had read his father's shelves of books about Borneo, the Californian had not, was no match for him, had to be grateful for the impromptu history lesson he got. Out from smiling Hugh the instances came, well documented. Certainly a warrior overcome in what the English would call fair fight was a head to be taken, hung in the place of honour over the *penghulu*'s mat. But no less so was the head of a child surprised on a forest path alone. Just as sacred would be the head of a woman attacked while she was washing clothes in a stream. A head – any head . . . The pounce. The grappling. The shrieks. The hacking. The bloodily burdened flight.

Hugh got his love of the green island from his father, no one could doubt that. And it was an informed love, and not all his learning came out of reports.

He knew, he'd been up the rivers. He'd gone up the Batang Lupar, gone up the Katibas, gone up the Baleh, he knew the Tingor and the Tutoh. He'd been too long in France and England, he only spoke a smattering of Malay and a few words of Iban, but when it was a matter of getting to places he wasn't easily stopped.

The hitch was, he was beginning to be well known, journals dotted about the world published what he wrote, and the Kuching authorities developed an irritating tendency to have their airport minions stamp *Not Permitted To Travel In The Interior* on his visas. He had already found that when he travelled up the Rejang as far as Belaga, say, and applied for a permit to go further up and further inward to the Usun Apau Plateau, he was generally revealed to be on the list of those to whom the police would not grant such liberty. The new offence to his passport simply confirmed him in his conviction that it was sensible never to ask to be allowed to do anything. Best simply to act, go where he pleased. Not always easy. More than once he was stopped, sent back, had to start again with greater guile, more circuitous approaches, friends who would harbour him, pass him on to other friends.

The first time the police laid hands on him Hugh Blakeney was on one of the fast ferries; they came roaring in from the sea toward the mangrove swamps and nipah swamps at the mouth of the Rejang. Sky light blue, sea dark blue, dolphins playing, the hull bursting through fantails of spray where rainbows shone. Hugh pulled his hat over his eyes – in the tropics he always wore one of those cricketer's white floppy hats. He leaned on the rail, he watched the dolphins' muscular shining backs, how they arched, how they dived. It was cheerful to think about the article on erosion he was going to write for *Nature*, the photographs he would take. Cheerful to feel the wind and spray on his face, see the green shore open before him as they swept into the Rejang. Infuriating to see a police launch detach itself from the distance, stop the ferry, range alongside. Two officers came aboard, thumbed everyone's papers, peered at the paltry cargo. The only white man on board was the only culprit invited to leave one boat for the other.

He knew. He'd taken action. He'd been to have a look. In a curious partial clandestinity often of late. But generally he had got where he wanted to arrive, seen what he wanted to find out about, moving shadowily, not precisely hiding but not advertising his presence either.

He had been to the Batang Ai dam where thirty longhouses had been evacuated, three thousand Ibans had lost their *ladangs* where they had planted rice, tomatoes, gourds, banana palms, chilli peppers; lost their forest where they had hunted, where they had gathered rattan and gutta percha and honey and herbs and nuts; lost their graveyards under construction sites and under water. In the Ulu Baram he had watched the longhouse women weaving mats. He had helped the men chip away at a leviathan of a tree until it was a dug-out canoe, he had paddled their craft with them to work their swidden clearings, he had gone into the forest with them to hunt. Sometimes they had come upon the gashes which were timber trails, thoroughfares of smashed branches and eroding top-soil where heavy vehicles had dragged logs. He had stood by rivers paved with rafts of tree trunks roped together, drifting down to the mills. His inquisitive love had taken him to trudge through the residual stands of a logged forest with its sparse canopy, with its damaged trees left dying where they stood, the ground littered with broken wood. He had tramped through such violated country all day and mourned the vanished animals and mourned for the singing too, for the birdsong which had been coextensive with the island but was patchy now, broken up and reduced here, silenced there. He had been to the lumber camps which were ugly with raw earth and huts and bulldozers, he had talked with the Chinese contractors and store-keepers, the Japanese timber company men, the Dayak labourers.

After each spell of wandering, of taking photographs, of writing in his notebooks, Hugh would come back to his father's verandah, to his father who knew more than enough about the attempt to save a garden of earthly delights.

Since his night torments in the bungalow on the Baram where the tappan trees had now been felled, Philip Blakeney had known that naming could be an act of love. Desperate love perhaps, love almost beyond endurance – but the true thing. Hugh would hand him his notebooks to read, would tell him what he had seen. Hundreds of miles of logging roads, Philip, he'd say, lorry after lorry grinding along laden with dead trees. He always called his father Philip.

What about such and such a region, Philip would ask, what about this river or that *kampong*? And Hugh would tell him, when he knew, or he would make a note of where he must not forget to go. Hillsides washed away, he would report, river banks washed away – and he would name them. And still naturally they used brute force to drag the trees along the skids to the roads, he would report. How else? Teams of tribesmen paid next to nothing to put rope harnesses on their shoulders and haul the trunks, I've seen them, Philip, he would say. Their hands and their feet latched to the bars of the skids. And sometimes of course a big tree trunk gets out of control and men are injured and men are killed. Eighty-six logging deaths in Sarawak last year. Heap them up in your mind. Eighty-six men.

What about Long Kai, Philip Blakeney might ask, what about idyllic Long Kai, have you been there? Long Kai where the stream flowed so cleanly you could see every fish flicker. Where the carved totem poles to commemorate the dead, called *kapatongs*, were still standing and had their magnificence. Where I heard an Argus pheasant call from the forest and they took me to search for it and we found the dancing ground they clear but we never saw the bird – who, for that matter, ever has?

How they talked, those two, how they named! It might be Long Kai where Philip and Danielle had been happy, Long Kai where the dead had left them in peace for a while, Long Kai with its Argus pheasants and hornbills calling, with its hospitable longhouse, its grassy slope of fruit trees and its children cavorting in the stream. It might be any other part of the violated whole.

A psalming, their talk, a psalming of hills, valleys, rivers, creatures, men and women and children. And as much a commemoration as any graven image, any *kapatong* with its carved and painted spirits and heroes smeared on festive days with sacrificial blood.

The dusky fruit bat, father or son might say, the Borneo horseshoe bat, the flying fox. The names! And then the other would take up the chant. The palm civet, the Kinabalu squirrel, the sun bear. Anything that was in Hugh's notebooks, anything that was in either of their heads, might be summoned, might be given its moment of love. Impressions, facts, passions, notions, whatever their epistemological status was . . . Words, anyhow. As if their world were composed of innocent beauties, and all innocence and every beauty were in danger and some were irretrievably lost. Yes, as if loveliness was so vulnerable that naming became a mourning, names were bells tolled in a land where the real keening was in the voices of illiterate natives, and the triumphant mockery was the voice of chain-saws. And the birds! When they got onto fretting about the island's birds they were positively musical. The mountain minivet and the scarlet minivet, one of them might murmur. And then the other would answer with a kingfisher or a warbler or heaven knows what, and they'd be away, the hymn was raised. Bornean blue flycatcher, paradise flycatcher . . .

Of course, Hugh Blakeney had other loves. For his mother to compare him to Don Juan was just her odd type of doting. But about the usual number of young women, or perhaps slightly more, passed through his hands. On the day of his silent declaration to Cassandra on her way down the aisle after evensong, he had wished to discover if he could imagine her apart from her church, imagine her freed at all. A little free . . .

Hugh couldn't stand her church.

It was not Cassandra's faith which offended him – it seemed he could always be amused, be dependably tolerant. No, it was Saint Thomas's unlucky church in Kuching. The bricks, the mortar. At least, that was the impression Hugh invariably gave, without duplicity you assumed. How could she frequent such a dreary building? he would tease her. Could she not *see* how ugly the place was?

She with her simple piety before God and her adoring admiration of her older brother would smile. Poor heathen Hugh, in her turn gently she would tease him, hadn't anyone ever explained to him that the building did not matter, the Lord's house could be any hovel? He needed catechising, honestly he did. She would arrange for him to have lessons, she would speak with Stephen Chai the very next day – smiling till she dimpled, knowing his dislike of priests, particularly of that priest. Or perhaps Hugh would prefer to attend the deacon's weekly Bible Study meeting at the bishop's house? She knew he admired the bishop's airy old wooden mansion among its trees on the knoll of Mission Hill, he had once declared that after the Astana it was the grandest house in the country. The Bible class was held on Saturday afternoons, Grace and Lily always came. Tea and cake the deacon offered also, and the household dogs were her friends, the new litter of puppies were sweet. Cassandra was charm itself when she teased him, everybody agreed about that, oh she did it prettily, prettily, and you could see she was mad about him, madder than she knew; but he knew all right, listening, grinning ruefully, acknowledging mock defeat, offering to perform any dire penance rather than be consigned to Chai for enlightenment. Then all of a sudden she would be grave. What was wrong with Saint Thomas's? Why was nineteen-fifties architecture thought to be lousy? He was to remember she hadn't been to Oxford, she hadn't read half the books he'd read. He was to stop teasing her for a minute, he was to explain, please.

Like his father, Hugh Blakeney loved the old churches of the East just as he loved the old temples and mosques and shrines. Like his father he was a reader of memorials and tombs.

He would expound their beauties to Cassandra – was a delight in the ecclesiastical architecture of the past not a taste they might share? And a delight in the shadowy presences of the dead? Together they would haunt damp-streaked aisles and overgrown churchyards, together! 'I'll take you to India,' he would announce, smiling into her eyes, seeing them light up. And he would describe to her the eighteenth-century churches of Calcutta. The Armenian church. The Roman Catholic cathedral which the Portuguese had built. Saint John's church with its *Last Supper* by Zoffany which had prominent men of Calcutta dressed as the apostles; Saint John's with Job Charnock who founded the city buried in the graveyard before the present church was built, with vultures eternally perched in its trees. To Madras he would take her too. To Fort Saint George, to Saint Mary's which was built in the seventeenth century and rebuilt in the eighteenth and had a cornucopia of instructive reading on its floor and its walls. Saint Mary's where Robert Clive married Margaret Maskelyne, where there stood that superb monument to Schwartz, Hugh would enthuse to his pupil, realising as he spoke that he was right, it was essential to get her away from Kuching.

It had been during one of Hugh Blakeney's meanderings through India in the cause of sound ecological policies that he had come upon a small hill town in Kerala with a church of such dilapidated charm that he had paused to muse in its cool, damp nave. It had been while strolling idly in its thickety graveyard, stooping as his father might have done to scrape the moss from the dates of a Scotsman who had taught at the school for an astonishing number of decades before he died there, that it had come to Hugh how far from Paris and from Oxford he would always happily feel, how he felt married to the East, how for him the East was Cassandra.

Born in Sarawak like his father before him, born therefore already at home in exile, the year before the fire Hugh was haunting the ugly church of Saint Thomas as before he had only haunted handsome churches, as if that despised structure housed the enigma he needed to unlock. He went when the place was deserted. He went alone.

The Lady Chapel is the Gift of Yap Ghee Heng, as a Thankoffering to God for His many Blessings. Not a sad haunting, like Philip's of the graveyard. Hugh would pace, would read, would wonder, as if in the scentless air an understanding were waiting for him, as if only in that unlovely enclosed vacancy could he discover whether between Cassandra Matlaske's Christianity and his scepticism a marriage might be possible. *The Chime of Bells in this Tower were presented jointly by Sarawak Oilfields Limited, The British Malayan Petroleum Company Limited, and Shell Company of North Borneo Limited.* The church was quiet except for his footfalls, except for children's voices from the grass outside, except for flies. He read, *In Memory of Madam Jummat Bay.* He read, *Remember before God Ellen Law Nyuk Kiaw.* He sat down in a pew. He dreamed. He recalled his father revelling in the story of how the first bishop of Sarawak and Labuan might during the Chinese rebellion have been too careful of his episcopal carcass, a touch too swift to pay homage to the President of the *kongsi* when he could see that the gory head stuck on a spear was poor Nicholetts's and not the Rajah's as the President maintained. But he had not always been timorous, Bishop McDougall, not by a long chalk. Alone in the church, Hugh smiled, recalling his father's story of how at the sea fight between *Rainbow* and three Illanun pirate *prahus* McDougall had helped to man the guns with conspicuous verve, had only with the most vocal reluctance been obliged before the shooting was finished to go below and tend the wounded. The epilogue to the tale was the bit Philip had liked most. All about how afterward the bishop sent a glowing account of the battle to *The Times.* How he was surprised and dismayed when in British religious circles this caused an outcry, fighting bishops being out of fashion it appeared. How he was a little consoled by the Rajah's approval of his manly pugnacity. And the best of it was, Philip had chuckled, that when a few years before, in fright, McDougall had sworn loyalty to a murderous Buddhist usurper, none of his fellow ecclesiastics had reprimanded him.

Conscious again of his surroundings, Hugh Blakeney frowned. Truly the place was hideous. He wondered whether Cassandra had ever asked herself if such poverty of creation betrayed in its creators a poverty of soul. No, no, he was wrong. Doubtless those who had endowed the refoundation had been admirable. Again he frowned. Restlessly he twisted in his seat, he read names. Pews had been presented by Mr and Mrs Julius Chung, by Dr and Mrs M. Sockalingham . . . By other Bornean churches too. Saint James at Quop, All Saints at Jessleton, Saint Luke at Simanggang . . .

Hugh had had affairs. They had not meant much. He did not want any more. So far his reasoning carried him. Cassandra was his East. So far his heart. But she . . . ?

In the church with its font presented by Chian Tiaw Swee,

with its heaped copies of *Songs of Praise* in Chinese, with its confirmation classes in Iban, Cassandra's face appeared before his mind's eye. She drew near, her eyes smiled. Philip would be delighted, why should he not be? Philip would bless them, that was good, was alone perhaps sufficient grace to justify the illumination which had come to him in a sultry Kerala churchyard, in a tangle of undergrowth studded with tilting headstones and lop-sided crosses.

And she . . . ? This church might be soulless, might be easy to deride; but her Christianity was his enemy. Would her devotion balk at his being officially her brother? Would she marry an unbeliever? In taut unrest, Hugh stood up from his pew donated in memory of Alfred and Alma de Rozario. Cassandra was a woman now, but she'd never been anywhere, never done anything. Did she really reckon to teach small Christian children to read and write and add up and subtract year after year, marry no one or marry perhaps that soft Chai?

He would take her to India. At Varanasi he would take her in a skiff on the Ganges before dawn, he would bale her in a shawl against the night chill, the quiet boatman would row them in the silvery first light, would row them by the stately *ghats* and the ruinous palaces when the sun rose and the pilgrims came down to the holy river to wash and to pray. In Burma they would voyage on a ferry up the Irrawaddy, by his side she should climb Mandalay Hill, arm in arm they would walk through the temples at Pagan.

Would she come? The church doors had been presented *In memory of George Frederick Hose, Bishop of the Diocese of Singapore, Sarawak and Labuan 1881–1908*. They creaked under the impact of Hugh's suddenly violent desire to find out.

To Cassandra Matlaske's unaccustomedly tumultuous heart, the passage from her brother's silent and diabolical and smiling declaration at the close of evensong, to her lover's voicing of the intolerable question aboard the *sampan*, was so prolific of recognitions and doubts that it seemed the time it takes a shooting star to blaze and fall and be extinguished, not the entire month of November which in fact tinglingly elapsed.

The recognitions came winging and trooping into her mind as if they had been the creatures coming to their sanctuary

in the ark with Noah ordering them to get a move on, the
water was rising – and there were a few snaky thoughts that
came slithering too. Pleasantly surprised by the eroticism of
her day-dreams, she was surprised too by how plainly it
stood forth that her worshipped Philip's love for her had its
restrictiveness, his elderly care was almost too protective. Or
was it some innate dullness in her that had let her live until
she was twenty-one without feeling anything potent or thinking
anything audacious, had let her find provincial Kuching with its
Mission School and its tennis parties, its Westernisation and its
corruption, world enough? For her adoptive father had never
prevented her from learning more or venturing beyond; if she
was limited it was not his fault; he had let her take to what life
she fancied. Her faith also, which he did not share but which he
had never murmured against – had it a little prevented her from
coming alive? Aghast by this thought, for which she hastened
to beseech forgiveness, she was dismayed also to find herself
wishing that her real parents were still living, not for their sakes
but so that there might be no conceivable impediment to her
union with Hugh, just supposing that one day he . . . For this
sinful musing too she earnestly begged to be absolved.

That his voiceless *I love you* in the nave had not, despite the
mischievous glitter in his blue eyes, been a mocking brotherly
tease, Cassandra could not bring her mind to try to doubt.
Particularly not when, late in the evening on the verandah
where for the good of the moths they had put out the lamps,
Philip would discuss the whys and wherefores of the killing
of Charles Fox and Henry Steele at Kanowit in 1859. Or it
might be the racket-tailed drongoes which flew after the bands
of macaques swinging through the leaf canopy because they
flushed insects for them, but the Dayaks didn't understand this
and used to call the drongoes the macaques' servants. Or it was a
porcupine which on the Baram thirty years before had wrought
fearful destruction in his neighbours' pineapple patch so they
had killed it and cooked it, had invited him to partake of the
feast, and the consequence of the beast's diet was that it had
tasted delicious. What did Cassandra care for this topic or that,
so long as on the verandah she could gaze into the gloom where
Hugh sprawled in his chair?

With the sophistry of the damned, the innocent girl allowed herself to dream more freely because she had constrained her head to inform her heart that there could never be any question of her passion being anything but a dream. God had given her to Hugh to be his sister. (That God had done nothing of the sort, that God had given her to an Irish Hussar and his mistress, that the merely human Philip Blakeney had given her to Hugh to be his sister, she allowed herself to believe later, when that belief was what her heart would find comfortable.) Sheltered by this idea, given fortitude by her conviction that she had decided that since she could not marry Hugh she would never marry anyone, she could admire him shamelessly, admire his body in a way she had not known how to before, admire as ever his travelling and his scholarship, his environmentalist crusading which impressed her inexperienced devotion as little less than a mission to save the world.

Of their evening hour in the *sampan* on the Sarawak river, of that hour of drifting and of mist and of birdsong and of motionless palms, that hour so apparently indistinguishable from a hundred other hours, an hour so cruelly branded by Hugh's intolerable question that Cassandra felt her jerking head had indeed been held in a vice and a red-hot iron applied to her cheek – of that ordeal afterward she remembered only a demented screaming whisper of *No No No* which was in her ears or on her lips or in her brain or in the twilight, she didn't know, a maddened and maddening echo that wouldn't die.

Of Hugh Blakeney's return from Timor to Sarawak neither Cassandra Matlaske nor anybody else had time to think much, so swift and irresistible was his commandeering of her to set off with him to Sabah, to the coast of the Sulu Sea, to find Thor Bernstein.

She had ten days' holiday for Easter, had she not? He was brisk, he was merry. On their journey he would have plenty of time to relate to her how the Indonesian occupying force was eradicating Timorese culture, how they were ramming their jingoistic Javanese cant down people's throats, how in the schools the children were not allowed to speak Tetum any more, were not allowed to speak Portuguese either for that matter, it had to be Bahasa Indonesia. Yes, and in the hill regions around Viqueque the invading soldiery were doing what they liked with village schoolgirls, and . . . Oh, he had an indictment . . . !

Did Philip and Cassandra not agree that Thor was the man for the expedition to the fire? Good for him not always to be let moulder on that island of his, too. As for Hugh's mother and his stepfather, he expressed his delight in seeing them again in the same breath as his hope that they would still be anchored at Kuching when he returned, and in the next breath his apologies for his inability to say when that might be.

Thor might not be on his island, did someone suggest? Well then, they would have had fun going to look for him. Hugh was not to be gainsaid. He would remain in Kuching for a day, not a minute longer. Shoving clothes into a light bag which she could sling over her shoulder, Cassandra just had the perspicacity to comprehend that he had timed his arrival for the beginning of her short holiday with impressive precision.

Through her bedroom window, she could hear him talking to his father. Energetic, committed, wondering, reasoning. With one burning idea around which all lesser thoughts circled. There'd be no deflecting him. His blood was up. The fire had taken possession of him, or he of it. Yes, already it was *his* fire.

6

If a malign fate had decreed that Cassandra Matlaske should with her brother give way to a sinful passion which must ineluctably consign those ravished souls to a tragic punishment, Hugh Blakeney's old-fashioned attempt to gain her consent to marry him could not on this second occasion have achieved a triumph more immediate, more simple and more complete.

The religious scruples over which she had agonised in the *atap*-thatched hut by the river, the hours of prayer which she had described in letters which had enchanted their recipient by their nineteenth-century tones, by that innocent seriousness of the pious maiden which might in the West be assumed to be pretty well extinct but still endured in a few enclaves of the Christian East . . . Had not the luckless Stephen Chai confessed with estimable honesty that he could think of no good reason why the Church should not bless this unconventional union if prolonged prayer revealed this to be the will of God? Had she not with a restraint she could not but subduedly pride herself on refrained from writing to Hugh for all of January and half of February, dedicated those weeks to the search for what was right? Had not Philip, though it was true that at her first confession he had seemed to see something which was hidden from her, recovered his affectionate gruffness, offered his blessing? Marriage was a holy sacrament, Cassandra repeated joyfully to her expectant heart as she stepped out of their small aeroplane at the shore town of Tawau, watched the propellers slow their revolutions and thicken their blur and come clear and fall still. Joyfully she attended to Hugh explaining to her that now they would have to find out about a ferry up the coast, a ferry or a fishing-smack, a vessel of some kind, because this dazzling azure before their eyes was the Celebes Sea and they'd got to make their way north and east toward the Sulu Archipelago. So often she had prayed for Philip's soul, so often she had been appalled by his indifference to religion. But now she prayed for Hugh and on her horizon, which only appeared to be this equatorial blazing sea, glimmered the possibility that she might – oh not yet, but one day! – be the humble means of his returning to God. She listened, she smiled at him. Distances, courses, men, costs . . . With him she would go anywhere.

So far Hugh had respected her plea that he should not repeat the intolerable question. Her mind felt as if it were made of glass – she had written that to him too. Now she rejoiced to imagine its fragile transparency in his care, her head cradled forever in his hands. As for the question, it rang joyously in the sea birds' cries, there was nothing intolerable about it now. It was in the sunlight that glittered on the sea, she didn't have to be afraid it had gone away, it lapped all about her senses, it played its manifold brilliances in her crystalline mind.

The fishing-smack had a tin-pot funnel, had a deck-house, had at the stern a winch and crates and buckets and nets. The skipper was a Malay; he had four teeth, which served to give stability to his cigarettes; he drowsed over his wheel. All day under the shade of an awning Cassandra watched the wooded hills and the mangrove shore slip by, gazed at a white-bellied sea-eagle when Hugh pointed it out, realised how little of the world she knew. Nowhere, she had been! Not to Sandakan, not even to Brunei! Now Hugh was telling her about the Coromandel Coast, a Hindu temple of the sun at a place called Konarak. Before her, the sea stretched invitingly.

At the *kampong* from which Thor Bernstein's island could be seen in the late afternoon sun, Cassandra admired the wooden houses built on piles at the river mouth; she admired the wild sea-teak trees and the yellow-flowered sea-hibiscus growing along the shore, in the village the kapok trees and rambutan trees. Yes, Thor Bernstein was in residence in his hermitage, they were told. The week before he had bought a load of fruit and a drum of petrol. That very morning he had come over in his dinghy with its outboard engine to refill his jerrycans with fresh water, his island having no spring.

Cassandra bought vegetables from a stall, listened to Hugh negotiating for a vessel. He did not need a motorboat, he insisted. A rowing-boat he might have the use of for a few days, that was all.

Hugh stood and pushed at his oars in the Bornean way. A mile on an unruffled sea was nothing; he rowed steadily, easily. The sky was unruffled too. As they pulled away from the land, high in the west glimmered the beginnings of gold and rose. Down-sun, Thor's retreat lay before them with its cliff etched hard and its greens very emerald. Perhaps it was the quiet creak and drip of oars which Hugh had wanted, or a harmonious expedition at sea to supplant a discordant one on the Sarawak river. With Sabah half a mile astern and Bernstein's detached, still uncorrupted, paradisal fragment half a mile ahead, he rested on his oars.

'Well?' he asked. 'Now . . . ' He smiled. 'Cassandra, will you marry me?'

To which in a faint but clear voice, with only a heartbeat's hesitation, she answered 'Yes.'

No one had ever visited Thor Bernstein on his island, except the local fishermen who on occasion descended convivially upon him to grill their catch on his beach or to enrol him for a marine hunt, and who to him had become as pleasing a part of the nature of things as the herons in his solitude's heronry. The only person he had ever thought of inviting was Philip Blakeney. As a young man in Vienna before the war, Thor's father had published a couple of books of poetry; but then in Oslo he never found his feet, he eddied from job to job, in his forties drank himself to death. Thor in his thirties had come to think of Blakeney as an honorary godfather. Of course he was too ill and frail to leave Kuching, it couldn't conceivably be him in the skiff creeping closer across this normally more protective moat, Thor knew it couldn't be. But still . . . Blakeney might be the most condemned and imprisoned of souls, but he had learned to think less of himself, had trained himself to think more of others, he had that measure of goodness, the hermit thought, and raised a hand to shield his eyes which were straining to make out who his invaders were. Perhaps precisely *because* Blakeney's soul had been so tortured and was still daily and nightly tortured he had in the end developed the ghostly heroism to free himself a little from himself. A little . . . but who else achieved it even minimally? Thor Bernstein stood on his shore, stared at the boat. The oarsman was taller than any of the villagers. The watcher lowered his shading hand, took a few paces along the cove. Often he had imagined Philip Blakeney at Kuching prison camp, he had seemed to see him help to succour the survivors, had thought he could hear that ghastly exchange with the wraith who remembered Andrew. As for Blakeney's desperate search for Nerissa, it was better not dwelt on. Thor turned back to the offing, narrowed his eyes. With surprise at his quick pulse of pleasure, he recognised the brother and sister.

Fishermen excepted, as visitors of irreproachable holiness, the hermit's Order was a closed one, the atheist was as dedicated to silent communion as a Trappist – or these things had been so until this invasion both hymeneal and incestuous. The last time he had left Kuching, where on her father's foliate stage the enchantress appeared always to be quietly and stilly present, effortlessly in command and infinitely vulnerable, the anthropologist had not even pretended to study his fellow men and their burial rites. He had headed straight for his island, which had received him back with the indifference he craved. Not at home in any society, ill at ease in the academic discipline he had hoped might give his thinking aerodynamic stability, he wanted peace. Whether any philosophy, any mere stance, was intrinsic enough to him to be inalienable, whether he was identifiable enough with any cast of mind to be natural to it, not to be shrugged off, time would tell. Time, solitude.

Thor Bernstein was not lonely in his solitude. He could not recollect ever having felt lonely in his life, he had other weaknesses. His hut was rudimentary, scarcely more solid than the slant-roofed *langko* the Dayaks construct to sleep in at night in their forests; but before it the sea-almond trees dropped their russet leaves on his pale sand. Overhead the feathery casuarina trees rustled, between two of them he had slung a hammock. His tastes were simple, he counted himself fortunate. It was

true that during the deluges of rain his hut's thatch leaked
so profusely that really it was more sensible to go for a swim
even if it was three o'clock in the morning and combers were
crashing on the shore; but he had found a cave up the hillside –
well, perhaps it was not to be dignified as a cave. In a crag there
was an alcove which was more or less weather-proof except in a
westerly, and there he stored things such as his few books which
it was better should not be too regularly soaked. Bernstein was
a strong swimmer, with his rusting harpoon gun he could kill
enough fish to live on. Toward each evening he collected fallen
wood and driftwood, he lit a fire. At twilight, herons flew from
the coast and from other islands, appeared winging over the sea
toward him. Over his modest peak they greyly circled, as night
fell they descended into his trees to roost. It was a thriving
heronry, perhaps because the island had no monkeys; nests
could brim with eggs and not be raided.

The snag was, his heronry on the Sulu Sea reminded Thor
Bernstein of the egrets on a Japanese river, how in Kyoto in
a snowfall he had watched the white flock fly like blizzard
ghosts from the whitened *padi* fields to the temple trees. The
Bornean herons brought back Keiko-san slight and dark in
their old wooden house with its sliding screens that creaked
and floorboards that creaked, with its cherry tree and its stone
lantern in the garden. Sitting alone with his back propped
against one of his casuarinas, Bernstein would again be walking
beside his wife through their quarter of wooden houses and
maple trees by the river, walking with her under the great red
gateway of the Shinto shrine because it was a feast day and the
traders were selling silks and statuary and weapons and icons,
or because it was April and the shrine's plum trees were in
fragrant blossom, or just because after work in the evening it
was good to saunter to the local shrine with your pretty wife
on your arm.

Days came when this most islanded man's melancholy was
such that it seemed his heliotropic idling would never cease,
might be the death of him, he'd just go on brooding beneath his
casuarinas and pacing his beach, a man the colour of mahogany
wearing faded shorts who strolled through the warm rippling
shallows, glanced to mark a fish's jump or a kingfisher's flight,

went on pacing. But then he would smile, remembering maybe some scrap of lore about Bornean ceremonies of death. Beccari had been a natural historian, but he had broken off an account of camphor trees to describe a Kayan who when dead was not only arrayed in his finery but had his *sirih* and a cigar placed in his mouth. Philip Blakeney had told him this – also that Beccari had added that if the Kayan women when returning from a funeral met a man they bespattered him with mud. Thus indolently stimulated, Bernstein might from his dry cranny exhume his notes on the *tiwah*, the death feast for which Borneo was famous. Often years after the demise of a great man the Katingans used to burn his first coffin, reduce to ashes any flesh that might remain, place the bones in a smaller vessel of ironwood . . . Crouched on his forest scarp over the sea, the scholar would turn the discolouring pages of his notebooks. Then for the second funeral a second slave, or latterly a second water-buffalo, was sacrificed: an attendant for the spirit in the next life.

Summoned by a bird's cry, the dreamer would let his notebook lie unread, go back to gazing at his moat. Either he was far too easily distracted ever to be a successful academic, or anthropology had only been a preliminary manoeuvre in a study of mankind which had now turned inward. Or lack of ambition, that might be his deficiency, it had occurred to him.

Thor Bernstein inhabited his moral solitude not only without loneliness, he was without anxiety too. Almost Olympian, the way he sprawled under his sea-almond shade and mused on the horizon and made his decisions about right and wrong, about more true and less true. It was a question of attention. Time would tell. Ringed by water-light, he waited to see what would come.

The outside world came to visit him in the shape of a skiff rowed by Hugh Blakeney dressed for cricket, a skiff with Cassandra Matlaske sitting in the stern. Diogenes, peering out of his barrel to behold the approach of the Emperor Alexander and his retinue, couldn't have greeted the onset with his surprise and pleasure better occulted by courteous reserve than Bernstein, as he waded into the glinting shallows to lay a hand on that battered gunwale.

Afterward, he remembered that moment very sharply. Hugh and Cassandra had come drifting toward him in their rowing-boat – it was just a cockle-shell, with room for the two of them and no more. They'd come bobbing toward him, but their vessel might have been on fire out of sight of land for all the chance they had. They might have been a Norse chieftain and his consort or his sister or both laid dead aboard a longship and the ship set alight and headed to sail out to sea, manned only by those two lying in state, to sail till all her canvas had burned to ash and then her mast, to burn till she burned to her waterline, was quenched, lay awash. They hadn't a clue, Thor wading toward them hadn't a clue, but it was so. And to confirm what thesis, to illustrate what justice or utility? It haunted him, that insanely pointless destruction latent in the event, that destiny already in invisible motion or rather in motion that only ever appeared other than itself.

Of course, what actually occurred appeared perfectly straight-forward, as usual, ensued roughly as you would expect.

Cassandra sat very still, her face in shadow beneath her straw hat.

Hugh was all hardly contained happiness, Hugh was forthright, Hugh was smiling. 'We've come to get you. I want you to come with me to have a look at this fire.'

Thor smiled back. He pulled the cockle-shell ashore. 'Will looking at it put it out?' He reached into the hull to lift the bag he saw lying on the floorboards, was bowed therefore when above him Hugh spoke again.

'And Thor . . . ' His voice was jumping. 'You've known Cassandra as my sister. Well, she never was that really, and now she isn't going to pretend to be it any more. She's just said she'll marry me.' Such was his delight that he gave a fluttering laugh. 'And now several minutes have gone by and she hasn't changed her mind. You *will* marry me, sweetheart, won't you?'

In Cassandra such transformations had been wrought by that day's voyage that there was irony in her amusement, was wickedness in her smile. 'Yes, my darling, I rather think I may.'

7

On the flight to Tawau they had seen the great region of smoke away to the south. The pilot had told them that in the harbour at Balikpapan the schooner skippers would not weigh anchor because they were afraid to sail in the fire's mephitic gloom. As for landing an aircraft there or at Samarinda, you weren't allowed to try.

But a week of happiness Hugh had to allow himself – no, less. Three or four days with Cassandra, days and nights of Cassandra . . .

Thor Bernstein might be tempted to explain this engagement to be married by reflecting that a Mission School maiden like Cassandra Matlaske would never make love with an admirer but might with a fiancé, yes, undoubtedly would, judging by this new voluptuous light in her eyes, by the softness of her laughter. That cosmopolitan turned Diogenes, as he insisted that his hut was at his guests' disposal and that after supper he would take his sleeping mat down to the end of the beach, might feel thankful to the chance which had dictated that he had never stumbled upon an opportune moment to tell Cassandra how she beguiled him. But to Hugh Blakeney the miracle now being made clear was how the past fell away.

The love affairs which had been part of the way of life at Oxford and in London – only part of the way of life. These were routed from significance, their sham intricacies and superficial sentiments dispatched to oblivion. Even Hugh's political tussles seemed for that first enchanted twilight on the island in the Sulu Sea to stand back from him a little way. How combative he had often been! Writing articles about the group of Kayans from the upper Baram who filed a suit against Sarawak Plywood and Marabong Lumber and the state government to defend their rights to their forest. Writing articles about the Penans who were arrested because they had blockaded a logging road. Now years of agitation seemed to recede, to allow him this interlude. He had worked to persuade the European Parliament to pass a resolution calling the Sarawak government to free the imprisoned tribesmen, calling the International Tropical Timber Organization not to infringe upon the indigenous peoples' rights to their forests. That had been a success, the motion was voted, not that calling did much good. Then that same International Tropical Timber Organization sent a mission, a politically well-judged mission dolled up with a British peer in charge, and they visited several towns and they held interviews but did not have time to travel far up the polluted rivers or deeply into the degraded hills, and they published their report which said that the State's forestry policy was admirable, the forests of Sarawak were among those best managed in all the world, and Hugh had written about that too. He would be combative again; but now, an interlude.

Monitor lizards a yard long gallivanted through the undergrowth. The evening sea was mother-of-pearl; over its tranquillity in the warm dusk the herons came. In the trees along Bernstein's cove, fruit bats began to flap their leathery wings. Cassandra put their few possessions in the hut which was just a low branchy bedroom raised a couple of feet off the ground. Hugh lit a driftwood fire. He strolled down to the shallows where his friend was gutting his catch with a fearsome dagger, where his lover, hatless now, was watching the evening fall on the strait. He listened to the ripples lap. A line came back to him, an inscription was it? or a motto on a painting. *Et in Arcadia ego.* But no, that was wrong. That was when you were in Arcadia and everything seemed splendid but then you found a skull leering at you. Yes, it was a painting – vaguely he could bring it to mind. Well, no doubt death was here too. A ray had been washed up; farther off, a big greeny-pink jelly-fish; they were fly-blown, they were rotting. Under the palms the old rotting coconuts looked like heads as they always did. And here was Thor hoiking innards. But mortality was not alarming, there was nothing bad about it. *Et ego in Arcadia* . . . He fiddled with the words. Now they caught his feeling. He too would have been in Arcadia. He was in Arcadia now. He was infinitely fortunate. He must remember.

Thor Bernstein might, as with practised jerks he disembowelled fish, regret that his island's hitherto ascetic air should all of a sudden be trembling with carnality. He might be amused by how, the fine ships of their cultures magisterially capsized by the typhoon of sexual love, Hugh Blakeney had been converted from a philandering sophisticate into a devoted monogamist, Cassandra Matlaske the demure Mission School teacher in a day had become a passionate lover and, perhaps stranger still, the beginnings of an ironist. But to the man whose love was magnificently returned and would that night be consummated in a hermit's cell requisitioned to be a bower of erotic delights, the falling away of the past was freedom. To hear a moment's faint crepitation in the trees, to hear it die into quietness again. In the brackish nightfall to watch Cassandra stand ghostlily by the sea's edge, to watch the driftwood fire flicker, to watch for the first stars. He was at a turning in his life, Hugh Blakeney couldn't doubt it. He had turned. A man could change himself, could change his world; he was changing momently. This wasn't necessity. This wasn't chance. This was free will; it was the victory of the hard, exacting will. The feeling was heady. Hugh walked away down the beach, he wanted a minute alone. This too he would remember, give thanks for. The past dispelled, the self-remaking will could look forward undismayed.

The nights warm but not hot, the nights calm – it was easy to be confident about the free man's dedication to making his soul in his own style. The hut's rough-hewn platform kept Hugh and Cassandra up off the insect-paraded earth. Its intermittently solid walls gave them enclosedness. Its *atap* thatch protected them from nothing worse than falling leaves. They made love, they lay whispering, they walked down the sand to bathe in the dark sea. If hand in hand they ventured a few yards up the forest slope, beneath the trees the intense blackness was lit only by the occasional amorous firefly and by decaying branches and foliage which were luminous, by a fallen tree which bore fungi that glittered with phosphorescent light. If they lay on the beach, the moonlight was bright. Once they saw a school of dolphins swim by.

One day they left Thor Bernstein to resume his isolation for a few hours; with the help of his stuttering engine they crossed back to the *kampong*. They stocked up with fresh water. They bought chives, chillis, lansats, mangosteens, rambutans, durians; they bought oil, they bought flour and rice. At a roadside shack they drank cold Anchor beer, they ate *nasi goreng*. But then they did not at once return over the strait but chugged along the shore to where there was a waterfall. She would like to wash her hair, Cassandra had said. Thor had replied that he generally just tipped a bucket over his head, but if she fancied a cascade there was one he could recommend.

If she had known! Cassandra Matlaske later grieved. If she had known how little time they were to be allowed!

But she did not know. Later, when it was of even less significance what she thought, she was heard to say that no one ever knew anything; but most people had stopped giving any weight to what she said by then. As they moored their boat at the mouth of the stream, as they climbed the path into the forest and heard the waterfall above them and ahead, Cassandra seemed to know a lot of things. But none of these truths warned her. And none of these illuminations fortified her much when her need for spiritual strength was a desperate one; and none lasted long, none endured as long as she did. If her ideas had any value it was as transitory as the hour, as their splashing in the stream where the fish shot away. The fresh water was cold after the sultry sea. The trees' canopy closed over the rocky defile, made a shade which was deliciously cool and pierced here and there with brilliant sunlight. These things were not poignant. They were instinct with gaiety.

Perhaps for a moment the clear glass of Cassandra's mind was clouded by anxiety about what people might say who did not understand that Hugh and she had never in fact been brother and sister. Or a shadow might fall which was trepidation as to what her spiritual adviser might think, what his view of her prayers might be. Perhaps momentarily she wondered about the brightness of Thor Bernstein's eyes, the thoughtfulness of his forehead. But these clouds were fleeting, and not really clouds, mere haze. Had her adored Hugh not miraculously fallen in love with her? Had her incomparable Hugh, who at the very least was Sir Galahad and Sir Lancelot rolled into one, not asked her to marry him? Here was a benediction to light up her consciousness's translucency with a play of peacock colours. Here was joy, as they scrambled up the rock ledges, edged around the deep pools, stopped scrambling for a moment, for a kiss which made her quiver.

Around the merry splashing of the waterfall, the forest stood motionless, shadowy, quiet except for birdsong. Alive with her new sensuality, Cassandra was sensitive as never before to the touch of water, the touch of air. Alert, smiling, she waded, she climbed. Where was the perfect pool, the perfect cascade, the perfect sheen of moss? She was not going to wash her hair in any old puddle and trickle. There must be sunlight on the rock she should choose, and some ferns, she insisted on beautiful ferns. Ah, here! Idyllic! Hugh was to spread their towel on that boulder. And look, there were butterflies!

Hugh washed Cassandra's hair in a sunlit, silvery fall. Feeling his hands lathering her head, she knew that in his love her glass mind was safe forever. The sound of playing water was a lulling music. Before her eyes the rippling moss shimmered, from a towering tree a swag of creeper hung over the pool, a butterfly flitted from shade to light to shade, settled on a rock. In a day or two she would set off for Kuching, for Philip, for his blessing. Hugh would go to his fire. He would come back. They would be married in Saint Thomas's. Even the thought of Stephen Chai marrying her to her godless lover who had always been so rude about her church could scarcely mist the shining facets of her happiness. He was rinsing the shampoo out now, she tipped her head back and shivered under the cascading glitter, he cradled her head, he smoothed the water through her hair. The chill splashing on her brow and on her closed eyes seemed a new baptism without this thought causing her unease. Through her thin eyelids the freshness of the bright fall struck piercingly, her mind was suffused with water-light.

Thor Bernstein whiled away the hours on his shore beneath his lofty casuarinas which around them had strewn a bed of their fallen needles, beneath his sea-almonds which were less tall, which shed a shade less faint than the airy casuarinas, a shade of sharper-edged and darker dapplings, which let drop leaves which the faint breaths from the sea puffed fluttering along the sand. He lay in his hammock. Restless, he got out of it, lay propped on one elbow. His fingers played with the sand, sifted, sifted. In his mind he could come up with no enthusiasm for this journey to the fire. But it was difficult to think of an excuse for *not* accompanying Hugh Blakeney. And there was no other venture he was enthusiastic about, no other idea, nothing.

Out in the belabouring sun Bernstein strolled back and forth along his beach that was so pale it was nearly white; he patrolled his solitude. For so long the only footprints in the sand had been his, but now . . . The world had set foot in his retreat. The world wanted to abstract him from his island kingdom, or abstract him from himself, was that it? In the last storm a palm had tilted over the beach; he shook his head irritably to dislodge the image of Cassandra Matlaske leaning against its grey curve. Abstract him . . . ? The hermit king frowned, he paced. Well the world was after him, that much was plain. Not that Hugh's causes were not all splendid, his indignations admirably righteous, but . . . But what? There was an indifference which Bernstein prized too. And his independence he prized – and here he was being shanghaied into collaboration, into participation; they'd make him that abhorrent creature, a member of a team, if they could.

His wish not to be enrolled where his sentiments and his opinions would quickly come to be assumed, then depended upon, then conditioned, made him argue to himself that the environmentalist cause would be more wholesomely served by spirits less shadowed by indifference than his. Or did he mean spirits less solidly founded on the bedrock of indifference? And what was it Philip Blakeney had mockingly but affectionately said, perhaps with envy said? *Unmoved, cold, and to temptation slow.* That was right. And here they were, dead set on moving him, damn them. A shame that the crusading son was such a poor, simple declension from the father. Something distasteful, too, about European so-called experts charging around the tropics making themselves feel good by blunderingly trying to save this, that and the other, brooded the man who could be sour too in his dismissal of the Third World's slavish desire to ape the Second and First. He scowled at the boat coming back across the strait. Enough of that. What would be the sensible thing to do? He thought indifference might be a virtue; Hugh was quite sure it was a vice. This either meant that they would be disastrous travelling companions or it did not. Or was the distinction to be made between spirits prone to feel all the correct sentiments and others liable not to feel them, not profoundly?

The afternoon sun tyrannised from a hard blue windless heaven. The sea glittered like tinfoil. The unwelcome boat's engine insisted, it invaded, it yammered. Irritated, Thor Bernstein's apparently casual beachcomber's sauntering became a desperate last defence of a citadel. Maybe Hugh Blakeney and his cronies from the charities were unreconstructed Victorian do-gooders, were district nurses who insisted on visiting those too ill to escape their moral ministrations, maybe they were just the latest generation of self-excusing colonials – but maybe they were not, and certainly along with considerable harm they did some good, and certainly it didn't matter much what you called them. Anyhow his mind could not be as jaded as often he feared, the solitary colonist of an uninhabited island reflected, if he pitched back into a romantic defence of his realm so helplessly. This foreshore was his rampart. To an obstinate garrison who had refused so many offers of a negotiated, face-saving capitulation, no mercy would be shown, the defender thought, and mocked himself for thinking anything so dramatic; but then reminded himself that this was not necessarily all overdramatisation, there were surrenders you could not indulge in with impunity. Now the mighty forest trees behind him seemed an old civilisation beset by barbarous hordes, they were an old disdain, an old poise, an old quietude. But easily destroyed. Here came brains clogged with arguments and hearts aswill with righteousness. A pity that for the besieged garrison any compromise would be total defeat. Here came belief in action, all manner of beliefs. Here came interest. Bernstein shuddered at his own love of coldness, frowned at the passion which the defence of indifference could arouse, resolved to be amiable. Be amiable . . . it meant surrender, he supposed gloomily. In which case perhaps he might try to put up a courteous but resolute fight. Already they had interrupted his mind's attentive waiting, spoiled that expectancy and openness which were intelligence; already they had blown dust in his light, muddied his water. Elements so easily clouded could never have been worth much. He waded into the sea. A second time, he laid his hand on their gunwale.

That twilight Cassandra Matlaske in her sarong and blouse sat on the sand by the driftwood fire, her mind shimmering with knowledge of time to come, of the procession of years in which she would walk beside Hugh.

Toward them, singly, in pairs, in ragged skeins, the gaunt herons flew over the sea, bringing Thor Bernstein his daily sadness.

Hugh Blakeney had lit a fire, had allowed it to begin to die down. With a stick he now raked some embers apart into a glowing bed, so they still had cheerful flames around which to sit but they also beside them had the means of grilling their supper. Thor with his harpoon gun had done them proud, the primitive black gridiron balanced on stones was covered with his kill, the smell was encouraging. Gingerly Hugh turned the sizzling fish, contentedly he licked his fingers.

'Well, Thor? Are you coming with me? I can't hang around all that long. In a day or two . . . '

'Am I?' Bernstein watched the dark grey herons circling in the pale grey air over his wooded retreat. 'You haven't yet told me what good looking at the fire will do. And getting anywhere near it could turn out to be a lot harder than you've imagined. You've realised that your presence will be unwelcome in some quarters, I suppose? Your . . . ' He hesitated. 'Your interest won't be to everyone's taste. Quite apart from the physical difficulties of closing in on the thing. Can you imagine what it must be like by now? Not sure I can. Say . . . Say ten Singapore Islands burned and the wind blowing the ash and down-wind another ten Singapore Islands blazing because it hasn't rained for months, not real wet season rain, nothing to do any good.' As he spoke, he realised that even if when Hugh and Cassandra departed they left him behind, if he remained and no longer had to play the unwanted ghost at their feast of the voluptuous, his refuge would have been irrevocably altered. Their sensual passions and their convictions would linger in the air. His inexistence, which had tasted of freedom as well as of melancholy, would taste of uselessness now. 'Have you worked out how you're going to move around this fire?'

'Oh, don't give up before we start.' Hugh was kneeling by his gridiron, with a knife he carefully sliced into a fragrant flank. 'Ready in a minute, I reckon. Come with me, it'll do you good. Then we'll go back to Kuching and you can be my best man. Well, you can if Cassandra can persuade her priest to let me anywhere near his altar. If not, we'll get the consul to marry us.'

'Am I suffering from something? Some malaise?'

Hugh's eyes met Thor's. His gaze was steady, affectionate. 'Aren't you? I mean, I know this island is paradise. But to roost here alone for month after month . . . But stay here if you'd rather. For heaven's sake, I don't want to spoil your peace. I just thought maybe . . . '

Hugh Blakeney felt so free of the discarded past, so confident as to what it was right to do now, so ebullient about the future, that it was with nebulous guilt that he remembered Keiko-san far away in Kyoto alone or not alone, remembered her husband's faltering career. 'But maybe you've got too much research to do.' In the air of the island without indigenous inhabitants the suggestion drifted. 'Or perhaps you're writing something you want to get finished?'

'No. It's not that.' Bernstein smiled. 'I'm a lapsed anthropologist these days.' He recollected a tiresome aspect of this. 'I've got practically no money left at all.' With his eyes, in the dusk he indicated his primeval, changeless domain. 'One of the advantages of my rotting here is that it's almost free.'

'I've got a little. We won't spend much.'

'And . . . I don't want saving, you know.' Thor Bernstein was being as amiable as he had resolved to be, but what he had not predicted were these waves of weariness of the world breaking in his brain. Well, he could always come back to his island later. He wondered if he would want to.

'No one's going to save you.' Hugh Blakeney grinned. 'Not a hope, don't worry.' The briny night had fallen. The fish were cooked. Delicately, with a knife in one hand and a stick in the other, he was transferring them from the hot bars onto a plate. 'I don't want to be saved either. Cassandra has a tendency to want to save people, but I promise I'll protect you from her.'

'And you won't save anything from the fire, I guess you've focussed on that?' He must learn not to sound so morose. Less grimly, with forced humour he went on. 'You'll just add your squeak to the hubbub of opinion.' He gazed into their crackling driftwood, as if in that innocent and beautiful burning he might comprehend the greater fire. 'You'll add to the politicking. You won't save a longhouse.' Heavy, the waves crashing down in his head. 'You won't save a tree.' He'd end by hearing only this plangent falling, then the retreating surf's roar.

'We'll see.' Hugh was smiling broadly at him. With liking in his voice he said, 'Maybe you'd better not come. Here's your fish.'

'If Hugh can't persuade you . . . ' Across the flames, Cassandra Matlaske regarded her host. 'If the fire in itself – if it doesn't – attract you . . . ' He met her eyes. With a play of seductiveness she asked, 'Will you go for my sake? Go with Hugh, if I ask you to? Keep an eye on him. Come back with him. Be his best man.'

Bernstein's brown eyes smiled into her black ones. Irresistible, to watch her being the coquette she was not, being the innocent she no longer quite was. And were men of nearly forty not supposed to like letting beauties of twenty-one twist them round their little fingers? Amply contemptuous enough of his own nature to consign himself to the conventional, he rejoined the wide stream of human inconsistency, he said, 'Yes.'

The victress laughed softly. 'I'll wait for you. Do you know what the Malay women used to do when their men were away? Philip told me.' Her voice was calm, was low. 'They made lamps out of split coconuts with a drop of oil and a rag wick. Little votive lamps. They sent them floating down the rivers at night.'

The defeated man lowered his eyes. The salt-imbued branches were burning with orange lights and violet lights.

THREE

Cassandra Matlaske's return from the Sulu Sea to the Sarawak river with the declaration of her engagement to marry her former brother, the man who on paper was still her brother, was greeted by Grace and Lily Chai, as soon as they had confirmed that their brother had not condemned the match, with a flurry of girlish enthusiasm.

Up the worn boards of Philip Blakeney's stairway their feet pitter-pattered. Up through the verandah floor their raven heads of hair and their ivory faces erupted. 'Let's talk weddings!' the sisters chimed. It was all too astonishing, it was wonderful, Cassandra must please quickly explain, recount, confess. What dress was she going to wear? When was the wedding to be? Which of her little friends were to be her pages and bridesmaids? There was no excuse for reticence, there could surely be no wish for it, she was to day-dream aloud. Their love for her demanded no lesser tribute. She was to satisfy their romanticism and their curiosity by commencing right now.

The Chai family were Hokkien Chinese. They had been prosperous traders in Kuching for a hundred and fifty years, and for three generations they had been Christians.

Very dutiful Christians, they had become – though it had all started in a chancy enough fashion. In the last century the Dutch authorities south of the watershed and the British to the north and west knew that the Christian sects would always squabble unless they were kept apart. The way they worked it out in Kalimantan was that the Protestant missionaries were corralled up in the south and the Catholics were let rip to the north. On his side of the mountains the white Rajah, when at

last he let the missions into his country, used his waterways
to separate them, so that up a lot of Sarawak rivers they
were all Church on one bank and all Chapel on the other.
The Chai family became Church of England because Kuching
was an Anglican fief. If they had been Foochow Chinese living
in Sibu, say, they would all have been Methodists.

The reasons of state of a Rajah dead for over a century, the
opportunism of some Hokkien merchants – the upshot of these
interlocking sagacities was that when Philip Blakeney used to
escort the little Cassandra to the Mission School he got to know
the parents of some of the other children, among them Mr and
Mrs Desmond Chai. Stephen was a quiet boy. They were his
merry sisters who made the playground shindy. He had grown
into a reserved young man when, ten years later at a wharf
waiting for a ferry, he introduced himself to the old man who
was a familiar spectre in the graveyard but never set foot in
the church. Did Mr Blakeney remember him? He held out his
hand, shyly but firmly. 'I am the son of Desmond Chai, I am
Stephen Chai,' he said. The *tambang* was coming, and to make
friendly conversation Blakeney mentioned that on the Baram
he had known boat traders with vessels no bigger and a lot
shabbier than this. They stepped aboard. In the cramped cabin
open at bow and stern Blakeney sat with his long legs carefully
folded. Yes, wretched little craft often, with a foot of freeboard,
with an *atap* shelter, and the Chinese traders would be away for
weeks rowing from longhouse to longhouse. Of course, Stephen
lived in a different Sarawak, but could he imagine . . . ?

The Hokkien of Kuching were always on good terms with the
Rajah. They took his side against the Bau *kongsi* in the fighting of
1857, remained warily loyal on that day of Bishop McDougall's
discovery that though to be brave was the simple duty of a
Christian when the weapons were in your hands and those of
your friends, it was less a matter of course when they were in
your enemies'. The Chai of the time was a considerable *towkay*,
with two shops in the bazaar, with a godown where he stored
his rattan before he shipped it to Singapore. This industrious
entrepreneur, having not been much spoken of by anybody
for a hundred years after his funeral, which was very grand
and was attended by distinguished men of all Kuching's races,

suddenly existed anew in the rambling discussions of Philip Blakeney and Stephen Chai. Because of course after their talk in the *tambang* Blakeney invited his young acquaintance to visit him any evening he pleased, come and have a look at some of his Chinese odds and ends. The student was shy – he became a bit less withdrawn as he proceeded through his twenties – but not too timid, having let a few evenings elapse, to take the offer up.

A T'ang dynasty platter unfortunately broken, a handful of indecipherable Chinese coins, a Ming celadon dish cracked and repaired, a Martaban jar, some chipped Annamese monochrome ware . . . Some of the odds and ends were quite impressive, if you liked that kind of thing. Stephen Chai had never before asked himself whether he liked it or not, but he decided the cracked this and chipped that were fascinating right away, took his lessons happily under adolescent Cassandra's eyes.

Those were still the days when Blakeney would now and then determine that he was going to reduce one or other of his mounds of notebooks to the lucidity of a chapter which would take its place in *A History of Borneo* – and naturally there were going to be chapters on the Sarawak Chinese. He never made much progress. But Stephen Chai came of an interesting family, and it turned out that Blakeney could tell him things about his forebears that he had not known, and the historian could pick up details from his pupil too, so their conversations amused them both. Often they were not alone on the verandah. Some of the young Kuching researchers were courtiers of old Blakeney's too, people who would never write anything as ambitious as his *History* but were far more likely actually to publish *something*, essays, a monograph. Well, he didn't write his *History* either. Occasionally Hugh was there. Chai and he were the same age.

Conversations with Philip Blakeney tended to be like meandering strolls on stepping-stones. You stood with him on one stone and you remarked upon the waterlilies and the dragonflies, you admired the irises and the carp; then you took a leisurely step to the next vantage point. If Stephen and he did not dwell on the Chai who took the Rajah's part in 1857, it might be the turn of his son. This Chai was a big shot in the opium trade, and along with the Rajah and the Datu Bandar and the Resident, and indeed for that matter Michael Blakeney, was present at the opening of the Chinese Court in 1911.

From Blakeney the theology student, who became a curate at around this time, learned a lot of things about his people and their adopted country which nobody else had thought to tell him, which he had not thought to find out for himself. He learned about the Hakka miners of the Twelve Company at Bau in the nineteenth century who when it came to panning for gold were of a sophistication beyond the dreams of the local Malays and Dayaks – how they built dams and reservoirs, canals and sluices, till the landscape looked like a region of China. Or it might be the Chinese labourers in the Sadong colliery they talked about, the wretches who crept through the galleries beneath Mount Ngili up to their waists in water, breathing the black damp.

From these illustrations of the benefits of autonomy at Bau and the miseries of servitude at Sadong, the talk might divagate to Wong Nai Siog, who was a Methodist minister and by agreement with the Rajah shipped the first batch of Foochow colonists to the Rejang in 1901. Sitting on his verandah with his glass of whisky, Philip Blakeney might remark, calmly and cheerfully, that he couldn't for the life of him understand how Wong then and Stephen now could get jazzed up about a whole lot of half-baked claptrap like Methodism or Anglicanism or Romanism. Sitting a few paces off with his glass of lime juice because he never touched alcohol, Stephen Chai might respond, just as calmly and cheerfully, that he looked for the forgiveness of sins, the resurrection of the dead and the life everlasting, or words to that effect – for the fact that he was reserved with all men and deferential with his elders and his superiors did not mean he lacked self-confidence. On the contrary . . . He had belief in abundance, so much that he scarcely needed to think about it. He had the equanimity which certainty lends, didn't give the impression that anything would ever torment him, didn't look as if anything would ever break him.

Then it was James Hoover and his wife they harked back to . . . Hoover who preached among the Foochows for the first thirty years of this century, and whom Blakeney as a boy had met in his plank and *atap* Mission House at Sibu. Hoover had founded Methodist chapels, had founded schools and taught in them, had planted rubber trees in the school gardens so they might one day to a degree be self-financing. Mrs Hoover had taught in the schools and had held Bible classes and had gone to teach in the houses of Foochow girls who were too old to be seen out of doors or whose bound feet made it impossible to walk to school.

By questions and answers, by convergent musings, they kept haunting back to the Rejang as Blakeney recalled it from when Andrew and Nerissa and he were children, the great Rejang three miles wide at its mouth and still over a thousand yards wide up at Sibu; the tramp steamers and the junks which went on higher up-river, traded as far inland as Kapit. Blakeney remembered the shop-houses at Kapit bazaar with their wide verandahs where the rattan and gutta percha were stored, the fort with its flame-of-the-forest tree. He remembered how the Dayaks used to cut swags of rattan in the forest, drag them to the river. When they were sere they would be cut into twenty-foot lengths, lashed into bundles to make a raft. Then on the raft the men would build a little *atap* cabin and so they would set forth, drifting and poling their way down the current to a bazaar.

The friendship between Philip Blakeney and Stephen Chai never had any great profundity, but it was never less than amiable either – or at least it wasn't until right at the end when there lay so much tragedy between them and such desolation within them that they had nothing left to say to each other. Not a word. Scarcely a glance. And maybe then their silence was as amiable as it was humanly possible to be. There were his sisters too. In the happier times of Cassandra becoming nubile and Stephen becoming a priest, to Blakeney's anxious watchfulness Grace and Lily were so reassuringly cheerful, so chunky, so chatty. Stephen was cheerful too – and he was well off. With him she would be warmly cocooned. True, he was a bit stodgy . . . But had not Blakeney determined that for the skinny consequence of the sexual passions of an Irish Hussar and an Iban dancer the Church of England would make an acceptable bulwark? It was a lair she had done nothing but snuggle deeper into. So let her marry into it one day – why not? For it occurred to him, as he watched his adopted daughter bend before Chai to pour lime juice and tinkling blocks of ice from her jug to his glass, that he might ask her and she might say yes. It was at this period that Blakeney and Chai discovered they had the Tay family in common, all that ramifying Tay cousinage up the Batang Lupar at Simanggang.

The trouble was that this felicitous discovery about the Tay lineage, who had been a power in the land up at Simanggang for as long as anyone could recollect, who counted among their number several friends of Blakeney's and who were connected in some obscure alliance with the Chai dynasty, coincided with Philip's discovery of his son's visceral dislike of Stephen. He supposed it was visceral, just a gut reaction – couldn't explain it in any other fashion. This was before he had any suspicion that Hugh might wish to lay amorous hands on Cassandra.

Hugh Blakeney was invariably civil to Stephen Chai. But he was never anything better than civil. And he could be civilly aggressive too. Long before he came galloping from Timor and stopped in Kuching to possess himself of Cassandra before charging off to the Sulu Sea, unluckily bumping into Stephen on the stair and grabbing the opportunity to demand of him why he had not preached a sermon on the subject of the fire . . . Long before then he had wanted to be told why no one from the pulpit of Saint Thomas's had denounced what was being done to the peoples of the interior and to their land. And there had been a famous verandah evening when he had wanted poor Stephen to allow that missionaries did more cultural harm than good, wanted him to come out and say so aloud. A man who thought he might persuade a priest to climb up his pulpit steps and denounce his missionary brethren! Well, Hugh was always an optimist.

Yes, it was a shame, that dislike . . . Because Philip Blakeney was coming to think that what he had dismissed as stodgy was a commendable evenness of temper and steadiness of feeling, and he was coming to sense that Cassandra thought so too, and the Tay clan were serving his turn very well.

What would occur would be that Chai, in his capacity as the girl's best friends' brother or in his capacity as her spiritual adviser, would be sitting on her father's verandah. And because they had already inspected the Ming celadon dish which had been cracked and stuck together again, and because there was nothing the Twelve Company had got up to that they had not palavered about, because there was nothing further to be said about the old Chinese sailing vessel called a *bandong*, they would fall back on chat about the Tays.

The Tays had been up the Batang Lupar in the mythic past before Rajah Brooke introduced brass currency, when one of the staples of Bornean bartering was the cotton cloth called *blachu*. Since then the number of Tays who had achieved mighty things was prodigious, and they served Blakeney and Chai in excellent stead. Had not two generations of Tay been Kapitan China at Simanggang? Had their family firm of Seng Joo not regularly supplied the officers at Fort Alice with victuals and liquor, for many years been awarded the lucrative tender to sell opium? Then there was the temporary decline in their trade with the interior in 1877 when in the longhouses cholera was rife. Not to mention the construction of the Simanggang theatre, in which Tay initiative and money had been manifest, the arrival in 1898 of a Singapore troupe who gave *wayang* performances which went on for a month.

The last thing Stephen Chai wanted was to be bluntly interrupted by Hugh Blakeney desiring to know what the Church reckoned to do about the destruction of a number of communities in its ministry. Of course, afterward everyone felt they understood. Those two had just been firing the first shots in their fight to the death for Cassandra's soul. Well, in the end neither of them got her – which possibly was justice of a kind. Maybe . . . if souls aren't for fighting over, aren't for winning and losing.

2 ∫

Several people remarked that after his adopted daughter's engagement Philip Blakeney seemed to put a good sane bit of distance between himself and his most penetrative thoughts. He appeared for a few weeks to have that ability. Right toward the end of his life, for a short period he was fortunate.

Yusof Badawi was a level-headed man. If his pilot's salary did not constitute wealth, it was a far cry from indigence; and that year he too was getting married, making a match beyond reproach. Indeed Yusof was perhaps the only creature of plain common sense much connected with Philip Blakeney – at least, the only one after David Matlaske was killed. Hearty Raoul Kahn was too infrequent a visitor to count. Not that Blakeney did not have good sense, did not manfully try to live by just that – but he had other mental faculties too.

While Yusof . . . He wasn't composed of shadows, like Akbar Nasreddin and Thor Bernstein. He didn't cart a creed around with him, like Cassandra Matlaske and Stephen Chai with their factitious strengths. Of course he was a Muslim – but it was not a matter he bothered about. He was not a man given to bothering.

Well, Yusof Badawi had no doubt about Blakeney being on an even keel. Naturally that practical man had suspected that Chai had taken a fancy to the prettiest girl in his flock. He had taken a fancy to her himself, while knowing full well that nothing could ever come of it. He knew enough about Christianity to know that Chai – and therefore, naturally, Cassandra – were sufficiently something called High Church to go in for spiritual advice, whatever that might entail. Clearly the priest had found that dishing out murmurous counsel to that demure nymph was one of his pleasanter duties. And he knew Church of England priests could marry, and he didn't think Blakeney would have had any objection – which would have been important, because it was terrible to envisage Cassandra's anguish if she were ever tempted to betray the man who, when she was a baby, had saved her.

That was the way she saw things, always – Yusof was right. That among the burning houses Philip had picked her up off the dust . . . Though of course she knew in fact he hadn't, it had been a *kampong* woman. That if they ever came to a division of their ways it would be her betrayal of him. Horribly clear glass, her mind. For if you had asked her why necessarily it should be so, she would have looked at you with surprise that you did not understand, had not seen that Philip's love was of a capacity, a fineness . . . ! Through years of love and suffering, of love and self-denial he had achieved a heart which was perfect, she would softly have pointed out to you – while she! any fool could see that she had so far to go she'd never get halfway. So it was a relief to Yusof Badawi when Chai came to offer the girl his congratulations – a relief because it knocked on the head the possibility that the pilot might have felt the obligation to bother. Yusof had just made his own modest effusion, was taking his first sip of lime juice, and it was a relief to see how smoothly the moment went.

Stephen Chai had not followed hard on Grace's and Lily's heels when they came bundling up the staircase. That afternoon he had been busy with his pastoral cares. He came after evensong, which that day the fiancée had somehow not got around to attending.

Of course the convention that all engagements were a cause for docile rejoicing helped. Danielle Kahn was there, her raffishness for this occasion set aside. She had embraced the suitably radiant Cassandra almost passionately. Now she was enjoying being the mama who might be observed to be making terrific efforts not to talk *too* much about her handsome and brilliant son – whose absence most of the party were fulsomely lamenting while one or two suspected it might be providential. Raoul Kahn was there, his bluff solidity an assurance that he would give the young couple a solid wedding present, a sum he would not notice the loss of but which would help them through their first year together in no uncertain measure. The engagement had held his attention for two minutes, now he was complimenting Philip Blakeney on his Glenmorangie, asking him the name of his supplier. Grace and Lily were there – indeed for the next few days they more or less bivouacked in the house.

Yusof Badawi watched Stephen Chai smile, watched him kiss the flushed, betrothed girl on both cheeks, heard him say, 'This is marvellous news! I'm so glad.' He watched him swing round to Blakeney and still smiling declare, 'You must be enormously pleased.' Stephen Chai who, Yusof reflected, had clearly been reserved enough never to let his sisters suspect that his feeling for their enchanting friend might have been other than friendly ... But the two girls were of an innocence – though Yusof lacked the acerbity to follow this perception far – which might more plainly be called lack of imagination; Cassandra's alliance with such doughy spirits was eloquent of her uneducated provinciality if anything was. Stephen Chai who, Yusof had occasion to ponder the following year when they coincided at the swinging door of the local bank, by all accounts never spoke a word against Hugh Blakeney in his life. No – not even when the temptation must have been excruciating ... And he knowing that Hugh didn't think much of him, though mercifully not that he was referred to as Cassandra's fat little priest.

Blakeney shook Chai's hand with vigour, held his gaze for several seconds. Of course his sentiments, in a sphere in which Hugh's reigned supreme, were nothing much. But he was an excellent young man, and Philip liked him. 'Surprised, Stephen, as I expect you can imagine. But, yes, delighted. I've been thinking of Cassandra's father. Old friend of mine from the regiment. That his daughter should marry my son ... Naturally it never occurred to either of us. But if it had ... I like to think he'd have been pleased.'

What Yusof did not hear was the exchange between Stephen and Cassandra when they obtained a minute's seclusion at a corner of the verandah.

'So ...' He was still smiling, but thoughtfully now. 'It's resolved.'

She was serious. 'It's all right – isn't it?'

'Certainly. If it is the will of God . . . '

Yusof Badawi did not take long to arrive at his prognostication that his host's ship had begun to sail on an even keel and would continue to do so unless battened upon by a hurricane not now visible on the horizon – he took an unworried sweep around the distances – at any point of the compass. Blakeney this evening was beaming – and he had not been in the habit of beaming since anybody could remember. No doubt in the early days of his marriage to Danielle he had lived such flashes of happiness – perhaps on the moonlit Baram beneath a boat's awning making love. And now he had plainly decided to let this revelation be just what it apparently was, what it ought to be, let it be a flash of happiness . . . And he seemed to be capable of putting this decision into practice, at least for an evening. The union of Hugh and Cassandra, the taking of his two paramount loves and making them one, was to be allowed to be a great good, a blessing to be given thanks for.

Others were more involved in the betrothal than he was; Yusof found himself chatting to Raoul Kahn, who also was peripheral, a little apart from the fizzy nucleus.

Yusof never forgot that evening – not because of the engagement, which when all was said and done concerned him little, was chiefly a matter of being pleased that Blakeney was letting himself be pleased. No, because of Kahn's braceleted carbuncle of a gold Rolex watch. They had been talking about oil palm plantations, about Raoul's business interests in Asia – he made his real money in Paris, but he liked to invest in the East too, have an interest in a factory here or an estate there. He used to say it paid for his sailing, paid for *Aigrette*'s yearly overhaul in Singapore. The yachtsman was explaining why he was hesitant about this particular fellow who wanted him to come in with him in oil palms on a fairly big scale, and Yusof's eye fell on Raoul's brawny wrist. It bore one of those watches that cost thousands of dollars and perform all manner of chronometrical tricks and are said to go on performing them hundreds of metres under water should you go down there.

A couple of years later, Yusof Badawi remembered that watch. He had just bought a copy of *The Herald Tribune* at an airport stall,

partly because it was a newspaper pilots read, partly for mere
sentimental attachment because Hugh had written one or two
pieces that had been published there. It was Singapore airport.
Aigrette was being overhauled in the docks there, though he
didn't know it. Danielle Kahn was in a hotel in Hobart, and
though he didn't know that either he began to suspect as much
as he read the sporting page. Raoul Kahn had been sailing as
navigator aboard a big sloop in the Sidney to Hobart race, they
had been up among the leaders when the vanguard of the fleet
ran into a storm. Notorious for foul weather, the Sidney–Hobart
– for damage, for losses. Several yachts were dismasted, and it
might have been better if Raoul's had been, but nothing broke
or anyhow nothing serious. They kept her sailing hard because
you do when you're in contention to win the thing, and they
were having a heart-stopping time of it crashing through the
combers and having the combers crash over the deck when she
was knocked down. A squall. Then one of those freak waves
you can't seem to see the crest of when it rears over you . . .
The sloop was knocked flat. Yes, better if in that instant her
mast had gone over the side. That takes the pressure off things,
that simplifies matters. The hull would have stayed upright. Of
course, she came upright again, she had been designed to do
that. But by that time two of the four men who'd been in the
cockpit had gone.

Yusof read Raoul's name, he laid the newspaper down on the
airport seat. He thought of Raoul going down into his black cold
vortex. He thought of him down in the roiled ocean with his
gold watch still telling the time for his dead eyes. For weeks he
thought of that wonderful watch telling the time as the wrist
it was latched to rotted. He thought of Danielle in Hobart, in
a hotel. Yusof always had respect for a beautiful woman, even
when she was thirty years his elder. The next time he was in
Paris he went to pay his respects to the widow. As he rang
the door bell he was still thinking about the watch and the
wrist . . . How long did they go for, those Rolexes? 'She's in
good health,' he said grimly to Nasreddin when he was back
in Kuching. 'She could easily live another ten or fifteen years,
even twenty. Quite a punishment. And she was innocent.'

Such was Philip Blakeney's good humour that in the next

few days he began to put his house in order. Of course it was not a house that could be reduced to much order, and even to the enchanted pair who made this bold attempt, even to Philip and Cassandra, it must have been clear from soon after they started their labours that their success was going to be limited. Certainly those, such as Akbar Nasreddin and Yusof Badawi, who witnessed this assault upon chests of drawers some of which had stood inviolate since Kitty Blakeney had last tidied them, never gave three seconds' serious thought to the possibility that much system might be introduced into the collection. And why should anyone care? It was delight enough to watch that beguiled pair in action. Yes . . . Because their joyful love quivered in the dusty air of those rooms like the equatorial heat of the afternoons through which they worked. Well, they called it working. To the observers it was rapturous play, heavenly and messy play . . . For they regularly left more mess behind in a room than they had found. But you walked into their devotion as if you'd strolled into a church and so naturally breathed the incense wafting in the quiet. There they'd be in their sultry shuttered dusk, their heads bent together over some chest . . .

Everyone knew that for years the Blakeney house had been rivalling Kuching Museum when it came to Bornean antiquities. When he was curator of the latter collection Tom Harrisson had teased Cassandra Matlaske's other godfather about this. His successors had enjoyed the same joke – especially when it was understood that the eighteenth-century Brunei cannon with its dragon mouth was among the pieces to be left to the official museum when the watcher over the unofficial one died. But for years it had also been true that the place was becoming more of a mausoleum than a museum. It seemed to be waiting for the dead hero to be laid there among his trophies. Or no . . . Because that infirm old wooden house couldn't last long in that climate. It was more of a catafalque – as indeed it turned out to be. A first, carpentered tomb for Blakeney to lie in briefly before he was carried to where he'd stay.

It had caused Philip Blakeney much anxious meditation, the question of who should be left what. That Hugh and Cassandra should be treated so far as was possible equally was not in doubt.

But the Devon house for his son and the Kuching house for his daughter . . . ? And their contents? Only he didn't want Hugh never again to be at home on the banks of the Sarawak river – after all, he had been born there. So the forthcoming marriage was a happy resolution of this dilemma. It was in these weeks that Akbar was commanded to draw up Philip's last will and testament, which bestowed everything jointly upon Hugh and Cassandra.

At last it appeared that Philip Blakeney had stood watching the river for long enough, he had seen what he wanted to see. He had waited, tall, gaunt, grey, still, among his nipah palms and sedge. He had watched for years until he knew what he wanted to know, till he saw his love victorious, knew what to do . . .

This altering of his will, this sorting out of his possessions, were very nearly the last actions he ever took.

Kitty Blakeney had been a watercolourist – a proficient one, nothing amateurish about her. She exhibited at various Mayfair galleries on and off for two decades. A view of a wooded scarp of Mount Kinabalu with a thunderhead louring was hanging on a wall in the Watercolour Society's rooms along Piccadilly when the Japanese shot her. Her masters were Girtin and Linnell and de Wint, John Sell Cotman above all, and with their examples to inspirit her she painted in Sri Lanka and in Bengal and in Sumatra as well as in Borneo. Three or four dozen of her pictures had remained in her surviving son's house: framed, unframed, hung, in solanders, propped here and there. Sometimes she had forgotten to date them, but they were all signed, and on most of them she had indicated the subject, if not at the foot of the picture then on the back or on the frame. Such and such a temple near Kandy, Philip Blakeney and Cassandra Matlaske would read, holding the painting up to a jalousie and blowing the dust off it. Or it was a scene of the harbour at Trincomalee, or of a garden at Mount Lavinia. Watercolours of pagodas at Palembang, of decaying and overgrown mansions at Bengkulu. Watercolours of the sea and lateen sails, of palmy roads winding off into the Himalayan foothills, of godforsaken little places in the Ganges delta. Watercolours of the dust and rain-trees and *ghats* and rivers, watercolours of the sun and wind . . .

With Hugh gone to the fire as men had gone to the war, his

father wanted his bride to know what everything in the house was – this was the start of their sorting, their naming – so that she might tell him when he came back, so she might tell him when his father who could explain and name everything should be dead. Where Kitty had neglected to indicate her subjects, Philip would write them on the backs of the pictures when he knew. When he didn't know with any precision, often he knew when his father and mother had visited a given island or province, so he wrote that as a rough guide. It was a loving game, this searching through the rooms with his darling Caz, this unearthing, this cataloguing . . . But he was playing it in deadlier earnest than the girl could suspect from his smiling companionship, deadlier than she was aware till later. It became vital to him that Hugh and she should know as much as possible. He wanted to give them as many things as possible – several gifts to the museum were revoked in the course of this survey, though Cassandra would protest that half the bundle of pre-war Murut embroideries would do, that Hugh and she would be fine with a mere half-dozen swords – and he wanted to give them as many facts as he could too. Objects, names, dates – so blessedly apparent. It was as if he were deploying his forces in his last defensive action. Hugh might have gone off to the fire with the righteousness and the panache of an early king of France into whose hand the abbot of Saint Denis had given the oriflame; but his ghostly giver of life, left to command the realm of the dead in the heir's absence, would do his duty, would not be found to have slacked. So . . . This was a Javanese kris from the seventeen hundreds. This one had had its blade broken because the Malays had believed that a kris which had tasted blood would thirst for it again, but a vendetta could be stopped if you snapped off the tip . . .

Blakeney was particularly happy to rediscover his mother's paintings of her brother-in-law's river and bungalow and garden. He remembered the place in Perak so well . . . Claud's hibiscus avenue, his bullock carts, the Tamil temple where as a child Philip had been garlanded with jasmine and sprinkled with attar of roses. Claud sitting on his verandah in his *tutup* jacket and sarong, telling his nephew about the Malays' spectral Huntsman who had lived in the forests so long that his thighs and chest were thickety with moss and orchids. Now Philip stood holding Kitty's rendering of a street of wooden verandahs and balconies in Taiping; he recalled how when one night he had been sent to bed in his uncle's bungalow a tapir had come snuffling under his floor. In a drawer of his desk in the saloon he found a ring which had been Claud's, a ring of reddish Mount Ophir gold with an emerald set in it. Holding it to the light, he said, 'If I give this to Hugh, he can give it to you.'

Astonishing, when you considered the bits and pieces that house was jammed with, the old man's memory. Of course, you expected him to know about the favourite things that stood on his desk. The ivory Buddha from Moulmein. The lacquered bowl from Yokohama. The hornbill's pale golden casque some Bornean tribesman had carved with a tiny tree, with tiny figures.

But the things that Cassandra and he disinterred from drawers which also yielded an impressive variety and plenitude of insects alive and dead . . . Take the innumerable fetishes. The girl would rout among the moth-eaten saris in a trunk and she'd come up with little fetishes carved in bone and carved in horn. 'Fishing fetish,' Blakeney would judge abruptly. 'Kayan. Got it near Belaga.' Or for a moment he might meditate. He might have been looking askance, looking at his fruit trees and his nipah fronds and the brown river. He might quietly have been saying, *They went to sea in a Sieve, they did, In a Sieve they went to sea*, because toward the tail-end of his life he often recited 'The Jumblies', used to say in his rumble that it was the only poem that to his mind still made any sense. Then he would frown at the carved figure she was holding out for his identification. He would say it was a Melanau sickness image. They enchanted the ailment from the sick person into that image and then the malingerer decided he was all right, he might do a bit of planting or hunting. Or he would say, 'The Iban used to stick them in the earth near a trap to lure game,' or whatever it might be.

Those afternoons in the wooden rooms when it was hot and the brass propellers of the fans fluttered the oppression over the father's and the daughter's heads and the insects whined. Hours on the verandah when they carried things out to lay them on the teak table. Hours of tropical haze, of steamy luscious quietness. Progress and Development bustled about on the south side of the river, and that was where the bazaar was tenebrous and fragrant and dirty and down-river was being pulled down. That too was where, across the tideway from Blakeney's scrutinising and naming and, as he dreamed, bequeathing, the fishing-smacks tied up and their catch was landed. On decks under the sun, sweaty men tipped buckets of water over their heads, handed chunks of soap back and forth, lathered their brown limbs. But the north side of the river was drowsy. It was for flying kites. It was for thickets which overwhelmed shingle roofs. It was well suited to exercises in naming.

A sixteenth-century Chinese hornbill snuff bottle. A stuffed black-headed oriole not yet quite tatty enough to throw away. A pair of razory spurs which had been bound to Iban fighting cocks' legs. A board for playing *congkak*. A French crystal bowl which had stood in the middle of Claud Blakeney's dining table before the last war, before the Great War too for that matter – Philip told Cassandra how his uncle had always had it brimming with lotus flowers. That reminded him that he had eaten more turtle curry in a month in that bungalow than in all his days since. Then he remembered the lotus lake far away in Perak. It was not always sunny and idyllic, that lake, he said – standing on his verandah half a century later with his long bony fingers touching the crystal bowl. In the reedy swamps, buffaloes wallowed. Out on the water, Claud's skiff pushed through beds of mighty leaves and pink flowers. Beneath looming clouds in the sweltering mist, with swamp and jungle all around, that roseate lake was the saddest, loneliest place on earth.

An Iban nose flute, a Bugis *kacapi* with two strings, an Iban fiddle called an *enserunai* . . . It was when they got to the musical instruments that Cassandra declared she would never recollect all the names and provenances and dates, she was going to write them down. Forth she sallied to buy labels. Back she came. This labelling of hers, which went on for several days, was the only time when to Danielle Kahn's affectionate amusement it really did look as if the two guardians of the shrine of things and knowledge about things were going to introduce some system into their clutter. Her lost husband's arcana might become legible – here was an advance!

'What's this?' the bride-to-be enquired, gingerly picking up an old gourd with bamboo pipes fixed to it. 'It's a *kediri*,' Blakeney replied. 'You don't find them on any of the other islands. Just in Borneo, I believe.' So she wrote: *Kediri, only found in Borneo*; tied the label neatly to the bamboos. Next a *sambe* with strings of copper thread, an older one with rattan strings. The following day, on to the weapons or the headdresses . . .

Philip Blakeney's mind was as much of a jumble as his house. Still, it was a jumble he knew his way about. Things had stories attached to them; stories reminded him of things. She must read the great Wallace, he told her. Mary Kingsley for West Africa, Alfred Russel Wallace for South-East Asia . . . The tropical world was illuminated by a handful of cardinal texts, he pronounced in his gruff voice, and these were two of them. And if she were going to read *The Malay Archipelago* she must read it in his first edition, which was on such and such a shelf.

They reached the volume down. On its fly-leaf he wrote: *For Hugh Blakeney and Cassandra Matlaske, for their engagement*. He wrote the date, his own name. He told her about Wallace's adventures in *prahus* in the seas off Lombok and Flores, at Makassar which these days they called Ujung Pandang, at Ambon and east of there. This brought to his mind the famous Malay captain Haji Sleh whose three-masted schooner the *Sri Lambir* was as fabled for speed and for loveliness as her master was for noble blood, courage, astute trading. Philip told Cassandra how the *Sri Lambir* was lost in twelve fathoms of water off Sematan. The wreck was celebrated for being caused by the vessel being blown into the whirling column of a waterspout. He was just recounting that while the schooner went down Haji Sleh was seen striding his doomed deck and brandishing his sword at enemies visible only to him, when he saw something that made him fall quiet.

The girl had only been listening with half her attention. Idly she had opened his Regency writing-box. Now she was standing before a tall looking-glass with his revolver in her hand. Smiling, she raised the gun, took aim at her reflection.

'Does this thing work?' she asked gaily.

'It would if you loaded it.'

He showed her the bullets, showed her how to load the chamber, spin it round.

They went to sea in a Sieve, they did,
  In a Sieve they went to sea:
In spite of all their friends could say,
On a winter's morn, on a stormy day,
  In a Sieve they went to sea!

Smiling faintly, Philip Blakeney recited, his eyes on his jacaranda tree.

And when the Sieve turned round and round,
And every one cried, 'You'll all be drowned!'
They called aloud, 'Our Sieve ain't big,
But we don't care a button! we don't care a fig!
  In a Sieve we'll go to sea!'
    Far and few, far and few,
      Are the lands where the Jumblies live;
    Their heads are green, and their hands are blue,
      And they went to sea in a Sieve.

The previous day's unearthing and naming had ended with a demonstration of how to cock the revolver, with lessons on how Cassandra would be more likely to hit what she aimed at if she steadied her right wrist by gripping it with her left hand, if she remembered the recoil, if she closed her left eye. She had stood before the looking-glass and had practised shooting herself in her reflected eye. Behind her back Blakeney had stooped, had set his head beside hers, laid his hand on her hand.

Now this evening they had mentioned the iron-working sites

which had been discovered at the Sarawak river mouth, sites which dated from a thousand years ago. They had mentioned the armoured river vessels called *kota-mara*, floating forts made of belian which the Dayaks had built in the last century when fighting the Banjarmasin War. The connecting link here had been iron weapons – they had been admiring the chased blades of Blakeney's collection of *parangs*. From the pitiful inadequacies of a *kota-mara* when pitted against a Dutch frigate, they had divagated to a Tinjar river chief called Aban Jau who, in the eighteen-eighties, refused to recognise the Rajah's jurisdiction over his territory, who strung a rattan across the river at Long Batan to mark the border of his realm, a rattan on which were posted signs warning the unwary and the presumptuous of the consequences of violating his domain or his laws. Then there was the tale of the first white man to penetrate the upper Mahakam, the ethnologist Nieumenhuis. The Penihing chief Blaney twice tried to have him killed because he seemed a presage of evil, but the Kayan chief Kwing Iran prevented the death. Blaney did not like to have Europeans come to that country which, as he expressed it, belonged to the natives.

Not a chance of the peoples of the interior fending off their present overlords from Kuching with a rattan tethered across a river, Blakeney had remarked wryly; but had said nothing more bitter than that. And then Cassandra had asked him why he liked 'The Jumblies' so much.

Akbar Nasreddin knew the answer to this; he had heard it among other elucidations of Blakeney's stoicism. He waited for the reply without particular alertness, therefore. Something gruff about how they were all at sea in a sieve, weren't they? Something amused about setting forth to no one knew where in leaking vessels. Something about spinning round and round, about thinking everything was all right when it wasn't.

But his old friend surprised him. 'The Jumblies' was all about the importance of going improvidently on adventures even when the sober bunch back at home shrilled that you were mad, he told his adopted daughter. For did not the Jumblies sail far and discover wondrous lands and purchase treasures and come safe home? The poem was a history of the East India Company in miniature, he genially declared. As for him, he admired the sailors in their sieve unreservedly. He liked the *beautiful pea-green veil* which was their sail. He liked how they kept their courage up with singing.

> The water it soon came in, it did,
>   The water it soon came in;
> So to keep them dry, they wrapped their feet
> In a pinky paper all folded neat,
>   And they fastened it down with a pin.
> And they passed the night in a crockery-jar,
> And each of them said, 'How wise we are!
> Though the sky be dark, and the voyage be long,
> Yet we never can think we were rash or wrong,
>   While round in our Sieve we spin!'

So determined to be happy, so contemptuous of wisdoms and of dangers – did Cassandra not agree they were irresistible? And then their success! How they sailed

> To a land all covered with trees,
> And they bought an Owl, and a useful Cart,
> And a pound of Rice, and a Cranberry Tart,
>   And a hive of silvery Bees.

Not to mention all their other glorious acquisitions. And then how twenty years later in their sieve they came sailing home again; and it turned out that while away in *the hills of the Chankly Bore* and elsewhere the voyagers had grown taller; and the stay-at-home lot naturally announced that now they too would go adventuring . . .

Even as a young man, even before as a groom he had been photographed sitting in state beside his bride, Akbar Nasreddin had hoped that if the apparent man was of impeccable formality, the abstract man might achieve an unsuspected autarky. And certainly his conventional good manners had protected him against dangers. On the day of Danielle's coming to confer with him about her divorce, for instance, when she had started spitting out those things about Philip's sexual anguish, Akbar had known how to play the quiet family lawyer. He had sat as immured in unexceptionable discretion as the stuffed oriole which yesterday Cassandra had brought out onto the verandah and dusted, which had remained on the table, its dead black head looking attentive among human proceedings.

Over the years, Akbar had gone on waiting for the ghostly freedom he had dreamed, not because he still thought he was likely ever to be initiated into such a communion with the time-less, but because he no longer had the mental vigour to change, to live more vitally. Not for him Hugh Blakeney's confidence in the will, in a man's ability to remake his thinking, his life. For hours Akbar would lose himself in the rich melodiousness of 'Ode to Autumn' or 'Tithonus' – he was the enchanted kind of reader, the kind who then sits with the book laid aside, who muses. Those voices sang to him from an England he had liked when he was at Gray's Inn, a Europe he had always been as innocently romantic about as Danielle Vernet and later her son, when detained in the West, had been romantic about the East.

Then on the warm grey evening of Raoul and Danielle Kahn's approach up the Sarawak river it had seemed his nebulousness might at last be rewarded. And now it was still sultry and it was nightfall again and it was May not March, and what Akbar had dreamed as the saddest of beginnings had had a little time to – to what? he wondered.

On that twilight of Cassandra's return with her bag of ram-butans and her declaration that she was going to stand by her father, Akbar had felt himself visited by that passionate man's dead, by Andrew, by Nerissa. In the dusk those piteous figures had appeared to stand before him. And now that Philip and the girl were labelling necklaces, now that they were marvelling at the intricate causes which had brought Renaissance Venetian glass beads to adorn the throats of Bornean warriors and their consorts, now that it was beginning to emerge to what a superb degree Cassandra was standing by her protector . . . Now the dead were here again. And if they were still piteous – for their sufferings had been atrocious, their sufferings were to be neither forgotten nor forgiven – had they not this time come also as celebrants?

The ice in Akbar's glass had melted, the whisky was tepid, he knocked it back. He relit his cigar. It was not just that Philip had given a surprisingly boisterous explanation of 'The Jumblies', had gone on to say what a fetching man Edward Lear had been, not just a fine painter – Kitty had admired his scenes of Egypt and of Greece – and not just an indefatigable wanderer, but by all accounts charm itself. It was that this was symptomatic of his being on what Yusof had called an even keel. It might be indicative almost – cautious Akbar made an effort to be as bold as his nature would permit – of Philip's final victory. For his dead, the piteous dead, were smiling.

Claud Blakeney a starving prisoner in a labour gang at Three Pagodas Pass dead of cerebral malaria, flung with other diseased carcasses into a purifying bonfire. Michael and Kitty Blakeney gunned down at Long Nawang, pitched into a mass grave – at Long Nawang with its longhouses smothered in trees, its *kampong* wet and unhealthy ... With Philip and Cassandra merry as they divided earrings according to tribe and labelled them, divided gold from silver, ivory from brass, bone from horn, Akbar Nasreddin was solitary. In his aura of cigar smoke he was impregnable against attack by mosquitoes, and his absentness had its protective haze too. He surrendered his mind to the shadowy; he was taken by it. He couldn't be wrong, the survivor's dead, if in their abstract fashion they might be imagined to exist, *were* looking on with contentment, weren't they? With smiles. With benedictions. In the grey arabesques of his cigar smoke Akbar seemed to see their eyes. Had Blakeney not at last won through? In '45 when he had fought to Kuching he had been too late; but now ... Even if the dead existed only as adumbrations in the brains of the living, that was reality enough. And the victory was in Philip Blakeney's being able to meet their eyes steadily; in his being able to lay the offering of his life before their deaths and point out that he had not survived in vain, had not been futile, not utterly. Philip might appear to be talking to Cassandra about jewellery. But he was really talking to his dead, and what he was saying was: Look, is this any good? At long last ... This young man my son. This young woman my adopted daughter. Their love for one another. All right ... ? My giving them things. My telling them things. A small triumph of love to set against evil's greater triumphs.

That the tortured and the killed should return as celebrants of a brother's survival conducted with courage and with love, with a self-control for which few had the discipline, a self-dismissal for which few had the sense of justice. That Akbar's deathly initiation had not been into unforgivable horrors, or not only into those but into their transcendence too. That ghostly eyes might be imagined to smile upon Hugh and Cassandra . . . Akbar's head was grey, grey too his smoke, grey the tropical dusk – but his fat fist resting on his fat thigh quivered as he softly clenched it.

He tried to think he had misread the signs, but he could not. Look, he demanded, debating with trenchancy against an adversary who was not there, the other evening they had even discussed the *sungkup* affair and Philip had not flickered. It came to be known as that because the men the Japanese arrested were carted off in lorries covered with *sungkup* sail-cloth. It all happened in West Kalimantan. In October 1943 people started being rounded up in Pontianak – Malay and Chinese dignitaries and intellectuals. Then the following July the names of forty-eight men executed for having been the leaders of a conspiracy were published. Had Philip not spoken of the episode like an historian born after the Japanese War was over? his lawyer demanded of the dusk with silent aggression. Spoken of it tranquilly, without that shadowed look of his, in his voice no hard edge . . . How later they had found mass graves. At Mandor they found a grave where the Japanese had buried more than a thousand so-called conspirators. Not that people let themselves be intimidated. In '45 when Philip Blakeney and the others in Z Special were fomenting rebellion in the Tamabo Range, the Dayak tribes from the upper Kapuas and the Singgau regions founded a guerrilla outfit called Majang Desa, began picking off a few of the invaders.

The small triumph of love, the greater triumph of evil against which it was outlined . . . The judge at Kuching Court, who had lived with such immaculate conventionality that almost everyone except Blakeney thought he was dull, clenched his fleshy paw a second time. The celebrants were too piteous. Their fates had been too cruel. Once Philip had said to Akbar that when he was dead and forgotten it would be as if Andrew and Nerissa and he had never lived and that would be good, would be the most grace that was possible. Though Philip might now in his enchantment with Cassandra and her engagement have let himself set aside the lucid justice of that judgement, poor Akbar could not, not for long.

Michael and Kitty Blakeney on the retreat inland to Long Nawang, not knowing what had happened to their elder son and their daughter at the fall of Kuching but praying that they might be alive ... Akbar Nasreddin was not a man given to strong feelings of any sort. But if he found he had to think of the grave at Long Nawang where there lay sixty bodies, anger and hatred were the only feelings which were morally decent. When then he thought of the pit at Mandor with more than a thousand bodies rotting in it; when he thought of other pits ...

Andrew Blakeney being tortured – first in this manner and then in that, in manners which Akbar sitting at nightfall on the verandah could not help imagining. Too often he had known Philip was imagining those tortures, too often. Andrew's body broken; his spirit broken; Andrew screaming for mercy; screaming. Andrew left to crawl away. His fellow prisoners doing what pathetically little they could to ease him. Andrew singled out again the next day. Philip at the freeing of the camp. Philip Blakeney in his Hussar lieutenant's uniform standing before a man apparently more dead than alive, a bony ghoul dripping with sores, teeth fallen out, hair fallen out, a ghost who had survived years of hunger and brutish labour and rough handling, who remembered Andrew. The officer. The ghost. The questions. The slow answers. The eyes. The knowledge.

The beginning in Philip Blakeney's head of an understanding he had feared but now had to know was the truth. In his head the beginning of questions and answers that never ended, of a screaming that would never die. Philip at Kuching Hospital trying to find somebody who had been there that Christmas Day of the invasion, someone who remembered Nerissa. Had they *all* perished? His desperate disbelief – was there never to be *any* knowledge? His maddened searching about Kuching, his haunting the women's prison camp. His searching all over Borneo – she might have escaped, was she hidden in some up-country backwater or eyrie? His endless meeting and asking and not knowing. At last, his belief. Nerissa in enemy hands. Nerissa raped tirelessly. Nerissa beaten, humiliated with all the ingenuity of military intelligence. Nerissa begging her torturers to shoot her, until maybe a man who did not think he would want her again did her that courtesy. Or she filched a length of rope or a knife.

One hand gripping his empty glass, the other his extinguished cigar, Akbar Nasreddin sat. His brain swam with horrors. His eyes glistened with tears.

With a shock, he realised that Philip and Cassandra had turned from the lamp on the table where they had been sorting through ornaments. They were standing shoulder to shoulder. They were looking into his eyes.

Akbar tried to smile. 'You looked . . . ' He raised a plump knuckle, he smudged his tears. 'You looked so wonderful together.'

In the garden a torch jigged. 'Philip!' called Danielle Kahn.

Cassandra Matlaske hardly had time to smile at the man she had elected to be her honorary godfather. Philip Blakeney hardly had time to reflect that his old friend not only lived through others but to a great extent for them too; that his compassion was as noble as his social adroitness was brave – the attempt to smile had been worthy of all praise, though his mouth had not worked, the whole performance had given the impression of a man trying to tear open a packet that was too strong for his fingers. Akbar himself hardly had time for a vision of the greatness of unknown evil transcending the known, for a jaggedly lit vision of a knot of the living dead wandering over dry treeless hills in the shadow of an immense wrath, a knot of pilgrims who looked like Andrew and Philip and Nerissa and who held one another by the arm and dragged on their way without hope, who on the grim land oppressed beneath an infinite thunder-clouded sky comforted one another with the words of an unbearable love. Danielle's footsteps were on the stair. Now here she stood in the light of the lamp.

It was not a strong lamp. It shed a puddle of yellowish light on the teak table where it stood; on a scatter of necklaces and bracelets; on a whisky bottle, glasses. Moths hovered around the shade, thudded into the bulb softly, beat their wings against it with a soft fast flittering. Around in the penumbra you could make out a shimmer of light on a Chinese gong embossed with dragons, on the glaze of a jar. Beyond, a dark rose wreathed a dark pillar, through the trees the lights of craft on the river gleamed. It was the hour when ferries became rare. Most of the *tambangs* were moored, three or four or five hitched to a pole planted in the shallows near the shore, others clustered around other slanting poles. Some of the boatmen had eaten at stalls ashore. Some had cooked on their little stoves, crouching in their glowing hulls afloat on the flowing blackness. They had rinsed their one plate and one cup, stowed them away under the floorboards. Now they sat by their hurricane lanterns, they talked, they smoked. Later they would lie down on their floorboards to sleep.

Danielle Kahn did not know that her chugging up the river to Kuching two months before had been for her first husband a disheartening instance of the way the past came back as just banality and cliché. Nor did she know that by the time *Aigrette*'s anchor chain had gone rattling out through the fairlead and the ketch had swung, had steadied, by the time Raoul in the cockpit had cut the engine, Philip had rephrased his despondency. His ex-wife was now, by virtue of being merely living, one of the relatively acceptable aspects of the past. By comparison with the dead, very acceptable indeed. She was the merest nothing, child's play.

She had, on the other hand, been aware that her arrival would perhaps make Philip gloomy and irritable, and this had seemed to her a shame. As she stood on the foredeck in the dusk and they came up-river and the scene of her first true love, of her great love, opened before her sixty-year-old eyes, she had wished he could be a little more magnanimous. Then she had given her thoughts a shake. Philip had always been magnanimous enough. It was his inability to distance himself from feelings, it was his hideous capacity to feel for others, that had driven him nearly mad. It was she who had abandoned him when most sharply he had needed her love, she reminded herself sternly. She had protected herself, had done him the further injury of depriving him of his son. To hurt still more a man already so hurt! No doubt Hugh's heart had its reasons; he was right to love his father, to like his mother. And if Philip was made only irritable by her arrival, made only a bit gloomy, it was to his credit. She reminded herself also that although when Raoul and she visited Kuching he was invariably charming to them, he had never in all these years urged them to come.

Raoul was out at yet another business dinner, Madame Kahn exclaimed, and she had not felt she could stomach yet more discussion of whether or not there was a rollicking future in palm oil, and she had heard that Cassandra was going to make one of her curries which put her own efforts to shame . . . So, in short, here she was. They might send her away if they liked. Though she had equipped herself with a couple of Raoul's finest bottles of claret, in the hope that by bribery . . . And look, she had even remembered to decant them.

Cassandra Matlaske's curry was excellent, and if Danielle Kahn partook of it meagrely this was not because privately she considered her own to be superior. The wine was better than anything customarily consumed in Blakeney's house, but if she drank several glasses it was not for this reason.

The fear which Danielle had sensed on her approach up the brown river that hot grey evening had returned. The fear that this might be her last meeting with Philip, it might be a definitive rediscovery and a definitive losing. Of course she was devoted to Raoul . . . And of course her second marriage had been what second marriages so regularly were, at once a terrifically sensible idea and an offence to the soul. But it was Philip Blakeney, as the four of them dined at one end of the verandah table and at the other end ornaments and jewels lay in the dimness, as a coaster coming to a wharf hooted, it was he whom Danielle wished would be more open with her. Not now, not in company . . . But even when they were alone together he was all amiable reserve. Well, she had forfeited him. Though the wedding meant that this year they would see more of each other, that was good.

Her old flame. Her man of night sweats and night cries . . . Proceeding from her first husband to her second, from one attempt to identify a more or less tolerable self and be it to another, had perhaps not been so reprehensible after all. Had

Philip one sweltering Baram night not said to her that if she was afraid of being sucked down into his vortex she was to desert him? Yes, he had insisted. In a cold voice. Wearing a sarong round his waist. His brown chest and shoulders dark in the lamplight. Whisky in his hand of course. She was to save herself even at the cost of depriving him of Hugh and depriving Hugh of his love. 'If you're scared, run away.' He had said that, smiling.

Only this evening things seemed to have gone a step farther; somehow Danielle felt she had both husbands and neither of them. And she had the liberty to try to find a decent self to be, as ever. And she could not, as ever – even though her standards were by Philip's measure ridiculously low.

Philip's rejoicing in Cassandra's passion for Hugh and in his for her, his good humour this evening . . . These had the effect of bringing back to Danielle, to her heart which had never been fully happy, their old Baram river bad nights. Philip drinking Scotch or Irish. She recalling what she had heard of her father on the Mekong in the late twenties drinking. Her father with a mistress. Her father then disgracefully in love or besotted. Her father holding a pistol to his sweaty throat. Then Philip's madness in the dominion of the unknown. Philip drinking so much whisky that he forgot Nerissa and wanted to make love but couldn't. Other nights when he didn't drink and didn't say a word and didn't touch her. He sat in a chair and gazed at the river hour after dark hour and would not answer when she spoke to him except to tell her to go to bed.

Cassandra's love was so wholesome! Danielle Kahn found herself taking comfort from this. Far too late to make much of a moralist out of me, she thought without regret, remembering the pleasure with which as a schoolgirl in Saigon she had dispensed with her virginity, remembering war-time seductions in Poitiers, a seduction in Penang a few days before she met the man who was now trying to cheer up corpulent tedious old Akbar who seemed rather glum this evening, Danielle could not think why. She hoped Hugh would like having a young and beautiful wife who would adore him. He must do, surely. His mother found herself curiously vague on the subject – but never mind. The girl would be faithful to him. Clearly she would.

While she . . . Well, not only she. The tender virtuousness of Cassandra's love for Hugh, her eagerness to be liked by her fiancé's mother, to that lady's sad and perverse mind brought back the Chinese businessman who with masterful calm had first possessed himself of the sixteen-year-old Mademoiselle Vernet. Then her second lover, the French junior diplomat, who had been anything but masterful, who had wasted evenings beseeching her, had turned out such an inept seducer that she had as if by right of natural stylishness ended up playing the leading rôle. And as for after her wedding, as for the Baram . . . But no, not only she.

She remembered hauling on her dressing-gown, chucking herself down in their bedroom rocking-chair which had rocked with a soothing motion that had made her even crazier. 'Why don't you try a few other girls?' in her humiliation and her frustration she had snarled to the naked man lying under the mosquito net. 'Not here, for God's sake. But go down to Marudi. Help yourself to one or two of the bazaar girls. See if they do you any good. See if they're fun, the bad girls.'

The next day he had set off down-river. Some excuse to do with work. She had known that what he really longed for were a couple of days away from her, the girls would be secondary if they were anything.

Her feeble assault upon the curry exhausted – innocent Cassandra was hurt to feel that her future mother-in-law did not think much of her cooking – Danielle sipped her claret, lit a cigarette. She recalled how with her husband away at Marudi bazaar she had taken his place in a rattan chair on their verandah overlooking the Baram. She had watched night fall on the river and on the tappan trees. She had thought, had thought.

Perhaps she had lied to Philip about being afraid of his voraginous whirlpool, later lied to Akbar about it too – or if she had not lied she had let herself be culpably superficial. Perhaps too there had been a flash of cruelty in her dispatching Philip, who was obsessed by men's use of his sister, to overcome that particular torment with the bazaar girls. Certainly when she had sat in his place alone at night with the river and the stars and her thoughts and then the moon had risen she had not been sexually jealous, not really.

She remembered the forest trees reflected in the silvery river. She remembered thinking inconsequentially that life was very long. In her mind, she had felt time growing as slowly as a great tree, so slowly it would never be done. And now thirty years later she thought that possibly in the fullness of time the tree had grown, she would have liked to show it to Philip, invite him to taste its fruits. However – she crushed out her cigarette – he showed no sign of having anything to say to her, of wishing to listen to her.

The next morning, the deacon invited Stephen Chai into his study in the bishop's wooden palace on Mission Hill.

'This proposed marriage . . . I suppose you know what people have said about the bride's mother?'

The tone of the question was even. Stephen answered steadily, 'Naturally I know her parents weren't married.'

The deacon was a cleric of the world. Very slightly, his shoulders rose; very slightly, his lips curled.

Stephen looked out of the bow window across the river to Fort Margherita on the opposite knoll. 'Is there something I ought to . . . ?'

'I didn't mean the mother's relations with Major Matlaske, but with Mr Blakeney.'

4

Cassandra Matlaske had inherited none of her mother's wildness. Of course sometimes she went out with her friends in the evening, but it had never occurred to her to dance for money. Not for her the coming home dark-eyed at dawn or not coming home, the nightclub friendships, the liaisons with Hussar officers stationed at Brunei.

Not that Philip Blakeney had ever told her much about her mother. Or rather, he told her lots, but only one kind of thing. What fun they had when her parents came to visit him on the Baram, lamplit dinners afloat, blowing the dust off his ancient record-player so they could waltz on his verandah, that sort of stuff.

He only told the girl one kind of thing about her father too, for that matter. Stories about how in the longhouse at Bario he danced a war-dance with a feathered *parang* clenched in his teeth. Stories about him in a dug-out on a river in spate, how he shot some infamous rapids with a crew of Kayans steering and fending off from the boulders, how the maelstrom roared and spray burst and David Matlaske sat in the stern with his rifle and grinned. All about what a gallant soldier he was, and the finest friend a man ever had. Nothing about his rake's ways when it came to wine, women and song.

In her bedroom Cassandra had a silver-framed black and white photograph of her mother and father outside the Church of Our Saviour at Labuan, she herself bundled in a pale shawl in the crook of her mother's arm, her godfathers and the parson flanking them. Blakeney had once even mentioned to her that it would not have astonished him if her parents had got married.

Well, if it would have served to lull her heart in comfort he would have done worse than that.

No doubt Cassandra's religious sensibility helped too, her guileless Christianity which Blakeney, when he saw it burgeon in her childish spirit, did all he could to foster, in his despair prayed might serve her well. Yes, if he might have ensured that she should never be exposed to the order of truths that he had been admitted into he would have sold any wisps of his soul that were still his, if any were.

Anyhow, for this reason and that, Cassandra Matlaske, who was the casual upshot of late nights and gaiety and music and bright eyes, who herself could be gaiety incarnate without apparently so much as being tempted by dissipation, who now at twenty-one was revelling in her discovery of love both true and sexual, had always had an extraordinary ability to share her world with the dissolute without being aware of it, let alone being infected. Perhaps it *was* her religion. Certainly none of the sinners around her were religious. Not her prospective mother-in-law, that worldly creature so amused by the girl's maidenly view of life. Not her adoptive father whose horror at his sister's probable fate had not prevented him marrying a wife whose svelte good looks and sensuality were a large part of her charm, had not prevented him either from making love with English debutantes and Bornean nymphs – in a lot of longhouses an unmarried girl could share her sleeping mat with whom she pleased. Not her brother and lover, whose past flings she was serenely untroubled by. Or maybe her intrinsic innocence naturally expressed itself in her Christianity and in her not being aware of a lot of things. Probably it was that, and her reluctance to what she would have called think ill of people. That and Blakeney's telling her which kris was from Selangor and which from somewhere else, but not about Kitty's affair with the Rajah, for instance, or his doubts as to the blood in Nerissa's veins.

Of course, Cassandra had taken the pleasure you would expect in men's admiration. There had always been Yusof Badawi with his brown eyes and black moustaches – for the most straight-forward of men he had unsuitably luminous eyes – teasing her by lamenting that she'd never look at a Muslim like him.

She had been aware of Stephen Chai's liking for her too – and not only because Yusof had bewailed that as her priest Stephen had an unfair unadvantage, it was his duty to tell her what to think and feel and hers to listen, he was even paid for it. But in the November of her realising that she was in love with Hugh, in those humid, sweaty Sarawak river nightfalls of her listening to him talk with his father, of her letting herself dream because all she was ever going to do was dream, of her evening after evening putting on her necklace of leopard's claws set in silver and the earrings which were two leopard's claws because she knew he liked them, it was easy to overlook that until recently she had softly hoped that Stephen Chai might, now he was a fully fledged clergyman, ask her to marry him. Watching the last fires of sunset over Mount Serapi, watching the coils of mist on the river – easy to overlook, to forget. Before, what had she understood of life? Now she knew!

When Cassandra returned from her second baptism in a waterfall on the shore of the Sulu Sea, when she entered the rejoicing occasioned by her engagement, a celebration which perhaps took added zest from people's wish to smother any possible anxieties in good cheer, it was likewise not difficult to treat Stephen simply as her dear and trusted priest on whose affectionate wisdom she would always rely. The house was so unaccustomedly alive with friends coming and going, with friends who stayed for dinner, with congratulations, with plans. There was her suddenly imperative need to be approved of and liked by Danielle Kahn. There was that lady's offer to be of any assistance she might in the organization of the motherless girl's wedding – 'If,' as she drawled with a smile, 'Philip will let me.'

It was later that Cassandra began to wonder. When May was over and still no word had come from Hugh and Thor, when soon she would be twenty-two. On those afternoons of naming, afternoons of being endowed, when Philip would seem to be reciting the inventory of his world or telling his godless man's rosary, when the burning light sweltered on the river and she would grow distracted, would pause with an object in her hands or a name in her ears or a question dying on her lips and gaze out at the windless trees and muse.

How she had changed! How everything had changed! Her mornings teaching at the Mission School no longer absorbed her. All her world had changed – except for Philip, his truth and his goodness never faltered, and he was a sceptic, what did this mean? Tying labels onto Penan quivers of blowpipe darts she frowned, fumbled her knot, had to start again. Quickly she reminded herself that Stephen was unchanging too. Then why of late had he sometimes irritated her? That evening when he had come to congratulate her, for example, and then in seclusion she had asked him if her engagement was acceptable to the Church. 'Certainly,' he had responded, 'if it is the will of God.' And with a thump of blood to her brain, in a sickening spasm of recognition, his reply had come to her as the most feeble she could imagine hearing. *If it was the will of God* . . . Did it mean *anything*? It was of a vacuity to make the mind reel. Did all thought have to be as inert as this, all knowledge this vaporous?

Cassandra had prayed for forgiveness for this crashing of dark blood in her usually limpid mind. And even after her engagement she had continued to beg for guidance for her enraptured heart. An engagement might be broken. A wrong engagement must be broken. Morning and evening she walked through the trees; she climbed the ladder to the *atap* hut with its piles in the slimy river bank. Balks of timber drifted by, a chicken coop, a bloated disintegrating dog, then a palm tree like a felled idol with its rotting top a headdress of superb barbaric plumes.

In the Sulu Sea she had felt herself changing momently and had rejoiced in her metamorphoses. In Thor Bernstein's hermitage she had tasted how to change is to be free. But now her lover who had swept her off her feet for less than a week had abandoned her with no word from him for over a month. Of course, communications with the interior, which were never good, in this time of national catastrophe might be expected to be worse, even if it was a catastrophe the nation was reluctant to acknowledge. Still, she began to fret about her ability to change.

Had she not in December prayed to God to grant her the strength never to ask Stephen Chai if the Church would let her marry her adoptive brother, then in February asked him?

Had she not written to Hugh that he was never again to ask her to marry him because her answer would forever be No? *This is true*, she had written, *please, please believe me*. This is true! Had she not then skipped off to sea and said Yes?

If it is the will of God . . . What did it mean? She had prayed. She had let herself believe her heart's desire was the will of God. Well, luckily it turned out that the Church had no objection. All the same, Cassandra found herself letting Danielle take in hand the preparations for the wedding – Philip had authorised this delegation with a curt laugh – relieved that it gave her more time to idle away on the steps to the *atap* hut. Often after praying that she was not deluding herself, that God not she was moving her, she came halfway down the rungs. Instead of doing anything useful, she sat under the nipah shade and listened to their rustling and watched the river, motionless except when she brushed away a fly. The *sampan* lay with its painter tied to a palm bole. There was a fisherman who often came, who let his dinghy drift; she saw him stand to cast his net time and again. When the tide was low, she looked at the detritus it had left on the muddy slope. She watched the loathsome mud-skippers scuttling, the crabs edging sidelong with morsels in their claws.

Cassandra found that during her talks with Philip her attention meandered off more and more fecklessly. Several times she labelled things wrongly, had to correct her errors under the regard of his indulgent amusement. Through those idyllic days on Thor Bernstein's island, through those nights making love, she had sloughed off her past, her old self – or so it seemed, for now her spirit was adventuring in a world made only of metamorphoses. Hugh had infused in her mind a new freedom, and now she was embarked upon change after change, her very spirit was not immutable, she had been renewed once and now she would forever be being renewed. She sat on the worn wooden ladder. The palms crepitated. Soon it would be the end of term. She had no wish to do anything except at Hugh's side, speak with anyone except him, not even with his father. Sometimes her changing and still again changing, the fluidity of her, the smokiness of her, made her gloriously dizzy. At other times that nothing was fixed pierced her with such alarm that she hastened up the top rungs, knelt in her tumbledown sanctum. If all were changeable – all . . . ! And yet with Hugh the self-renewing world had quivered with promise, nothing that existed had been less than sheer promise. And still now often her mind was radiant with light. Her mind – her mind, of all small modest mechanisms! – was as changeable and as beautiful as the light.

During the first onsets of mutability, or during her first recognitions of them, Cassandra had prayed for steadiness. She had prayed to steady herself, prayed that she truly was who she had hitherto believed herself to be, that she always would be. She had prayed that the changeless tenets of her faith should endure in her as invariable as before. She had prayed to steady the whole world, which had come bewilderingly to resemble a bird which Philip had once told her about called the changeable hawk-eagle, an eagle of which you would not find two with exactly the same plumage, of which even individual specimens changed, would not always from year to year – *could* she have been paying attention when he explained this? – be feathered the same.

Then after consultation with Stephen Chai, to whom she had confessed the agitating new feelings ebullient in her heart, her prayers became praise of the vitality of God's creation. Certainly all was not subject to change, Chai had assured her; but within the infinite grandeur of God's design the altering forms of life testified to the eternal truths within them. By all means let her rejoice in nature's metamorphoses, in the play of brilliances in her mind. All was God's loving work. Her delight in the promise in all things was one of her ways of loving Him. She was not to be afraid.

Those were probably the hours of Cassandra Matlaske's life when her religion gave her most joy. Superseded, the simple devotion of girlhood; transcended, for a while, her fears . . . On her knees in the hut over the river bank where sunlight glinted through the slats and fell dappled through the decayed thatch, where she heard a coaster chug or a cock crow, she marvelled at the changing forms and colours of creation; she prayed that in the end Hugh might see that the whole eternally evolving miracle was God's design. She would come out of her sanctum with peace instilled in all her being. Then her mind would change. She would remember how she had sworn one thing and done another. She would worry about whether *If it is the will of God* meant anything much. She would fret because she hadn't heard from Hugh.

Stephen Chai was a person of innate innocence too. Of course he was thirty, and if he had not precisely knocked around the world he had acquired a smattering more knowledge of it than Cassandra. And his calling brought him into some reluctant familiarity with wickedness. Afterward, some people maintained that his innocence served him better than his beautiful parishioner's served her. What they meant was, he got off. In their view this was reassuring for everybody, not just a damned good thing for Chai, because it meant that innocence *can* save, some notable instances to the contrary do not scupper the whole idea. Of course there was the other view of the thing. This line of argument ran that innocence and guilt made not a scrap of difference, that was an irrelevant question to ask. When it came down to solid facts, this school reckoned it was simply a matter of how you were tested. How hard you were tried. Quite often it was the less innocent who contrived to get through life without being tried more cruelly than most people could put up with – they allowed relative guilt and innocence that much importance, no more. Whereas the good sometimes blundered into trials it was preferable not to think of.

The year of the great fire, no, late the previous year, before it broke out, the trials of the Reverend Stephen Chai commenced with his stupefied apprehension that Hugh Blakeney and Cassandra Matlaske were flirting.

He was far indeed from being an authority on flirtation – but even to his celibate sensibility the aliveness of the air between the pair began to be unmistakable. He could not, like the hermit Thor Bernstein when invaded the following Easter, count himself lucky that he had never let the girl know of his tenderness for her – surely in his manner toward her she must have sensed his feelings. But he was relieved that he had never declared his gentle passion, at the same time as he suffered a twinge of regret that he had not charged right ahead while the going was good. Only maybe the going would never have been good.

That Hugh and Cassandra were not really brother and sister, that there was no reason why they should not fall in love ... Why, why had it never occurred to him? So often he had heard the schoolgirl babble about the undergraduate's brilliance and his handsome face till she had set Grace and Lily giggling, the young woman with more calm enthusiasm praise the scientist and political campaigner. She had used to bring him Hugh's articles, leave the reviews and newspapers with him after church, ask him next day what he thought of them. And there had always been Philip Blakeney to hymn those two each to each. Chai was too modest a man to let himself think for long that Cassandra had shared his dream that one day they might be man and wife. When Hugh was in Java and she confessed to the proposal and her need to know the Church's judgement, Chai was too generous of spirit to suspect her of sexual gamesmanship, of the smallest unkind duplicity in his regard. But for a pacific man his unhappiness was nasty enough; it hurt like earache. All his self-possession was required to ensure that he treated her with the sympathetic respect she had a right to from her parish priest, to let none of his disappointment and jealousy show. And Chai was too honourable to take refuge in disliking Hugh.

Stephen Chai's admiration for Philip Blakeney had been impulsive, and he had been ready to like his son. But Hugh's contempt for religion was so cheerful! his convictions were so vehemently declared! his flamboyance gave so little quarter! And although Chai agreed with Hugh that it was heinous the way Kuching politicians and businessmen made prosperous careers by disinheriting and exploiting the peoples of the interior, he was also aware that a number of sanctimonious Western environmentalists were making careers founded on the distress of others too.

Still, after Cassandra's confession of Hugh's proposal to her, Chai redoubled his efforts to think well of him. Some occidental battlers for civil rights or forests or what-have-you might be arrogantly taking possession of others' causes, indeed he knew the Church was often accused of such interference, but Hugh's passions were of irreproachable sincerity. Did he not insist that his job was not to save and develop other people's societies, a task they had to perform themselves, but a little to educate his own? And there were plenty of issues they agreed about, though Stephen Chai's statements of his views always came out sounding so moderate and Hugh Blakeney's so warlike that you had to be alert to find them at one. That cabinet ministers were hypocritical when they preached cultural plurality, paid lip service to the rights of the native tribes. Did their every policy not operate to promote the supremacy of one culture only, the opening up of the interior as the dominion of the exterior, the rape of the land with Five Year Development Plans, the coercing of peoples who had before been self-sufficient into becoming labourers in plantations and mines? Hugh would whirl his argument around his head like a sword; but then if you listened carefully you would hear Stephen murmuring, 'There's a lot in what you say,' or 'I'm afraid you may be right.'

A consonance of minds among the habitués of Blakeney's verandah wasn't unusual. Hugh might remark that the only difference between the old poor and the new poor was that the old poor had to an extent been their own masters, each longhouse had made its own decisions, while the new rich were making sure the new poor belonged to them. People would nod, or they'd grunt their assent. Someone not rendered quiescent by the heat might say that this subjection had been going forward for a hell of a long time and wasn't likely to be reversed now. No, what marked Hugh out as if the abbot of Saint Denis really *had* thrust the oriflamme into his hand was that he didn't just think and talk, he reckoned to do something.

It was a pity that Hugh Blakeney took absolutely no trouble to succour Stephen Chai's Christian attempts to like him. Even that day when he eloped with Cassandra – for that was what it boiled down to. That day he shanghaied her . . . He might have spared Stephen a bit. He might, thudding up his father's rickety stairs as the parson was mildly descending them, have forborne to demand merrily of him when he was going to stand up in that pulpit of his and tell the truth about the fire. For a start, the implication that Chai was not, in the pulpit or anywhere else, in the habit of speaking the truth outraged him, naturally enough, though he was nice enough not to say so. Perhaps above all that day . . . Because when Hugh had commandeered whatever she was – his sister, his lover, his bride, his all the things the girl so passionately was, his unswerving adorer, his saviour as she dreamed – when they vanished toward the Sulu Archipelago to evict Bernstein from his melancholy peace of mind, they left behind them in Kuching a trembling of the sultry air. And it was luckless Stephen Chai who had to inhabit the dying quivers of the aura of carnal excitement in which they moved. He had to live as best he might with his certainty that the die was cast. He had to try not to think of them making love. It was he who found a further humiliation in his not altogether disliking to think of it. Let her be given her fill of what she so desired. Let her have it . . .

In time Stephen Chai began to permit himself some small comfort from the fact that he had, during the blushing and hesitating Cassandra Matlaske's consultations with him, behaved well. He had known her nearly all her life – and had he not of late studied the sweetness of her nature with particular delight? – so now, if truly she was in love, and surely she had never entertained an untrue feeling in her life . . .

He had treated her with all the gentleness and tact he could muster. And no, it was impossible that in her timorous but bold confession, in her earnest questioning, in her modest but agonisingly intense declaration of her heart's hope – impossible that there should be veiled coquetry. And even if she had suspected his past intention of offering her his love, she was perfectly correct to behave as if she had never intuited anything of the kind. Had she not a right to bestow her affections freely? Chai gave thanks to Our Lord, Who had made him able to give kind advice to a young soul filled with Christian love but overshadowed by the looming tragedies of the past, wrung by anguish at difficulties not of her making.

It was true that he had touched on the prospective groom's lack of religion. He had felt it an inescapable duty to allude to this, though very gently; and then had been thawed by

Cassandra's rapturous avowal of her hope that God would show her how to bring Hugh to Him. He had mentioned her beloved's escapades too – they had never been a secret. Cassandra had been blithe. 'Oh yes, girls at Oxford, girls in Paris and London, girls everywhere. But that's all in the past, don't you see? He loves me. We've always loved each other. Now we love each other more.'

When she had returned from Bernstein's retreat and Chai had gone to her father's house to congratulate her, he had liked Blakeney's firm handshake, the smile he had received from those old blue eyes. In the next few days he had convinced himself that he would know how to transcend his merely personal longings, leave his disappointment behind. Then came his interview on Mission Hill. He sat looking past the Cantonese deacon's head across the river to white stocky Fort Margherita where as a boy he had admired the cannons and the flag. He remembered that once he had suggested to Cassandra that even if now, even if after weeks of prayer, it did not seem to her that her love for Hugh was the love of a woman for her brother, perhaps deep down it was, she might come to find it had always been. He remembered her answer, her clear voice, her clear eyes. 'Of course I loved him as my brother long ago. But that was just a little girl's adoration. I'm a woman now.'

In the next few days Stephen Chai felt his mind pounded by doubts till it felt like one of the ironwood troughs in which the Dayak women husked rice with poles as tall as themselves. Every time the grains, husks and dust in his brainpan began to settle, down the pestles came crashing once more. It was an ordeal he had to endure alone, too. To whom could he turn? To the gossips of the island who had murmured the scandal? He did not know such people. If he had been in the habit of frequenting those circles, he might have been forewarned. The deacon? No ... He had got the impression that the deacon expected him to deal with this business alone, return to him preferably with an achieved solution, only as a last resort come for advice. And the deacon was so urbane; and Chai was not urbane in the least.

Stephen Chai's respect for Blakeney made him shrink from the notion that Matlaske and he had shared a mistress – though he had to acknowledge that among the dissolute such things occurred. He dreaded to think of Cassandra's sufferings should she come to know that an accusation of promiscuity, even of whoring, was laid against her mother. He dreaded that he might be the man whose duty it would be to tell her. To inform her that she could never marry Hugh. To suggest to her that Blakeney had adopted her because her flighty mother had been his houri too. And if he acted on the vaguest of unsubstantiated rumours; if he chose to put his faith in evil-minded chatterers and to disbelieve Philip Blakeney who was the very figure of an honourable man; if he refused to marry Cassandra to Hugh and gave this shadow of doubt as his reason . . . People might say that he had found a pretext to break the girl's heart so she might in five years or ten for want of real love marry him. Poor Stephen tormented himself with the fear that, even if others were not so malicious, he might be unable not to suspect this.

He must go to Philip Blakeney, he must tell him what he had heard. Almost certainly it would be useless. Without doubt it would be horribly embarrassing. But if there was a ghost of a chance it might do good . . . You never knew, there might turn out to be a splendidly simple explanation of how the rumour had taken wing. Or maybe there would be proof it was a slander. Maybe all through the weeks when Cassandra must have been conceived her mother and Blakeney had been at opposite ends of the country.

Chai had never felt his pastoral cares more onerous than when he observed Cassandra enter Saint Thomas's for evensong, which was to be conducted by the Reverend Paul Wong, than when he walked down to the river, boarded a *tambang*. Would Blakeney tell him the truth? Of course it was not his habit to lie. But in this case he had decided that the marriage would make the two living souls he loved happy, so the stakes were high. Nervously the priest decided that if Blakeney gave him a straight declaration that the girl was Matlaske's daughter, if he discovered no reason to doubt his word, he would consider it his duty to believe him.

Somewhat bolstered by this resolution, he stepped ashore. Then he remembered that Blakeney was an unbeliever. Perhaps the idea that the marriage might be incestuous, that the love affair might already be incestuous – Chai's erotic fancies returned to humiliate him – perhaps this dallying with sin would not bother Blakeney at all. If Cassandra was probably Matlaske's but just possibly might be his – he might smile to himself, decide to let things ride . . .

Stephen Chai was not at ease among such profane attitudes. In conflict with such unprincipled wisdom he would lack stratagems. It was with these perturbations compounded by his horror that he risked performing a null and void marriage service that he climbed the familiar stairs.

Philip Blakeney had been writing a letter at his desk in the saloon, his brown scalp with his short white hair at the back bowed near a brass lamp. He waved Chai to a seat. Over their heads, the brass propeller of the fan turned. Leaning against the wall was the collector's latest find, the carved door of the *penghulu*'s apartment in a longhouse that had been abandoned, a door wrought with animals and gods.

If the older man was surprised at the younger's initial embarrassed speech he showed no sign of it. When silence fell, he assured his guest that he was not offended.

'I haven't a clue how this unpleasant talk arose. You'll have to ask your deacon that. I'm slightly disappointed that he should lend himself to such twitter. But never mind, that's his concern. For my part, I can promise you that Cassandra is Cassandra Matlaske, she's who she seems. I might add . . . ' Blakeney had been wryly grave, but now his eyes glittered. 'The parson who christened her had known us all for years.'

When Stephen Chai said goodbye, his host levered himself to his feet with his walking-stick. As they shook hands he enjoined him, 'You'll know better than to make her unhappy with this nonsense.'

Between his longing to feel relief and his dread that his longing should not be satisfied, Chai tried to smile. 'I hope she need never come to hear of it,' he replied in what struck his listener as the tone of a prayer.

The following Sunday after holy communion, Cassandra

Matlaske asked her spiritual adviser if she might speak with
him. They strolled beneath the trees in the bishop's grassy
desmesne.

'We've heard from Hugh.' Her soft voice danced. 'Thor and
he are fine. And I've decided . . . ' In the dappled shade she
halted, faced the cassocked priest. In celebration of having
word from her lover, she had put on the leopard's claws
he liked for the elegantly pagan adornment they gave to
her throat and her ears, their air of the ancient and the
sumptuous which he found attractive. 'I'm going to him.'
In a recess of her small leather handbag she had the ring
of Mount Ophir gold with an emerald set in it which had
been Claud Blakeney's. The rubber planter's surviving nephew
had given it to her that morning, with instructions to take
it to Hugh. 'So he can put it on your finger,' he had said,
smiling into her eyes. Now she laid her hand on the bag
hanging from her shoulder as if it contained an infallible
talisman, a charm that would see her through. 'We know
roughly where he is,' she added gaily. 'I ought to be able to
find him.'

Chai's first thought was that the wild pair were perfectly
capable of getting a missionary to marry them up some burning
mountain, up some river no one had heard of. His second was
that he had not yet reported his conversation with Blakeney to
the deacon.

'When are you thinking of setting off?'

'Soon. In a day or two. Term is over,' she said with such a
light heart that Chai wondered whether when the next term
began she would be among the teachers resuming their duty
at the Mission School.

'Is it a good idea for you to go on such a journey alone?' Till
a few months before, their friendship had been so stable. She
had been as stable as he was. Now often she altered from hour
to hour. 'Is it safe?'

'Terribly dangerous, I expect.' Neither she nor any other
woman had ever addressed him with such a smile – was there
mockery in it? – and such half out of control gaiety. 'Do you
think you ought to protect me? You can come with me, if you
want. Would you like to take me to him?'

'Cassandra, I think it would be wiser for you to wait for your fiancé here.'

'But if you come with me to the fire . . . There's a condition. Do you remember Hugh asking you why you hadn't preached about what's going on?'

'I don't accept conditions. I hope I shall know where my duty lies.'

'Will you preach a sermon on the fire?'

5 ∫

At Fort Sylvia we met a man with no hands, Hugh had written. He was sitting under the jacaranda tree by the fort, the stumps of his arms sticking up like cart shafts. 'Don't dynamite fish if you don't know how,' Thor said – but to me and in English. 'Don't anyhow.' I gave the fellow some money.

Left alone, Philip Blakeney turned back and forth the stained pages of the notebook in which his son had written him a long letter, had written what they had done and what he had thought and what Thor Bernstein had said, the journal which before they disappeared up the mountains to cross the watershed out of Sarawak he had parcelled up and given to someone going back down-river to take on the first leg of its passage to his father in Kuching. He thought of the mutilated man sitting under the jacaranda tree, the wretch who had to beg, who looked as if he had been the victim of an Islamic court's verdict of guilty of theft, whose eyes saw what his hands had done. He remembered the tumid Rejang, still river enough to take sea-going schooners even a hundred and sixty miles up-stream at Kapit where now the cheap dirty lodging house was more of a brothel, Hugh wrote, a place used by lonely lumber men and destitute Iban girls. He remembered the little fort's wide eaves and the trellis-work beneath them which let in fresh air. He remembered thunder clouds over forested hills. Then fallen trees clogging a tributary where Andrew and Nerissa and he had paddled a leaking *sampan*, a stream which became so narrow that sometimes tangled branches and creepers met across it, had to be cut away with swipes of a *parang* before they could go on. The thud of the blade, splashes, his aching arm, Andrew laughing, saying, 'Come on, put your back into it.' Screw-pines growing in the water, rotting there. Rafts of floating grass. Then how in the rainy season you could scull away from the streams into the forest, scull on slowly from towering tree to tree.

Stiflingly hot in the ferry's cabin, so we perched on the roof. Mighty fast these new river boats, and the engines deafen you. Under that sun, in the burning wind of the boat's passage, Thor and I spent most of our energy keeping our hats on, keeping our necks and arms in the shade. Not like the leisurely way you used to travel this river.

Stopped every hour or two at a longhouse or a logging camp. People went ashore onto the pontoons, climbed up their ladders or their notched poles to the bank. Other people came down the mud, came aboard. Every now and then a plank and shingle chapel, white, small, against a backdrop of dark trees. Remember? It reminded me of that long walk I once did up the coast of Kerala toward Goa. Miles and miles of golden beach, fishing boats pulled up – no nails or screws, just like these longhouses, they stitch them together with the rope they make – and then the trees to my right would have been cut back a bit and there'd be a church. But as we came past Kanowit and then on up here to Kapit it was the Rejang which is the colour of coffee with milk in it, not the Indian Ocean.

Now we're in the bazaar with two bottles of beer. Judging by his face, Thor is thinking gloomy Scandinavian philosophical thoughts. I feel wonderfully lighthearted. To know Cassandra will marry me. (To her he had scribbled a few words on a scrap of paper shoved in the journal: Don't change your mind, honey – I never will. The fire first, then our wedding, then India.) To know that at last I'm on my way into the centre, into the heart of the problem. I doubt I'll ever face an evil greater than this. I'll never have a better chance to do a little good. Up the Pelagus rapids tomorrow.

Blakeney thought of Hugh in a head-splitting cacophony of turbines roaring up the river which in '45 Sochon and he had slowly fought their way down with the current on their side and the Japanese against them. Hugh going on next day up-river from Kapit in a smaller, slower boat, with a hundred or so miles to cover before he got to Belaga. The Pelagus rapids which after rain you could hear a mile before you saw them – but Hugh wrote that the river was low, it hardly ever rained, and when it did, after an hour or two the sun returned. The Pelagus rapids where in his day the Chinese traders had often had to land their cargoes and portage them for two or three miles before they could be loaded again, while the lightened longboats were hauled up through the cascades and the spray rock by rock. Belaga where the Rajah had not had a fort until eighteen-eighty something – reading, musing, Blakeney could not recall the precise year, got up to rummage among his indexes – and where Hugh and Thor would be out of Iban country, would be among Kayans and Kenyahs. His limbs seizing up, painfully and inexorably dying in a rattan chair in Kuching, his mind ventured on inland. Above Belaga, the river branched into the Batang Balui and the Batang Belaga, both with further branchings, both with rapids, dry season shoals.

In the latticed shade beneath Philip Blakeney's house, which long ago had been painted green and white, the bob-tailed Bornean cats dozed on the dust. The windless sun beat down on his shingle roof, his carved eaves, his gables with their pinnacles, on his nutmeg tree, his jacaranda, his frangipani. Upstairs in the saloon with its five-angled bay window, the tusks of elephants shot in Perak by Claud Blakeney gleamed palely.

Once the sportsman's great-nephew, who was as vociferous in defence of elephants as of whales, had threatened to carry the tusks down the garden and chuck them into the river. His father was as fervent as he was when it came to the protection of species, but he didn't see what good purpose sinking the tusks would serve. Best hang onto them, he had said. With the ban on new ivory, the old fetched good money, and these animals had been killed before the 1914–18 war. When Hugh mismanaged his affairs hopelessly and was penniless, he'd be glad he had these tusks to sell, Philip had said – who was intermittently alarmed by the young man's indifference as to whether he made any money. Anyhow, he had managed to save the tusks from him, save them for him, with the help of the story of how Claud was one of the few men ever to have shot a right and left of charging elephants. Hugh admired courage. He admired his father's, he cultivated it in himself, and his great-uncle's steadiness impressed him.

There had been a number of witnesses, and when Philip dug out a book of press cuttings and found *The Straits Times'* report Hugh forgot about lugging the tusks to the river and pitching them in – anyhow someone would be bound to see him, come at night and dredge them up. How Claud had got himself in the way of a charging herd was not clear, but everybody seemed to have agreed that he stood before them calmly. The two elephants fell just in front of him, the rest of the charge divided round their bodies, he was left standing in the dust cloud they left behind.

Philip Blakeney sat in the saloon, he looked at the tusks. He thought of Claud who had known not to shoot at the massive bones of the brutes' foreheads even with a heavy rifle, who faced with the pounding charge and the trumpeting had taken aim at the base of the trunk or the mouth, fired, swung to the other – who as he fired never dreamed that after his death the creatures of the wild would be massacred, the seemingly eternal and unending tropical forests would cease to be.

Claud had taken him to his pepper garden, showed him his rambling pepper vines supported much as hops were rigged up and festooned, the Malays picking the berries when they began to turn red, winnowing them. Claud had taken him into a coconut wood, they had paddled up narrow streams where you still occasionally saw an alligator, they had lain low in the skiff and glided in the gloom below the nipah fronds. Another time they had climbed a hill to a clearing from which you could look down over miles of forest and see that it had mange where man had intervened, but in those days you could also see how small the uniform plantations were, just a few deserts dotted about the oasis. Claud had showed him how, although people were right when they said you did not see many flowers in equatorial forests, if you got up above the canopy and looked down you saw the efflorescence, the pink and yellow shoots. Those were times when it was still possible in distracted moments to dream that the fantastic invasion of men and machinery might pass away, the jungle close in again as it had been before.

Blakeney thought of Hugh who disliked to recall that his grandfather and his great-uncle had been big-game hunters, Hugh who spoke so naturally with the voice of righteous indignation which Blake said was the voice of God. Of course, it *wasn't* the voice of the divine in man, that was just pretentiousness. In most mouths it sounded like the cackle of poultry, had occasionally the sonority of a donkey's bray. But in Hugh's case . . .

He was ambitious for his son. Since he had become too decrepit to do anything himself he had lived, he used to remark self-deprecatingly, largely through Hugh, who luckily was tireless and thus kept him almost unduly alive. And the young man would play up to his father's humour. Half the time they'd be talking about Philip's arcana. About the unsuccessful British attempt to found a station at Banjarmasin in the sixteen-nineties. Or how certain tribes used the fat of the python or maybe it was the boa constrictor as a medicament, anyhow they were also invaluable while still alive, kept down the rats in the rice stores. But if they were discussing Hugh's plans for action – and Hugh Blakeney invariably had a lot of plans for a lot of action – you might see the adventurer smile, ask his father what experience he felt like vicariously living next.

Dogged, really, the way Philip Blakeney, who in Borneo had found time so illusory, went on writing *A History of Borneo* in his head if not on paper, went on trying to endow at least a few of the rhythms of his time with some apparent actuality. There was a rather Buddhist-sounding line he used to quote sometimes: *Knowledge increases unreality* . . . But regularly he behaved as if he hoped the contrary might be true. As if above all now when the peoples of the island were having their cultures eradicated, when uniformity was being imposed like a coat of paint and a lot of the past obliterated and other elements adjusted in politic ways – above all now it was vital to give solidity to Borneo's so vaporous history. As if people without history could never be redeemed from time, and even if the embittered teller of times did not believe redemption was ever on the cards, at least one might have some fecund intricate time to live and die in. Had he not squatted at night on longhouse mats while ancestries were recited and myths rehearsed and heroes sung? Strange, some people felt, for the man who knew the hideous realities which the determination to arrive at knowledge could introduce you to. Or perhaps he had learned still more from his search for Nerissa, from his maddened questing to embrace a knowledge that could not be known, embrace a ghostly love. At any rate, the involuntary Faustus veered between his hopes and his fears – he who knew that Faustus could only do what he did, having been created who he was; he who knew that he too could not have decided not to try to know. Dogged too, and rather odd when you thought about it, the way he who knew so vilely much about the vanity of action went on being enthusiastic about his son doing this and doing that.

Of course, Hugh Blakeney was better informed than anybody about his father's discoveries as to knowledge, as to action. In their long evenings on the verandah there was nothing they didn't mull over. That was one of the ways he took the measure of his father's love for him. He saw close up Philip's enormous simple hope that their worlds might be different, he might know evil only at second hand, at a safe remove. He might know that spirits can be broken by omnipotent evil – but not at first hand, might himself not be broken. So – in Borneo where so much time had neglected to get itself made into written history, where so much oral history was being returned to meaningless air, where time could seem possessed of dizzying intensities of abstraction, they told one another about the ups and downs of mining for antimony, mining for cinnabar. Dogged . . . They planned what Hugh should do . . .

Blakeney's ambition for Cassandra might once have been that she should live and die in sheltered unawareness among the well-to-do of Sarawak; but his son was to be a great man, the great man he had not been. In contemplation of Hugh's coming glory, Philip Blakeney could appear to shrug off his own ruin, that ruin of the soul which nobody except he believed he had suffered but which he knew was absolute. Because naturally he did not acknowledge the goodness which others saw revealed in him. The admiration and the choking pity he aroused in Akbar Nasreddin . . . The selflessness, almost the transcendence of mere personality, which Thor Bernstein and Cassandra Matlaske had by unconnected approaches come to marvel at in him . . . To the man himself, these were nothing, just silly talk. What could they know, with their superficiality?

Yes, Hugh was heading for high things. It was really rather endearing, the way the old fellow talked about his son. The

discussion had a terrific tendency to wind back to that scholarship at Oxford. Or to what he had just written for *The
Independent*. Or to how the directors of the Asian Progress
Bank or maybe the Development Bank honoured him with
a desire to drink his blood. Those were the days in which
the pernicious wiles of the World Bank were fairly common
newspaper fodder, but this Asian Development mafia was only
beginning to have questions asked in parliaments about its free
and easy ways. To no one's surprise, Hugh Blakeney was one of
the first and fiercest dissectors of its venality. No listener on the
verandah could recollect the sums he reeled off, the loans, the
interest rates. Still, the indictment was roughly that this bunch
of chiefly Japanese financiers were buying up political parties and
individual cabinet ministers too in Bangkok and Manila, in Kuala
Lumpur and Jakarta like nobody's business, getting governments
in debt to them for this development project and that, acquiring
in this way power over territories and peoples.

Anyhow, Hugh Blakeney's straight morals and straight thinking and straight talking could only mean one thing, according
to his fond papa. Was the lad not barely thirty? Had he not
already achieved this, written that? Hugh was going to write
books. You couldn't help smiling as you listened. Hugh was going
one fine day to be elected to Westminster – the Blakeneys were
social democratic in their sympathies, or liberal, or thereabouts.
Hugh might even be going to end up United Nations High
Commissioner for – for something marvellously important . . .
And indeed, why should he not have done? He *was* already
making a reputation. He had the brains, the drive. Or he might
have fetched up having to sell the tusks. Probably it would have
hinged on whether he felt arrogant enough to have to succeed,
or so carelessly proud he did not feel like being seen to try.

When Philip and Hugh Blakeney could not talk they wrote
letters. It was typical of the son to keep a journal which was a
letter to the father, send it to him before he really got lost in the
interior. It was typical of the father to sit on his verandah or in
his saloon and read the scrawled pages, listen to his son's voice
talking to him, in his turn silently reply. So Blakeney's mind
became a sort of echo-chamber.

The river was all serpentines and getting narrower, Hugh

had written from beyond Belaga. The forest closed in on either hand, we were shadowed. Different kinds of pigeons, woodpeckers – you'd have liked the brightness of plumage in the air. Often the settlements have rafts where rice is germinating moored to the shore. In one longhouse where we spent the night they had a little pet gibbon, the kind they call a wah-wah, very affectionate. Tame birds too – a red-breasted parakeet, a Malay lorikeet. A great feast that night – one of the hunters had killed a deer. You know those longhouse evenings of lamps flickering, pigs rootling down below, exhausting hours of raucous horseplay sometimes but everyone disarmingly friendly. We had brought a lot of presents to give people, still have a fair amount of stuff left.

Then off the next morning. Mist on the river: ghostly, dank. And the other boats setting off in the dawn too, little *sampans* with a man, a woman and a child off to their *ladangs*. We passed the clearings – blackened stumps of felled and burned trees sticking up through the *padi*, huts on stilts. It made me remember I have relations living this life. Then all day up-river between high walls of vegetation, steamy heat drowsing on the water. This valley hasn't been logged yet, though I understand a licence has been granted, so it's as it has always been. Up here the water is cleaner, takes on some of the green colour of the reflected trees. Still, it isn't clean enough for us to see all the snags, and the river is so low that the propeller of our outboard keeps hitting gravel or rocks. When this happens the alloy shatters and we can't steer, so the thing to do is to jump overboard and hang onto the boat to stop her being swept away and capsized. Needless to say our two guides are far better than we are at keeping their feet in the rapids while we haul the boat to the next deep calm reach, and then outdo us at fitting one of the spare propellers.

Blakeney turned the pages, he smiled. Hugh would be equal to the adventure, equal to the fire. Had he not written of how good it felt to be getting toward the heart of things? Of how he liked the sensation that he would never face a greater evil than this? Great indeed, for reports were of two thousand square kilometres burned. Hugh would be up to this opportunity to do some good.

The forest so luxuriant, so thickly woven – high palisades of leaves between which we rattle and splash. A dream of abundance and peace. And if we land, walk away from the river . . . Trees which rise sheer for over a hundred feet before putting forth their lowest branches. Air which seems to have settled immoveably dense and fragrant and moist. Does this at all bring back your jungle wanderings? Trees with their trunks invisible in their lianas and epiphytes. Strangling figs which have writhed around the trees they're killing till all you can see are their twined roots clasping and the long straight roots that fall from the canopy to the earth. Climbing mosses, orchids, ferns. The barbs of the rattans, which hook into our clothes, into our hair, into us. Leeches everywhere. But nothing irritates me: not broken bolts, not rattans, not leeches I can't feel while they're sucking my blood – have they got some kind of anaesthetic they infuse in the cuts they make? – till Thor points out what a pretty sight the back of my leg or arm is. Yesterday as we were heaving the longboat up some shallows a snake fell out of a tree and swam away. Thor keeps saying this is a fool's errand, but quite often he forgets to pretend he's not having fun.

Around the time the scribbler of these impressions was born, his father had walked for two days with a Penan of the Ulu Baram to visit the man's family, give them presents of sugar and tobacco and salt, be fed on sago and mouse-deer and river prawns. He remembered paddling up a lost stream – no outboard engines with their frailties in his day – so peacefully a big deer, a reddish wide-eyed sambur, raised its head from drinking to stare, and his Kayan boatman reached for his *sumpitan* but Blakeney put a hand on his wrist and then the deer was away. He remembered streams which you could wade one day but which the next might be torrents raging twenty feet deep, so at night you moored your craft with the rope well up a tree. Nights spent with Penan hunters shivering under a downpour in the makeshift shelters they called *sulaps* – how blue the lightning could flash, how the tempests of rain shook the trees, the water slimed down the trunks. Then after a storm sometimes a hillside of forest would suddenly slide, would collapse, go cascading down into the valley below. More often where deforestation had caused erosion, flash floods. He had started up drenched and shaking in the blackness to hear, miles off, that crashing roar.

Up among the limestone peaks there were no streams, every drop of water seeped away down crevices, vanished into the maze of passages and caves in the hearts of the mountains, came out in the foothills. High on the crests which the tribes believed to be the haunts of the dead – well, a lot of them *had* believed that, the Kelabits had when Z Special came floating down the sky with the blessing of rifles – you scrambled through acres of moss, of rhododendrons. Blakeney remembered the insectivorous pitcher plants named after Nepenthe the goddess of sleep, how those baroque jugs had seemed to hold the promise of a merciful oblivion.

Left alone in his saloon with his tusks, with his array of *sumpitans* and their decorated quivers of darts which Cassandra had labelled before she left, he recalled how because water ran off the limestone so quickly you sometimes got droughts up there. The vegetation became desiccated, liable to catch fire. There had been drought in East Kalimantan before this fire broke out, this incomparable destruction which had summoned Hugh from Timor, was now drawing him toward it, drawing Cassandra after him too.

Blakeney did not like to think of her travelling shadowed by a priest, though *some* escort was sensible. His last meeting with Chai had made him remember that you could never trust the religious. In the last analysis, their loyalty would always be to their faith, not to people, not to moral decency.

The old man shifted unquietly in his chair, made himself think of something else, of Gunung Api which meant Fire Mountain where conflagrations had been reported over the years. Nothing drastic, a hectare burned here or burned there. Warnings. Admonitions. Signs. Oh, nonsense. And a fire which blazed for several weeks had been observed from Limbang in '29, though that was probably on Mount Benarat where there were still barren patches near the ridge. The Berawans thought the fires were caused by rocks falling on rocks and striking sparks. Most of the Europeans thought lightning was more likely to blame.

It was good that Hugh had gone up one of the last unviolated valleys, it would remind him what a paradise the island had been. Probably he was over the watershed by now. Blakeney had never been able to stand back from his passions; now with elderly tenacity his nearly extinguished mind followed his son inward and upward where he had launched him. It was good that it would be Hugh who wrote the fullest first-hand account of the fire, gave the straightest version of events, it would do his career no harm at all. Naturally in government press releases the pontificating and the misleading, once the fire had got too big to deny altogether, had begun. But Hugh would set the record straight.

Philip Blakeney's *memento mori* of a head nodded. He dreamed. A fly settled on his arm without being brushed away. He and his Kayans were poling up through boisterous rapids in the headwaters of the Baram. Then at evening they moored. He was lolling beneath an awning of pandanus leaves reading poetry to the girl from Hampshire who was a painter, who had fallen in love with Sarawak and had wanted to put up her easel on every river beach and in every *ladang*, who had fallen in love with the District Officer and gone some way toward consoling him after Danielle's departure with Hugh. Very pretty, Tanya Mayhew had looked, wearing a palm and rattan hat made by a woman in Bintulu, a wide slightly conical hat painted red and black and blue, ornamented with shells, a hornbill's feather for a panache.

Asleep, Blakeney gave a faint moan. Up-river he travelled, past poles swagged with calico which marked Dayak graves – though the time when the desecration of graves was punished by death seemed to be passing. He was high in the interior where rivulets gushed deep under limestone mountains, where at dusk the big bats called flying foxes glided by. In the forests, flying snakes swooped down. Hugh came out onto a ridge over a rumour of rushing streams in an evening humming with insects. The dreamer's arms tried to do something, his head flopped. The fly buzzed in a circle, again landed on him. Hugh saw the orange sunset light up a glimmering limestone scarp, saw mist wreathing among gnarled trees. All the kingdoms of the earth . . . Only the kingdoms were on fire. Over them the air burned red, it was a risen hell. From the fired forest the birds flew up with their feathers in flames. A voice echoed: *And I saw an angel standing in the sun.*

Madame Kahn leaned over her husband of long ago, gently shook his elbow. 'You cried out something,' she said – she who remembered what he used to call the red ant swarm in his mind.

6

'Poor old Philip.' Danielle Kahn stood looking down at him. For a moment her mouth trembled, her eyes glistened. 'My poor old darling, are you all right?' She turned her head aside, took a a couple of steps away.

Blakeney woke thinking not of the apocalypse but of Tanya Mayhew in her hat reading *Meru*, Tanya who had been twenty-odd years younger than him and had not looked a bit like Danielle thank God, Tanya with her red hair and her freckles and her green eyes. After the Slade she had come out to visit her cousins in Sarawak, someone had said she really ought to see Kitty Blakeney's pictures.

Of course after Hugh and Thor set off for the fire and then Cassandra and Stephen went in pursuit Blakeney had not been left all that alone, not really alone. Akbar Nasreddin was as faithful as ever, or only slightly less so. It was Danielle Kahn who had the effect of making him a little less loyal. He told himself that it must be pleasant for Philip to talk to her privately sometimes, but the true reason for his abstentions was that he knew she didn't think much of him.

Raoul Kahn had flown to Paris, would fly back for the wedding as soon as the betrothed pair re-emerged from the interior and a date could be fixed. Danielle had remained, living aboard *Aigrette* anchored off Philip Blakeney's nipahs with their twenty-foot fronds. The happy justification for her remaining had been her son's marriage, though without his bride or him there was disappointingly little arranging for her to do.

Often in those days Danielle's thoughts returned to the mother of the bride, that young dancer tattooed on her throat and arms and fingers like a good old-fashioned Iban damsel, that beauty with silver tinkling on her breast, earringed and braceleted, necklaced and ankleted. Was it the Ibans or the Kayans who, Philip had told her, believed a tattoo acted as a torch to light your way in the land of the dead? Fervently Danielle hoped the dancer was stepping along a lit path. She thought of her running out of her burning longhouse with Cassandra in her arms, running straight into the rifle fire, falling on the dust mortally hit with her baby by grace missed, by grace alive.

In those weeks the only person doing much to prepare for the wedding was Akbar. Originally he had decided to give Hugh and Cassandra his family's old Malay silver teapot, but his wife had objected. Then he hunted for a similar piece to buy, but could not find one with comparable chasing. At last he bought a blue and green and gold cloisonné jar.

Wiping her eyes behind Philip's back, Danielle Kahn recollected how in the first year of their marriage, long before her dismissing him to the girls at Marudi bazaar, she had asked, 'What's it like? A kind of prickly heat of the mind?' And he had answered, 'More like a swarm of red ants.'

Danielle liked being left alone aboard *Aigrette*. Her sharers of that curve of the river were the quiet fishermen who paddled by, and she liked the faint splash and the hoop of ripples as a flung net fell, the solitary brown men standing in their *sampans* to watch, stooping to haul. Her haunters were the brown Brahminy kites overhead. She liked the weatherbeaten wooden hulls of the coastal and river traders, forty or fifty foot overall, the fishing-smacks at an equal remove from the spick and span, the rusty hulls of the more twentieth-century vessels.

If she went ashore on the south bank she was content to stroll down the street of tailors and watch the alley girls playing shuttledore. It was hot; she drifted. Here were Muslim Food and Tea Coffee Dust Sold Here and Bee Hin, Goldsmith and The Sarawak Wharf Labourers' Union; her past was still here. She remarked the beauty of a Malay boy with raven hair down his back – Danielle would never be indifferent to male good looks. She rested for ten minutes in the Min Heng Café where often thirty years before she had sat with Philip, in the Min Heng with its round marble tables where they set boiled eggs, bananas, tea, with its white-vested smoking Chinese, with its grimy walls. Contentedly she breathed somebody's clove-scented cigarette, watched the trader next door sell a saw or a *parang* or an axe. She walked on past a Chinese club where the old men were playing billiards under a revolving fan with the chairs of ebony and marble set back against the walls. It was a shame that Philip was too frail to accompany her on these saunters as he had in the old days, but never mind, as she meandered she was at peace. In the bazaar she admired a mound of hirsute coconuts under a filthy tarpaulin. She hesitated in the gloom before stalls selling uncountable types of dried fish or dried herbs, stalls selling pots and pans, stalls selling guava and jackfruit. She liked the crates and sacks and chests and urns, the calling and the heaving and the laughing and the sluicing down. Then she liked untying *Aigrette*'s tender, setting off past the *tambangs* which the men rowed from the bow with crossed oars, boats which had been painted yellow and green or pink and blue but had weathered to river camouflage.

At evening there was almost no traffic on the water. Trees dipped their foliage, a fishing line tautened and dripped. Danielle sat in the cockpit of the ketch, she watched the eddies and counter-currents slide. Mount Serapi stood etched very clear in dark silhouette against the mother-of-pearl left when the reds had died down.

Philip Blakeney was too weak to handle his *sampan*, of late he had only ventured on the river with Hugh or Cassandra to row him, so he did not visit *Aigrette* unless he was fetched. But often in the evening Danielle Kahn rowed to the north shore, moored her dinghy by Cassandra's bare and now deserted sanctum, walked up beneath the white flowers of the frangipani. There had been the excuse that, although the girl's curries and her own curries might have their merits, Philip was the acknowledged master. There had been Hugh's journal which had arrived, which was to be perused and discussed and reperused. Blakeney was scrupulous to treat a thirty-page letter to *Dear Philip* as if the writer had addressed himself equally to his other parent.

Generally, when his divorced wife climbed the stairs, if he was not reading he was pottering among his collections. Once she found him polishing the throne of tappan wood which had been the seat of sovereignty of his father's friend, the down-at-heel ruler of a unprofitable east-coast sultanate chiefly consisting of malarial swamps. This sultan had loved his fighting cocks more fiercely than his wives, and had known his historical ill-luck, his manifold interlocking weaknesses which meant he would be the last of his line. Under Dutch hegemony he had declined – he who had been poor to start with, his authority compromised, the European epaulettes he insisted on wearing on state occasions threadbare, his shako of equally obscurely derived dignity a battered one, his ability to strike terror not ranging far beyond one muddy delta settlement. Under the Japanese he had died, leaving a decree that his tappan throne was to go to Michael Blakeney. When peace came back, it was shipped to Philip, who was sad to think of his father's old friend whose autocracy had been efficiently subverted by the Dutch, who apparently was then treated with such contempt by the Japanese – not physical savagery in his case, just contempt – that he died of what appeared to have been despair. Well, the Indonesians would have finished off any stateliness that remained. What had become of his shako nobody knew. Where his wooden palace had rotted, these days stood a petrol station.

This morning in the longhouse I was the first awake, Danielle read, opening Hugh's journal at random while Philip, still thinking of Tanya Mayhew and her slightly hooked nose and her extraordinarily white skin, was fetching the whisky bottle and the water jug. **I got down the ladder without waking anybody, then along the walkway to the water-steps. Cool mist rising off the river, the sky beginning to turn pale, wah-wahs hollering. While I was bucketing water over my head I saw sandpipers flying up-stream. Soon smoke was curling up from the longhouse. It had rained briefly in the night, men came to bail out their boats, paddle off to inspect their nets and traps. I bailed out our boat. The mist was changing from grey to grey blue to blue pink.**

Later when she looked back to those peaceful evenings with Philip it seemed to Danielle that she should have sensed a warning, a kris ought to have rattled in its scabbard at the advent of danger as the Malays used to think they did. But there were a dozen krises in the house and none of them rattled. The proud mother read on.

Rough travelling all day, one lot of rapids after another. But then we'd drift forward into a quiet green reach and it would look like heaven. Trees reflected in the clean river, creepers festooned, suspended orchids flowering, fish that jumped. Deep blue sky, small white cumulus clouds. Curve after curve of the sultry river opening before us and closing behind. We heard a hornbill's laughter – not a common sound any more. A lot of kingfishers, they sit looking very brilliant on branches over the water, fly up as we go by. A superb country, a peaceful country – I could travel on and on, lose any wish to arrive anywhere.

Then I think how people want to destroy it all. Isn't it foul, the way commonplace man wants to conquer all nature but himself, how he has to make a desert and call it progress, has to cockadoodledo? I know I'm no better at conquering myself than the next man – but a dash of self-hatred is a necessary virtue, isn't it? – like courage, without which all the other virtues are just talk.

Now it's twilight, we've pulled our longboat up on a stony beach. I'm writing on my knee. Thor is roasting a leaf-monkey which one of our guides, a man called Kadir, shot with his twelve-bore. A mind without self-hatred is a violin without a bow, strings just plucked sometimes, Thor says, scorching his monkey over the driftwood. Is it Schopenhauer he's read too much of? We sit side by side on the stones, down-wind of our blaze so the smoke gives some protection against mosquitoes, red-eyed, coughing sometimes. We've seen a number of wild pigs floating down in various stages of putrefaction, it may be that higher up there's an epidemic of swine fever.

On the wooden leafy stage of the verandah, Hugh's journal brought alive in his mother her years in Sarawak. Cruising along the coast, at night Philip had pointed out to her the medusae flickering deep in the black sea. They had sailed to the coral islets off Santubong where the turtles lumbered ashore to lay their eggs. She remembered a day when silvery sea birds whirled against storm clouds, then against a golden sunset the same birds were shadowy. Flocks of Malay sand-plovers on the beaches – Danielle had loved the birds, and in the peace of being isolated with Philip again half a lifetime later they seemed to come winging back to her. Bittern feeding at the rims of ponds, a stripy tiger-bittern waiting with its beak looking straight up to God like a mystic. Shrikes in the casuarina trees along the shore, gaudy little minivets in the treetops, a pitta hopping away over the forest floor, a big coucal swooping through scrub and over the grass. How had she lived all these years without being revisited by the birds? And funny things too. How an exceedingly manly Dayak had explained to her that the clouded-leopard, which lived shyly in the trees and never attacked anybody, was always regarded as female irrespective of its sex, while the honey-bear which could be aggressive was invariably male; how she had smiled and the fellow had been hurt. And that time in a clearing when the young men had been walking on stilts so high they had to get onto them from the longhouse verandah, and Philip amid jovial rejoicing had a go and didn't do half badly till he fell – she had taken a photograph of him grinning among the other stilt-strutters, it must be somewhere.

Danielle Kahn had made nothing of her first husband's infidelities. How should she resent them, she who had dispatched him to the bazaar girls, who had sated her appetites where she might? And Philip had never been a man to drag her down into the vortex of his despair. She made herself confess that now. He would have shot himself rather than endanger Hugh's spirit or the boy's mother's.

No – what had been terrible had been his stillness, his silence. He had sat at night in that chair and had looked at the Baram hour after hour and had not moved and had not spoken. She had tried to sleep and had tried not to think of what he was thinking and had tried not to think ill of him for his impotence, which came and went, and his despair which never went. She had come out in her nightdress to where he sat like a carved king who would survey his forest and his river for all time, had knelt by his chair and with all the softness she could command had begged him to come to bed, to lie down, to let her stroke his tortured head. And he had said things like, 'Don't worry about me, I'll be all right.' The silly thing was, he had told her afterward, his difficulty sometimes in making love because of Nerissa had only been a problem for ten years or so after the war, for the years of his marriage; with the passage of time, he'd been fine.

Now with everyone away she was alone with him once more. To be beached beside him on an island – that was what it felt like. The tide had gone down, they had been left high and dry like the skiffs the Malay fishermen pulled up the sand into the shade of the trees. She laid Hugh's journal down on the teak table. Yes, the verandah was a stage, she was islanded on it with him. It was as if they had been marooned here together, the way the warm lush night lapped all around them, the moths at the lamp performed their sad dance. She wondered if he had known at the time that her divorcing him had been mere cowardice, if he knew now that she knew it now. And her feeling that she was married to both husbands and to neither, that at last in the fulfilment which Hugh's marriage somehow strangely offered she knew who she might be, in that plenitude was beginning to be herself . . . ?

'Listen to this,' he snorted, picking up the morning's news-paper, preparing to read to her from it as if she had been Akbar Nasreddin – whom indeed, she reflected without bitterness, as a companion for dinner he would probably have preferred. She must remember to pass more evenings alone aboard the ketch, let the two men enjoy their accustomed ways undisturbed.

'*The Session Court at Miri was told yesterday that the Penans involved in the blockade at Na'ah were praying when the forestry officers arrived to arrest them. The prosecution witness Encik Abu Seman said his party had to wait nearly half an hour before the one hundred or so Penans had finished their prayers.*' Philip Blakeney was as passionate as his son when it came to the doom facing Borneo, fire or no fire, he read with a gravelly voice. If these politics vanquished, would not practically all the rain-forest by the close of the century be gone, just a few enclaves be left, two or three per cent of the whole maybe, in the shape of national parks degraded by tourism? '*They were praying with their hands raised to the sky, Abu Seman testified at the trial of twenty-seven Penans who were charged under Section 90B(1a) and 90B(1b) of the Forests Ordinance for obstructing officers sent to dismantle the barricade across the timber trail. The episode took place at Ulu Akah on 16 September of last year.*' And with their forests felled would they not lose the vestiges of their self-sufficiency and the holy places of their gods? And would they then not be herded into Model Villages to labour on Development Schemes which so far had a record of losing money and laying men off? Generally an astute move, if you wanted to subjugate a people, to uproot them first.

'Cross-examined by the defence counsel John Terang, Abu Seman said the Penans' praying did not frighten him or his fellow officers.' Blakeney glanced up from the page. 'Men of steel! He explained that when the order for the arrest was made known to the Penans most of them ran away, leaving only twenty-seven who claimed they were the leaders of the blockade and should be held responsible. He added that they looked aggressive and were all armed with parangs and blowpipes. When asked if the Penans had used their weapons to threaten the officers he said he could not remember.' Blakeney had forgotten Tanya Mayhew's white body; he had forgotten the meaningless chimera to whom he was reading. Revelations was echoing again. Babylon is fallen, is fallen ... Thrust in thy sickle and reap. He scowled through his gold-rimmed spectacles at the newsprint. 'The Penans did not resist arrest, although they were reluctant to surrender their weapons. In response to the prosecution counsel, Lim Heng Choo, Abu Seman declared he had no problem in identifying the twenty-seven accused, as their features, their hair and their clothes were utterly different from those of urban people. The trial before the Session Court judge, Puan Mariah Ahmad, continues today.'

Philip Blakeney tossed the paper down, his mind ringing with contempt and grief. Yes, the Dayaks would end up as estate labourers growing this tropical cash crop or that. And if Hugh or Cassandra or Akbar had been there he would have told them his last night's dream. He had seen the fire expand from the centre of the island outward. In concentric circles it had grown, until all the people and all the creatures not burned were huddled along the coasts. Then the fire had reached them, they had leapt like lemmings into the sea.

Danielle Kahn was more concerned with her presentiment of plenitude than with whether Puan Mariah Ahmad was going to sentence twenty-seven Penans or not. As for the fact that after their barricade had been knocked down the felling had proceeded, already off those hills the dust was blowing – it never occurred to her. In the dusky silence, she smiled. Hesitantly she confessed, 'You know, Philip . . . With Hugh marrying Cassandra, I almost feel I'm being married to you again. Not really, of course. But a kind of abstract marriage.'

Philip Blakeney's laughter was gruff. 'I'm damned glad we're not.'

And that was as far as she ever got, Danielle Kahn lamented with light hardness to Yusof Badawi when he visited her in Paris. The flat which Raoul Kahn had bought for his third marriage was big. The drawing-room where they sat by the fireplace had a lot of dim air around its chandelier, had pilasters, had alcoves, had shadows. It was a summer evening, neither the fire nor the chandelier was lit. The windows stood open onto chestnut trees.

That was as pathetically far as she had – as she had got with her . . . The widow's mouth twisted. Opposite her, Yusof's dark luminous eyes shone, he manhandled his luxuriant moustaches. With her presentiment of – of fulfilment . . .

Of course, she had known not to be put off by Philip's gruffness. He had been gruff for years. Had he ceased to be there might have been cause for alarm. She had persisted a little; gently and with gathering sadness had tried to explain a little. How it was as if all her life a tree had been growing in her mind, a tree like those handsome tappans by the Baram, the tappans swagged with honeycombs, and at last she felt the tree was mature, her tree of time. No credit was due to her. She had merely lived. She had possibly just taken a foolishly long time, sixty years, to grow up, to *be* very convincingly. But now with this miracle of their son marrying his adopted daughter – yes, she would stick by her word, it *was* a miracle – she was conscious of a drawing together of spirits, a flowering of her tree.

'You know as well as I do,' she told Yusof, 'my plenitude didn't last long. And perhaps it was nothing of the kind, an illusion. At any rate, that conversation with Philip must have been in July, so you see . . . In a month it no longer mattered what I'd felt, whether I'd felt anything.' With a corner of her handkerchief, she touched the corners of both eyes. 'In August we . . . In September, in October, we were married so there was no divorce.'

'Married?' wondered Yusof, who when he was away from Kuching missed his young wife.

Beneath the eaves, swallows had built their nests. The parent birds swooped up to feed their young. From the boulevard beyond the garden, engines droned.

'It was like . . . It was like when a ship sinks and the swimmers are sucked down with her.' Through her tears, she smiled. 'We were married so there was no divorce.'

Yusof gazed in pity at the elegant elderly lady who was married to one dead man and more irreparably married to another, who had once dreamed she might emerge beyond the marriages she had not been very good at, emerge alone, herself.

'Poor Yusof, I'm sure you don't want to hear all this.' His hostess stood up. 'Now I'm going to switch on a light and fetch you a glass of orange juice. Such a shame that you're not the sort of Muslim who drinks wine. The Prophet did.'

On his feet, Yusof protested. 'Orange juice would be delicious.'

Suddenly, in the evening air the chandelier was refulgent.

'Next time you come to Paris, bring that pretty wife of yours. I scarcely know her.' But then as she was crossing her Persian carpet Danielle stopped. She stood straight with her arms tensed at her sides, with her head flung up. 'Do you understand?' Her voice cracked with the desperation of her love. 'We were so married . . . !'

She turned on her guest. He swallowed. He nodded. He mumbled, 'Yes.'

'He and I. At last. ' Then she smiled. She drawled, 'And then he left me.'

7

Right from the start, that fire was all things to all men.

To the authorities in East Kalimantan, where it was raging, it was yet more proof that the indigenous slash-and-burn farmers were a menace. These primitive natives would have to be stopped living freely in the back of beyond – well, bureaucrats don't tend to like wanderers. The troublemakers were to be settled in villages where the government could control them. Could provide them with hospitals – this was the popular part. Provide them with mosques and churches, with schools which went down well too, places where they could be civilised a bit, would learn to pay taxes and consider themselves Indonesians and wear more clothes.

To the environmentalists, what was significant was that the wildfire roared through areas which had been logged, where the canopy was sparse and the ground littered with tinder, but made far less impression on virgin forest.

To Danielle Kahn it went without saying that it was a terrible tragedy, but it was most immediately annoying because it meant that her son and his lover were off righteously cavorting in the interior, when she wanted them in Kuching to talk about bridesmaids' frocks. To Stephen Chai it was a lesson from God, matter for a sermon possibly one day – for he was ready to take up challenges when they were flung down. And in the end he did preach his Fire Sermon, just like the Buddha. Well, perhaps not quite like the Buddha, poor devil.

To the fabulists, the fire was a fable. To the naturalists, it was a list of species perilously reduced and a shorter list of species wiped out. To the moralists looking for a way of threshing out the brave and the cowards, it was a test of physical and moral courage.

To a crusader like Hugh Blakeney, it was a crusade; it was a disaster to measure, explain, learn from, so it might be prevented from occurring again. It may have been more Hugh's fire than anyone's, but so many people appeared to appropriate it that it didn't have much objective reality left. To Cassandra Matlaske, it was somewhere you went because your true love was there. To Philip Blakeney, who from the earliest days had intuited how nebulous even an inferno that great would seem, the burning hills and valleys came to be the unredeemed world where he sent his son to find out if any good remained to be saved.

In its small way, Hugh Blakeney's writing was all things to all its few readers too. Look at how Akbar Nasreddin read that first journal with his reflected, milder version of Blakeney's satisfaction that their young stalwart was doing exactly as they had expected. Was his voice not unchanged, not just what they loved and believed in: sensible, forthright, cheerful?

Or take Cassandra Matlaske. She was in the house when that first parcelled-up journal made its way to the coast to be read in peaceful Kuching. She was on the verandah when its first reader handed it to her to be its second, took off his glasses, gruffly pronounced, 'The lad sounds fine,' which interpreted meant 'I'm proud to say I reckon he'll do a splendid job.' She watched Akbar announce his pleasure with such a puff of cigar smoke that his large round face was clouded over.

Naturally she was overjoyed to know that Hugh was well, or had been three weeks back; and naturally she lapped up his news; in the days before her departure she would pick up the battered notebook when people left it on the teak table, read a few pages. But for her that thirty-page report by the son for the father was principally important because of a scrap of paper inserted in it for her. *Don't change your mind, honey – I never will. The fire first, then our wedding, then India*. India . . . ! she dreamed. The journal meant that she knew her lover's plans, could be sure roughly what his movements would be. When Blakeney gave her the Mount Ophir ring and she tucked it away in an inner pocket of her handbag, it was wrapped in her scrap of love letter.

The last time Thor Bernstein had seen Cassandra was when Hugh and he walked with her to the airfield at Sibu, just some rough grass at the edge of the little river town. They had come from Tawau as a trio. Now the two men were off up the Rejang. She was to fly back to Kuching, to her Mission School. They stood on the dusty grass in the sun, and Hugh Blakeney told them that a survey had concluded that there at Sibu, in the heart of Iban country, three hundred of the local women whored.

He was in a campaigning humour, he was coming out with that sort of information or polemic. Whereas in the bad old days, he said with an exasperated laugh, when his grandfather had been Resident and Kitty in a hat had set up her easel, when Mr Hoover had planted rubber trees in the Methodist School garden and Mrs Hoover had taught in their houses the Foochow maidens whose bound feet meant they could not walk – there would have been a minx or two who fucked for money to be sure, but only a few. And now, three hundred. It gave you an idea of how the timber business distributed wealth and poverty, eh?

Bernstein looked at Cassandra Matlaske, at her rippling black hair lustrous in the brilliant light, at the high black arches of her brows which gave her black eyes that thoughtful, innocent look. Of course it was shameful that the local people should have been reduced to be the serfs of the Malays and Chinese and lumber company Japanese, and she was half Iban and she was listening and at another time would have been interested, but now . . . ? Tall, flamy-haired, white from shirt collar to tennis shoes, Hugh Blakeney stood very handsome against the green field, against the shanties where the girls were available. A head shorter than her fiancé, she stood before him looking up into his eyes, slight in her sarong and blouse, her leopard's claws to lend her barbaric splendour, lend a touch of sumptuous cruelty to her pale throat and pale ears.

Unobserved by the lovers saying goodbye, Thor Bernstein allowed himself to smile a moment at the girl who had seduced him from his island, was making him compromise his indifference. He did not resent her charming victory over him. He wished her all the luck in the world, all the victories her pure spirit could aspire to. Now she would return to Kuching with the triumph of her engagement. Alone. Almost as if bereaved before she was married. With Hugh soon vanishing beyond the humdrum world of post offices and telephones, she would have to bear the burden of their engagement alone – to his surprise, Thor found himself thinking of it as a weight. So frail she looked, so vulnerable. He remembered that slenderness when from the headwaters of the Rejang the first journal was dispatched China Sea-ward. He meditated that when it arrived, when on the Blakeney verandah her lover's voice sounded in harmonious confirmation of hers, the responsibility for the engagement to marry, for that unorthodox and perhaps dangerous triumph, would be shared, she would no longer be so alone.

Nobody had yet had his days darkened by having to witness the way Philip Blakeney and Cassandra Matlaske would end up standing by one another. But even at Sibu, even as the pilot and seven of his eight passengers began to walk toward the little aircraft and Cassandra hurled herself into Hugh's arms, the ex-anthropologist, as he turned his eyes away, was aware of how by giving her body and soul to the son the girl was standing by the father.

What more could she do? he wondered as she followed the others toward the plane. She was casting her soul into the balance to try to save her old Faustus all right, she would bring him what grace she might. Not that love of Hugh Blakeney had yet become a call to self-sacrifice, she wasn't yet hastening toward that pyre. In those days it was unadulterated sensual delight, it was the dancing together of the two lightest hearts and boldest spirits which anyone in Sarawak had ever been amazed to see could exist uncontaminated in this polluted world – even Thor, who had not rated Hugh in the same moral league as his father, was beginning to smile on all this revealed happiness. But it was of the utmost importance to Cassandra that their wedding take place in church, and watching her wave to them as she clambered into the poky fusilage Thor, with a jolt, realised why.

Loving Hugh Blakeney as she did, she very likely would have consented to marry him under the profane aegis of the French or British ambassador at Kuala Lumpur. But loving Philip Blakeney as she did . . . If her marriage with Hugh could bring solace to

Philip's soul, which he persisted in describing as lost but which she named the most selfless, the most good – and if that balm might be administered by a priest before God's holy altar . . . No wonder she had tackled Chai. The burden of mysteries in that slight and beautiful head of hers! Thor Bernstein, as he watched her borne up into the blazing sky, felt something akin to awe. For surely they must seem mysterious to her, the diabolical forces which held her adoptive father in thrall. His despair against which her love and hope and faith wrestled must seem implacable beyond comprehension. Balm, Thor found himself murmuring as they strolled toward the wharf. Balm, balm . . .

For reasons best known to Akbar Nasreddin, Hugh Blakeney's passport had been defiled with no prohibitions. It was not until they were in the mountains that they found themselves the wrong side of the law. So their progress up the Rejang had many of the aspects of a holiday.

Indeed they might have started by flying as far as Belaga – which is what Stephen Chai and Cassandra Matlaske did when trying to catch them up. But Hugh wished to take no risks with officialdom. In Tibet, in Burma, in Timor, in Borneo – he had been turned back on too many ventures to want to tell anyone his name, not even a clerk, make himself unnecessarily visible. For instance, at Kapit they ought to have got police permits to go on to Belaga. The merest formality. But when Thor Bernstein suggested they drop into the office and pick them up, Hugh refused. 'The more ghostly the better,' he said. 'I've done more of these kinds of adventures. Trust me.' And who knows, maybe he was right. He *was* the author of reports researched against governments' pleasures – while Bernstein's harmless sojourns in remote communities had never attracted the ire of even the most tinny politician . . . well, if you excepted the Rangoon gang who on principle thought ill of all men. And when Hugh and Thor and Kadir did need to disappear, it was undubitably a terrific advantage to start with no one knowing who was disappearing or where or when or in what direction. Hugh Blakeney's mastery of the clandestine finished by impressing quite a lot of people – might, his nearly unfleshed and irrevocably unsouled father had occasion to comment, have got him a steady job. It was not only Cassandra who thought he would have made a successful guerrilla or commando. At any rate, Hugh told Thor he would have flown if he could in one flight have got damned near to his objective. If he could have flown to Tanjungredeb or to Samarinda on the Straits of Makassar, he would have risked policemen who might know his record. But those airfields had been closed because of the smoke.

After the turquoise moat around Thor Bernstein's Sulu Archipelago hermitage, the earthen Rejang. After his white-bellied sea-eagles, kites and black eagles and serpent-eagles. After his grey herons which reminded him of white Kyoto egrets flying in the snow, ibis which reminded him of them too. After his pale immaculate sand, pebble beaches and mud banks. To his island's coves were washed dead sharks, dead conger eels; their cleaned bones whitened. Turtles were washed up; their flesh rotted away; their shells weathered. Once a visiting fisherman had worked for hours with a makeshift razor-blade knife slicing away the enamel to sell. At one Rejang river camp Bernstein watched a Dayak hunker down beside a turtle which in alarm had withdrawn its head. It was a peaceful evening, the man waited patiently with his *parang* ready. At last the turtle, reassured by the stillness and quiet, put forth its head, the blade came down.

After the sea breezes and dry heat of his sanctuary, humid forest heat. After his solitude, the incessant companionship of Hugh Blakeney and their guides. He found the merriment in the longhouses depressing, too. It was better when they made their own camp. He could sit apart and muse, watch Hugh writing in his notebook, watch the river flow. He could wander into the forest, into the bird-loud shade. Somehow it seemed to the lapsed husband and lapsed scholar that in the interior things would be better – but this was a premonition of hopeless vagueness. It started merely with the supposition that in the mountains the longhouses would be few and far between. He who as an anthropologist had delighted in living among the tribes would find his solitude again, find it all around him, find it within him once more. And indeed beyond Belaga his spirits began to rise.

The forested hills were as beautiful and as peaceful as the Sulu

Sea, might they not grant him freedom in equal measure? The green lapped about his mind as enchantingly as the blue had done. The boat in which they travelled leaked, it reminded him of that poem Philip liked, the one about a sieve, it made him smile. Every reach of the river opening before them seemed to entice him deeper into the core of peace. Thor half forgot the tragic nature of their mission – or would have done if Hugh Blakeney had not kept talking about it. If he sat in the bow of the longboat with the others behind him he could feel himself alone, could let his thoughts be mesmerised by the gleaming curves of the river, the high walls of greenery that were always the same and always changing. The country ahead was so immense, they in their craft were so few and so small, that the taut nervous mind with which he had set out on the journey began to unclench. He who had found himself a lapsed almost everything took heart.

He had wanted time and solitude in which to discover whether any philosophy was intrinsic to him, to discover what mode of thought would not lapse, would endure, would be him. Well, up in the Hose Mountains ahead, maybe . . . And perhaps it had not really been such a defeat when he had let Cassandra tempt him into action. As for all that gloomy nonsense about not being able to surrender with impunity – what had he lost? Nothing, of course. And one day he should know how to take the mental action he longed for. In the bow of the longboat he day-dreamed more optimistically. His island was the summit of a sea mountain, and there were magnificent summits ahead now, a latter-day Diogenes might find a pleasing barrel on any one of them. Nor need he always stick with Hugh; he could meander off on his own pilgrimage. No he couldn't, damn it, he'd promised Cassandra he'd keep an eye on him.

Thor Bernstein was getting on with Hugh Blakeney better than he had feared. He was beginning to allow that he was not such a disappointing son of his father, find traces in him of the old soldier he had of recent years elected to be his honorary godfather. For a start, Hugh was admirably good at being convivial in longhouses. Unaffectedly he made friends, and he had a blessed ability to make jokes in languages he could not speak. When it came to repairing their outboard engine his patience was exemplary. And though his mind might be aflame with zeal he kept commendably quiet about it, when he spoke was modest and humorous. Thor's asking him if looking at the fire was going to extinguish it had stuck in his mind. 'Just going to take a glance at this fire,' he would say, 'and put it out.'

Sitting by their camp fires in the evenings they talked about how the tribes had believed a good *antoh* or spirit would send an omen bird to warn of danger ahead, so that if a certain kingfisher flew across the river the *prahus* would turn back. They remembered that among the Penihings to see a large tree fall had been the grimmest of omens – so what horrors must their ghosts be suffering now? Then there was another tribe who thought that in the life to come a thief was condemned perpetually to carry what he had stolen on his back. Their heaven must be aswarm with timber millionaires each bowed under a log.

Talking with Hugh was very like talking with his father, Thor Bernstein found, and warmed to him. The chat was a similar Bornean hotchpotch. And indeed Hugh and he quite often began, 'Philip once told me . . . ' So Blakeney had his spectral presence in their boat, at their camps.

Early one morning they watched a dead woman being rowed away through the mist to her grave. Questioned by Hugh, the devotee of burial rites told him how the guardians of the dead had been carved on the *kapatongs*. If you looked closely they were often a pair of lovers, the most vigilant watchers because they did not sleep. Thor confessed that he doubted he would ever write his study of Bornean death, but he talked about it cheerfully enough. They had not encumbered themselves with books, and to tell stories at evening came naturally, as camp fire by camp fire they entered the interior where half the people were still illiterate, where immemorially tales had been remembered and rehearsed. So Thor talked about ironwood *kapatongs* which were the roughly sculpted images of a benign *antoh*, or of a man or bird or animal the *antoh* had entered. When the carving had been finished, the *blian* or holy man invoked the *antoh* to possess it, he smeared the statue with the gore of a sacrificed pig and danced and sang before it all night.

But Thor might not go on. He might be distracted. Their

conversations rambled hither and thither, often without much rhyme or reason. So Hugh, who had been brooding on the fire, recalled that hatred was one of the eight perils referred to in prayers to Tara, the Buddhist goddess of compassion, and its symbol was a forest fire. And another time Thor saw something in the water which made him remark, 'I suppose they really *have* slaughtered all the poor old crocodiles in this river?' So Hugh told him a story of Philip's about how some tribe or other used to consider them excellent *antohs* and only killed them if they had eaten a man. They caught them by suspending over the river a strong stick sharpened at both ends, with an ill-smelling dog or monkey for bait. A rope was fastened to the middle of the stick, so when it wedged between the crocodile's jaws the brute could be hauled ashore.

Hugh Blakeney had written to his father in the forthright voice which came naturally to him and which he knew would give satisfaction. *I doubt I'll ever face an evil greater than this*, he had scrawled, perhaps with arrogance – who of course knew that flame in itself was no more intrinsically bad than it was intrinsically good but had no qualms about judging the incineration of the tribes' lands now to be bad. *I'll never have a better chance to do a little good.* His morality had been suffused with hope. Cheerfully he had disregarded the aid agencies' doctrine that you should limit yourself to helping people help themselves, piety he too had professed while knowing its inconsistencies. But now in the paradisal *Ulu* he spoke to himself in a more grave voice than that in which he had written to Philip, written also for the eyes of Cassandra, Akbar, Danielle. Spoke to himself, spoke silently to his father. Bernstein's warning that he wouldn't save a longhouse, wouldn't save a tree, haunted him with its good sense and with his knowledge that to content his pride, if for no sounder reason, he was going to try. As they headed up the Rejang his companion had also remarked that all they'd do would be to add a footnote to the long history of white men being idiotic in jungles, and Hugh did not wish to make a fool of himself.

He was aware of Tanya Mayhew. So was Danielle Kahn, for that matter. But the son knew more than the mother about that green-eyed red-head, that painter with her Roman nose and her freckles, with her hats and her voluptuousness. He knew that she had been the reader of poetry which Danielle had not. Tanya had read aloud to the divorced District Officer beneath awnings, in bedrooms. It had not been Danielle's fault that he had been happier with Tanya for a year than with her for ten, Philip Blakeney had with wry sadness been scrupulous to tell his son. Probably it was just that in his forties he had been more capable of loving and being loved than at any time since the war. And certainly, Hugh had reflected, the years of horror and despair had reinforced his self-control.

'Perhaps you would have been happy married to Tanya,' he once suggested to his father. He had seen photographs of her, he could picture her on a bed under a mosquito net as she stretched her arms and arched her back – for she had done that, Philip told him by way of beginning to answer, had done that many times but once in particular. She had stretched, she had arched, had half turned and half smiled. In a gay soft voice she had said, 'You can ask me to marry you if you like.' And he had lain looking up through the swags of enfolding net which suddenly seemed a veil he would never see through, a knowledge he was swaddled in, a life he could not die from, and he had replied, 'I'd love to, but no one ought to marry me.'

However, it was not as the girl who had wanted to marry his father that Tanya Mayhew now came to Hugh Blakeney. Nor as the young woman who back in Hampshire had begun to exhibit her paintings in Winchester, in London, had either married somebody or had not, he must remember when he got back to Kuching to ask Philip about that. It was as a reader of poetry that she appeared to him. A reader of 'Meru' – of which Philip had more than once commented in his growl that the sestet might be resoundingly platitudinous, but the octave was clairvoyant and no mistake. Hugh heard her voice, he thought of the girl just out of the Slade lying under a nipah canopy on a *prahu* to read to Philip who was beginning to lose his grizzling hair but was still handsome, the woman who must be fifty-something now somewhere in the world.

Civilisation is hooped together, brought
Under a rule, under the semblance of peace
By manifold illusion; but man's life is thought,
And he, despite his terror, cannot cease
Ravening through century after century,
Ravening, raging and uprooting that he may come
Into the desolation of reality:
Egypt and Greece, goodbye, and goodbye, Rome!

No wonder 'Meru' had echoed in his father's head, Hugh thought. No wonder ... In the walnut head of that student of the vanished civilisations of India and Java and China, that lover of the glorious pasts of Malacca and Brunei and even of the far more modest but undeniably civilised way of life which had been conducted at sleepy leafy little Kuching.

Yes, it was plain enough why when his lover had asked what she should read he had more than once asked for 'Meru', his son mused, as after supper he unmoored a boat and paddled alone up a confluent, for he had belatedly inherited that habit. Philip's life had been thought. Living after war in a semblance of peace he had known civilisation to be a tissue of illusions; Faustus' ambitious, enslaved mind had broken through. And Hugh went sculling alone up streams by the light of the stars into the forest because he was beginning to be aware of the magnitude of the evil ahead of him, no longer invariably felt as positive as he was accustomed jauntily to sounding, not now as he advanced toward the desolation.

He remembered some of the evils he had known, had tried to combat. In Sarawak in the last ten years, six hundred workers had been killed in logging accidents. They were crushed by falling trees or branches, they were crushed by logs on the skidways, by trucks which overturned. That was the kind of appearance which evil had assumed for him. Then there was that Ministry for Forestry statement in '82 which had noted, with reckless objectivity and insufficient attention to public relations: *Even fatal accidents are soon forgotten in places where labour is cheap and abundant.* But now night after night as he left their camps, as he paddled away where the night creatures rustled and cried, Hugh Blakeney was conscious of evil as never before and he took to naming as his father had done. His paddle would drip, an owl would fly across from one bank to the other, and faced with the fire he would recite the names of trees and plants and creatures. All the innocent victims, he wanted to hymn, all the losers.

Philip Blakeney on the Baram, in order not to sleep and not to think, had named the hills and rivers and the flora and fauna as if making an inventory of his world, a reckoning for the last trump. And now for a region the size of some small nations the trump must have been blown when no one was listening, when people were eating or sleeping or walking about. It was the end, the country was being consigned to the flames.

So Hugh mourned for the dead. For the heron and egret and bittern he grieved. For the curlew and whimbrel that flew up from the mangroves. For the snipe that loved the rice mire. For the fire-back pheasant, for the Argus pheasant and his dancing ground. For the sun-bird and the flower-pecker and the humming-bird, for the minivet and the bulbul and the babbler, the weaver and the drongo, the golden plover and the green pigeon, the sandpiper and the tern. Or he would name the different civets and squirrels, the different orchids and butterflies.

Sometimes where the phosphorescent lichens on the creepers falling to the black stream glimmered most arrestingly he laid down his paddle, in his shorts which were already muddy and damp he rolled overboard and swam beside his boat. He would swim away in the starlight and sometimes in moonlight, watch his humble vessel drift with the current like a log, hear a bird call or a fish jump. Sometimes eddies tried to lay hold of him, or in the water something rubbed against his flesh and made him start. He thought of the vanished species ghosting the hills they had lost. He thought of the tribes too, Philip talking about *the howes of the silent vanished races*. Their languages and arts, their marriage rites and funeral rites, their histories and religions, their lives hooped together by manifold illusions . . . Civilised, barbarous, it didn't seem to make much odds what word you used. Not less civilised than the society triumphing over them. He was drifting beside his vessel one night still a long way from the fire, still north-west of the watershed where his loggish drift would in time have brought him to the China Sea, not south-east to the Straits of Makassar, when he noticed that the stars were not so multitudinous and not so bright as they should have been. It was marginal, and he could not count the orbs or calibrate their resplendency, but . . . Smoke had dimmed the heavens, this was new. A few nights later, he smelled the burning. It was so faint that he at once doubted he had sensed it. But the following night in the fragrant stillness he was sure. Awash in the warm dark flow, he shivered. Far, far off – but he had been touched by that hot breath, this was it.

Not only Hugh Blakeney's journals addressed as letters to his father were composed when the two expeditions wormed into the interior. Stephen Chai was trying to write his Fire Sermon.

It was not coming together well. A few jottings . . . When he tried to formulate his thoughts, after the opening movement of his argument they were disappointingly amorphous, sometimes downright treacherous. That the fire, terrible though it appeared, was a necessary part of God's scheme for our salvation . . . His sermon would start, he felt, with this premise, if he ever preached it. That the island of Borneo, which time out of mind had slumbered in sinful darkness, had been singled out for exemplary punishment. Then that many of its people he feared were unworthy of this chance to have sin burned from their hearts. There were many who denied the fire, who would not confess to it, who turned away from this divine purgatory and light. For yes, Chai was sure that his sermon would proceed from the fire suffered as a redeeming punishment, to the fire seen at last as the light of our salvation. There were many who had forgotten that all trials, however cruel, worked for good in the Christian soul. There were many whose belief in that good had faltered, who no longer knew how to discern it.

So far, perhaps, so good. Lucid enough. Not obscure. Not intolerable. But when it came to being clear about the fire as light . . . When more tormentingly still for the believer it came to perceiving that the suffering not only of the guilty but of the innocent also might be ordained by a loving God . . . Stephen Chai's reasoning became tortuous, his conscience was lacerated as if by rattans. In truth, since his recent interview with Philip

Blakeney, since his return to the deacon for a second discussion, his mind had been in tumult. The constant companionship of Cassandra plunged him in misery too.

The deacon had been polite, even sympathetic, but he had not minced his words. He had expressed his surprise that Chai should accept Blakeney's word with such simple faith. He had made worldly observations as to English officers and gentlemen. When Chai had pointed out that he had no reason to believe that malicious tittle-tattle about the dancer having been a courtesan, having been Blakeney's mistress as well as Matlaske's and perhaps contemporaneously, the deacon had rejoined that he had not conducted much of an enquiry. As to Chai's absenting himself from Kuching for two weeks to fly with Miss Matlaske to Belaga, then in the hills consign her safely to her intended, the deacon had conceded that the priest was indeed due for a fortnight's holiday but he had forcefully recommended against uniting the young couple. It was only when Chai had convinced him that Cassandra was not to be stopped, it was merely a question of whether she went escorted by her adviser or foolhardily alone, that the deacon consented. He added two pieces of advice which, if they did not have the form of orders, had that ring to them. That Stephen should let matters go not an inch further without making a thorough investigation of the rumour; and that the young lady in all fairness should be made aware of the danger she ran.

It was then that Chai had realised he did not even know Cassandra's mother's name. Such was the oblivion which engulfed the girls of the island, whether they were dancers or courtesans or not, whether they died old on their mats or ran still young and with their babies hugged to their breasts into rifle fire. And to augment Chai's unhappiness there was the awareness that had come to him while Cassandra and he were talking on the clipped grass beneath the bishop's well-grown trees on Mission Hill. She *was* teasing him, perhaps in all her recent consultations with him had been. In her intoxication with her lover, half out of control of her behaviour, Chai liked to think kindly, in the gaiety of her abandon to that overmastering desire, she had mocked him, she had flirted. How could he forget? *Terribly dangerous, I expect. Do you think*

*you ought to protect me? You can come with me, if you want. Would
you like to take me to him?*

Possibly Cassandra Matlaske had let herself be blithe about
how straightforward a matter it would be to catch up with Hugh
Blakeney and Thor Bernstein, who had disappeared weeks ago
into range after range of scarps, run them to earth in that already
violated Eden. Possibly in his turn Stephen Chai had to the
deacon made light of the difficulties, had not been thinking
of them, haunted as he was by the passion with which the
two lovers would find one another again, the light hearts with
which up some hillside still lush or already ashen they might if
he were not there startle some outback missionary into making
them man and wife. Certainly when his two weeks were up,
the pursuing second detachment was nowhere near the heedless
vanguard.

His agitations wired tight by the impossibility in that wilderness of leaving Cassandra to her wild devices, leaving without
protection or guidance she who had been demure but was now
revealing her inheritance of her mother's debonair high spirits,
wired tighter yet by the impossibility of long extending his journey without complying with the deacon's recommendations,
Stephen had just marshalled the courage to tell Cassandra of
his dread when she confronted him.

She had left the longhouse where they were to sleep that
night; she had gone to the women's bathing place; there in
the river had washed her clothes, washed her hair. They were
close enough to the fire for the sun to have been gauzily overcast
by smoke all day; now it was below the hill. The softness of
evening was a smoky shroud. Dimness was gathering between
the columns of the trees. In the clearing, from a fire a plume
of smoke arose. As Cassandra strolled back, she came upon
Stephen sitting under a tree to watch the river. Boys were
diving from a pontoon, romping in the brown water. A barge
freighted with timber chugged by. A man back from labouring in
his *ladang* silently paddled his *sampan* to the jetty. She sat down
beside Stephen. He lifted his brooding eyes from the water. Flies
jittered around them, a mosquito whined.

She asked, 'Why are you so miserable these days?'

Knowledge of the poison he was going to drip into her

innocent spirit struck Stephen Chai as a prefiguration of his own guilt – for he knew she was good. Her flirting with him was nothing. Her imaginable fornicating with Hugh even to his priestly mind was nothing. For him she would always be incarnate innocence. Sitting with his elbows on his knees, he bowed his face into his hands. He prayed to God that what he was about to do was right. He raised his head, looked at her with wincing eyes.

'The deacon told me that people said your mother was Philip's lover too. That you may be his daughter.'

On her lips her cheerfulness and her affection died. Her eyes widened with religious terror. Rigid, she sat on the river bank, her wet hair shining on her shoulders, drying tendrils curling on her brow.

Her voice when it came was a ghastly whisper. 'Have you asked Philip?'

'Yes.' Stephen swallowed. 'He said it was all nonsense. He – '

'Of course it's nonsense!' she cried her arrogance, her voice cracked. But for Blakeney she could weep. Glistening, her tears fell. 'Oh, poor Philip! How he must be suffering!'

'I thought . . . I think we ought to talk to Hugh.'

'Hugh?' she asked with soft wildness, her soul writhing with her first taste of the tree of knowledge of good and evil, with her first knowledge of all her joy being wrenched from her, the grace being drained from her world.

Stephen Chai was her spiritual adviser; he could not turn tail; it was his duty to think the business through with her to its end. 'I'll talk to Hugh,' he suggested gently, 'if you like. But probably you'd rather do it. You will, won't you?'

'What? No. Yes, I suppose so. Yes, of course. But it doesn't matter.' She laughed jerkily. 'Do you think Hugh cares?' Her demand was spat fiercely at her priest. 'Do you think Hugh gives a damn who was whose lover long ago? Do you think he cares who I am?' If to extort a confession her torturers had been laying their first hideous touches on her body, she could not have cried her questions with such desperate pain. 'He loves me, don't you understand? Do you think I know who I am? Do you think God . . . ?' In fear and despair at the muddying of her mind, she screamed. Through a gush of tears, she cried, 'I believe my God . . . !'

In his wretchedness, Stephen said, 'God will lead us to the truth.'

Cassandra sprang furiously to her feet. Hugh's Christmas Day letter from Singapore echoed in her ears. *Supposing Philip and not David had been your real father – I wouldn't love you differently or love you less, and I defy you to pretend that your feeling for me would be merely sisterly. I'd commit incest with you happy in the knowledge of our innocence. I'd love you truly all my life happy in the knowledge that we were more profoundly married than in any union Church or State could fix us up with.* Where was God going to lead her? Where? Her fists clenched, she gazed around at the dusk, swung her welling eyes back to Chai.

'All right, you've done your work!' she cried. 'Get away from me. Go back to Kuching.'

'I . . . ' Appalled, scrambling up, he stammered, 'I'm your priest, I don't think I can leave you like this.'

But already she was furling the swathes of her self-control about her. She was entering the inner silence in which she suffered and prayed for so long.

'I'm sorry, I know it's not your fault. Just leave me, now, please, for an hour.'

He watched her walk away alone beneath the trees along the river shore. Her fingers rested on the handbag at her side.

In the forest, Cassandra knelt down. She remembered: *And the Lord went before them by day in a pillar of cloud, to lead them the way; and by night in a pillar of fire, to give them light.*

FOUR

So there they vanished, the product of Oxford and that of Harvard, then a couple of months later the priest of Saint Thomas's and the Mission School teacher who never taught again, into an interior that was one of the unluckiest places on earth.

Unlucky? People took different views. Stephen Chai was as aware as the next man that a lot of the effects of Development were injurious. But he couldn't deplore the success of the Christian missions, though it was a shame that in West Kalimantan the greatest number of converts were to Catholicism. Yes, too many of the Protestant ministers were of a severity which repelled the Dayak tribesmen of the inner hills, while the Catholics were often grounded in the rudiments of anthropology, were prepared in the short term to let the villagers stick to some of their superstitious ways, were of formidable tolerance and patience, played a far-sighted game. And Hugh Blakeney never put anything down to luck. No, for him events always had causes. They weren't the nebulous powers of darkness that were battening on the great island, that were ravaging hills, were corrupting hearts in communities where often till well into living memory theft had been unknown. They were organizations with names, men with names. The Sarawak Timber Association. The Japan Lumber Importers' Association. What he called the Asian Progress Mafia Bank. The Sarawak Land Development Board . . .

But for the longhouse crones whose idea of time did not extend to the fact that in the Niah caves a *homo sapiens* skull had been disinterred which Carbon-14 dating methods gave as, what was it, thirty-five thousand years old ... ? For those dodderers with their bunches of brass or silver rings in their ears which stretched the lobes until their magnificence brushed their skeletal shoulders ... For they who did not know that on walls in those caverns were drawings of the old death cults that might antecede the Prophet Mohammed and for that matter antecede Our Lord Jesus Christ too, but which the new generation was being taught to despise; who did not know that the Bornean boats of the dead were figured on those rock walls, but would not have minded dying in the indigenous manner, shipping in the old way to the old afterworld ... Bad luck.

Bad luck for the *Orang Ulu*, the people of the interior, when the Minister for the Environment remarked: *If every longhouse wants to have a communal forest, we might as well stop logging right now*. When in the Seventh Division the Chief Police Officer told a meeting that *applications for communal forests should not be investigated*. Yes, bad luck in the hills where the timber companies bribed the forestry officials who were meant to protect the Reserves, often also bribed the *penghulu* of a longhouse so that at the cost of making one man rich the livelihood of a village might be destroyed. Where along with polluting the rivers with diesel and sewage they had now started poisoning trees – sylvicultural treatment, it was called. What it meant was, forest species declared uneconomic were poisoned. This contamination was perpetrated up hill and down dale; it infected the soil, the water. The old diversity was going, the old habitats were going, the loss of genetic resources was irreparable. Bad luck when a forest was selectively felled and might in, say, fifty years have regained a semblance of its old splendour, but after twenty-five years the tractors came back – well, the concessions weren't for all time. Bad luck, the malaria spreading in logged regions, bad luck the dengue fever. Bad luck, the saw-mills smoking, the dust lands blowing, the rivers bringing down dead fish.

Not that admonishments were not uttered, the national disaster not foretold. *I beg you to listen to what I have to say* ... Thus the second Rajah to a sitting of the Council Negri in 1915. *Has it ever occurred to you that after my time others may appear with smiling countenances to deprive you of what is your right*

– that is the very land on which you live, the source of your income, the food of your mouths? If this is lost, no amount of money will recover it. Be warned, or you will lose your birthright to strangers and speculators who will become masters and owners, while you people of the soil will be thrown aside, be nothing but coolies and outcasts of the island. Then there was the Dayak elder who raised his voice, who made his protest a couple of generations afterward when it was too late. *How can the government say that all untitled land belongs to itself when the people have been using the land before the government existed? We love our land. We farm it, plant fruit trees, build our houses. We hunt, we gather rattan. Beneath it are buried our grandfathers and their fathers. The land belongs to the countless numbers who are dead, to the few who are living, to the multitudes not yet born.*

Hugh Blakeney had watched Dayaks smear their thumbs with ink to sign their petitions to officials who never replied. He knew they believed they lived in a time of unaccountable misfortunes now that up the Baram the loggers did not stop at dusk, a new shift with lights worked all night. Farmers had told him that since the forest had been depleted the wet season brought floods such as had never occurred before, the dry season came with drought so the *padi* never sprouted, and he had tried to explain why. For a newspaper he had written that food was scarce in the uplands, there were not the deer there had been, not the sambur, not the barking deer or muntjak, not the little plandok, the mouse-deer which in Bornean myth was fabled for cunning.

That was the kind of place the interior of Borneo had become.

Hugh had helped to clear *ladangs* by felling and burning. To dwell on that was one of the ways he concentrated on the fire ahead when one of their Ibans turned back down-river with the big longboat and the engine, when Bernstein and Kadir and he ascended where you chugged into the last of the old quietude with the old splashy slowness. In the area to be farmed, the shifting cultivators cut the trees, left them till they were sere. They made fire-breaks around the field. Then just before the end of the dry season, under the midday sun they put torches to the tinder. As the fuel blazed it caused a wind to blow into the heart of the conflagration, Hugh had seen fire-storm whirlwinds, seen flames spiral up a hundred feet, two hundred, higher . . . Afterward he had trudged over the warm cinders, had kicked up a cloud of ash. He had walked choking and blackened, ash in his mouth, his eyes, his hair. When he came to the next stream, he had stripped off his clothes, had bathed.

The trouble was that the Fifth Malaysia Plan alienated for development regions which it denominated 'idle' native land, but which were not idle. It was land left fallow, which the farmers would return to when it had regenerated. The trouble was that with forests logged there was less land on which the Dayaks could cultivate their *ladangs*, on which they could grow their rice and their maize, grow their pumpkins and cassava and gourds, their sugarcane and ginger and Job's tears.

In the headwater longhouses toward the frontier the people lamented their graveyards bulldozed, a bridge built in such a manner that their vessels could no longer pass. People complained that the loggers cut down their engkabang trees from which they could sell the illipe nuts at the down-river bazaars. This was one of their only sources of income and the trees were supposed to be protected, but they had been felled. The loggers had boasted that if a case were brought they could bribe the authorities to have it dropped. People said the wild boar were shot by the timber company men, were scared away by the vehicles and the saws. They said that platoons came to their settlements and fired their rifles in the air to frighten the women and children; when the men protested they were taken away.

More than seven hundred miles long, the border between Sarawak and Kalimantan. Time out of mind it did not exist, the tribal chiefs acknowledged no sovereignty but their own. Then the Governors of the Dutch East Indies and the Rajahs of Sarawak never bothered much. The demarcation was not surveyed.

By the time David Matlaske's body was devoured there and rotted away, by the time his goodness was made one with the forest's cycle of nutrients, the border was a border all right, it was real enough to shoot across. But twenty years later, if you came on foot with nomadic Penan guides in the old manner, you still could not declare with any precision when you crossed the

line. Not unless you came by one of the main paths to one of the
– what? four? six? – checkpoints, which was scarcely necessary
when traversing a range of mountains that wild. The *Orang Ulu*
hunters and gatherers still crossed and recrossed the watershed
freely – a liberty which offended the governments on both sides,
made them renew their exertions to depopulate the forests, coop
the wanderers up on plantations.

Stephen Chai and Cassandra Matlaske, in a hurry and
equipped with Indonesian visas, stumbled openly along one
of the immemorial trade paths zigzagging through the crags.
Hardly speaking to one another, they plodded through the green
shade from lost scrappy settlement to lost scrappy settlement,
arrived at a *kampong* on the Indonesian side.

A border guard took their papers, left them in a shack drinking
tea with some bony children gawping. He reappeared. Their visas
were in order, he said; but because of the fire, because of the
difficult national situation, he feared it would not be wise for
them to go on. Stephen began to recount the important Church
mission on which he was engaged, but Cassandra gave him a
look, he took the guard outside. When he came back, it was
permitted that they should proceed, the guard himself would
recommend guides to escort them to the next village.

Ruthless, Cassandra Matlaske, in her fashion. As for poor Chai,
it never occurred to him that he was being used. Or rather, he
considered it his duty to be of use.

After he had dripped the venom of truth or falsity into her
mind, alone on her knees among the columns and festoons
she had prayed. Then a second time, but temperately now,
she had urged him to return to Kuching, to resume his
accustomed life, to let her go on. He had said it was his
duty to accompany her. Since then she had spoken to him
only of practical things. It was some consolation to Stephen
that she did not give the impression that it was particularly in
him that she did not wish to confide. He did not feel singled
out. Her coldness was all around her, was in her. Then he
realised that far behind on the Sarawak river a gaunt man
was declining toward his death, for whom every night in
the gauzy shrine of her mosquito net she wept. Then he
realised that far ahead in the smoke-overcast basin of the

Mahakam river was a heart to whom fearlessly she would open her heart.

Each dusk before supper Stephen Chai said evensong, on the verandah if the longhouse were a Christian one, in a glade if the people were Muslims or still held to their ancient gods and myths and enchantments. Then kneeling together Cassandra and he would pray silently. She no longer told him the nature of her prayers. He wondered in vain, in an agony of compassion for her and fear that he was unworthy to feel that compassion. She no longer asked his advice on any matter beyond the reading of maps on which, as they advanced, were written with irritating frequency *Unsurveyed* and *Relief Information Unreliable*. She no longer confessed to him her paltry sins, if she committed any.

They were neither of them experienced travellers. Of course they had both read books from Philip Blakeney's shelves. They had read Hanbury-Tenison and Hansen, they had read Hong and Ngau, in theory they knew a fair bit about the interior. They had flicked through yellowed numbers of *The Sarawak Gazette*. But neither of them had undertaken a venture like this. Their town bodies were unused to the rigours of rain-forest travel. Often the food upset their stomachs. Bitten by ants, their ankles swelled; their shoes lacerated by river rocks, their cut feet did not heal. Still, their minds were tough. They were not enjoying the trip, but they did not complain.

They knew it was unadvisable to journey alone in strange country, so at each longhouse they acquired guides to escort them to the next. Money was not a problem. Cassandra had enough for her needs. Stephen had apprehensively brought plenty, almost delighted in getting rid of the stuff, it seemed to salve some nerve or other. It might have been better if money *had* been a problem – though at a pinch to be able to corrupt a border guard was vital. But word travels fast in the rain-forest – travels on occasion more swiftly than you feel you can account for – and Chai's reputation for being ready to pay over the odds for boats and men preceded the unlucky pair. This meant that they could never leave any settlement without being fastened upon by the money-grubbers in the community. It meant longer and longer bargaining sessions before the next day's travel – colloquies there was only one way of abbreviating.

It meant companions who would agree on a wage for a journey of three days, but then after the first day demand more.

Hugh Blakeney and Thor Bernstein and Kadir had a merrier time of it in the forests. They paid their Penan guides with twelve-bore cartridges, doling them out day by day. Hugh and Thor had travelled in the forests before. They knew how impossible it was to get Penans to take you in anything resembling a straight line, knew their need to keep divagating to search for the aromatic wood called *gaharu* which they could sell when they came to a bazaar. They had steamed pork and rice in lengths of bamboo. They had eaten the flesh of pythons and monitor lizards, of squirrels and bats. They knew how quickly you got tired climbing ridges latticed with undergrowth, scrambling over fallen trunks, around trees' buttresses, over slippery roots. They knew the bridges made of a single log often had no rattan rail. Even if you didn't topple off the slimy thing it sometimes broke under your weight, pitched you down through bushes into a ravine of mud. Your friends had to cut their way to you with their *parangs*, haul you out bruised and cut. They knew how you got disoriented among streams which doubled every-which-way, so when your mocking guardians asked a simple question like, 'Where is the border now?' you pointed the wrong way. For days you would not be able to see more than a hundred feet; then from a precipice you had not known was there would fall a glittering cascade, it would crash into a gorge of mossy boulders and cast a silvery haze up into the pendent boughs.

Before a storm, the insects would stop humming and the birds would stop calling. No animal would cry. Glimmers of sunlight would no longer come lancing through the canopy. After lightning and thunder came blasts of wind which could bring branches down. Penans would not rest under trees with dead wood, or which showed signs of termite activity. Then you heard the deluge of rain roaring toward you through the darkened jungle suddenly possessed by St Vitus' dance, suddenly creaking, groaning, thrashing. Tempests of wind could bring trees down, could start a concatenation that would level a patch of forest. The thing to do was to select a tree with mighty buttresses and huddle between them so while your pillar stood you were safe. Rain slithered greyly down the bark. Afterward when you walked on, for a long time the leaves pattered, the dimness dripped.

Hugh and Thor knew how Kalimantan men would cross into Sarawak, if they were lucky find work at a lumber camp – underpaid work, the contractors knowing these indigent souls had no permits – and a year or two later tramp home over the mountains carrying a sewing-machine or a chain-saw or an outboard engine. Crews would pole a longboat as high up the streams as she would float; hack a path over the pass; haul the boat up; then with rattan hawsers to steady the hull's plunge begin the descent into the first gully the other side, the first trickle of a stream.

As for their own penetration deeper into the heart of the island – Hugh did it in remembrance of his father's 1945 struggle to emerge, to fight his way free, be reborn from that hatred of his mind's impotence to alter things, to do good. As for their slipping across the border, their clandestinity – was he not entering into his freedom to discover truths and take actions, was he not about to take up an inheritance bequeathed him by his father, a knowledge, a power? That exalted and determined young man thought he was. Reckoned to live up to Blakeney's expectations of him, certainly – but dreamed of revenging his father's perdition too, or achieving a frail good to offer him to set against the too easily triumphant evils, or something cloudy like that. Very young he was, in some respects – despite being thirty and quite a man of the world, a man of great cities and great wildernesses. Young with a wild, indefatigable innocence . . . And he was the only man apart from Akbar to whom Philip had ever told what those Japanese did to Andrew, told what he knew, what at the freeing of the prison camp the informing ghoul had brought himself to utter. And . . . Well, it wasn't Hugh's innocence that was defeated.

So there he vanished into the shadow of the smoke of the fire, into a country where for months the sun was just a pale splotch in the murk – the equatorial sun! that hitherto immitigable force! – and vanished shadowed by the past too. His grandparents had got as far as those ranges but no further, and naturally he remembered that. He remembered too that it had been to Samarinda that the five survivors of that party had escaped – to Samarinda on the Straits of Makassar where he could not follow in their footsteps because he had the fire in the way.

But Hugh did not feel shadowed, or only in the grave, joyous way of having a responsibility to take up. The enormity of what they saw impressed him right enough, Bernstein recounted afterward. But while they were still in the trees and couldn't see a damned thing, his spirits seemed as high as the dipterocarp temple they wandered through. That was before their lawless presence in the back of beyond was signalled to authorities aware of what they might witness and what they might describe. Before military helicopters took off to look for them – took off from some tatty grass at Long Akah but also from Bario as it chanced, from Bario where the first primitive airfield had been cleared by Harrisson and Blakeney and Matlaske and their Kelabit warriors back in the heroic old days.

Buoyant, Hugh was . . . Only he must unwittingly have picked up the Sultan of Sukadana's diamond, Thor Bernstein felt. Yes, by the time Hugh in the Hose Mountains had dispatched one journal back to Kuching, and on the eastern slopes of the Müller Range below a summit called Batubrok, and then below another called Nyaan, was jotting notions down in a second, he must have picked up that stone which was the loveliest ever to come out of Borneo, men said, but of implacable ill-luck.

Either that, or he had shot a paradise flycatcher. This occurred to Bernstein at the time of his return to Norway, of his discovery that so far as university careers went he seemed to have missed the boat. He was in the Museum of Natural History in Oslo, standing before a case of tropical birds. Among the other glamorous plumages there was a paradise flycatcher from Sarawak. Thor remembered how the Dayaks called them the rajah bird. They used to say it was death to kill one, their white bodies and their royal blue heads were so fine.

2 ∫

They say he is already in the forest of Arden, and a many merry men with him; and there they live like the old Robin Hood of England. They say many young gentlemen flock to him every day, and fleet the time carelessly, as they did in the golden world.

Philip Blakeney gave no letter to Cassandra to take to Hugh in the interior. He just sent those lines from *As You Like It* copied out on a sheet of paper. And of course he sent him the girl herself, and the Mount Ophir ring.

Nothing curious about Blakeney imagining his son and his band of outlaws or fire-fighters or whatever they were as Shakespearean aristocrats in plain-living, idyllic exile. What was remarkable was that, in those mountains and rivers and forests and logged dead lands and burning dead lands, a mere two or three weeks after crossing the Kalimantan border the girl trudged into that palmy clearing with her man of God at her bloodied heels, blew that famous wolf-whistle of hers, brought her lover galloping along that longhouse verandah, hurtling down the ladder only touching one rung in ten.

In that doomed interior, which may have resembled the forest of Arden in some superficial particulars but did not have its inviolability, Cassandra Matlaske ran Hugh Blakeney to earth because of his plan. This famous plan of action was not committed to his journal in order to bring his nymph haring over colls and passes to his side, Thor Bernstein was adamant about that. And indeed that day you could not doubt his genuine surprise, that day of her ear-splitting whistle and his flying down the ladder with such haste that he deserved to sprain his ankles, that minute of embraces so joyful that to behold made your throat contract.

No, the plan was written down in order to impress upon his father that he was setting about his escapade with the requisite practicality. Also probably to convince himself that he had a chance of achieving something. A bit of method might be encouraging, even if so far it only existed on paper. And as it chanced they stuck to their first plan pretty closely, which was amazing, since the fire obeyed no law but its own. Otherwise Cassandra might have trailed her parson around *kampong* jetties and rain-forest paths till the crack of doom or till their visas expired or their alliance with the outlaws became known – for that was another hitch, they had to locate Hugh and Thor without being seen to look for them and without betraying where they were.

This obstacle bulked formidably among Cassandra's worries, but it turned out to be fairly simple to get round. For a start, outsiders trekking in the interior were so rare that often, quite spontaneously, people recounted that a few weeks back two white men and an Iban had gone such and such a way. And the Dayaks of the *Ulu* were not especially enamoured of officialdom in either its Malaysian or Indonesian manifestation. Recently there had been a case of a European who went missing in the forests, lived peacefully with the Penans, a line of conduct the authorities found insufferable. But whenever the military thought they had closed in on him, his jungle hosts spirited him away. And the hunt for Hugh was hardly up yet; when they really went after him, Cassandra was at his side.

About this time the fire spread over the border into Sabah – but Hugh never knew that. What he *did* know when Thor and he were elaborating their strategy was that in East Kalimantan there had been drought. Not for the first time. In the eighteen-eighties droughts had befallen Borneo which caused starvation among some tribes – you couldn't be Philip Blakeney's son and not know that. And now again for months only a few showers had fallen, agricultural production had just about stopped. Fresh vegetables became scarce. Fruit trees died. The peat swamps and the swamp forests were desiccated. Water-levels fell so that navigation in some rivers ceased. Rafts of logs being floated down to the mills went aground. Sticks and leaves on the forest floor dried out. Why previous droughts had never resulted in comparable conflagrations was probably because the Dayaks had always known how to control the fires with which they cleared their *ladangs*. But now Kalimantan was being what they called opened up by Javanese immigrants, by businessmen from the squalid coastal boom towns who hired labourers to clear land for plantations. Why the fire had grown with such horrifying swiftness was not difficult to imagine. The smashed trunks and branches left by loggers were ready fuel. The lack of canopy meant that timber and leaves were drier than they had ever been, than it was natural for them to be. With fewer trees, the wind-speed increased. Roads into the forest became corridors of blowing flame.

Hugh's instinctive grasp of the situation was accurate. That the fire would wreak its greatest devastation in logged forests – the final figure given by the German Agency for Technical Cooperation was 1.4 million hectares of residual stands consumed. Yes, the only proper study of the fire was conducted by Germans. Borneo remained true to its passivity, to its tradition of being regarded from outside – Philip Blakeney would not have been surprised. The ruin of the within was contemplated from without. And Hugh was right about one apparently minor detail which turned out to be fatal. The natural fire-breaks were the rivers; but for the first time in history, bridges had been built over a lot of them. Wooden bridges, naturally, constructed by logging companies for their vehicles. Bridges by which the fire crossed. When he had realised this, it was straightforward to make the destruction of bridges his purpose. It became his answer to Thor Bernstein's laconic objection that he wouldn't save a longhouse, wouldn't save a tree. The fire had the sea on its east flank – his language was getting terrifically military, as if the fire were an enemy army of occupation and he were a guerrilla. But if in the hills to the enemy's west the rivers could be made to resume their old service as fire-breaks . . . Here was a job of work to undertake. Listening to him, you got the feeling that before he had been bored, or rather had just decided that he must have been. Anyhow, luckily all was going to be splendid now that he had awoken to the importance of demolishing bridges, burning them in a contained way before the fire went crackling and flaring across them, now that his standing up to the fire had assumed this admirably clear-cut shape. At last a project to get his teeth into . . . You sensed he saw it like that, was satisfied it would prove worthy of his father's son. Its first unlucky consequence, of course, was that he could be branded as a terrorist.

As for the country over which this dashing campaign of his was to be waged . . . The younger Blakeney's romanticism and protectiveness, like the elder's, might be primarily focussed on Sarawak, but he had travelled in Kalimantan. He knew the kinds of thing you expected him to about the oil industry. About the timber business too, naturally. Upward of four thousand square kilometres of forest were being destroyed each year. This meant – what? – ten, no, more like twelve square kilometres a day . . . And he was great on the monkey business the International Timber Corporation of Indonesia got up to without apparently bothering to conceal it very cleverly, about the nefarious antics of Weyerhauser and Georgia Pacific, of Mitsubishi and Sumitomo, of a whole crowd more only he could remember.

A lot of what he had absorbed was not of much practical relevance, that had to be allowed. Philip had told him about the magnificence of the Sultan of Kutai's palace at Tenggarong. Michael Blakeney had been received there before it burned down in '36; had recalled the throne room which was sixty feet wide by a hundred and twenty long; had recalled the Chinese and Japanese porcelain, the Belgian carpets, the Venetian chandeliers, the tiger-skins spread out in radiating lines in a semi-circle with their heads toward the throne. And Hugh had drifted in a *sampan* on Lake Jempang. That had been one of his days in Arcadia, and no death's head had leered at him, *Et ego* . . .

Fortunately in the jumble in Hugh's head were some elements which might be more use to him when making his plan and executing it – be of more tangible help than the Kelabit war charm which Philip had been given at Bario in '45, and had carried when Sochon and he and their Iban fighters attacked fort after fort down the Rejang. It was a figure two or three inches high carved from an antler, which the father had handed on to the son, was in his pocket now.

Hugh was dependably informed as to the villages of the Apokayan not being so isolated as they had been, because the pilots of the Missionary Aviation Fellowship had started regular flights – though during the fire it was likely these had been discontinued. He knew the Kayan river was navigable through the highlands, but before you got down to Tanjung Selor you had to face twenty miles of rapids through which not the most adept boatmen, the legend told, had ever passed. Certainly before the war a crew of eight Dayaks renowned for their prowess in white water had attempted to run a vessel down through that deafening maelstrom of rocks and spray and had been drowned. In those days a path was kept clear so that goods might be portaged to the higher settlements like Long Nawang, but for a generation the way had been overgrown.

Hugh remembered that generally it was not difficult to travel up the Mahakam as far as Long Bagun, three hundred and sixty miles from the sea. But now recent reports were that fires were raging on both shores of the river, and how much water was flowing higher up? Before, it had been possible to ascend the rapids above Long Bagun when the water-level was high. You had to get hold of a boat with two powerful engines. Then if you didn't load your craft too heavily, if you kept your engines running wide open, you could inch butting and jouncing up through the welter of spray. But now? How much coming and going in and out of eastern central Borneo still went on? And the prices charged for fuel, for any commodity that had to be brought up from the coast, had always been higher in the interior, where the people were the poorest in the island, than in the down-river towns; if any remained to be purchased, he probably wouldn't be able to afford it. Ah well, even in peaceful pre-fire times the customary way to travel the streams in the foothills of the Müller Range had been to paddle slowly, tranquilly.

Armed with pages torn from Hugh's first journal, pages scribbled with encouragingly detailed specifications of valleys and tributaries, with soldierly talk about relief contours, about latitude and longitude, Cassandra Matlaske carried the anguish in her head south and east.

She tramped and scrambled with energy; her slender legs grew fit; she ceased to be troubled by the small rucksack on her thin back. She had not brought many possessions. Just a change of clothes, a few simple medicines, a mosquito net, her Bible, what more did she need? She invariably walked in front of Stephen

Chai. When their track lay plain she walked in front of their guides too, strode ahead of her modest entourage with her head held high, except when she had to duck through palisades of undergrowth, her mind held high and borne forward with the treachery of the world, the treachery it seemed sometimes of consciousness itself, gnawing it within.

That was what it had turned into, the venture proposed with such lighthearted devilry beneath the tembusu trees in the bishop's garden on Mission Hill, beneath the tembusu which stood eighty feet high or more where for years she had passed with the Church an invincible power for good, with the creamy tembusu flowers making the air of her girlhood fragrant. Bernstein had been right when at Sibu he had shaded his eyes and seen her rise into the blue blazing sky: what she had been fired by wasn't just any girl in love's sweet enough longing for her wedding day. Yes, she desired to be standing before the altar in that soulless Saint Thomas's of hers, wearing a white dress, with Hugh Blakeney beside her dressed up posh too if he could be cajoled into such a performance. But from the start through the tissue of this happy thought had kept slashing her cruel need for Philip Blakeney to give her away. Which naturally he would have done. For him too it shimmered ahead as a moment of crowning. Faustus might be consigned to life-long hell and to death-long dissolution; but he could stand stiff and straight like the old officer he was, he might have his proud glistering moment to fling in the face of evil – that was the way he saw it. The way *she* saw it was that she would bring him to the altar. It might to the uncomprehending clergy and congregation appear that Philip would escort her up the aisle to be married. But God knew and Cassandra knew that she would be bringing him toward redemption. It was this thought that made her eyes dim with tears of religious passion; and after her interview with Chai on a river bank a few days out of Belaga it was this thought that made her mind scream. That their drawing near to Our Lord's holy table side by side might never occur. That the world might betray her and, most hideously evil of all, might betray Philip yet again; that godly bliss might never come . . .

Luckily her sense of humour bore up. One night in a Kenyah longhouse she was dog-tired but the women would not let her sleep. They insisted on arraying her in their finery, for an hour she was for communal admiration to be transformed into a Dayak princess. An intricately embroidered jacket; a bonnet of stitched beads of great price; necklaces and anklets and bracelets and combs of a profusion and a splendour to dazzle the most imperturbable . . . With chatter and laughter they worked away on her. Yawning, she reminded herself that this might be the only bridal bedecking she ever got. But then when at last she was permitted to curl up she could not sleep.

God will lead us to the truth . . . Stephen Chai had said that – Stephen in whom she had scarcely noticed she had ceased to confide. He had blurted those words out in honest distress: how could she doubt him? The emergence of the slander or the truth was not his doing. If there were a *just impediment* to her marriage it would not be the fault of the deacon with his calm Cantonese face whom she now found it annoyingly difficult to think of with her habitual pious admiration.

Where was God leading her? To what truth? How would she know it if she arrived where it were? Not away from Himself, that could not be. But if not toward the *holy estate* of which she had dreamed, where? Then she would remind her panicky heart that to Stephen's straight question Philip had returned a straight answer. So what difficulties might there be? All would be well.

Or no . . . That the past could reach out as if with malignancy was a terror she had never known. Her adoptive father had nurtured her in such a tranquil enclave, and she had taken to innocence so thoughtlessly, that now against insinuations of depravity she was without defence. That David Matlaske might perhaps with nonchalant amusement have lent his mistress to his friend. That the nightclub dancer might have lived by her lovers. That Philip Blakeney, to whom it had never occurred to portray himself to her as a libertine, might at her christening have had his wry wonderings, at her adoption might have suspected he was simply taking back his own . . .

To what end had God plucked her from her knowledge of the world? She was still sufficiently the Mission School chorister to conceive in such terms her being driven out to wander where it seemed nothing would ever be established or disproved again. Vile enough that Philip who was the soul of honour should have his word doubted for an instant – and by her, ungrateful foundling! More vile that she – she who might be anyone, what did it matter? who was no one – that she did not rejoice that she might be Philip's child, shrank from the possibility because she had conceived a reprehensible passion, no, a true love and honourable desire to marry ... It was only the distasteful presence of her companions that prevented her moaning aloud, sitting down on the leaf-mould to cry. Nor for long could she stop herself knowing that Stephen had felt a tenderness for her and she for him. So why now did he have to be the mouthpiece of these loathsome accusations, of the malign? But it might not be the malign. Our Lord was all powerful and all wise. It might be a sign – meaningless truths or falsities as to her origins might partake of a higher order of truth. This might be God's way of leading her. Still, it remained more than she was capable of, not to find Stephen's panting presence irksome. And they were both weary of explaining to strangers that they were not man and wife.

In her *atap* sanctum on the Sarawak river, the mutability of creation had brought home to Cassandra how illimitable was God's mind. To live as the most insignificant flicker of consciousness among His eternal metamorphoses had assured her of the infinity of His justice and mercy, it had been humbly to share in His glory, it had been to hope.

In the interior she carried her newborn sense of the treachery of knowledge in the bone urn of her head on her dignified neck from *kampong* to *kampong* as she drew closer to Hugh. Not that she could silence the fear of renunciation crying in her ears. Not that she could long for her beloved's arms with her former gaiety. But she prayed that by his side she would be able to reason about things more sensibly. Several times she came to settlements where she hoped he might be. As they proceeded into the centre often the longhouses were desolate, everybody had fled from the fire.

And when she found him ... Oh, the scene was charming enough all right. At the stream's edge she splashed her hands and face, she brushed her hair. Evening was falling. She trudged into the clearing where there grew three or four durian trees, a clump of pandanus, a clump of bamboo. It was an old longhouse, ridge-poles sagging. Abandoned, seemingly. They had been met by no children tending swine and hens, no dogs barking, no women washing clothes.

Cassandra stood still, weary. Between hope and dread, she put her finger-tips in her mouth, gave that whistle of hers. Hugh had taught her to wolf-whistle years before, it consorted delightfully with her Mission School mien.

She brought him down as if she had been a Penan with a *sumpitan* and he a macaque.

Then the stage began to fill up with actors. Bernstein and Kadir and a forester who had befriended them appeared, looking surprised. Very theatrical, longhouse verandahs. They had been laying their fire to cook supper, in another minute smoke would have been wisping up. Chai and a guide came into the glade after the heroine – onto the lower stage. And then . . . It was curious. Hugh Blakeney when he heard her summons had leapt up, but at the foot of the ladder he checked. Motionless. She didn't stir either. For moments they stood marvelling at one another in the overcast, green dusk among the palms. Then she slipped her rucksack off her back, dropped it. She ran toward him. He waited, he gathered her up in his arms.

Nobody could hear, but holding tight around his neck and with her feet still off the ground, among those first kisses she must have whispered to him. Because when he set her down he grinned over her head at Stephen Chai and said cheerfully, 'To hell with the Church.'

To which with praiseworthy good humour, if you considered that Stephen had escorted Hugh's darling over a biggish range of mountains on foot in order to be greeted with this blithe brusqueness, he replied, 'Not to hell with anything. Just a difficulty we must sort out.'

Cassandra fumbled in her little leather bag. 'Philip gave me this to bring to you.'

Gazing into her black eyes, Hugh took her hand. He put Claud's gold ring with its emerald on her finger.

She stood without breathing. She looked at her ring. But then something went wrong with her. She stared wildly around at the gloaming, she gasped some words no one could understand, she burst into tears.

Which was behaviour everybody felt it sickeningly easy to account for. Her circumstances were grim enough. At Stephen Chai's brief explanation, Thor Bernstein turned aside. And the girl cheered up. She let Hugh sit her down on a log. She appeared to be herself again.

What Cassandra could never admit to Hugh was that in that instant of seeing the Mount Ophir ring on her finger – well, Philip's son was never going to have wavered in his striding forward for a mere religion, was he? you couldn't imagine he might – at that pitch of plenitude she had heard a call. Her dread had seized hold of her soul.

God will lead us to the truth . . .

And if He were? If He were beginning to lead her, if for her He had prepared some harsher destiny, some lonelier end?

What she said at the time, sitting on that log and wiping her eyes and giving a flimsy smile, was, 'Today's my birthday. Hasn't anybody remembered? I'm twenty-two.'

3

'I expect you'll want to get back to Kuching.'

Hugh Blakeney's suggestion was delivered through the smoke of the longhouse fire on which his fiancée's unappetising birthday dinner was being cooked – a few fatty chunks of boar, an emaciated eel, rice. Stephen Chai appeared to have been expecting the challenge, or at any rate he had made up his mind.

'No, I'd rather stay and help you, if that's all right,' he said simply. He even smiled. 'If you think I might be able to make myself useful.'

'Of course.' Hugh grinned. 'That's wonderful. We need all the help we can get.'

You had to feel sorry for Stephen: that first evening with Hugh and Thor and their merry men, all the sensual delights and ascetic sufferings of the succeeding nights were already alive. It was a presage of the time they still had left, the less than a month they had left. There were eight or ten merry men that evening – about average. They never numbered more than a dozen, and their one young woman with the leopard's claws which from that day forward she never took off her throat, and the engagement ring she never took off. There was Kadir who, when he had heard what they were up to, had decided to stick with them and was now far out of his tribal territory – the other Iban boatman of their ascent of the Rejang had as soon as he returned to civilisation reported their names and what he had understood of their intentions to the police. There was a Malay forester called Nazim Bokhari who revealed himself the type the timber businessmen would be unable to bribe. From the Indonesian side of the frontier, a few Kenyahs, sometimes a Kayan or two.

Never enough for the job, Hugh used to remark in his capacity as resistance captain, but a lot better than nothing; and he would remember his father in the Tamabo Range forty years before, rallying men. Never enough for the illegal, dangerous, necessary job of burning bridges. A task you might have been forgiven for assuming that the administration of the state of East Kalimantan would have undertaken as part of their policy for controlling the fire: but they had no such policy.

Quite how dangerous this assault on the fire's means of crossing rivers was, Cassandra realised that first evening when she watched Hugh spread out a map, heard him discuss the coming days' movements with his companions. He always consulted everyone equally, which was wise, because his maps printed on paper were generally a lot less illuminating than the pictures of the circumambient hills and valleys which the Dayaks would quickly set out with twigs on the forest floor or on longhouse planks. How audaciously Kadir and Nazim, Thor and he carried the fight to the borders of their enemy's country . . . How often it was a race to get to a bridge an hour before the fire reached it; how because waterways meandered this sometimes meant you were on the same side of the river as the advancing flames . . . Her eyes must have betrayed her agitation, because Hugh took her hand, led her along the verandah to where now that night had fallen you could see, far off, the great fire. 'There it is,' he said quietly, but with all that tremendous seriousness of his quivering deep in his voice. She gazed. Along the horizon to the east, an orange light was blossoming. Orange, red . . . Hugh said, 'That's what we're up against.'

Of course, Stephen had suspected that his arrival with Cassandra would signal not a release from his trials but their intensification. It had been predictable that Hugh would begin by brushing aside all qualms, though the gaiety of his dismissal of Christian scruple was daunting. 'Caz my darling, I think it's splendid that my sinful old father may have gone to bed with your beautiful mother, don't you?' And with a sparkling glance at Stephen, 'When I get back to Kuching, the first thing I'm going to do is ask him if he really did.' His contemptuous mirth on the subject of the deacon's taste for gossip about soldiers and houris was predictable too, though Stephen found his lack of respect offensive – and he was tired when he walked into that glade, tired when he heaved his pack up into that longhouse. Indeed that was a problem for them all in those last weeks. No one was getting enough sleep.

No one was getting enough calories either, for that matter. That afternoon somebody had grubbed up some bamboo shoots, they contrived to enhance Cassandra's birthday party a little; but by and large in the interior their diet was wretched. Stephen was pudgy no longer; the others were lean. After weeks in the rain-forest, Thor had lost his tan. His hair was no longer bleached by sun and sea, you noticed how grey he was getting. Hugh's cricket whites looked as if he hadn't taken them off all season. They bathed in the streams, but it was impossible to keep clothes really clean. And because they were all exhausted, day by day it seemed they never had time to think issues through properly, never had time to feel things in this way and then in that until they arrived at the right way – at least, this was one comment Thor Bernstein made afterward.

For Stephen to comprehend that he could not just dump the girl in the burning interior, could not turn his back on her hopes and perils, had been plain sailing. As her priest, he confronted a truth which had been stated with clarity. *For be ye well assured, that so many as are coupled together otherwise than God's Word doth allow are not joined together by God; neither is their Matrimony lawful.*

For him further to resolve that it was his duty to serve alongside Hugh and Thor, in their struggle to limit the damage done to the environment, or in their arrogant folly ... Well, in Borneo the delinquency of the instituted powers was beyond mistaking. And as Stephen had plodded and puffed after Cassandra there had in his equable soul stirred the beginnings almost of exaltation at the sense that he, who had been considered cautious and conventional, was as capable as more flamboyant creatures of taking a moral stand. Yes, if he were accused of unlawfully destroying lumber companies' bridges he would plead guilty with a cheerful mind.

Their outlawry was something they all took in different ways.

Hugh Blakeney seemed positively to welcome it as an honour accorded him. He even knew the Malaysian law under which he expected to be arrested and charged: The Emergency (Public Order and Prevention of Crimes) Ordinance – its Section Three, apparently. And doubtless he would be arraigned under whatever the Indonesian equivalent was called too. Thor Bernstein was despondently aware that his being beguiled into this defence of the last forests, which if they were not burned this year would be felled the next, signified the end of his residence permits – for him it was the last of Borneo. The few Kenyahs and Kayans who, instead of fleeing with their fellow tribesmen, stood firm and joined the only effort they knew of which was being made to defend the land of their birth, realised they risked a few months in prison and a fine they would not easily pay. Afterward, one of Akbar Nasreddin's last actions was surreptitiously to pay some penniless men's fines, including that of Kadir the Iban whose gaol sentence he tried to get suspended but without success. Nazim Bokhari perhaps risked the most. The man whose job was the safeguarding of forests should never have crossed the border, his superiors pronounced at the subsequent enquiry, and certainly should not have taken the law into his own hands. They sacked him. Stephen Chai did not believe he would be defrocked, but he was pretty sure that his extended and unexplained absence would be regarded ill.

Stephen weathered the imaginable faint mockery in Hugh's acceptance of him in his requisitioned quarters – would he really be as effective as the others? was his profounder motive the wish to keep his priestly eye on Cassandra, keep a steadying hand on her wildness? Half an hour later, at one end of the verandah he said evensong.

Foreshadowed, all their individual solitudes that were going to be endured together for their remaining twenty-something nightfalls; foreshadowed in that moment when Stephen and Cassandra withdrew down the creaking crepuscular barn of a building and knelt side by side. Funny, too, in its fashion. Funny how each of them locked in the cell of his self was so confident he had the keys to the others' doors.

At first glance it might all have seemed pleasingly familiar, you might have thought people were in things together. Food being prepared over a fire – reassuring enough. The voices of Hugh and Thor on the kind of topics they had both discussed with Philip and now discussed together . . . Such as the missionary who had complained that each time he tried to hold a service in a longhouse a gang of inebriated heathens a few paces off would burst into song, around the crate he was using as an altar a pack of snarling curs would start a fight. Or it might be Lieutenant La Rivière who commanded at Long Nawang early in the century with two officers and forty soldiers and a doctor. How in those days the voyage from Long Iram up to the Apokayan settlements by *prahu* and on foot always took two months and sometimes three, and the mail only got through three times a year. How La Rivière considered it would be difficult to eradicate head-hunting because, as the Dayaks would explain to him, the spirits demanded the practice; and they would ask him when he was going to leave Long Nawang so they might take heads again. Facts – things to have in common, base your thinking on. Stories – reassuring sort of talk. At the verandah's end, the two figures kneeling in Christian worship shadowy against the darkening jungle, the familiar words of their prayers.

Of course, everybody was cheerful. You had Thor Bernstein who decided to sacrifice their last bottle of Scotch, the one they had been hanging onto for emergencies. Plainly there were things he couldn't know. That when Hugh had washed Cassandra's hair in that waterfall on the coast of the Sulu Sea it had been a godless baptism of a kind; both the man smoothing the cascade through those black tresses and the girl with that cold brilliance splashing on her eyelids had thought it an initiation, a new start. That when aboard the *sampan* on the Sarawak river Cassandra had confessed their passion to Philip Blakeney, before the old man could recover his composure he had seemed to face something that was uncomfortable to face. That now she was haunted by his look in that river dusk . . .

But Bernstein knew enough. That the fight for Cassandra Matlaske's soul had been joined in earnest was horribly clear. A duel between the faith of one and the will of the other . . . And that fights for souls were bad. Were destructive of souls. Pitiless. So when she walked back from being blessed, he handed her a tin mug with a tot of whisky and a splash of boiled stream water in it; he raised his own drink to her. With a grave smile, he said, 'Welcome. Your arrival has been declared an emergency.'

You had Stephen Chai, who not surprisingly took a less gloomy view of what they were up to. Hugh Blakeney might believe that Cassandra Matlaske would be his until death; as soon as the fire relinquished him, they would be off toward India; ensconced on a sumptuous flying carpet, they would soar over the Natuna Islands and then over the Nicobar Islands . . . But Stephen was not much concerned with Hugh, whose pride showed no indication of softening, and he knew that before God the couple were not united. Unfortunately when after their humble service they walked back down the verandah, past room after room which the Dayak families had abandoned, Stephen could not help recollecting that tonight the solitary member of his congregation would go to the room Hugh had adopted – she had already left her rucksack there. But after weeks of prayer the priest had put behind him his old bashful longing for her. Lying awake in longhouse after longhouse, he had managed to suppress thoughts of her body – though tonight it would be hard not to know Hugh was unbuttoning her shirt, unwinding her sarong.

Still, on the whole he returned from evensong with the refreshed calm he had hoped for. It was true that by law Cassandra might marry Hugh in a civil ceremony. But Stephen was confident of her Christianity, he did not think she would commit an action she feared might be a sin. It was true that Blakeney had denied the allegation, and that his word had a nobility in her ears which Stephen was happy to respect. But the sovereignty of the Church was absolute. And had he not helped her mature in Christian virtue from adolescence on, witnessed how self-disregardingly she grew, how her spirit seemed apt for the most perfect oblations? And not only Blakeney but also the deacon and even he himself had their authority in her sight.

The responsibility was awesome. Stephen resolved that tonight yet again he would beseech guidance. At their last conversation the deacon had spoken gravely of the dancer's scandalous way of life, of Blakeney's and Matlaske's notoriety in those days. They were in the hands of God, Stephen reflected – but without the grimness of mind which before evensong he had found he had to guard against. Either it would be right for him when they returned to Kuching to accede to this woman's request to marry her to this man or it would be wrong. The mortal web was inextricable. Matlaske and his concubine dead ... Even the parson who had christened the baby was dead. But with the web's very fibre the humanly unknowable, surely Our Lord would provide a resolution. And he had been at fault, Stephen realised with his renewed serenity, at fault to be disappointed that Cassandra confided in him less, much less, not at all. No doubt she would open her stricken heart to her priest when he gave her the example of opening his to her. Tomorrow when they prayed together he would utter his misgivings aloud. He would try to make her see how they were all in the palm of God's hand and how fortunate they were, how rich in grace it was to be so held. Under his breath, as they sat down on the planks by the cooking fire, he said, 'Amen.'

It wasn't a cheerful scene, despite the flickering firelight, despite Bernstein's rendering up of his last reserve of whisky, despite the lovers being united. Very desolate, a deserted Bornean longhouse. When they were all convivial activity they could be oppressive enough if you were a dog that liked an angle of kennel to himself; but when they had been abandoned ... !

For a start, of old they were rarely just left standing there. When a community decided to up and off they generally half dismantled the place, removed any timber that could be used again, could be floated or carried to the next site. Less laborious, often, than hewing new posts and boards and beams. And the reasons for decamping were traditionally such as to leave the old position with a sombre feel to it. Increasing poverty of soil or poor hunting; the encroachments of an enemy tribe in the past and of loggers in recent years; massacres or epidemics or fires; such evil omens that the shamans insisted ... You'd go ashore where jetties were rotting on a river bank, shove through the brush to where two or three hundred people had conducted their lives. You'd find some of the vast upright posts still standing but the forest coming back, young trees growing tall, creepers entwining the ruin. The Dayaks believed that those who had lived and died there would haunt an abandoned longhouse.

But that place of Cassandra's twenty-second birthday party had been deserted with such haste that the people had taken with them only their Chinese jars and gongs. It did not look like a departure which had been debated, put into action with method. Terror of some atrocious augury, perhaps. Or they expected to return, but then something occurred which they had not foreseen. Or some official arrived, ordered the removal with such abruptness that there was no time to be systematic, make provision for the future. Or that blossom of flame shaking in the acrid, dimmed sky infused them with horror, they were blown away like leaves. In a lot of the rooms there remained boxes, garments, utensils. There was firewood cut, stacked above the fireplaces in the island manner. In the rafters were traps and baskets and nets.

It was sad among the vestiges of life to sit around one clay hearth where fifty were cold. It was sad to hear the wind wandering along the verandah in the sultry blackness. It was sad, Hugh said to Thor, that only outsiders were here to witness the end of the old way of life of the interior. Thor replied that it made him feel like a trespasser. Of course, he could imagine what the people felt whose country was being burned, but he couldn't know.

The mosquitoes had not let themselves be ordered away by holy men or by government men, nor had they succumbed to panic. There was a plague of flies, too. Everyone was always slapping their elbows and ankles, brushing at their heads. Moths kept flying into the fire.

As became their custom, Hugh and Cassandra held court on what had been the *penghulu*'s mat in the place of honour roughly in the centre of the verandah. Some smoke-blackened skulls bound in rattan still hung above them. Which was balefully indicative enough, was evidence to justify Thor Bernstein's silent mourning for the cultures of the interior undone, their rituals fallen into desuetude, their vision of their annihilation unrecorded. Those crania which had been the incarnation of the community's spiritual strength ought, with appropriate ceremony, to have been conveyed to the new dwelling place.

Maybe the village had already been converted to Christianity or to Islam, the ancient trophies had lingered aloft astutely tolerated for a while by the new dogmatists, still mutely revered by the old, forgotten by the young. Maybe the flight had been an undignified turmoil indeed. Anyhow, for good or ill, there the death's heads hung, over the heads of the living, as they had used to do.

And there the living had their bivouac. *Under the greenwood tree* . . .

No, not really. They could all agree that it was good to be a long way from those dispiriting settlements where the Chinese antique dealers had discovered that all things sacred or profane had their price, where they had bought every jar or god or hunting-knife which might have reminded people who they were or who they had been. His listeners could agree with Hugh Blakeney when he argued that even education might be a mixed blessing; just because social engineering was new to Borneo it did not mean that its insidious corruption of minds had not been chronicled elsewhere – it depended on who taught what to whom. Why were so few Dayaks taught by Dayaks, the teachers in Sarawak and Sabah predominantly Malays, in Kalimantan predominantly Javanese? Researchers had begun to document how children from the inner hills were brought to down-river schools where they learned to despise their parents' hard toil and their rites, their language and their dress.

His listeners did not disagree. They had all seen what a lot of modernisation came down to. When the uplifting rhetoric of Progress blew away, what you got were towns of shacks where people were decreed to have been integrated into the national economy, which had no jobs for them. You got swindlers, you got pimps. You got boatmen who turned out to know waterways no better than you did yourself, guides who drank themselves imbecilic.

No, it wasn't that . . . And Hugh's rejoicing in his repossession of his darling was enchanting enough, though she looked wan with weariness, didn't say much. Proud, his delight in her who by air and water and hill had come hundreds of miles to appear in that glade at twilight, among the palm trees stand before him like a miracle, dark, slight, still. Proud and tender, the way he kept gazing at her as if he could scarcely believe she were there.

It was not that he had become unreliable in his facts, either. Or that his logic was in any sense impaired. When it came to thesis and antithesis and synthesis you couldn't often trip him up. But his indictments were more scathing than they had been. You could perceive that he was right about how the degradations of East and West were being jumbled together, and without the refinements of either, to make a new barbarism; but you could do so while regretting the times when he had said things less bitterly. After weeks of fighting his campaign against the fire, the strain was putting jaggedness in his humours. Destroying bridges had been his idea, and he felt responsible for the men helping him.

So that birthday party was not the idyllic evening it should have been, and this was not because the gobbets of boar which were not fat were gristle, nor because the eel was all bones, nor because the bamboo shoots were fine but very few and the durians fine if you could contrive not to inhale their stench. Perhaps it was silly to have hoped it might be. The island was not what it had been. The dead lands had grown and the living shrunk. The spoliation on which Philip Blakeney had written hundreds of pages of notes was nearly finished now. The interior was not the sanctuary it had been. No longer could you retreat up-country and reckon to be left in peace there. The next day during their advance toward the fire – that was the rhythm Hugh had fallen into, after each skirting round they made a fresh attack – they heard for the first time a helicopter clatter above their sheltering trees.

The souls gathered around the *penghulu*'s mat beneath the skulls were unquiet, their harmony was not what it should have been. There was no call for Hugh to tackle Stephen as to how he was getting on writing his Fire Sermon. The girl had come to him, she had his ring on her finger, what more did he want? But perhaps there were the calls of his mind which had to be right, of his will which had to carry all before it.

At any rate, for the edification of their peers they went at it hammer and tongs – or maybe for the benefit of the moths that wouldn't stop fluttering and dying. Not for the last time.

Those two made other evenings unreal in the same manner. Haunted . . .

The problem posed by the fire was the problem of evil, Hugh might commence – friendly always, hard as iron always. If God existed, as Stephen believed, did that mean evil was part of His design? If it was the duty of a Christian to love the working out of divine purpose, did Stephen feel that he had to want what God wanted? Did he have to love the sufferings of the innocent, love the burning of creatures to death? Was that good? And God . . . ?

Just as friendly, just as hard as iron within for all his outer mildness, Stephen might say something about how the love of God was a difficult love. It was necessary that we should school our hearts in adoration of depths of the holy mystery we could not fathom yet.

That was the kind of way they'd carry on. Tonight, Thor found himself feeling this was a hell of a birthday for the girl. He turned to her. Of course, he had intended to say something distracting, something frivolous. But then suddenly he wanted to know what was going on behind those black eyes of hers.

'What do you think of all this?' he asked.

The other two had got on to how you defined innocence, or something highfalutin. When Cassandra turned her gaze on him, in the fire-light Thor for the first time saw the mad brilliance in her eyes.

Scarcely audible, but it was a scream. 'I want to go free!'

4 ∫

Charming, this talk of incest which Cassandra and Stephen have turned up with, Hugh Blakeney wrote to the man from whom he had inherited his former free and easy ways with girls. It lends a piquancy I rather like. Reminds me of Nerissa, too. In this family we appear to go in for girls whose fathers may not be who they seem.

No, he never really changed, Hugh Blakeney. What with exhaustion, and being watched for by two armies, and feeling responsible for his friends doing dangerous work, right toward the end his opinions may have been expressed a shade more raspingly than was called for. But his high spirits were indomitable, his forthright mind never changed. Nor did his cavalier way with sin, his gaiety which blew reeking smoke into Cassandra Matlaske's mind, which had been translucent, but was a miasma now that she was helpless in the grasp of her fear that she might have to give him up. Because when, back in Kuching, she had sworn to her priest that in marrying Hugh one of her fiercest prayers was that hers might one day be the humble hand which led him to God, she was telling the truth. When, indeed, did Cassandra *not* tell the truth? What increasingly gave her doom a degrading air of futility was that people didn't believe her, or not until it was too late. So now she was horrified by what might become of his soul if they were separated, of his soul never bathed in Christian love . . .

Her next way of tormenting herself, naturally enough, was to resolve that, if she did have to renounce love in this world, day and night she would pray for him. No soul would have grace invoked for it with more dogged desire. God was omniscient, how could He not fathom Hugh's innocence?

In Hugh Blakeney's fire journal, that was the only reference to the girl's parentage. Oh, except for the remark: **If Stephen had any real liking for her, he wouldn't worry her with his nonsense.** His conversation didn't show much concern for her religious terrors either. She could not be damned, she was innocence itself, and anyhow damnation did not exist. The only hells were made by man. Wars. Concentration camps. Environmental devastation. The fire. He would marry his sweetheart in Saint Thomas's in Kuching or he would marry her in a registry office in London or he would not marry her – what could it signify, their two souls already being one? He would take her to India. They would visit temples. Arm in arm, they would wander through overgrown churchyards; they would read the nearly obliterated commemorations of East India Company men and their wives, of navigators and builders, of ayahs and children.

Stephen Chai was useful at first because he had more money than the rest of us put together. In those days, we had got hold of a longboat with an engine that actually went. He very decently bought fuel at the crazy prices people asked. This made getting from bridge to bridge a lot quicker, as you can imagine. But then that engine broke down like the engines before. And now we are nearer the fire, and there are no spare parts, and there are no people to sell anything. We tipped our last cans of diesel over a bridge, it went up like a firework. But they're all dry, they burn.

To be fair, Stephen pulls his weight. We paddle and pole our boat, but on the rivers we're too conspicuous, we keep hearing helicopters just in time to bolt under the cover of the waterside trees. We take to the timber tracks, carrying our kit. Dusty, stifling, smoky – a ghastly business. And the problem is the same, in the logged regions the canopy is too sparse to hide us. The only sure refuge is virgin rain-forest, but it's slow travelling and there isn't enough of it left and it isn't always where we want to go. Odd, but the nearer to the fire you get the safer you are. No one to betray you. And the helicopter pilots don't fly all that close to where it's actually burning. Blessed, protective

smoke ... But I'm sick of breathing it, and we've all got bloodshot eyes.

Nothing like as sick as I am of hearing our padre say that God has visited the conflagration on this pagan island to punish us for our sins, that we now live in this foul greyness and we see this light raging in the sky because for centuries the peoples of Borneo haven't seen his bloody divine light. A trial which is necessary for our salvation, he says. A trial we must strive to be worthy of, he says.

I don't know if anyone has yet been killed by this fire. No intelligence reaches us, and we transmit none. We're all still alive and kicking, though we don't look up to much, all scratches and grime. But I've got close enough to forest in flames to watch the creatures come stampeding through the trees, I've stood the safe side of a river and watched boar and deer come to the far shore and fling themselves into the water, I've seen flocks of birds flee across the sky. In areas where the fire has passed, I've walked among the black rotting bodies of animals burned to death. I've smelled them. I've stood beside Stephen and looked at a monkey's carcass half melted away. Of course, you can't see into the fire, it is a blinding light, it is a mindlessness impregnable to thought. But afterward you can contemplate what it's done, and with a dash of imagination you can conceive its nature, its activity, its effect. Stephen's ability to look at torture and refuse to call it evil, victorious evil, is astonishing. You show the man black, he says he can discern some white in it. A part of God's love which with more pure belief we may come to comprehend, he says. He makes me so angry I could spit. Indeed, Caz told me that the last time I was cursing him to his face, cursing his religion or philosophy or whatever he thinks he's wadded his heart with, she saw the poor fellow wipe his cheek.

It was true, around then his arguments with Chai were getting unpleasantly forceful. With Bernstein, Hugh Blakeney went on having the inconsequential type of conversation they had both enjoyed on his father's verandah. All about the Buddha's thought on the subject of *becoming*, and how interesting it was that Heraclitus, born a generation or two later and at a mighty distance, had similar ideas. Or it might be about the mason wasp which built its mud cells on a longhouse beam and into each cell stuffed lots of green caterpillars for the nourishment of its offspring which would hatch there, while the carpenter bee on the other hand bored a hole into the woodwork. But with Chai . . .

It was not that they didn't acknowledge each other's worth. They had both heard Philip Blakeney recollect in his growl that all that was necessary for evil to triumph was that good men should do nothing, and in that sense they had no trouble recognising one another as good – though the priest would have adjoined that evil's final triumph was not possible. But it seemed they could not leave it at that. Once Hugh Blakeney remarked that it would be no bad thing if the Malaysians or the Indonesians locked him up for a bit. Not for terrifically long, he hoped. But if his report on the fire were written from gaol . . . If his articles on the politics of ecological ruin were also the prison letters of a man convicted for taking action against it . . .

Stephen Chai demurred. He was sure Hugh was correct when he said he could get his cause taken up by Friends of the Earth or whoever it was. Doubtless it was correct too that his allies at *The Sunday Times* or perhaps it was *The Observer* would rush his testimonies into print. But was there not something cynical about his taste for publicity?

That really got the crusader going – on the magnitude of the tragedy, on the need to fight with any weapon you could snatch up. They were sitting on a stony, muddy bank at dusk. Murky river. Grey stones, grey mud. Mosquitoes. Smoke-laden night falling. It was gloomy all right. You had Hugh being coldly eloquent. By then he thought only of the fire. He ate the fire, he breathed the fire. You had Stephen whose calm spirit never budged an inch. You had Cassandra, who gazed at the one and then at the other with her black eyes in which glittered the terror of where God was leading her, the terror of the fire He had led her to. You had Thor, who saw her turn her suffering mind from one of that fine pair of antagonists to the other and back again, like a girl condemned to watch tennis eternally, to watch the senseless ball being whacked senselessly back and forth. Compassionate Thor. He had overheard her pleading with her lover that they should abandon this benighted interior, they should escape from this fire which paralysed her soul with horror, they should flee as normal people had fled, it was madness to remain. Yes, and he had intuited that she was as afraid of Hugh Blakeney's fixation as of its object. And he had heard his friend's cheerful refusal to run away.

It's more or less bearable when you're in the forest. You can't see. But when you come out of the trees . . .

How could you not love Hugh Blakeney? Admire him, love him, want to stand beside him. If he had hardnesses, he had fewer than most of the righteous. And then his pride in his father's confidence in him! and his being so in love with his opportunity! For he may have appeared to sit aboard longboats with Cassandra Matlaske, to trudge along forest paths with her, to set fire to bridges not exactly with her, because generally he would send her back on some pretext or other when he went forward . . . But several of his companions in that idealistic business came to the conclusion that his cardinal love was his opportunity to do good. To take action, however inadequate, however long too late, however consolatory. When he was underfed and unshaven, when he was hunted as a criminal, when he was bedevilled by a priest who informed him that God was omnipotent and God was love and that – this was the last straw – before God he couldn't have his girl even if he stood up to hell-fire and got her clear away from it . . . Even then, Hugh's overriding passion was for his chance. In his apparently all-conquering enemy's array, he had identified a weak point where even one man alone might strike: bridges . . . His opportunity was the spirit bride who sat veiled beside him on board those leaking longboats, and Cassandra knew it, that was the appalling thing. *The fire first* . . . Had he not written that to her? The scrap of love letter which had made her happy became a knell she couldn't forget.

I had seen what the lumber companies left, I had seen the eroded hills and the clogged rivers, seen the wet season floods and landslides, seen the dry season dust bowls and dust clouds, the country surveyed, razed, made ugly and valueless now. I had witnessed how this great, beautiful island which had never acted much on the world's stage was being acted upon. What had started with Malay control of the

river mouths and therefore of trade, what had started with a bit of bully-boy extortion, had progressed by my day. I had seen the desolation left by increasingly efficient plundering, seen the rapacious souls of the coastal Christian and Muslim bourgeoisie mirrored in the inner desert they made.

Remember when the forests provided the tribes with their game and their fruit and their medicines, with their materials for building and for craftsmanship. Remember when Dayak civil and religious law was the only law. Remember when land was revered because it held the graves of the dead.

But now when you come out of the trees, when you see what the fire has done ... The desecration, Philip! Hills of ash, valleys of ash. Emptiness, the inane. . . The charred, putrefying creatures. The whole world black and grey, fuming. No sunlight of course. Clouds of ash blowing, blowing ... Then on the horizon, which is a lot nearer than it ought to be, a black pall where the fire is burning now, and miles of flame erupting into the sky. Yes, it is horribly beautiful. Forest trees blazing like flambeaux send gouts of flame hundreds of feet into the air, they are towers of fire. I remember you saying that in the forests time could feel eerily abstract. But here now it is almost impossible to conceive of time at all. There are no events, no leopards mate, no minivets nest and sing, even the termites have been eliminated. On these ash plains and ash ranges where among the black stumps of trees you stumble on the sooty mess that was a monitor lizard decaying where it burned alive, nothing happens except that the wind drifts the ashen air this way, that way. I remember you saying that in the forests' rustling shade the sense of oblivion could descend on your mind with an awesome suddenness and power, transience could seem to triumph more effortlessly and more totally than elsewhere. But now even the coming of oblivion has been transformed utterly. The living do not lie down to die in the green forest shadows, that is no longer the world which at death is forgotten and forgets. Ash, Philip.

No indication in that fire journal that the writer was afraid. No indication in his behaviour either. Well, probably he was not afraid. And as for Cassandra's fears . . . Sooner or later the *landas* would blow, the rains would fall. The fire would die down. On the journey back to Kuching he would have time to cheer the girl up.

No, in that second notebook addressed to *Dear Philip* he just went on talking to his father in his usual tone of voice. Naturally they did not live in the ash country, although occasionally they risked traversing a burned region as fast as they might before returning to the harbouring trees. It was uninhabitable, no men or animals or birds lived there – though it was repellent how soon vermin appeared to feed on the carrion, how maggots reappeared. But in deserted longhouses, at forest camps, at river camps, he would write in the smoky evenings.

Of course, he knew the kind of Bornean chat Philip liked, and he wanted to please him – and beyond doubt the unaltered state of his relations with his father was a strength to him. So alongside soldierly talk about which tributary of the Belayan river they had fired a bridge on the day before, he recollected how in 1878 after five months of drought the botanist Burbidge steaming toward Sandakan saw jungle fires along the coast, how the monsoon was dead against them, they met native craft flying before it laden with pearl-shell and *bêche-de-mer* for the markets of Brunei. That journal was the last utterance in the dialogue between father and son. It was a silent calling from the heart of the island to the outside.

Did Philip remember how one night in 1706 at Banjarmasin – *was* it at Banjarmasin? – the Sultan and three thousand warriors burned the English settlement? They had deserved it, by all accounts: a haughty, invasive bunch. The English retreated to their four ships anchored in the bay, but only two vessels got away to sea. The others were attacked by the war *prahus*, set alight. Their crews were burned, except for those who swam off and were butchered or made slaves.

Did Philip remember how the little tarsier could turn its head not, as the Dayaks would tell you, right round, but through half a circle? So that if it were clinging to a vertical surface it could, without moving anything but its neck, look straight back into your face if you were standing directly behind it. The last act of the naming which he had learned from his father, those scrawlings of Hugh Blakeney's. The tarsier, the loris, the Sunda shrew . . . Burned, burned. The fruit bat and the horseshoe bat, the grey leaf-monkey and the silvered leaf-monkey. All of them, it seemed he had to mourn. The gibbons and the porcupines and the pangolins, the otters and the martens and the civets, the squirrels and the rats . . .

He was true to himself, his voice didn't change. Except right on the last page he scribbled a few sentences that made you think maybe the strain was beginning to tell.

I see you everywhere. I see you crossing and recrossing the island, looking for Nerissa. That search of yours haunts me. I see you travelling, endlessly travelling. Stopping to ask, to be disappointed. Going on. What Borneo did you find? In your head what did you find?

No help to Cassandra, evening talk about how the tribes used to stun fish with a narcotic made from a plant they called *tuba*, how they pulped the roots in water which became white, they bailed this potent froth from their craft into a river, the stupefied fish floated to the surface where they could be speared. No protection, talk about how the white Rajah's government used to pay a reward of thirty cents per foot for every crocodile killed. No consolation, the famous python which was twenty-two feet long; the hamadryad which measured twelve feet; the snake called *Chrysopelea ornata* which at the turn of the century the naturalist Shelford discovered had hinged ventral scales which it could contract and thus make its underside concave, which explained how it could glide out from a tree – he experimentally hurled his specimen from the verandah at Kuching Museum. Information no longer stabilised her world. In the interior where Philip Blakeney had felt that facts could exist with disconcerting faintness, now she too was bereft of knowledge. Her old certainties no longer composed her. She was entering into her inexistence, it had begun.

If God exists, my soul is married to yours, her brother and lover had written from Singapore. *If God doesn't exist, my soul is married to yours*, he had written – the man with whom at night she made love and then terrified herself when she realised she was not terrified it was a sin. Her Christian faith was rooted deep; but it was now, when faced with a myriad creatures burned to death, that Cassandra began to understand Philip's unappeasable despair. Yes, Bernstein was right, it was grim the way she was being torn apart. Between belief in the sacraments of the Church and belief in the sacrament of two human hearts. Between evil ordained by God and evil ordained by man. Between torture called only a temporal evil, torture permitted by Our Lord as part of the mystery of our salvation and therefore in some sense good, and torture called nothing but evil. Even then, when they were still resisting the fire, she was not much more than rags and tatters. And that tooth of her faith had healthy roots . . .

She had followed what she had believed to be God's pillar of fire. Now here they were, cut off from the outside world, in an isolation made of logged forests and burned forests, made of foul water, foul air. And she had seen Hugh tackle the fire and it had horrified her. She had watched Thor and him clearing fire-breaks at the heads of bridges – since they had run out of fuel for their chain-saw they had thrown it away, they used axes. With a belabouring heart and a dry mouth she had watched how, with the greater fire advancing its black and red fury of death across the country toward them, methodically they lit their lesser fires. She had watched them as in their filthy clothes they fell back across their burning bridges. She had watched the posts and planks flare up and be consumed till there remained only a few charred uprights in the brown flowing water like the ruin of a weir.

Cassandra Matlaske saw the fire by day and by night. She dreamed of the fire at night. Like her father or her adoptive father before her, she prayed to be released from the interior, released from the swaddling cocoon of her helplessness. But Hugh was immoveable, he smiled at her fears. Was there not work still to be done, a fight to put up? The enemy might be outflanked here, held up there. When the rains came, they would be free to go home.

Christians and Muslims, animists and sceptics, all alike besought the heavens for rain. But it seemed the heavens had changed, they were no longer their old selves, they were ash and smoke. No rain fell. Or if it fell it was a mockery, for an hour it splattered ash, then nothing again.

Cassandra was condemned to unknowing. *If God exists . . . If God doesn't exist . . .* Her mind had come to hinge on the word *if*, it was crazy but it was so, *if* was the fulcrum of the universe. *If . . .*

She was condemned to be patient, to await the fire's pleasure. If God would only have mercy, would send rain . . . ! When Hugh was asleep, Cassandra lay awake beside him, she prayed to comprehend why God had led her to this doubt. And why were Hugh and she shackled to this fire which tortured and reduced to cinders, to this fire which existed but into which her thoughts could not penetrate, this evil which was unknowable but true? They were not salamanders, they could not live in fire, by fire.

Why would Hugh not believe her when she pleaded with him that they were in mortal danger? It was not loving of him, it was not kind. Why would he not yield to her when she pleaded that they had done enough, they had done more than anyone else, they might escape now? It was not natural, he was possessed. She felt bound hand and foot in ignorance, her horror had clamped hard on her mind, it would not let go. What did the fire mean? What was it whispering devilishly to Hugh? What was it saying to her?

To be reborn out of this miasma, to go free . . . ! Some nights Cassandra dreamed of rain, of clean rain. She dreamed of the sea with its deep blue translucency, of sea winds salt and pure.

Away from the fire they would go, down clean rivers. In the mornings they would wake to the dew sparkling on palm fronds, to golden mist wreathing on the water, to birds which sang. The camps they pitched at evening would be ever farther from the ash lands and closer to Philip.

In Cassandra's dreams, day by day their longboat drifted with the current toward the China Sea. Sometimes idly Hugh and she plied their paddles, sometimes they just steered.

Through green forests, attended by kingfishers . . . *As they did in the golden world . . .*

5

Thor Bernstein dreamed of the sea too, by day, by night. Condemned to dust and mud, condemned to tumid rivers and dry river beds, condemned to sweltering ash and smoke, he longed for his island hermitage.

It was not a desire likely to be satisfied. They were being pursued, he suspected, only in a desultory way. Why should the military police risk unnecessary dangers? Hugh and Cassandra and the others and he were like deer whose coverts were being destroyed; sooner or later they would have to come out into the open. All the Indonesians on one side of the island and the Malaysians on the other had to do was wait.

But to get back to the coast of Sabah and gaze out to the little islands in the offing which seemed to float suspended like mirages, in his dinghy to set forth over the strait toward his freedom, his peace . . . ! To return to that blue sea, that blue sky . . . ! Bernstein remembered schooners' sails. He remembered a sea snake the fishermen had told him was dangerous but which had been of a beauty to make you catch your breath, blue-black barred with gold, but a sailor shot it and the wounded creature swam down, down into the darker blues. He remembered coming inshore to the river mouth aboard a fishing-smack when the tide was low and they ran aground on the bar. He jumped into the lumpy yellow sea with the other men, set his shoulder to their barnacled hull. Heaving and splashing they stumbled forward over the sandy shoal, and the others knew when to hang onto the gunwale, but he went down into the suddenly shelving depth like a drowning man. Then the river lay tranquil, glinting in the sun; it was good to come to the *kampong* houses built on stilts, to *sampans* toing and froing, kapok trees, sea-teak trees. He remembered lightning which played on the horizon all night, phosphorescence such that when you rowed the oars stirred molten silver and you left a silver wake. He remembered how, when sailing off Borneo, you always had to be ready for a squall. Far off you saw clouds the colour of slate. The first cats' paws of a chill breeze reached you. That was when you struck sail, left your vessel under bare poles, let her run rocking wildly through the combers and scudding spindrift before the gale of wind and rain.

Week after week, the man who had loathed the idea that he might become a member of a team toiled beside his fellow outlaws. He had long since given up wondering whether or not indifference was a virtue, though he noticed that being indifferent to what you were doing did not stop you doing it dependably. He had given up his old watching and listening, his patient attention to what notions came and went or remained to haunt him, perhaps to be him. He no longer hoped that on a Sulu Sea island or on a Bornean mountain he might isolate the rhythms of thought intrinsic to him, less extrinsic than others to him. He was too tired to do much hoping. When he heard helicopters above the trees, he recalled that this was not the first time the world had come after him. This was not going to be the first violation of a fastness, not the first time he was routed out.

Had none of the others understood how paltry were their successes? Had no one but he realised the inanity of their struggle? Paddling ash-blackened rivers with aching arms, Thor Bernstein remembered gliding his skiff into mangrove swamps at high tide, how white egrets rose from the shallows, how you slid past the arched roots in the dappled sunlight, in the lapping quietness you cast your net. Wielding his axe to hack a fire-break, he stopped for a moment, he straightened his back, mopped his forehead. In his mind, he paced the pure pale sand of his retreat. His feathery casuarinas sighed, his sea-almonds fluttered their green and russet leaves. Turquoise ripples whispered. High overhead, a white sea-eagle soared.

Restless toward nightfall, often Bernstein would stroll away from their camps alone. The chatter around the cooking-fire bored him. Hugh Blakeney's and Stephen Chai's convictions dispirited him. So, for half an hour, solitude.

The last evening he slipped away it was into primary forest. They were close to the fire, you could see it across the country on the other side of the river, the air was horrible to breathe. The day had been miserable – hours of slogging at their paddles. Higher up-river there was thought to be a logging bridge which they wanted to reach tomorrow before the fire reached it; they would be afloat again at dawn.

But now, a respite. Perhaps his old expectancy would return to him, his openness when the sea-light had washed in and out of his mind. He walked into the columns, the green shade. He remembered how the forests had been sanctuaries, how his immaculate hermitage's trees had felt like a civilisation, a quietude, threatened by barbarians. Why did people have to be so avid to master and to destroy, so damned interested? Still, it was pleasant again to be alone for a while in the primeval peace even if it did reek of burning. Back amidst what he had imagined to be an old disdain, a poise – well anyhow, amidst the indifference of nature which he had always found congenial. Student of religious rituals that he had been, of the tribes' rites for the planting of rice and for its harvesting, rites for the welcoming of a freshly severed head to a longhouse, rites for birth and marriage and death, he had come to feel that the most sad thing about the devastation of the forests of Borneo and the obliteration of the life which had been conducted in their shadows was the loss of religions. To each land its native people, to each people their native gods . . . Idealism, maybe – but was this not best? Walking, Thor Bernstein shrugged, he shook his head. Mere sentimentality. Perhaps no way of life, no stitching together of amorphous experience with observances and beliefs, was so valuable that its annihilation should be much grieved for. But all the same . . .

Straying through the trees with his hands in his pockets, not going anywhere in particular, he mourned for the past before graveyards had been bulldozed for logging tracks, before sacred groves had been chain-sawed, the past when certain ancient trees were revered as holy, certain rocks were shrines and you found them garlanded. He mourned the carved images set around a longhouse to ward off evil – they hadn't stopped the loggers, they weren't stopping the fire, but even so . . . He remembered how some tribes would enthrone the dead for whom they were keening, would bind them to a rapidly constructed death seat. They surrounded the corpse with worldly goods like brass pots and shotguns and transistor radios without batteries, furnished it with coins and sweetmeats and cigarettes, decked it with finery. Memories . . . Decades after the people had abandoned Long Miri, in his anthropologist days he had sought out the graveyard which had been a famous one, where were sepulchred the great Tama Tiri and his followers. From the river he had made out the mausoleums where they still stood – very durable wood, belian – among the encroaching trees. He had scrambled up the shore to the place of the ancestors. Massive mausoleums on five thick pillars, loftier ones on two pillars only. The jars were there, cut at the shoulder so the bodies could be inserted, sealed again with dammar. Not hard to imagine that the forgotten indigenous gods and goddesses were there too. Or maybe not. When a world went, its spirits went. *Anima mundi* was ephemeral.

Bernstein sat down, leaned his back against a tree. Of course often the extinction of a people and its spirits wasn't sad in a romantic way like the tombs above Long Miri. It was just sad. Messy . . . He remembered Newington's report of how in 1912 he came upon the last of the Tabuns, a dying race. The old chief had expired a few weeks before, but they still had him in the longhouse, sitting in a large jar the neck of which had been removed. He squatted with his knees up to his chin – what was left of him. A lot of his flesh had gone. They had stopped his eye sockets with boiled rice. He was noisome, but family life was going on all around him. The juices of his putrescence ran from the bottom of the jar through a bamboo tube, dripped to the soil beneath the house where the pigs were rootling.

But still . . . Under his tree, Thor Bernstein grieved. This fire was an auto-da-fé, but they weren't burning the local heretics, they were burning the local gods. And now in the evening below the leafy canopy he was sad for the forgotten myths, the beliefs or illusions with which people had made sense or nonsense of their lives. Innocent enough. Almost, if he harked to soughings and flitterings, if he gazed into shadows . . . Almost, he could sense the last of the genii ghosting away through the trees.

He started. Cassandra was walking toward him.

She too had thought herself alone. She approached him hesitantly, she smiled. 'You were dreaming. Shall I leave you in peace?'

Thor had never been indifferent to Cassandra, he was not now. He shook his head, he met her smile. She sat down by him on the forest floor.

As if it were the most natural thing in the world to resume an exchange of theirs of weeks before, an understanding broken off before it could grow, musingly he asked her, 'To go free . . . ?'

She turned toward him her face which was blotchy white with tiredness, which was framed by hair that had been lustrous but was lank now. 'And you . . . ? Don't you regret promising me you'd come to the fire?'

'No.' His brown eyes smiled into her serious, black-eyed questioning. 'I don't regret anything.'

'I've often been afraid you did.' Her smile was the most hesitant he had ever seen. 'You seem very abstracted, sometimes. I've thought you might wander away. One morning you would say goodbye. And off you'd go, you'd vanish on some adventure of your own, on some pilgrimage only you knew about.' She appeared to be scrutinising his shaggy hair, the beard he had grown. 'Tell me . . . When you think of freedom, what do you think of?'

'Oh . . . ' Once more the waves of weariness were breaking in his mind. 'These days I suspect that if I ever emerge into freedom it'll be useless to me. If after all this ridiculous fire-fighting . . . ' His voice was too harsh, he tried to make his mockery more gentle. 'If I get locked up, or I get slung out of Borneo – into a new freedom? into a new desolation? – who shall I be?'

She was grave. 'I believe you'll be who you are. A marvellous man.'

Thor's lips twisted. To sound a more cheerful note, he said, 'I think of Philip. He's the only man I know that I'd call free. After years of suffering . . . He's freed himself a little from himself.'

'You're right!' Her eyes shone. 'Yes, yes! Trust you to understand.'

'And you, Cassandra?' He smiled. 'But,' he added gently, 'you have your Church.'

She gave a flutter of laughter, but when she spoke her words were unsteady. 'I don't have my Church anything like as much as you think. Stephen talks to me about what he calls his spiritual anguish, but I don't reckon he knows what the words mean. Unburden your heart to me, he says – things like that. I say No. He urges. I scream No.' In her soft voice, her pain jarred. 'I don't think much about the Church any more.' Her wan cheeks flushed hectic. Thor tried to swallow the pity clogging his throat. 'But I think about God all the time. I'm in the palm of God's hand.' Her laughter came shrill, staccato. 'In God's hand! But it's not a good place, it's not a safe place. I thought it was. But sometimes I can see His fingers curling up, Thor, I'm going to be gripped! He'll throttle the spirit out of me!'

His mouth drawn hard, ugly, he set his hand on her knee. 'Cassandra, you mustn't be afraid.' What comfort could he think of? 'The fire will die down. You'll be married. It'll be all right. I'm going to be Hugh's best man, remember?'

'*Hugh!*' It was a shriek for mercy. 'How can I renounce him? How can I know if God demands that I should renounce him?' Feverishly her eyes glittered. One of her hands scrabbled at the leaf-mould, flung the dust away into the gloaming. 'How can I know anything? There is no truth! None – do you understand? How can I tell Hugh that I can't marry him, I mustn't be his?' She was choking. 'Is it nothingness which has got hold of my soul?'

Thor knelt beside her, put his arms around her shoulders. 'Shh,' he murmured. He rocked her. 'Shh.'

Against his chest she wept her words. 'How can I forget this mad idea of God? I love and I cannot love, I believe and I cannot believe! How can I ever go free?'

'No God worthy of your love could want you to be this unhappy,' the sceptic said. And then, 'Think of happy things. Think of India.'

Cassandra sat up straight. Thor was relieved to see that she was trying to pull herself together. For some moments he looked away, he gave her time. It was nearly night, they ought to go back to their river camp.

But when he turned back, her eyes were too bright, her lovely mouth was warped. 'If I have to renounce Hugh . . . ' Her voice had ugly quaverings. 'If I have to give up everything I've loved . . . '

In his distress, Thor stood up. He reached for her hand, raised her to her feet. 'It's late, Cassandra. Let's go. And don't give up anything. It's a bad idea.'

Her eyes lifted to the forest canopy where the darkness was gathering, she breathed her prayer very softly. 'At least let me bear Hugh's child.'

They walked in silence. It was not until they came in sight of the camp fire that she gave a light, bitter laugh.

'Our child, Hugh's and mine . . . Our child for me to carry away wherever I go, to love whoever I become. Hugh's child, for me to be proud of.'

The usual drill at a bridge was to clear a fire-break on the safe shore. Then at the dangerous end of the bridge, where the fire was going to come, they set the planks alight. The bridge burned from the dangerous end back to the safe end in a nice controlled manner. The band of malefactors, looking like a troupe of piebald and skewbald clowns on account of the smuts, waited in the fire-break to beat out any sparks that flew across. Simple. But on this occasion they had come wearily paddling round the last bend too late to cut a line to hold, so they decided to smash down the bridge with their axes, starting at the dangerous end, of course, where any minute now the trees would be on fire.

It wasn't much of a defence, that river. Less than a hundred yards wide, the brown current flowed low between its mud slopes on account of the drought. But there was no mistaking its value as the meandering and sluggish and unclean division between the indifference which would let you live and the indifference which would not.

Of course on the untouched bank the air was nauseating to breathe, and you heard the fire; but for all that there lay an extraordinary calm, there was an unmovedness. Swags of creeper dozens of feet long hung from the boughs without a tremor. Even now it was difficult to imagine that this repose was not immutable. Hugh had told Kadir to wait aboard the longboat with the kit – it was going to be vital for them all to get quickly away – and sitting there he had a stolid, enduring look to him. On a fallen tree a big lizard crouched, stared at the men who were scrambling up toward the bridge, stared at the young woman with them who stopped, for a moment gazed back at that scaly head, immobile except for the tongue which flicked. Not a frond fluttered. A butterfly alit on a fern, was still. Hurrying after the others, Cassandra glanced back. The lizard had not stirred. Nor had the butterfly. Even the twigs and leaves she had trodden on seemed to lie once more with an enchanted stillness. While before her, beyond that narrow flowing separation, across that ribband of saving water . . .

Up-stream, the trees stood green and somnolent. There apparent eternity remained; the air would be moist. Down-stream, the river shore was a roaring palisade of flame. At a great height, in the clouds of smoke, wheeling birds preyed on the swarms of insects the conflagration had driven up.

It wasn't much of a bridge. Spindly piles stuck crooked in the river-bed, piles the multiplicity of which had been intended to compensate for their individual lack of strength and fixity. No guard-rail. Some beams missing. If you had been required to drive a truck across it, you would first have demanded repairs – tearing the bridge-head ramp balk from balk Thor Bernstein's thoughts were getting disjointed, that was one of the more consequential.

But if you had to chop it down with an axe, that bridge was monumental. If in a world abruptly limited to a few yards of heat and smoke you had to hack at those planks, they had a hardness . . . ! That ramshackle obstruction to the free flow of the water, that line of weakness which would betray one forest to the fate of the other, seemed to have been made by master-builders, made to last for all time. The joists had been lashed across the posts, and even the ropes could take a couple of blows to cut before the timbers could be heaved to fall into the river.

With the tumult of the flames, they had to yell in each other's ears to be heard. Burning branches were crashing down. The heat beat them back, they were a few paces out over the water when Thor realised they might be going to lose the bridge to the fire. Unless they could demolish a good big section in the next minute or two, they would end up pelting away from the advancing flames.

Working back joist after joist, Hugh and he bellowed words like, 'Now!' 'Pull!' 'Right!' His throat felt raw. His eyes streamed. His mind would concentrate on one beam, he would know nothing but its weight, its grain, its awkwardness – but then his feckless ideas went skittering away. He thought that really he must write to his mother more often, though he doubted whether in her senility she knew if he wrote or not. 'Back!' Hugh's axe flashed, the bridge under Thor's feet tilted, he fell, on hands and knees scrambled away. He thought, The last thing I must do is fall off this damned thing.

Then again Hugh and he were slashing at knotted ropes, they were struggling to manhandle a beam away. He was aware of Hugh's blackened face, blackened hands. Perhaps he would let himself write to Keiko-san. No, better not. Thud, thud, of his axe. Was there beginning to be a useful gap between the fire and them? He thought, I must be sweating like a pig, but my clothes are dry. Then he heard Hugh shout to Cassandra to go to the boat.

She refused to go without him. For a few seconds they howled at one another in a demented kind of way. It wasn't pleasant, in the scorching air, in the eddying smoke. Then Hugh ordered Nazim and Stephen to take her away. 'Drag her!' were the last words they heard him call.

It took those two all their strength to haul Cassandra back to the safe bridge-head. Down the mud slope to the waiting boat she would not go. It was ugly, those poor wretches grappling with the fighting, screaming girl.

We need those men here, Thor thought, why can't she go quietly? Then he noticed how Hugh, once he knew Cassandra was safe, never glanced back. Faced by the fire, choked by the fire, his energy was ferocious. In his soot-caked, singed shirt and trousers, his arms and legs kept bending, straightening, bending, straightening. His lips open, he was gulping the fire's air. Thor wondered if he was as singleminded as he looked. *No* distracting fears, stray ideas, phantasms? With his last ounces of strength, he kept his axe-blows falling as fast and as hard as Hugh's.

They must have demolished fifteen yards of bridge, Thor guessed. Maybe twenty. Not enough. He bowed his head again, concentrated on where his axe was coming down, saw Hugh's arms lifting a beam.

'Christ! I'm sorry!' Thor yelled, seeing blood rinse down Hugh's wrist. 'Are you all right?'

But he must have jerked back just in time. It must have been a glancing blow. Hugh hadn't stopped heaving. He shouted, 'Yes!'

Then before their eyes some big trees started to fall, to bring down other trees . . .

Kadir saw it all. First there were Hugh and Thor, in the red shuddering light and the swirling blackness, swinging their axes like devils. Then the spars of flame fell where they were, sparks volcanoed up. Nazim and Stephen let go of Cassandra, all three ran forward into the smoke where Thor had staggered clear.

Kadir watched Nazim and Stephen dance with mad gesticulations at the edge of the blaze. He watched Thor grab up an axe, saw Cassandra and him dash into the burning.

Out of the fire on the bridge ran a man and a woman in flaming clothes. They leaped into the water.

6 ∫

'I protest by your rejoicing, which I have in Christ Jesus Our Lord, I die daily.' Stephen Chai's voice was even, though it rang with a harshness which was new. His eyes looked as if he had forgotten sleep. *'If after the manner of men I have fought with beasts at Ephesus, what advantageth it me, if the dead rise not? Let us eat and drink, for tomorrow we die. Be not deceived: evil communications corrupt good manners. Awake to righteousness, and sin not; for some have not the knowledge of God. I speak this to your shame.'*

Brown river before, green forest behind. A scruffy up-country settlement: dilapidated bazaar, wharf, impoverished houses, godowns. Smoky sky. A tiny church of white planks with a shingle roof. In the earth around, a few wooden crosses of the simplest making.

'Now this I say, brethren, that flesh and blood cannot inherit the kingdom of God; neither doth corruption inherit incorruption. Behold, I shew you a mystery: We shall not all sleep, but we shall all be changed, in a moment, in the twinkling of an eye, at the last trump (for the trumpet shall sound), and the dead shall be raised incorruptible, and we shall be changed. For this corruptible must put on incorruption, and this mortal shall put on immortality. So when this corruptible shall have put on incorruption, and this mortal shall have put on immortality; then shall be brought to pass the saying that is written, Death is swallowed up in victory.'

At first, Stephen's care had been for the living. With Nazim's and Kadir's help he had hauled them from the water. He had wrapped them in wet towels, laid them in the longboat. His relief that Cassandra and Thor were alive at once became fear that they would die. Their hair had burned, their faces were mottled red and white, were blistered – how much smoke and burning air had they inhaled? They coughed soot. How long could he keep them breathing? And patches of their heads and hands, of their chests and arms were blistered brown and black, and did not seem to hurt like the red patches, this meant all the skin and nerves were gone, didn't it? Chai's lack of medical knowledge maddened him. In the medicine box he found a little morphine, that was good. But would they die of fluid loss? Of shock? The fire crossed the bridge, soon the longboat was making its escape down a corridor between walls of flame. He praised God for the morphine, but even with it their sufferings were ghastly to see and to hear – and how long would the morphine last? While Nazim and Kadir paddled, Stephen consulted the maps. To get away from the fire! Away from these ash lands, out of this labyrinth of rivers! Where was the nearest doctor, where was civilisation? His next fear was that in the medicine box there were nothing like enough antibiotics. He swathed them in the cleanest cloths he had. And surely all that wet, half-destroyed tissue would become infected within hours, let alone days. In this heat, in this filth, corruption would enter their blood.

It was at this settlement where Chai was now reading the service for the burial of the dead that he had written a short letter to Philip Blakeney, had entrusted it and his two patients and Hugh's second journal to the regional doctor to take farther down-river to a town where aeroplanes came. From here Nazim and Kadir and he had returned two days up-river for the dead – two days with an engine for which he had paid double its worth. Not much hope that they would find what might remain of Hugh Blakeney. But they did. Where the fire had left its nothingness. Among the charred trees and charred bridge posts, mud and water and ash. A shapeless black festering thing which had been a man.

No, it was no wonder that Stephen Chai looked haggard. He had lifted that dreadful burden in his arms, had baled it in a tarpaulin, brought it back down the river. His last labour had been to help dig the grave. He must give the atheist decent burial, some farewell, some obsequy.

'Man that is born of a woman hath but a short time to live, and is full of misery. He cometh up, and is cut down, like a flower; and he fleeth as it were a shadow, and never continueth in one stay.

'In the midst of life we are in death: of whom may we seek for succour, but of Thee, O Lord, who for our sins art justly displeased.'

There wasn't much of a congregation. The local priest, a young Dayak, who had lent Chai a simple vestment. He had lodged him in his bungalow too, for that matter, had lent him clothes, had with his own scissors given him a hair-cut. The local policeman, who happily knew nothing about public enemies, who was a Christian and was impressed by the priest from the cathedral in far-away Kuching who had endured horrific trials in the *Ulu*, who had brought down the river his wounded to heal and his dead to bury, who had insisted on committing to police paper with an official stamp on it an account of scarcely credible events – the survivor had decided that only the exact truth would be tolerable. A few pious souls from the settlement who had nothing urgent to do that overcast, sweltering afternoon. Kadir, who had been brought up in an Iban longhouse supposedly converted to Protestantism but who had the haziest notions of doctrine – it hadn't occurred to him that Hugh Blakeney's sufferings might not be at an end. Nazim Bokhari, who of course had been brought up as a Muslim, who certainly should not have attended the service. But he had fought the fire beside Hugh too long to turn aside from him now. He stood furthest from the grave, at the outer rim of the small group. In his bitterness remembering the Koran, perhaps. *Enjoy your unbelief a while; but the Fire shall be your home.*

As for a sermon, most people vaguely expected the expression of dutiful hopes customary when arrant sinners were committed to sacred earth, the customary mealy-mouthed evasion of the issue, a few words about what a splendid fellow the dead unbeliever had been. It would be short, anyhow, which was good, the preacher had no notes. One or two members of the congregation felt that under the circumstances it might have been better to say nothing, just stick to the sentences printed in the Prayer Book. And afterward when Kadir with tears running down his cheeks was shovelling clods into the grave, when Nazim had suddenly found it necessary to walk away on his own, there were those who suspected it was lucky that neither the bishop of Kuching nor the deacon nor anyone with a nose sensitive to sniff out unorthodoxy had been listening.

True, the Dayak parson was there. But if he heard any heresy he kept his counsel, perhaps out of pity for the tormented spirit he had housed. Anyway, it appeared that Stephen Chai was not quite so half dead as he looked, had a bit of fight left in him. He seemed aware of a challenge to take up. Not that it was much of a sermon, really – in some ways more of a prayer, or an asking. He took as his text some words from *Job: Shall we receive good at the hand of God, and shall we not receive evil?*

Chai began by saying bluntly that Hugh Blakeney was an atheist. He would have been just as content to be buried among his fellow men if they were of any faith or no faith. He would perhaps have been happiest to lie under the greenwood tree. But he, the speaker, was a Christian priest, and it was more than he was capable of to deny the dead man any portion of sanctity which might comfort his forlorn soul. There was also, he would explain for the benefit of those who did not know the circumstances of Hugh's life, this consideration. He had been engaged to marry a young lady of impeccable Christianity who would undoubtedly wish her fiancé to be given a Church funeral. He invited the congregation to remember before God that afflicted soul and her friend who also had been cruelly burned in the attempt to save Hugh, who now in hospital were still in danger of death. He urged all present to pray that they should be cured, to pray especially for Cassandra Matlaske to whose agony of body had been added – Chai lowered his eyes to the roughly fashioned coffin – terrible agony of heart.

Her impeccable Christianity? But you could forgive him that. Had he not suffered with her in what he knew of her anguish? Hardly his fault that he had not guessed its depth, which she hid from him. He believed that when the crisis was resolved her serenity would return. And you couldn't not like Stephen Chai that grey, sweaty afternoon by the pit in the earth. He stood by Hugh and Cassandra very well. Listening, it was impossible not to think he came clean, came nobly clean. Not that he got much in the way of thanks or recognition afterward; though when he was back in Kuching he and Philip Blakeney remained on good terms. On friendly terms . . . Scarcely exchanging a word . . . In a silence which shook with abstract screams till you wanted to weld your hands over your ears. Well, it didn't last.

When the preacher raised his eyes from the grave, for several seconds he was quiet. People thought that maybe he had finished with the death of Hugh Blakeney. But then he asked once more: *Shall we receive good at the hand of God, and shall we not receive evil?* He said that in easy times it was even conceivable that God might smile on our slack way with our faith in His truth, but that . . . His voice was low, he spoke the sentence with a curious humility. In his opinion, times of fire called for truth of fire, for clarity.

Stephen Chai *had* finished with the burial of the dead – you got that impression distinctly. But what was far more plain, in the meditation or whatever it was that followed, in his expression of his dread and his wonder, was that he was talking to the spirit of the dead man, to that immortal essence in which he believed but Hugh had not. He kept fixing his eyes on those of the congregation who had known Hugh, trying to convince them of something perhaps, or trying to learn from them. Then he would look over their heads, appear to see or imagine a spirit there, address his old antagonist directly as if to continue their discussions. Or as if to give proof of some quality they both had hoped to embody which was far more important than the mere chance of their like or dislike for one another, an immanence more true-hearted than any wrangling. Yes, as if to bear witness to some hope. His voice was gentle. He hesitated between his sentences.

He just had a few observations to make, Chai said, a few questions to ask which the fire had seemed to ask him. In mild times, people let themselves believe pretty much what they fancied. That was his experience – and he had grown up in mild times, gone to theological college and taken holy orders in mild times. Most of us took to our hearts a mish-mash of the Church's doctrines and called ourselves Christians. We had faith in God, even if we rarely pondered our grounds for this, or asked ourselves what we had faith in the Almighty to be or to do and why. Faith in God – the vast, simple concept seemed to cover our case. With the excuse of our mortal ignorance, we left it at that. We hoped for grace. We believed in the redeeming power of charity – we had to, existence would be unbearable if we did not. But for the rest . . . We grew slack, undemanding of ourselves. For instance, a lot of people let themselves believe in heaven but not in hell, which not only was bad logic but was in contravention of what Christ's Church had taught for centuries.

But now . . . Now we lived in times of fire, and he felt the need to face the starkness of the spiritual choices the fire confronted us with. He had seen burned to death a brave man trying to fight evil. He had seen the survivors disfigured, survivors no less brave and no less good. He had seen the believer and the unbeliever tortured; he had heard their cries; he did not think God intended him to forget their cries.

A sceptic such as Hugh Blakeney had been, and a Christian such as he himself hoped he was, could agree that man was free to choose between good and evil, though for Hugh the matter had ended there, while for him there stretched a further dimension, which was that Our Lord had created this freedom for us so that we might work out our salvation. Still, that the one thing of supreme importance that went on in this world was the battle between good and evil they had agreed. And they had both tried to be on the right side. He would be the last man to affirm that they had always succeeded – but he thought he could vouch for the intention. Likewise the question of whether they had achieved anything, either of them, whether they had done any good . . . This too he would leave to one side.

He was not concerned today with evil which was the consequence of the abuse of our freedom, which issued from hearts which had lost sight of good or lost the strength to cleave to it. The question around which his mind had come to circle like a moth around a flame was evil which was no one's choice, Job's evil which we receive at the hand of God. Evil which seemed innate in creation. The sufferings of little children. Evil which simply *was* . . .

This was the question, Chai said, which it seemed to him the fire asked. He had no brilliant answers, but he begged them to bear with him in his questioning.

When he saw the fire, what had he seen? For the sceptic, the world was as it appeared – at least, this was the sort of existentialism Hugh Blakeney had professed. If you saw a child sicken and die that was the whole truth, in this case evil had been victorious over good. For the Christian, the appearance was only the appearance, and although it was often sickeningly cruel there existed a deeper, spiritual reality too. At the unfathomable heart of all occurrences lay God's truth; and that eternal truth, though it might go masked in temporal evil, was ultimately good. So, at any rate, he believed, though in these last days the hideous sufferings he had witnessed, the apparent triumph of evil he had witnessed, had made his soul cling to faith in the final victory of good with a belief more tenacious than ever before.

Chai swallowed. He seemed to have difficulty in beginning to say his last few sentences. He had closed his prayer book in order to offer his homily, now as he held it at his chest his knuckles were white. Rigidly he gazed just above the congregation's heads.

What, he asked again, had he seen? Had he watched a sinner burned to death for his sin? He knew the question was an atrocious one, but it was no use dodging it. Holy Church had always taught that atheism was a sin deserving of damnation. Christian doctrine was either right or wrong, it was all or nothing. Heaven and hell existed or they did not, divine justice existed as we had been taught or it did not. And those two whom the fire had mutilated but, he prayed, not killed – were their tortures explicable on any level except that of chance, blind destiny, void rule? Could we truly claim that their pain had been necessary for the spiritual victory of good? How did we know? What spiritual victory?

These were questions which would not go away. The fire was burning still. It asked us to believe everything or to deny everything. To have faith that God was good was necessary for moral sanity – that was what his heart told him, and it was probably best for us all to trust our hearts. But in times of fire the need for that apparently mad faith could terrify. Yes, he concluded, and bowed his head, not only insensibility to God could appal. Faith did not always comfort, it could terrify.

Late that night, the Dayak priest found Stephen Chai kneeling by Hugh Blakeney's grave. No moon, no stars. The white plank church glimmered very faintly, you could hardly make out the raw earth over the dead man. He apologised for disturbing the mourner. He would leave a lantern burning on his bungalow's verandah, so his guest could find his way home when he had finished his prayers.

Stephen thanked him, but said he was not to bother. He would keep his vigil all night. Then, still on his knees, in a trembling voice, 'When I'm no longer here . . . When I've gone away down the river . . . '

'Yes, I shall do what you would wish for.' The other's voice was warm, was resolute. 'You did not need to ask, Stephen. I shall pray for his fiancée, for his friend. I shall kneel here as you are kneeling now. I shall pray for him, for you.'

'I have an idea it's desperately important.' He rubbed away his tears. 'Pray for him. Pray for mercy.'

'I will.'

'*A mystery* – remember? *We shall all be changed* . . . All, all! *In a moment, in the twinkling of an eye* . . .'

FIVE

5

In Balikpapan Hospital a letter was forwarded to Thor Bernstein from his wife. She wrote that she wished to marry again. Her lawyer was preparing the documents for their divorce. Would Thor please sign them? And indeed the next week a second envelope arrived from Kyoto. Thor signed the papers, he sent them back.

That was the period of Cassandra Matlaske's screams. Bernstein and she were lucky, very lucky: their bodies recovered. The regional doctor had shoved antibiotics into them. Now their wounds were cleaned. Drips in their arms, the septicaemia was checked. And Thor didn't appear to suffer much mental deformity. He might be without profession, without creed, without family, he might be without a mother country, might for years not have spoken his mother's language or that of her adopted country, but he was tough; perhaps because of these alienations or freedoms he was tough. Anyhow, he had a notable ability to keep his abstract sufferings to himself. That most detached of men, that wanderer on the face of other people's lands, that wanderer among other people's philosophies, came out of the fire unchanged, except that he looked hideous. Or he was refined; he was more intensely his sad self. But Cassandra screamed.

Trauma, people said, when she woke up shrieking that she was in the fire. Ah the poor creature, they said, when she shrieked *Hugh!* For of course her love of Hugh Blakeney was the shirt of flame she could never take off; that was the intolerable passion in which it was necessary to her to burn. Why had he not listened to her warnings? she cried. Why had he not believed her? Why had he left her so alone?

They gave her sleeping pills, she woke from her nightmares howling. Awake, she whimpered, she wept. They gave her tranquillisers – the other patients had to have quiet. When Stephen Chai visited the ward, she screamed with all the force of her lungs until he left the room. They sedated her. Partly in order that the unhappy priest might return to her bedside, might make the sign of the cross over her face which was loathsome now, her remaining hair shaved off, her wounds being grafted. And partly because of the things she would cry in those days, which were causing the staff to resort to sedation more frequently than was desirable. She had followed God, but He had led her farther and farther from Himself, she would cry. A pillar of fire! Rain, rain! His Church was a mockery, she would not take the host from hands not burned. God had no love for His creation, she would cry. And then *Hugh!* till her voice cracked. *Hugh! Hugh!* as if her clothes were still on fire, and only he could take them off. Unhinged, people said.

The one man who could do anything with her in those days of the tooth of her faith being wrenched out nerve by nerve, was he who had been in the fire with her, the other grotesque. Naturally, in hospital he was put in the men's ward and she in the women's. But earlier, in the longboat . . . He would lie beside her and say things like, 'It's all right, Cassandra. He's dead, it's all over. But you and I have got to live. He would want you to live. He would want you to be strong.' Listening to Bernstein's voice, she would become calm. And when they were sufficiently healed to leave hospital, they were inseparable, those two. She liked to see his scarred face, his scarred hands; they meant something, she would say.

When they were all back in Kuching, Stephen Chai tried again. He came into the garden with its areca palm and its nutmeg tree, its jacaranda and its frangipani. Philip Blakeney was sitting on his verandah. Using his walking-stick, he got up, came to the rail. Chai stood on the dust in the dappled shade, looked up at that sunken countenance, met those blue eyes which toward the end glittered ever more fiercely with their grief and their love. He asked if he might see Cassandra.

Blakeney turned, hobbled into the house. He came back, he said she would not see him.

Chai said nothing, he walked away. The next day he came back, with a letter which he asked Blakeney to deliver to the girl. He had written of Hugh's funeral, he told the dead man's father. He had cited a sentence from Job, given a brief notion of his homily by the grave. He had besought her to come to holy communion. He had asked her to forgive him. Blakeney took the letter. Chai waited, under the jacaranda. Blakeney returned. Cassandra thanked him for the letter, he said. But Stephen was not to write again. And she would not speak with him. Would never speak with him again.

Cassandra Matlaske was tranquil by then. She had entered her last, terrible tranquillity, which a lot of people reckoned was madder than the screams had been. The screams, after all, you could understand. And as for her refusal to meet Chai . . .

Of no avail to him, his lifting her from the water into the longboat. Of no avail, his trying to protect her wounds; his crouching hour after hour in that narrow hull to hold to her burned lips the cleanest water he could find; his desperate paddling day after day down the river to search for a doctor. Thor thanked Nazim and Kadir and Stephen handsomely for saving his life; Cassandra never. Perhaps she *was* mad, no longer felt things like gratitude. Chai's going back to look for Hugh, his giving what was left of him Christian burial – none of it counted. He hadn't gone into the fire with Thor and her. After that, he was nothing. Sitting on the tappan throne in the dusky saloon, she would say these things, in her still voice. Of course, she was obsessed by the idea that they might have got that burning branch off Hugh's legs. Chai had not braved the fire, his religion was just talk. Her mind wasn't a miasma any more, it was very clear glass again, but the lights that played in it were different. Then she might stand up, cross that wooden room with its bookcases, with its brass fan and brass lamps, with its dragon jars. In her sarong and blouse, she might stand at the five-sided bay window. She might look out through the trees, watch people strolling or bicycling along the lane. She might remark that it was strange, for her now it wasn't just Stephen Chai who had no goodness in him, no truth. All of them who hadn't stood up to the fire – they had no souls, they didn't exist.

Probably Chai would have got on better quoting the Book of Job to Blakeney. Anybody in Kuching could see *the tabernacles of robbers prosper*. And Philip Blakeney had a fair amount of Job in him by then. *Mine eye shall no more see good . . . My soul is weary of my life . . . Wilt thou break a leaf driven to and fro?*

Kuching had not changed, Kuching with its shops selling Dayak weaving, gods, weapons, musical instruments, its streets where everything was turned into money. The Court House with its Doric capitals. The Post Office with its Corinthian capitals, with its pediment, with DUM SPIRO SPERO. Vile alleys where among those uprooted and those dispossessed you could hear the warning of a dead rajah: *Coolies . . . Outcasts of the island . . .* And in the middle of that city a house with pinnacles and lattice-work, a house which years before had been painted green and white, a house beneath which bantams scratched . . .

Not really in the middle of the city. On the north shore, not far up-river from the Astana. On the north shore with its bungalows smothered in greenery, where lads coaxed their raggle-taggle kites up into the mother-of-pearl evening skies. A house where that September and October they conducted a way of life, if you could call it that, which . . .

A way of something. Philip Blakeney and Cassandra Matlaske were ghosts locked in their embraces of their dead, in their embrace. What you couldn't forget were their eyes. They would plumb each other's depths with slow gazes which were a lot too brilliant. Their minds, their souls were precarious. Locked in a watching, in a listening. Locked in their waiting. Perhaps it was one another they were waiting for. A truth, a moment . . .

Yes, in the end Akbar Nasreddin got his deathly initiation. He saw the cobras of despair in Philip's and Cassandra's minds were awake, had raised their winged heads.

2 ∫

All things considered, Danielle Kahn took Hugh's death bravely. It was clear she would never properly recover; but she behaved with self-control. Her first husband and she would sit in their cane chairs on the verandah from which you could look across the brown river to the bazaar portico, the Brooke dockyard, the mosque. They would talk about their son, smile over the tales of exploration and piracy he had delighted in as a boy. Quietly they would weep for him.

If Danielle felt closer to Philip than ever before, if in her grief she felt in some abstract sense more married to him than she had ever been . . . If this was some consolation to her, it was a dream which Blakeney was magnanimous enough, or maybe simply courteous enough in his old-fashioned gentlemanly way, to let her believe in, let her take to her heart.

Madame Kahn was useful, too – kept herself busy, which no doubt was sensible. It was not enough to mourn for the dead young man. Bernstein and Nasreddin and she knew that now they had to tempt Philip and Cassandra back from the brink, stop those two circling down together in that vortex of theirs which might be a union of illimitable love but was also a *pas de deux* toward death they were dancing. For instance, Danielle would cross from *Aigrette* to the market, she would buy food, come back over the river, cook for those wraiths. They went through the motions of eating.

Was Cassandra Matlaske mad when she sat on the tappan throne among the Dayak masks and spears, when she remarked that she had been left in a moral solitude with the mad idea of God to love or to hate as best she might? She *sounded* lucid. Was she crazy when she stared before her with her black bright eyes and told you that if God existed He was neither good nor evil? When she turned her cropped head and her ugly face toward Thor Bernstein's and called him her brother in fire, said he had been right all along, indifference was a virtue? Impossible to tell. But in those moments you knew for sure that those two were back in the fire. Again on the bridge in the gusting flame and smoke they had found their opening, they had seen Hugh lying there with his smashed scorching shins. His cries in their ears, they had reached him. Their eyes would fall on each other's disfigured hands and you would know they were back in those few seconds when they had struggled to lift that branch but had failed; Cassandra had been dragging at Hugh's shoulders when Thor started swinging his axe at his legs; when the flames blew their way . . .

Cassandra had no doubts as to her mental condition. Once she smiled, she said softly, 'I've never been so sane in my life.' And Philip Blakeney backed her up, in his gruff voice. 'Cassandra's had a damned bad time, but she's going to be fine.' That was the sort of thing he said. 'No, it's not much fun right now, but we'll pull through.'

It was an extraordinary performance, to the last. Some evenings she would take him on the Sarawak river in the *sampan*. A glamorous blaze of sunset beyond Mount Serapi, on the river with its golden glints and silver glints she sculled him slowly by the palmy shore, through the mist where the bats whirled. Back on the verandah after nightfall, moths fluttered around their lamps. They sat together, they looked into one another's eyes. Motionless, in tears, she talked gently to Hugh. His father listened, the furrows in his face graven hard, dark. Why had he not heard her cries, her upright Hugh? she asked the warm nights. Was he listening now, her man of justice, her man of truth? She had learned how to love him, she would never renounce him. In a whisper she swore it. She would come to him, her darling, her true love.

Cassandra's friends' great hope was that she might live for her child. Yes, though she had not known it, when she ran into the fire she had an embryo alive in her, and amazingly enough her pregnancy proceeded normally. Indeed if in all this story there were some almost miraculous good, some touch of grace, it was the child who began to form in Cassandra's womb.

At this happy news, everyone began to dream, to take action. That Hugh's baby should be alive in Cassandra despite her ghastly injuries, the fluid loss, the shock, made Danielle Kahn weep all one afternoon in *Aigrette*'s cabin – weep with renewed sorrow, weep in an agony of love, but also with joy. The next day she set to work purchasing things, knitting things. Hugh's child! Philip's and her grandchild, a child for Cassandra to live for . . . ! Akbar Nasreddin too was suffused with hope. He saw here the possibility of doing some good. He consulted his banker. He set up a trust fund for Cassandra and for the child who should be born. He wrote a cheque of such generosity that his sons-in-law were furious. Raoul Kahn doubled it – good, bluff, hearty Kahn, whose ways with mines and dams and plantations Hugh and Cassandra had always scorned. Chai and Badawi made contributions too.

As for Philip Blakeney, who had let himself believe in happiness for Hugh and Cassandra, who had loved their love . . . Blakeney who this time had awoken from a good dream to find that the old, evil dream had been true all along, turned out to be more deeply true . . . The Fisher was reeling him in now. Andrew and Nerissa tortured to death. Hugh tortured to death. Cassandra tortured. He was calling to his dead with immitigable love and with unwavering despair – Akbar could hear, Cassandra could hear, Thor could hear. *My days are vanity . . . On my eyelids is the shadow of death* . . . And yet when the girl told him she was pregnant he smiled. 'Another child to pick up,' he said. 'Just like when David was killed I picked up you.' That was the only time they referred to her vexed parentage. They scarcely needed to say things, those two. He had spoken, had given Chai his word. She would not have him doubted. Seamless, that loyalty of theirs.

Not that, in the house where the abstract fire was burning, things did not in many respects carry on as before. Akbar had managed to get Thor a six-month residence permit – in Sarawak he had, after all, committed no offence. He helped him to find cheap lodgings. At twilight they would cross aboard the same *tambang*, see *Aigrette* lying at anchor with her riding light. They would walk together into the garden with its *atap*-thatched hut where Cassandra no longer went to pray.

Hugh Blakeney's adventures in knowing and in doing might be at an end. Cassandra Matlaske might have outlived the faith he had derided as a low form of cognition; she might have outlived all her sustaining concepts, her constituent elements. Philip Blakeney might be near the end of his madness or clairvoyance in the possession of the known and of the unknown. But at dusk on the verandah with their glasses of whisky or of lime juice they discussed Sulu ponies. On that leafy stage the actors kept it up immaculately. In the haze of Nasreddin's cheroots they talked about whether Nicobar pigeons had been sighted lately, whether golden plovers still nested at Kuching race-course as they used to do. Their old accustomed kind of talk – if it meant anything, if it didn't mean anything. Or they might get out one of Philip's Dayak swords to admire, a *mandau* with its hilt plumed with human hair. Or a case of butterflies. There was a rajah-birdwing which Cassandra would pore over for minutes.

A communion of shadows. They chatted about the old Malay sailing *prahus* with outriggers, with two masts, with bowsprits. Only ... Only then Cassandra might say, in her still voice, 'Philip.' He would turn his eyes to hers – to their luminous, darkness which was all that remained of beauty in her lumpy, discoloured, patched face. 'Good and evil – they just ebb and flow, don't they?' she might ask. 'Ebb and flow ... ' And he would answer, 'Yes.'

Until one afternoon she – mad? rational? clement, weary of horror – took a new step in their *pas de deux*. Blakeney was sitting on the verandah. No one else was in the house. In the saloon she stood up from the tappan throne, crossed to the desk. The jalousies made the air dim. From the Regency writing-box, she took out the revolver, slipped two bullets into the chamber.

Peace. Peace. Why should Philip any longer be constrained to know too much, live in the toils of demonic imaginings? Why should she? And when in terror of having to renounce her love she had conceived a child – then she had not yet flown up free from God's hand, or those fingers had not yet parted, let her fall. Still, for a moment Cassandra stood holding the gun in one hand, her other hand laid softly on her waist.

Then beneath the turning fan she knelt down. Death would be a grace. Soon, soon it would be as if they had never lived. The fire had finished speaking, she had understood.

She set the muzzle of the revolver to the base of her throat, just above her leopard's claws. She whispered, 'Hugh.' She pulled the trigger.

3

The rains came late that year, but they came. With tempests of wind, with rough seas breaking on the coasts, with lakes and rivers choppy, all over Borneo the deluge fell, putting out the fire.

The rain fell on Thor Bernstein's island where in a crevice his books began to rot, where the monsoon battered to smithereens his hut, where the hermit never came back. Neither the Malaysians nor the Indonesians brought him to trial, but both countries chucked him out, the six months Nasreddin obtained for him were only a stay of sentence. Hugh Blakeney's eloquence had been the danger, and with him dead the authorities decided that the fire would be forgotten most swiftly if the other foreigner guilty of the destruction of companies' property were denied the theatre of a court. Stephen Chai was not tried either – though this may have had something to do with his family and his calling. And it was remarkable how quickly the fire faded from people's minds. The Indonesian Forestry Minister pointed out in an interview that much of the area burned had been designated for development, so what you had was land cleared without cost. After that . . . It seemed you could reduce to a waste land three and a half million hectares of fine country and soon it would be almost as if no one had noticed. That old prophet Philip Blakeney would have smiled grimly. In a year, the fact was less substantial. In five . . . Reality itself appeared to disperse, to blow away.

In the interior, the rain fell on the last virgin forests where the last leopards crouched; fell on logged regions and turned the hills to mud cascades, the valleys to floods. The rain fell on lumber camps. It fell on longhouses where the last shamans were growing old, where people had forgotten the words of the death songs. It fell on mausoleums still decorated with heads. It fell on settlements where they were still afraid of the mythical head-hunters, the *penyamun*, though these days the superstitious believed them to be in the pay of the government or the foreign firms. They must need heads, to give strength to the oil-rigs which stood in the sea.

The rain fell on the river where by day Chai had kept the sun off the injured man and woman lying in the longboat's bilges, had tried to keep the flies from their wounds; where by night he had brushed away the mosquitoes. The rain fell on the ash lands, made them black mud; fell where none came to witness the desolation, not a hunter, not a dragonfly. The rain fell on the pit where Michael and Kitty Blakeney's bones lay; on their grandson's grave where between the downpours a Dayak priest came, knelt down.

In Kuching, the monsoon drenched the Christian graveyard where Philip Blakeney and Cassandra Matlaske lay. Stephen Chai had persuaded the bishop to let him stow them in the hallowed earth which neither of them, according to the book, deserved. Chai's working friendships with the bishop and the deacon never satisfactorily recovered from the Cassandra Matlaske affair. His career lost momentum. From being the youngest priest at the cathedral church in the state's capital, and thus well positioned for ecclesiastical advancement, he was dispatched into the countryside to Lundu to do what pious work he might among the plantation labourers. Several years later, there was no suggestion of his being recalled.

In the event of his son and his adopted daughter dying without heirs, Blakeney had left his estate to be divided between two Iban families. Not that it amounted to much. Just the Kuching house and a few thousand dollars in the bank and those of the Bornean artefacts which had not been left to the museum. But it would be a bit more when the Devon house was sold too. One half of the proceeds was to go to Cassandra's mother's lot, the other half to the descendants of Michael Blakeney's mistress of before the First World War.

Akbar Nasreddin had a boring time tracing these surprised

people. Akbar was not just sad, he was unmanned. He thought damned nearly only intolerable things, and he thought them damned nearly always. You would see him footling about Kuching. He had retired. He had nothing to do but organize his one friend's bequests. He did that in order to keep existing, punctilious until he maddened the luckless Bernstein. Even the curator of the museum, who was paid to cluck, said he'd never met a hen like him. At least to begin with the two Iban families thought that he was magnificent and wise. Then they both decided the division of the spoils was not being as just as it ought to be. Which of course was rubbish. But that didn't stop them believing it. And he was rich and a Malay, poor devil, so he had to be bad.

On the north bank of the Sarawak river, the monsoon drummed a tattoo on the shingle roof of the Blakeney house. Boisterously the flood rose up the nipah palms, up the posts of the deserted *atap* sanctum. From the higher ground, brown torrents swirled beneath the house, the trees stood in rain-belaboured shallows.

Restless in the saloon with a watercolour of lateen sails in his hands, Thor Bernstein thought of Hugh Blakeney. He remembered how some tribes believed the souls of the dead embarked for the life to come on a *prahu*. Others had the soul wander through the forests till beyond a mountain ridge it came to a ravine spanned by a wobbling bridge, a single spar suspended by rattans . . . Oh, nonsense. Those old, half-forgotten fables . . . The combers of weariness thundered on his mind's shore. 'What do you think we ought to do with these paintings?' he asked. 'Put them in a sale in London?'

Akbar Nasreddin glanced up from the papers on the desk. But he did not see the man standing between the lamps in the shadowy room, did not hear the squalls of rain lashing the house. He saw again his storm-lit vision of the lost, but there were more of them now. Andrew and Philip and Nerissa, Hugh and Cassandra. Over grey treeless hills they toiled on their way through an infinite loneliness, comforted one another with the words of a love never to be assuaged.

4 ∫

Even when the rains stopped, the days were cloudy, difficult to remember.

It turned out that Hugh and Cassandra must have breathed new soul into Philip Blakeney, for a while: he had written a few last poems. Akbar Nasreddin found them in a drawer in the desk in the saloon, when he was muddling about with heaps of notebooks and journals, with bundles of letters and photographs. They were in a book of the sort in which the Mission School children wrote their lessons, which Cassandra had sometimes brought home to correct. Rough drafts, rejected stanzas, final versions written out immaculately.

What Blakeney never knew was that on the other side of the world critics were beginning to take an interest in him. A professor who had been commissioned to write *A History of Modern Poetry* or something grand like that sent a polite letter to which Akbar replied. In time, his stuff started to be chosen for anthologies. Answering these enquiries was one of the last twists to Akbar's grief. Just before his own lonely death he opened a letter addressed to his old friend in which an editor suggested publishing an edition of his work. There had been no obituaries of the poet in the English press, there was no reason why scholars should have known of his torments, his destruction.

The Blakeney house was in the process of being sold, Akbar still came over regularly. What should be done with all the books – there was that kind of thing to see to. Of course the Iban beneficiaries must get their market value – but in a South-East Asian provincial capital what value *had* a turn-of-the-century

Tennyson or a pre-war Tauchnitz *Fathers and Sons*? Or a *Yeats* which appeared to have been dropped into a *prahu*'s bilges? At last a dealer from Singapore heard that the collection included some first editions of people like Louis MacNeice, paid a derisory sum for the lot, sold the fifty volumes which had commercial value to the university library in Kuala Lumpur for three times what he had paid the Blakeney estate.

Well, Akbar had to have excuses for haunting that house, he was even unhappier in his own. Oddly enough, he too died in Philip's saloon, in that catafalque. He had gone there yet again, to check some final detail about the sale and to answer letters, or to sit alone in silence and think about the dead. Heart failure. He seemed to have been reading Keats. At least, 'The Eve of Saint Agnes' was open on the desk before him. If so, he must have been transported a long way from that brown tropical river, from the lush steamy air drifting in from the frangipani. Once, to the verandah company, he had recalled that he had first read it at Gray's Inn, had glanced up, through his study window seen for the first time snow falling. But this time his fat carcass had just slumped a bit; it stayed propped in the chair.

Raoul Kahn had been in Paris for months, but his wife had not been able to tear herself away. She would rejoin him, of course she would. But she kept putting off talking to the maritime agency about *Aigrette*, she put off booking her flight. A little longer . . .

She made her visits to the graveyard in the evenings. Like Philip before her, now she too knew well the Christian dead of Kuching. She knew Rose Lance who had died in 1902 aged eighteen. She liked the mighty trees wrapped in their strangling figs, she liked the hibiscus hedge.

There they lay, side by side. Their births half a century apart, their deaths the same day. The involuntary Faustus, his Angel who toward the last had tried to save him but had failed. Andrew somewhere near.

One warm dusk when Danielle Kahn approached the graves she saw a lady standing there.

The stranger hesitated, appeared about to withdraw. But then she stood her ground. She waited.

'In a moment I'll leave you in peace. But it seemed churlish to turn tail.' She held out her hand. 'Madame Kahn? We've never met. My name is . . . '

But then she paused, for it was clear from Danielle's eyes that she was beginning to know. From talk, from a photograph . . . With a sad smile, the newcomer let her face be studied.

The red hair had faded, was cut shorter now in middle-age. But her skin was still very fair, and her eyes were green.

'Tanya Mayhew,' Danielle Kahn said, and she too smiled. 'Unless . . . '

'No, I've never married. That is my name.'

In the twilight the two women stood together among the dead, in the air where even the abstract screams were dying away.

'I read about Hugh's death in the English papers,' Tanya explained. And indeed his colleagues had done him proud. The son got the obituaries the father was not given, though then he was forgotten. 'I've travelled a lot in recent years. I paint in odd crannies of the world. I was planning to return to this country. So I thought . . . ' She lowered her gaze to the two headstones. 'But I arrived too late. I've heard . . . ' She turned to the grey lady beside her, to that stricken face. 'You'll wish to be alone.'

'No,' Danielle said simply. 'I am pleased to meet you.'

Tanya Mayhew regarded Cassandra Matlaske's engraved name as if by reading the letters she might understand her despair.

'Twenty-two,' the elder woman said softly. 'Like her mother. And she . . . Did anyone tell you?' This Danielle Kahn could not say without her voice betraying her. 'She was going to bear Hugh's child.'

Her companion faced her with wide, green, brimming eyes.

'I suppose she wanted to release Philip?' Tanya felt her way. 'She must have known he wouldn't go first, wouldn't abandon her. She must have known that if she went ahead he'd follow her.'

'He heard the shot. Slowly, he stood up.' Danielle had never been so close to Philip as she was now. 'Slowly, he went in. I think . . . I think it must have been as if he'd found Nerissa at last. When he saw Cassandra lying there. They were his – his two . . . More than me. More than you.'

'You're right. Yes, after searching for so long. To embrace a love which couldn't be saved.'

'He knelt down . . . '

'And then, for a few minutes, perhaps for an hour, alone . . . I imagine him tired, utterly tired. But also . . . ' Tanya smiled. Her tears still glistened in her eyes, did not fall. 'Did he ever talk to you about Nepenthe? I'm sure he did. And about pitcher plants?'

'He called them claret jugs, he called them oblivion plants.'

'Perhaps at the end Cassandra was his goddess of sleep. He saw her holding out to him a glass of forgetfulness.'